THE OTHER VICTIM

By the same author

A Fool for a Client

The Other Victim

David Kessler

Hodder & Stoughton

First published in Great Britain in 1997 by Hodder and
Stoughton
A division of Hodder Headline PLC

10 9 8 7 6 5 4 3 2 1

British Library Cataloguing in Publication Data

Kessler, David
    The other victim
    1. Genetic engineering – Fiction 2. Perfumes industry –
    Fiction 3. Thrillers
    I. Title
    823.9′14 [F]

ISBN 0 340 68902 1

Typeset by Palimpsest Book Production Limited,
Polmont, Stirlingshire
Printed and bound in Great Britain by
Mackays of Chatham PLC, Chatham, Kent

Hodder and Stoughton
A division of Hodder Headline PLC
338 Euston Road
London NW1 3BH

To Simi and Nomi
the friends of my childhood.

PART I

GOLD

'Who chooseth me shall gain what many men desire.'

William Shakespeare,
The Merchant of Venice

1

'Am I my brother's keeper?'

Genesis 4:9

A streak of red hung over the horizon like a wound in the sky.

It hovered in the wake of the setting sun, as if reluctant to acknowledge the day's departure. There seemed to be no force holding it in place, no invisible hand dangling strings to suspend it from above, no breath of power to prop it up from below. Yet it stayed in place, held there by an inertia so final that not even the encroaching darkness could dislodge it.

It was a trivial sight. But it held Tony spellbound for a few seconds as he stepped out of Leicester Square Tube station. When the moment passed, he turned right and walked out into the warm air, pausing again, to take a deep breath, against the humidity. He felt someone tugging at his sleeve, puncturing his daydream with an irritating blast of reality.

'Come on, Tony!'

It was Phil. Cool, unemotional, impatient Phil. No wonder, Tony thought, he's the mathematician and I'm the chemist. He has no emotions. Even his dabbling in witchcraft is just a parlour game.

3

In time with their first few steps across the red brick pavement into the throngs and glitter of the square, two pairs of eyes followed them, focusing squarely on Tony . . . and two pairs of feet kept a steady distance between them. But the brothers walked on with the carefree casualness of ignorance.

As they walked, Tony pondered the differences between them. Of course, words like 'mathematician' and 'chemist' were stretching it a bit. They were both in that limbo of waiting for their A-level results, and both had taken each other's subjects: physics, chemistry, pure maths and applied maths, in fact. And both were eagerly awaiting the piece of paper that would tell them whether or not they had got those coveted four A passes. They had both been offered university places for substantially lower results. But there was a certain amount of personal rivalry, and it would have been deeply humiliating to either if the other had done better in his chosen subject, or for that matter if one had excelled over the other in their neutral subject: physics.

Certain amount of rivalry? Well, it was more like a massive amount, although it never spilled over into animosity. There was a special bond between the Neuman brothers, as there so often is with twins. To look at these two smooth-featured, somewhat athletic-looking blue-eyed blond boys, one would have been forgiven for thinking that they were attached to each other by an umbilical cord. They were very rarely separate in their spare time, delighting in doing everything as a pair, and their rivalry was more like a game which they used to keep themselves in tune and at the peak of their mental and physical fitness. They did not correspond with the usual image of nerds or anoraks at all. They looked like a couple of young Nordic or Germanic athletes, and it was hard to imagine either of them holding a test tube over a Bunsen burner or sitting huddled over a computer terminal at four in the morning.

They also didn't look Jewish. But then again, since their father had died, neither they nor their mother had practised the religion to any significant extent. Tony still thought of

4

himself as Jewish, but at the cultural rather than the religious level. At any rate, neither of them dwelled on religion, not even in terms of Phil's witchcraft pretensions. They just wanted to enjoy life, like any normal boys of their age.

They felt hot and sticky under the collar as they walked along in the evening air. But it wasn't just the claustrophobic feeling of the London Underground transport system, although the Tube could be stifling enough. London was sweltering in the heat of an Indian summer, and tempers were fraying easily in a way that would have left New Yorkers feeling at home.

'Let's check out the Hippodrome,' said Tony.

The black marble lower façade of the Hippodrome to his right provided a backdrop for a pair of skinny microskirted pubescent girls who had been denied entry to the nightclub. The girls stood there sulking and smoking and arguing over what to do next. There were plenty of places to go, but at the other nightclubs it would probably be the same story.

'It's a waste of time,' said Phil. 'Everyone goes there 'cause it's the nearest to the station. Let's check out the rest of the square first.'

In a corner nearby, propped up against the wall, sat a decrepit, bearded tramp, watching life pass him by in the form of the affluent carefree youth that could afford to ignore him. In a way this scene was something of a paradigm for his life – life had passed him by, and for whatever private reasons were his, he had let it.

Tony felt sorry for him, realizing how close his family had come to poverty after their father had died, his endowment policy long since lapsed without their knowing. He suspected that Phil had never truly realized this, as if Phil had maintained a blind sense of euphoria while he and his mother had struggled to get the family's finances under control. Of course, that was partly because Tony was closer to Mr Rubin. It was Rubin who had really been the emotional crutch for their mother to lean on, and Rubin who had helped them financially, even though as a teacher his own means were limited. Tony was Rubin's brightest pupil. So it was

5

only natural that Tony, more than Phil, should have been aware of what was going on.

Perhaps, Tony thought, that's why I'm more concerned about making money now than Phil is: because *I* know how close we came to losing everything. Perhaps that's why I'm ready to work for people like Hassan. Perhaps that's why I'm ready to help him create —

He cut the thought off, not wanting to think about what he had been doing, or how he was prostituting his ability. He wasn't really sure about the legality of what he was doing. But he knew that it was certainly morally questionable. And morality and ethics had been the one part of his father's teaching that he had tried to cling on to.

Perhaps that was why he was haunted by the sight of the old tramp, and the indifference of the other teenagers who passed him. 'There but for the grace of God' was a phrase that never entered their heads, let alone crossed their lips. Like religion, adolescence meant different things to different people. For some it meant the transitional phase marking the emergence of social awareness and the refinement of a child's simplistic moral code. For others it was a time to gain a sense of belonging by wearing a *de facto* uniform, joining a clique and practising mystical rituals. For some it even meant engaging in battle with members of other cliques in the fight for territory and to proclaim the superiority of their way over the 'infidels'.

As religion was to history, so adolescence was to maturation, a phase in the process of growing up. Just as no modern atheistic society could have reached its current status from primitive barbarism without having first gone through a religious phase of development, so no child could have reached adulthood while bypassing adolescence. And Tony was nearing the end of his adolescence, waking up to the fact that he was a man in a difficult world and that, as such, he had moral responsibilities to himself and to others. It was sorting out those moral responsibilities which was causing him so much discomfort and confusion.

6

If I am not for myself, the great Rabbi Hillel had once said, who will be for me?

But if I am *only* for myself, the saying continued, what am I?

This was the great dilemma that Tony found himself confronting, and it was this dilemma which had prompted him to worry when he saw what other work was lined up for him. The trouble was that it paid good money.

He would have liked to have gone out clubbing every night, or at least every weekend. But he didn't have the money for the best clubs in the centre of London. So hitting the West End had to be an occasional exercise for him and not a regular pastime. Of course, things would be different when Hassan came through with the rest of the money.

He regretted now having squandered most of the money on the watch. It was just that he'd always wanted a Rolex watch. He'd tried to wangle a second instalment on his advance. But they told him to hold off for a while longer, and that left him in limbo.

The entrance to the square was marked by an interlacing pattern of red bricks. But when they crossed over on to the large stones of the main square they both felt that pang of being engulfed by glitz. The square was a place of bright lights, a pedestrian precinct that was far from pedestrian, packed with cinemas, nightclubs and restaurants. On their right was a multiplex cinema offering a dazzling array of films on its ten screens, its blinking lights giving it an almost futuristic aura which its interior couldn't quite live up to. Phil shook his head, as if to say: *There's nothing there for us*. Which in turn meant *There's nothing there to appeal to the intelligence*.

For a few indecisive seconds they stood outside an Italian restaurant with fancy green metal tables spilling out on to the pavement on this warm summer evening. But its customers looked too square for the square, as if they didn't really belong there, or at least should be quarantined at the side and kept well away from its bustling centre and throbbing heart.

The young couples were out in force to explore the night life, and the pairs and groups of teenage girls were congregating outside the Equinox, one of the glitziest of all the nightclubs, displaying bare thighs, midriff and cleavage in what seemed like an open invitation. Having reached the age of consent, they were out for their first taste of sexual experience, looking to lose their virginity. He'd read somewhere that girls of this age were looking for smooth-skinned, pretty blond boys of their own age, like himself and his brother. But that never seemed to be the case with the ones he tried to pull. The microskirt was back with a vengeance, but there was a total absence of colour in the clothes that the teenage girls wore: the skirts and jackets were black, the shirts were white. And there was a preference for leather.

'That's where we should go,' said Phil, pointing to the Equinox.

'We can't afford it,' Tony replied, his frugality getting the better of him. 'It's eight pounds just to enter, and then we've got to buy drinks.'

'I thought you'd been saving up for this,' said Phil, a hint of disbelief in his voice.

'I don't know why you thought that.'

'Well, blimey, you told *me* to save!'

'That's' cause I already *had* money —'

He broke off, realizing that he had said the wrong thing.

'Well, if you've got money, what's the problem?' asked Phil, exasperated.

'I had some expenses,' said Tony defensively.

'What, like that gold Rolex?' asked Phil, unable to conceal the anger.

'I didn't think about it. I thought I was going to be getting some more money soon.'

'From whom? Those mysterious people you've been working for?'

Tony recoiled at the words. He had taken elementary precautions not to tell anyone, not even Phil, anything except the bare minimum. But Phil was the computer wizard, and it was hard for Tony to keep secrets from him, especially as he was the one who had taught Tony how to keep secrets on a computer. He sometimes wondered how safe his computer files were against Phil, even the encrypted ones.

'Look, I just haven't got the money. Why don't we go to a pub? Or a movie?'

Phil's eyes sparkled with their usual exasperated anger.

'Because I didn't come all the way to Leicester Square just to go to a bloody pub! If you're not going in I'm going on my own.'

'Oh, come on, Phil. I haven't got the money.'

'Well, I have!'

'For both of us?' asked Tony, his voice gently stressing the appeal.

'No,' replied Phil. 'Just for me.'

Tony's expression turned from appeasement to anger.

'Well, fuck you! Brother!'

And with that he turned away, without waiting for Phil to respond, and walked on into a crowd of Japanese tourists meandering off into a side street. Phil sprinted after him, leaving their two anonymous pursuers in danger of becoming separated from them and unable to catch up amid the thick crowds at that particular corner.

'Hey, Tony!' Phil called out after his brother.

'What?' Tony shouted back, barely turning.

'Fancy a bowl of lentil soup?'

A few yards away the two stalkers were engaged in an excited exchange.

'We may have got lucky,' said the younger of the two.

'Why?' asked the elder.

'They're splitting up. Looks like they were arguing.'

'That's a bit of a break considering we almost lost them.'

'Yeah,' said the younger, with a sneer in his tone. 'Those Japs get in everywhere.'

'So what are we going to do?'

'We'll keep on Tony's tail. All we need is for him to go somewhere quiet.'

The elder stalker seemed nervous at this prospect.

'I thought we were going to wait till he went to the toilet?'

'We were, but now we may not need to. Now that he's alone any quiet side street is good enough.'

'I don't like it,' said the elder.

The younger one became angry.

'Look, don't chicken out on me now. You've got as much to lose in all this as I have.'

The hands on the Rolex watch stood at nine-thirty, but somehow it felt later. People swept past in slow motion as he was carried along amid a horde of strangers who happened to be moving in the same general direction, each in pursuit of his own pleasure or escape from reality. The meandering people around him were like a glacier, cold and drifting aimlessly, while he was like a living body in suspended animation, frozen into immobility by this pack of human ice.

All the while, the two stalkers remained on his tail, watching him from a discreet distance, knowing that he was unlikely to glance back – except, perhaps, to ogle a pretty girl now and then – and realizing that if he did, he was unlikely to notice them. As he was just bumming around the square there was no reason why the same people shouldn't keep turning up again and again. That was what Leicester Square was for, bumming around until one met the right people or decided what to do.

A few minutes later, the stalkers followed him into a flashy electronic pseudo-casino, full of colour and noise. Like a genuine, adult casino, it gave the kids who frequented it the *illusion* of pleasure. But cash payouts from the machines were few and far between. He watched a few others wasting their money, and then left. The odds in these games were always stacked heavily in favour of the house.

His two pursuers watched him as he entered an old-style pub with wood panelling and Edwardian-style lamps and tailed him as he left less than thirty seconds later. They stood a discreet distance away as he argued with a multiracial group of evangelizing preachers out to save souls in this modern Babylon or Sodom, moving on with him when the preaching and haranguing had run their course. By eleven o'clock the square was still packed, with people milling about outside the nightclubs, restaurants and cinemas. But it was beginning to get boring for him.

With his stalkers in hot pursuit, he left the square for Piccadilly Circus with its huge bright neon advertisements, stopping briefly to admire the statue of Eros, and from there into Regent Street, which despite the throngs was wrapped in a strange nocturnal lethargy that couldn't quite detract from its regal opulence.

He walked down to Oxford Circus and turned left into Oxford Street past shops long since closed for the night, heading for the Marble Arch end. As he walked he looked up at the majestic hotels that loomed above him. Again, the adolescent fantasies raced through his mind. He was frolicking on a thick white plush-pile carpet with a voluptuous pair of pliant blonde twins as rain lashed into the windows and streaks of lightning cut wounds across the sky. He smiled at the thought, and felt himself hardening in his trousers.

It was when he finally took a detour down a completely abandoned side road that they finally made their move. They took the same turn and swiftly but quietly closed the distance between them and him. As the gap closed, their efforts at stealth finally failed, and he turned in response to the resonating squeaking of their soft shoes against the pavement.

'What do you want?' he asked.

'Just your wallet and watch, Tony,' said the younger of the stalkers, grinning.

'Is this some kind of a joke?' he said.

'It depends on your sense of humour,' said the younger of the two. 'We don't actually want the wallet or watch. But we're going to take them anyway.'

The elder of the two, dressed in a baggy tweed jacket, said nothing, and looked rather out of place in these sleazy back streets. By this time the gap between them had been closed to almost nothing.

'Look, would you mind telling me what this is all about?'

The boy was now beginning to get angry. His evening on the town had been none too successful, and he wasn't in the mood for any lip from these two.

'Well, it's very simple,' said the younger one, slipping a hand into a pocket. 'It's all about —'

At this stage the speaker broke off as a knife plunged into the boy's abdomen, just below the liver. An inch higher and the assailant would have been splattered in blood. But he knew exactly where to place the blade and any shout that might have emanated from the boy's throat was muffled by his right hand clamped firmly over the boy's mouth as he slumped to the ground.

'Is he dead?' asked the elder one squeamishly.

'Yeah,' said the younger one, sounding rather more blasé than his partner. 'He's dead. Help me get him to the side, quickly.'

The elder one bent down and between them they carried the body to the side, by the litter bins, where it was less conspicuously in view. The younger one lifted the boy and reached inside the hip pocket to get the wallet.

'Get his watch.'

The elder one obeyed, fumbling with sweaty hands to unfasten it quickly. As soon as the watch was freed from the wrist, the pair of attackers rose quickly and scurried away down another side street. Minutes later they were sitting at a corner table in a screened-off booth of a nearby pub, planning their next move.

The elder one took out the watch and looked at it admiringly, saying, 'A Rolex.'

'Are you crazy?' said the other. 'Put it away now!'

The elder one obeyed sheepishly.

'I'd rather like to keep it for myself,' said the elder one.

'Don't even think about it,' said the other.

It was surprising to see so many lights on in the house at

almost three in the morning. Usually when he came back this late from clubbing in the West End, the place was as quiet as death. His brother had probably made a noise when he returned, and his mother must have woken up. He could picture the whole scene. He knew how easily his brother and mother could get into arguments. It was as if he put so much effort into being patient and containing himself that every now and again he flew off the handle, the pressure of bottling up his emotions too much for him.

But as he drew nearer to the house, he was gripped by a grim foreboding, a sense that something was not quite right. It wasn't just the lights, it was the whole atmosphere. And then he noticed something else, something that he had probably perceived subliminally through his peripheral vision but only become conscious of now. There was a police car parked a few yards past the house.

He raced the last few steps to the entrance and ran in, a current of heat rising up in his stomach like molten lava bubbling up to the rim of a volcano.

It's Mum, he thought. Something must have happened to her. He must have found her and called the police.

He threw the door open and staggered into the house, grabbing at the umbrella stand by the door to keep his balance. He caught a glimpse of shadows in the living room, but before he could recover his footing he was stunned to see his mother, Miriam, emerge from the living room, her face contorted by tears. She was being partially restrained by a female police constable. In that moment, he felt the pain and anguish of a moment before vanish, to be replaced by a wave of confusion.

'What's happened?' his voice cried out, his mind struggling to assess the situation.

'It's Tony!' wailed his mother. 'He's been killed.'

There was a moment of shock flushing the blood into his face and then a wave of fear twisting in the pit of his stomach as he felt himself gasping for breath.

He fell into his mother's arms sobbing, the grief they

13

had shared barely more than a year ago sweeping over them. As their sobbing ebbed away to a quiet murmur, he inexplicably remembered the sunset outside the station.

2

'If you seek him, he will be found by you . . .'

I Chronicles 28:9

The rising sun exploded into flame over the Grand Union Canal, its orange fire glinting in reflections off the still waters. It was as if the sun were smiling on Emmett Freeman as he drove along the winding road.

Through the windscreen of his Jaguar, Emmett Freeman saw the dual rows of pine trees lined up by the sides of the road as it curved towards the mansion. They looked almost like soldiers on parade, although it clearly wasn't him that they were saluting. In his limbo years, after he was stripped of his physics degree, Freeman had effectively blackmailed Fabian Digby into retaining his services as a business consultant. But he had never been invited to Digby's house. Digby had made it clear to him that he would pay him his 'hush money' but would never regard him as a friend or even a trusted confidant. So this was the first time that Freeman had been really close to a display of Digby's personal wealth, and he was somewhat overawed by it.

He wondered what could be so important that they had to summon him out here instead of sending a middleman to his office. But when the secretary to Fabian Digby

15

summoned you, you didn't ask too many trivial questions – at least not over the phone. Whatever it was,
they would tell him soon enough. It couldn't be patent
work, as Freeman didn't do that sort of work any more.
And he never felt comfortable mixing science with law.
The bitterness from his ten-year struggle to clear his name
still twisted in his gut. It couldn't be legal work, because
although Digby sometimes used Freeman as a consultant,
he employed a large firm of lawyers in the City of London
to handle all his corporate litigation. The only thing that was
certain was that it would be lucrative. Fabian Digby always
paid well.

These pleasant but idle speculations were brought to an
abrupt halt by the appearance of a burly, mean-looking
guard in the middle of the road before the main entrance to
the mansion. The guard was struggling to restrain an even
meaner-looking Doberman. Unfortunately, he appeared to
be fighting a losing battle, and Freeman, whose hard-boiled
manner had a tendency to evaporate in the presence of any
member of the canine family larger than a poodle, was
beginning to have reservations about whether he should
even get out of his car.

This is ridiculous, he told himself. Who's going to hire a
lawyer who's scared of dogs? Gritting his teeth, he stopped
the engine, opened the door and gingerly stepped out on to
the roadside. Surprisingly the dog appeared to calm down
and more or less came to heel.

'It's the car,' said the guard, responding to the puzzled
look on Freeman's face as if he had seen it countless
times before. 'He hates cars, especially when the engine's
running.'

'I'm glad I'm not a car,' said Freeman, thinking that bit of
stand-up comedy would alleviate the tension. A bad review
came back at him in the form of an evil-sounding growl
from the Doberman.

So everyone's a critic now, he thought uneasily. But this
time he kept it to himself.

'You can go on in,' said the guard, jerking his head

towards the door as he maintained a tight grip on the dog's leash and collar. 'They're expecting you.'

A few quick strides carried him to the majestic oak door. But he wasn't sure whether he was expected to open it himself or ring the bell and wait to be let in. The guard had told him to 'go on in', but to open the door himself seemed like an impertinence. Also it would somewhat degrade his rank. He was, after all, an invited guest, albeit one who was probably summoned there on business. Still, as long as the business was unnamed he had the right to behave like any other guest and expect to be treated as such.

He pressed the large bronze button that rang the doorbell and waited. In the quiet of the morning, he fancied that he could hear staccato footsteps crossing a marble floor in the few seconds before the door opened. Then he found himself facing a besuited man who seemed to be too young to be a butler, but too deferential to be anything else.

'Yes, sir,' said the butler.

'My name is Emmett Freeman,' said Freeman. 'I have an appointment to see Fabian Digby.'

He wished he'd taken out his card before ringing the doorbell and had it at the ready. But it would look silly if he reached into his pocket now and fumbled with his wallet. The butler looked at him sceptically, as if weighing up the presumptuousness of this clumsy man who clearly lacked the social graces of the aristocracy. Freeman half expected to hear the words 'tradesmen's entrance round the back' uttered in a tone of peremptory dismissal. But instead the butler replied politely, if rather too forcefully for a servant, 'With the *secretary* to Fabian Digby.'

Properly put in his place, and not to say somewhat mystified, Freeman was led into a huge, high-ceilinged, marble-floored lobby and told to wait.

The butler left him there, the staccato sound of his feet traversing the marble floor, so reminiscent of a goose-stepping German soldier, reverberating through the house. High ceilings are good for echoes, thought Freeman, but only if one likes an echo. After a while, he guessed, it

17

tended to grate on the nerves. Or perhaps one got used to it.

In the absence of human company, Freeman began pacing. His own soft-soled shoes didn't make much noise, except a faint squelch. But he was conscious of it all the same. He felt eyes upon him from a distance, as if he were being watched by someone who disapproved of him. He dismissed the thought as lawyer's paranoia, a neurosis not mentioned in any medical textbook, but as real as any other.

'Mr Freeman.' A man's voice rang out, particularly resonant, even allowing for the echo. He looked around, trying to trace its source. 'Up here.'

He looked up to the top of a large spiral staircase – maybe four storeys up. He saw a man leaning over the edge. The man, whoever it was, looked more the way Freeman imagined a butler than the young man who had answered the door. Maybe it was the footman who answered the door, thought Freeman, remembering a TV series he used to watch in the 1970s.

'Yes,' he said, trying not to raise his voice, and knowing that it would carry far enough anyway.

'Would you come up here, please.'

He took the stairs slowly, ignoring the gaze of the man who had summoned him, and dismissing from his mind any speculation about the other man's impatience. He wanted to get the feel of his surroundings. For what purpose, he didn't know. He just liked to know where he was. He was out of his element and to a man in his profession that always meant danger. He wanted to orient himself in case a sudden danger materialized from out of nowhere. He noted the whereabouts of windows and corridors on each landing as he made his way up to what turned out to be the fifth floor.

'Sorry I took so long,' he said when he finally arrived and found himself standing before a middle-aged man. 'I was admiring the surroundings.'

He realized that he was being mildly rude, but he was beginning to feel resentful of the behaviour of his hosts. They had summoned him to this country house miles away from his normal haunts and now they expected him to climb five flights of stairs just to keep an appointment that he hadn't asked for. The money had better be good to justify it.

'Come this way, please,' said the man.

He was led a few more steps down a short corridor and into a rosewood-panelled office. The man closed the door behind him and then sat down at the desk – a large desk, also made of rosewood, that emphasized the opulence of the environment.

'Sit down,' said the man, indicating the high-backed, fur-upholstered chair opposite the desk.

Freeman sat.

'Cigar?' asked the man, holding out a silver box.

The man didn't have to tell Freeman that they were from Havana. A wry smile came to his lips as he remembered the old story about Havana cigars being rolled between the thighs of Cuban girls.

That Castro must have some real Madison Avenue types working for him, thought Freeman.

'No thanks,' said the detective. He felt an urge for a cigarette. But he had kicked all his bad habits a year ago when a bank manager of his acquaintance was diagnosed as having lung cancer. In the end, an armed robber got him before the Big C could. But Freeman could never escape the feeling that his friend's ill-timed show of heroism was the only form of suicide that a Catholic could permit himself.

'Drink?'

'No thank you,' said Freeman, gritting his teeth. By now he was getting tired of all this aristocratic professional foreplay.

The middle-aged man sat down.

'First of all,' said the man, 'let me introduce myself. I am Alan Nielsen, secretary to Fabian Digby.'

'How do you do,' said Freeman, but he did not extend his hand.

'Tell me, Mr Freeman, how well would you say you knew Fabian Digby?'

'Well, I was a business consultant of his for a decade.'

'You mean you were *retained* as his business consultant.'

'I was always available to give him advice if he asked me,' said Freeman. 'He just never did.'

'Considering the circumstances in which you *became* his business consultant, that's hardly surprising.'

'Well, I'm sure you didn't invite me down here to reminisce about the past, or to remonstrate.'

'No indeed,' said Nielsen stiffly. 'What I meant was, how much do you know about Digby's current business activities?'

Freeman recognized the game immediately. It was the old 'let's see how much you *think* you know then I can score a few points at your expense by showing you how *little'*. He took a deep breath and prepared to show off.

'Well, like I said, he never fully availed himself of my services, never really confided in me. So basically all I know about his current, or past, business activities is what appeared in the the popular and business press.'

'And that is?' asked Nielsen.

'Well, I know that he's a billionaire. That he inherited a small fortune and turned it into a large one. He doesn't dominate any one field or put all his eggs in one basket but has a diversified portfolio. He has interests in most of the old industries and some of the new. Publishing in London, mining in Africa, oil wells in the North Sea and Texas, and now he's had the sense to buy into computers in Silicon Valley and the Pacific Tigers.'

Freeman could see that Nielsen was getting irritated.

'He's also now the owner of La Contessa Perfumes,' said Nielsen, mentioning Fabian Digby's most recent and spectacular acquisition with obvious annoyance.

'Oh yeah, I forgot that one,' said Freeman, twisting the knife.

'It was in all the papers,' said Nielsen, 'and I believe it was covered by independent television. So even *you* should have seen it.'

'I only watch BBC 2,' Freeman lied. 'But now that you come to mention it, I think I did hear something about it. But I wouldn't have said that Mr Digby *owns* La Contessa Perfumes.'

'Why not?'

The voice was frayed at the edges. Freeman sensed that he was getting at Nielsen more than he intended, and he decided to stop. It was going beyond mere sport and he didn't want to lose a potentially lucrative client by starting off on the wrong foot.

'Well, he had to borrow a large sum of money to make the purchase, from some sort of private banking consortium. So I would have said that Mr Digby was more the . . . *custodian* of the enterprise, holding it in trust for the customers of the banks.'

He hoped that his formulation had not come over as unflattering. Once he had started it was hard to get out of saying what he meant.

'Yes, I think that Mr Digby would certainly approve of that characterization.'

'Now perhaps we can get down to business,' said Freeman. 'Maybe you can tell me what I can do for Mr Digby.'

'There's probably not much that you can do for Fabian Digby, but you may be able to do something for his wife, unless he turns up, that is.'

Freeman remained silent for a few seconds, digesting the words while Nielsen let them sink in.

'He's missing?' asked Freeman.

'Since three days ago.'

'Was Mr Digby having any business problems?'

Nielsen was silent. He looked at Freeman as if the lawyer had crossed some inviolable line or broken some sacred taboo of upper-class etiquette.

'Whatever you tell me will remain confidential,' said Freeman, encouragingly. 'Whatever you tell me will not leave this room.'

'All right, then. As you said a moment ago, in order to

finance the takeover of La Contessa, Mr Freeman had to borrow heavily from a syndicate of banks. The banks are in Liechtenstein and the Cayman Islands. It isn't known exactly who the financiers are. Even *I* don't know. Mr Digby was playing his cards very close to his chest. That wasn't like him. He didn't usually have secrets from me . . . business secrets, I mean.'

'Do you have any suspicions, like who he might have met in the run-up to the deal or something like that?'

Nielsen remained silent.

'Look, the less I have to work with,' said Freeman, 'the less I can do to help.'

'There have been rumours that it involved certain Middle Eastern connections,' Nielsen said at last.

'Is that something you *know* or something you suspect?'

'Something I suspect. In the run-up to the deal he was meeting with a lot of people, and he was being very discreet about it, but I know he'd done business with the Arabs in the past and I suspect that they were behind it.'

'Why the need for secrecy? The Arabs are able to do business here quite openly. It's not something politically or militarily sensitive.'

'I suspect, and I stress this is just a suspicion, that there was a quid pro quo involved. *Possibly* something military.'

'You mean something like a bit of unregistered lobbying?'

'With his press interests he wouldn't have needed to do that. I suspect that it was more on the lines of shipment diversion and bypassing the restricted list.'

'You mean illegal arms shipments?'

'Yes.'

'That would certainly be grounds to make a man disappear. Who do you suspect? Mossad? Or could he have fallen out with the people he was dealing with?'

'It could be either,' said Nielsen wearily.

'But you're sure it was the Arabs who were his business partners?'

'I'm not sure of anything. But that's what I suspect.

The only thing I'm sure of is that he was up to something.'

'I might be able to make some discreet enquiries. But first I'd like to piece together his movements up to the point when he was last seen.'

'I'll help you in any way I can. I've put together some preliminary information. That should reduce the number of people you need to talk to. We don't want to advertise the fact that Mr Digby is missing. It would cause the stock price to collapse. So far we've managed to keep it out of the papers.'

'How did you manage to find anything out without alerting people?'

'When a private secretary asks other staff members if they've seen someone or know where he is it doesn't mean he's missing. It just means that a panicky secretary is trying to find his employer quickly. It's not unusual for a businessman to be out of contact with home base.'

'Doesn't he have a mobile phone?'

'Not since the brain tumour scare started. He does in fact have a mobile phone in his car. And usually he can be reached at whichever office he has a meeting. But when he goes to the washroom or takes a lunch break he doesn't necessarily feel the need to touch base. He's his own master and as such his time is his own.'

'So what if you have to get a really urgent message to him?'

'He has a pager. Anyone can send him messages. But there's no way we can be sure if he got them . . . until he returns the call.'

'Before we get down to business, there is of course one small matter that we have to discuss.'

'Yes, of course,' said Nielsen. 'Your fee.'

Freeman was about to say 'That's right' when he saw Nielsen reaching for a brown leather attaché case and placing it on the desk between them. The secretary opened it and spun it round towards Freeman. Emmett Freeman's heart skipped a beat and his eyes practically popped out. The notes were twenties and there must have been at least fifty K in there.

'What's that?'

'That's your fee.'

'You're handing over that much cash? How much is in there anyway?'

'Seventy-five thousand.'

'You're handing over seventy-five K just to make a few enquiries?'

'I want you to try your best. There's another one seventy-five if you find him.'

'Are you sure there isn't something you haven't told me? Like maybe he's been kidnapped and you just want me to play delivery boy for the ransom?'

'No, Mr Freeman. There hasn't been any ransom demand, nor indeed any contact since he disappeared.'

'If you're giving it to me in cash, does that mean I don't have to pay tax on it?'

'That's between you and the Inland Revenue.'

'And if I do declare it don't you want to claim it as a tax deduction? Or does it come from Digby's slush fund?'

'The money is quite legal and has been properly taxed as Digby's personal income. The reason I'm giving you the money in this form is that I don't want any record of a paper transaction between the Digby Organization and a private detective. That sort of thing would be likely to set tongues wagging.'

Freeman closed the attaché case and placed it by the side of his chair. But his mind was racing. It could be a scam the secretary cooked up for bilking Old Man Digby. There could be an accomplice waiting in the wings to mug Freeman and relieve him of the money before he could get it to a bank or somewhere for safe-keeping. Then they'd have Digby released and make it seem as if the dirty private detective had swindled them. That would explain why Nielsen had brought the case to Freeman's one-man band instead of one of the big security firms.

However, he decided not pursue these speculations for

the time being. If Nielsen really wanted to set him up he would have needed a witness to the payment of the money, something which was conspicuously absent.

'OK,' said Freeman, 'let's get to work. When exactly was Digby last seen – the last positive sighting, that is?'

'When he left his office in Canada Tower at Canary Wharf at a quarter of eleven on the first of July.'

'Who saw him?'

'Well, his secretary saw him leave through her office.'

'I thought *you* were his secretary?'

'I'm his *private* secretary,' said Nielsen. 'He has a business secretary at his Canary Wharf office.'

'And that would be . . . what? The headquarters of La Contessa? Or the holding company?'

'The latter. The Offices of La Contessa are in Centrepoint.'

'So the only witness to the fact that he left his office was his secretary. What's her name, or is it a he?'

'Oh no,' said Nielsen. 'Lots of people saw him leaving. Executives, clerks, I think even the girl who brings the coffee round. But I can give you his secretary's name if you need it. Although I'd urge you to be discreet.'

'No, it's all right. I'll hold off on that for the time being. What I'd like to know is did he say where he was going? And for that matter I'd like to know all the appointments he had for that day. The ones he kept and the ones he missed.'

'He was on his way to an eleven-fifteen at the La Contessa offices. As for the other appointments, I took the liberty of making a photocopy of his desk diary and marking off the appointments which he kept. They were all at his Canary Wharf offices.'

Nielsen opened a desk drawer and handed over the prepared sheet.

'What exactly was this appointment at La Contessa? And why did he go over there? Why didn't he just summon the people to Canary Wharf?'

'It was a meeting of the full board of directors of La Contessa. So naturally they met at La Contessa's head-quarters.'

'So you have no idea what the meeting was about?'

'His secretary told me that he said something about boosting the sales of La Contessa's product. So I can only assume that it was a sales strategy meeting.'

It seemed strange to Freeman that Digby should discuss sales strategy with the full board. Normally only *executive* directors are involved in the day to day running of a company. But he kept the thought to himself.

'Was anyone with him when he left the office?'

'Like I said, the last people to see him were the staff in the office at Canary Wharf. If anyone had been with him, then someone would have seen him after that.'

'I mean someone that the staff didn't know. He might have left with someone that *he* knew but that they *didn't*. After all, if foul play was involved then obviously someone else *did* see him after that. But the question is who's the last person who saw him who can be *traced*?'

'Well, all I can tell you,' said Nielsen, 'is where my own, preliminary investigation came to a dead end. And that is when he left his Canary Wharf office . . . alone.'

'So does that then mean that he was planning to drive himself to the meeting at La Contessa?'

'Oh yes. Mr Digby always drove himself. It was part of his philosophy of life. He liked being in the driver's seat.'

'What was he driving?'

'A white Bentley – actually cream-coloured. Registration number FD2.'

'Two?' asked Freeman, looking up curiously.

'He had six other cars on this estate.'

'What are they?'

'Is that relevant?'

'It could be.'

'A 1912 vintage Rolls-Royce. That was FD1. A large Volvo station wagon, which was FD3. A two-hundred-mile-an-hour Porsche, FD4, and a very large minivan which carried the registration number FD5. He used the minivan when he drove his friends out on to the estate for a barbecue. Then they have a Burgundy Rolls-Royce and an army-green Jeep.'

'FD6 and FD7?' asked Freeman tentatively.

'VD1 and VD2,' said Nielsen flatly.

'VD?' asked Freeman, sheepishly.

'Veronica Digby.'

'His daughter?'

'His wife.'

'Wasn't that rather cruel of him, not to say crude?'

'What?' asked the secretary, innocently.

'Subjecting his wife to that sort of indignity.'

'Oh, it was *her* idea . . . or perhaps I should say her idea of a joke.'

'Is Mrs Digby a young woman?' asked Freeman.

'No, Mr Freeman. But she has a young woman's sense of humour, or maybe even a young boy's. Not that any of this really has anything to do with the case.'

'I'll decide what has to do with the case,' said Freeman, putting his foot down firmly.

Nielsen held up his hands and spread his fingers in a token of submission.

'OK,' Freeman continued. 'Are all his other cars accounted for?'

'Yes. They're all here. When he travels abroad he usually hires cars.'

'And what about the car that he was using on the day he disappeared? The cream-coloured Bentley?'

'That was found in the car park at Canary Wharf. It looks like he never got to it. Or he was kidnapped *when* he got to it.'

'Any sign of a struggle?'

'The police said no. They said if there was no sign of a struggle and no ransom demand then there was no evidence of abduction. With no evidence of abduction they say it may be a voluntary missing person. However, they haven't ruled out abduction, and they've assigned a detective chief inspector from the area level to the case, which suggests that they're taking it seriously.'

'I'll need his name.'

'*Her* name. One Karen Rousson.'

'A woman?' said Freeman, realizing, too late, that such a statement of the obvious was rather puerile.

Nielsen nodded.

'And where's the Bentley now?'

'The police have it. But they said that Mrs Digby can pick it up any time she likes. It's no longer evidence in an active investigation.'

'Why Mrs Digby?'

'She's the next of kin of the owner. Of course, she can give someone else written authorization to pick it up. As a matter of fact I intend to in the near future. I just haven't had time.'

'I'd like to pick it up myself. I may have a few ideas of what to check out.'

'I'll arrange it,' said Nielsen.

'Now, you said that when he travels abroad he hires cars.'

'Yes.'

'Does he have a hire card? Or does he have a preference for a particular company for that matter?'

'He has no preference.'

'How much money did he have on him at the time of his disappearance?'

'Oh . . . I would say . . . between one thousand and two thousand in cash, in a mixture of currencies.'

'Where did he keep it?'

'In a platinum money clip in his left trouser pocket.'

'A platinum money clip? Sounds like he enjoyed advertising his wealth.'

'More than some billionaires, but less than others. I think this was his idea of a joke. The clip was in the shape of a pound sign.'

Freeman nodded.

'Loose change?'

'He kept a hard leather money pouch in the same pocket.'

'Cheques? Credit cards?'

'A brown cordovan leather executive wallet in his left inside breast pocket. Visa, Master Card, American Express.

28

Again, all platinum cards He kept a full set of personal cheques on him, although he virtually never used them.'

'Drawn on which bank?'

'Coutts. He also kept five thousand in traveller's cheques, dollar-denominated, American Express.'

'Any particular reason? He could use his credit cards abroad surely.'

'I think as a sort of back-up. Sometimes the magnetic strip can get damaged. It was just an added precaution. He didn't believe in taking *unnecessary* risks.'

'So if he tended to travel at short notice, maybe this was one of his spontaneous jaunts?'

'His Gulfstream G-V is still in its hangar in the City Airport.'

'I stand corrected,' said Freeman, smiling. Of course, Nielsen's logic was far from impeccable. No matter how attracted Fabian Digby may have been to his luxury executive jet, that didn't mean that he was earthbound without it. But he let his reservations pass for the time being.

'Has any money been drawn from any of his accounts? Or weren't you able to check, if you'll excuse the pun.'

'Yes, with the formal authorization of Mrs Digby I *was* able to check, and no, not a penny's been withdrawn. Of course, I'm only talking about the US and European accounts. There may be accounts in the Bahamas and Caymans that I don't know about.'

'Or that you know about but can't find out about without Fabian Digby's authorization.'

Nielsen smiled but said nothing.

'Have Digby's credit cards been stopped?'

'Yes. Veron . . . Mrs Digby had them all cancelled.'

'But the bank accounts are presumably still open?'

'Short of actually withdrawing the money, the accounts can hardly be closed to one of their named co-holders. He's only missing, don't forget.'

'Has anyone tried to use the cancelled credit cards?'

'The police haven't informed us of anything like that. Nor the banks.'

'Does he have any other places of residence?'

'He has a private island in the Bahamas, a permanent suite at the London Hilton, a duplex in the Trump Tower in New York. He also has a mansion, somewhat smaller than this one, in California, and a chalet in Switzerland on his own private Alp, complete with ski runs and chair lifts, of course. Finally he has a twelve-room triplex in Paris, overlooking the Champs Elysées.'

'And I assume he hasn't turned up at any of these places.'

'I left messages for him at all of them.'

'But they wouldn't tell you if he turned up there?'

'Not if he told them not to. But there's no reason why he would.'

'Did he have a change of clothes with him?'

'No. Look, I have to say, quite categorically, that I don't believe that he disappeared of his own free will. I think . . . I am *convinced* that he was abducted.'

'Nevertheless *I* am the one who has been hired to find him, and until I'm satisfied in my own mind I have to consider all the possibilities, and not just accept your judgment.'

'Very well. I just want to put my views on record with you.'

'Noted,' said Freeman. 'What was he wearing when he left the house in the morning?'

'A dark blue single-breasted three-button suit.'

'Pin-stripe?'

'Solid blue. He hated pin-stripes.'

'Shirt?'

'Pale blue, almost white. Wash-and-wear.'

'Can you give me a picture of him, if possible in the suit he was wearing when he left?'

'I'll find you one.'

'Have there been any changes in his lifestyle recently?'

'Such as what?'

'A new religion? Gambling debts? Taking to drink? Doing drugs? Yoga? A new mistress?'

'No to all of the above. Actually I can't say about the

last, but I know he never smoked and only drank with his evening meal, a good Burgundy or claret usually.'

'Was he a puritan?'

'If he had been, I could have said no to the mistress, couldn't I? He was a man who valued his health. A clear head and a clear set of lungs were as important to him as success in business. In fact they were part of the means that enabled him to become successful – and to stay that way.'

'OK, now I have one more question which you've already answered once. But I want you to think about it again before answering. Could Fabian Digby have had *any* reason for going into hiding, or wanting to disappear?'

Nielsen hesitated for a moment.

'I think that he may have been afraid of his business partners. You see that's a double-edged sword. It could mean that they had a motive to kidnap him . . . or that he had a motive to go into hiding to run away from them.'

'Fair enough. Now tell me something else. Did Digby have any children?'

'Three. Two by his previous marriage, one by the present one.'

'Tell me a bit about them.'

'The eldest, Nicola, is twenty-eight. She's a spoilt brat. She expects everything and does nothing.'

'Is she pretty?'

'She's beautiful,' said Nielsen, resentfully.

'That means she can get away with it,' said Freeman.

'Exactly. Her younger brother, Michael, is twenty-six. He was the very serious and studious one. He has a PhD in physics from Cambridge.'

Freeman felt a stab of anger at the these words. He remembered his own physics degree, won through two years of hard work after an unpromising start in his freshman year. Then it was taken away by a university kangaroo court on the most circumstantial of evidence. He thought of the ten years when he could have been moving back the frontiers between the known and unknown in the realms of quantum mechanics and cosmology. Instead, he was reduced to hustling for business from science-based companies while striving to clear his name. It was a struggle that had brought him a law degree and the satisfaction of ruffling a few establishment feathers. But it could never bring back the wasted years or the flexibility of mind that goes with youth. And he knew in retrospect that the satisfaction of felling the mighty had been no more than a pathetic consolation for being thwarted in his efforts to fulfil his childhood dreams.

It had been a bitter pill to swallow. Made all the more bitter by the knowledge that you only have one life, and if you fail to make the most of it, you will never get another chance. Except in the dreams of Buddhists, life doesn't come around again. The saddest part was that in his mind's eye he could see upon his grave the saddest and most bitter of all epitaphs: 'He failed to achieve his potential.'

He became aware of Nielsen's eyes upon him, and he knew that he had been day dreaming. They had been talking about Mike Digby, Fabian's son.

'Does he support himself?' asked Freeman.

'No. I think his father supplements his income.'

'To what extent?'

'Enough to make his sister jealous. Nicola is always complaining about that, although Mr Digby insists that he gives them both the same.'

'I guess that when you're a spoilt brat, nothing is ever enough.'

'That's certainly true. Also, I think that Michael is a better financial manager. He makes his money go further, probably through sound investments. At any rate he never tries to draw more than his allowance.'

'You said there were three children . . . one by the current marriage if I'm not mistaken.'

'The youngest, by his current marriage as you say, is John. He's seventeen years old and a rebel. He's into motorbikes and girls and Greenpeace.'

'And drugs?'

'He probably smokes pot, but I couldn't swear to it. I remember his father taunting him about it once. "You protest the pollution of the atmosphere but pollute your own body," he said. To which John replied, "At least it's mine to pollute."'

'It sounds like there was a bit of hostility in their relationship.'

'Not hostility exactly,' said Nielsen. 'I would call it tension. The dynamic tension of a father and son who love each other but disagree fervently on matters of politics, economics and ethics. Is there anything else you want to know?'

'Nothing more that you can tell me, at least not for the time being. I may have more questions later. But now I'd like to speak to Mrs Digby.'

'Very well,' said Nielsen stiffly. 'I'll see if she's ready to see you.'

He rose and left the room, looking decidedly uneasy.

While he was gone, Freeman looked around the room. It was old-fashioned, but very little that was in it was actually *old*. The rosewood desk looked almost new. Of course, they had servants to keep it well polished. But there were always tell tale signs. Not even the most enthusiastic servant can clean the dust away from those awkward corners where the wood meets the chrome drawer handle. And of course chrome was the giveaway. So Fabian Digby was a man who didn't like things too modern but liked them to be in good condition.

Freeman caught sight of his reflection in a bronze mirror, a dark-haired man of just above average height with dark eyes that shed rays of anger on everything they touched.

The door opened and Nielsen returned.

'She'll see you in the library.'

The secretary sounded more like a butler than ever. Freeman said nothing as he followed Nielsen down the labyrinth of corridors to the library.

When he stepped into the grey-carpeted room he felt a sensation of awe, the old Temple of Knowledge syndrome that he remembered from his college days. He looked around the library and saw that it was panelled in mahogany rather than rosewood. But even if this was only the prince of woods rather than the queen, the room looked every bit as opulent as the secretary's office. Freeman craned his neck, looking up to the high ceiling and the internal balcony that ran around the room. It was the balcony which made many of the books accessible. Even so, Freeman suspected that one needed a small step ladder to reach the upper shelves in the lower section of the room. What impressed him most was the fact that the books were leather-bound, although as he looked up he noticed the paperbacks safely stashed away out of the immediate line of sight.

The room was flooded with light, not from the reading lights and floor-standing lamps in the corners, but from the huge window that looked out on to a beautifully landscaped garden and a dolphin-shaped water fountain. In a way the garden depressed him in spite of its elegance. It made nature look artificial, which to Freeman was no better than doing away with nature altogether. But when he returned his attention to the library, his sense of aesthetic equilibrium was restored.

In the centre of the room, on a white-leather upholstered armchair, sat Veronica Digby.

'Mr Freeman, I presume.'

It was hard to say what struck Freeman first: the fact that she was almost fifty or the fact that she was beautiful. It was all mixed up in his mind, a first impression that could not be unravelled or resolved into separate components. The only thing he saw was the whole: the maturity and the beauty. Not that she was without imperfections. There were one or two grey hairs amid the ash-blond and one or two lines on the face. Yet there was a kind of marble exquisiteness about her cheeks and forearms, about her full figure and the upright way in which she sat, not slouching with youthful indifference or bent with tired age, but with poise and self-control. And there was something about the blue eyes, that was almost frightening. They looked right at him and held him, not forcing him to look away . . . but forcing him not to.

'I understand that you wanted to ask me some questions about the disappearance of my husband.'

'That's right.'

'Didn't Nielsen give you all the details?'

'He thought he did. But there are one or two things that I'd like to ask you . . . with your permission.'

'By agreeing to see you I have effectively given it.'

Freeman rubbed the back of his neck with embarrassment.

'Perhaps it would be better if we talked alone.'

Out of the corner of his eye, Freeman caught Nielsen trying to say something, probably a murmur of protest. But Veronica Digby silenced him with a flick of the wrist, an almost imperceptible gesture that Freeman would not have caught had he not been looking out for it. He wanted to know who was in charge here. The information could be useful later on.

'For my part it isn't necessary,' said Veronica, 'but if you prefer it . . .'

She half turned her face towards Nielsen. He shifted uncomfortably from foot to foot and then left, salvaging his dignity by saying 'I'll be outside if you need me' as he reached the door.

'Maybe you could get me that photograph, Mr Nielsen,' said Freeman, emphasizing his control of the situation.

'Yes, of course,' said Nielsen, deferentially. Freeman suspected that the deference was not directed towards him.

Veronica Digby looked at Freeman as if assessing him. He almost expected her to pull out a pair of pince-nez or even a lorgnette and study him like a painting or a prospective son-in-law. But instead she merely nodded towards another armchair facing hers across a mahogany coffee table.

He followed her cue and sat.

'Now, Mr Freeman, how can I help you to find my husband and spare me from the awful wave of rumour and gossip that will assail me if he fails to materialize in the near future?'

Freeman looked around awkwardly, and felt the tension

rising in him. He was normally in control of his cases, but here he was dealing with a woman who had probably seen more of life than he, and who certainly knew how to wield power.

The next question had to be asked delicately . . . but it had to be asked.

'Were there any problems in your, and your husband's, personal life?'

'Such as what?' asked Veronica.

He hesitated, wondering how to put it without giving offence.

'In your . . . relations.'

'We had an active sex life,' she replied, not smiling. The tone seemed to be almost dismissive of his reticence about asking the question.

'Had . . .?' Freeman continued, tentatively.

'Up until the day before he disappeared.'

'So you don't suspect him of infidelity.'

'Define infidelity,' she said, with stubborn pedantry.

He thought to himself for a moment. Then, with comparable pedantic stiffness, he replied: 'Infidelity, marital. Carnal relations by a married party with a partner other than one's spouse; enjoying connubial bliss outside the bonds of holy matrimony; sexual activity with one while married to another; having a bit on the side.'

He smiled awkwardly, embarrassed by the frankness of his own formulation, wondering, in the face of Mrs Digby's stony expression, if he had gone too far.

'Does your definition not take account of the state of the other party's knowledge? – knowledge of the *intellectual* variety, I mean.'

Freeman looked at her blankly. She continued, 'I notice that your definition failed to distinguish between covert and overt extramarital relations. A skilled advocate could present a plausible case for excluding overt extramarital activity from the category of infidelity on the grounds that no deception is involved.'

Freeman nodded gently, impressed by Veronica Digby's

argument and by the underlying intellectual precision that it demonstrated. He had read about the Digby couple in the *Tatler*, and had always assumed Mrs Digby to be one of those elegant but middle-brow society wives, organizing charity dinners for Third World refugees and salons for the latest literary lions. But listening to her now he realized that there was an active intelligence behind those elegant gowns and sparkling jewels, and quite possibly, he suddenly suspected, the real brains behind the Digby business empire.

'You mean you had an understanding?' he asked, bringing the language back down to what he thought to be the appropriate level of crudeness for the subject matter.

'I mean that my husband did what he liked,' she said flatly. 'And when I had a mind for it, so did I.'

He looked at her appraisingly. That she had a *body* for it went without saying.

'So when you said before that you had an active sex life . . .' He trailed off, once again lost for the right word or phrase.

'I meant that we had active sex *lives*,' she amended.

'He had a mistress?'

'Mistresses.'

She stressed the plural significantly.

'I stand corrected,' said Freeman. 'So he didn't have anyone serious.'

'Oh yes he did,' Mrs Digby corrected him a second time. '*Me*.'

Again the bewilderment swept over Freeman's face.

'Forgive me,' she said. 'I've embarrassed you.'

'No you haven't. Just confused me.'

'Well, then, let me explain. My husband, like so many men of his age, thought that sleeping with young girls rejuvenated him. And like so many men of his age, he was right. Whenever he came home in the mood for a feverish night of passionate lovemaking, I knew that he'd spent the afternoon with some busty blonde that he'd picked up in a laundrette near University College.'

'That's where he picked them up?'

'He didn't like call-girls or streetwalkers. He said he liked them with a bit of brains, a modicum of class and a lot of enthusiasm. College girls fitted the bill.'

'Didn't it bother you?' asked Freeman.

'Mr Freeman,' she replied, 'when you sit before a warm glowing coal fire on a cold winter evening, does it bother you that men risked their lives down a dank, dark coalmine, inhaling dust and soot so that you could enjoy the warmth?'

Freeman nodded, comprehendingly, and rose to take his leave, realizing that there was nothing more to be said.

Ten minutes later, attaché case and photograph in hand, he was being escorted to the door by Alan Nielsen.

'Mr Nielsen, there's one more thing I'd like to ask you. You mentioned before that you suspect that Fabian Digby's partners were Arabs and that the Israeli Mossad might be involved. Does that have some bearing on the fact that you picked me?'

Nielsen looked away, evidently nervous.

'How do you mean?'

'I mean did you choose me to investigate because I lived in Israel for a number of years?'

'I understand that you were in the Israeli Army. I thought perhaps you could use your contacts.'

'The Israeli Army and Mossad are two different things.'

'Let's just say that you're in a better position than most. If you come back in a few days and say that there's no point looking any further, I'll understand not to ask any other questions.'

'You think Mossad killed him?'

'I wouldn't put it past them. They probably killed Gerald Bull, when he tried to help the Iraqis build a super-gun. They would certainly have been ready to do the same if they thought that Mr Digby was smuggling weapons to the Arabs. Or they might have kidnapped him like they did with Vanunu when he spilled the beans on their nuclear secrets.'

They had reached the door.

'In this case,' said Freeman, 'they wouldn't have needed

to do either of those things. All they'd've had to do was make the evidence available to the Crown Prosecution Service and have him prosecuted.'

'Only if the evidence was adequate. We had a recent fiasco when businessmen were improperly tried for selling arms to embargoed countries. Also, Mr Digby had the kind of connections that might have made the authorities reluctant to prosecute him. I'm sure you know about those kinds of connections.'

Freeman tensed with anger.

'I stand corrected,' he replied.

3

*'Where you die, I will die and there I will be
buried.'*

Ruth 1:17

'Yisgadal veyiskadash shemai raba.'

She was still drowsy from the tranquillizers, but Miriam
Neuman thought she could hear the sound of choking in her
son's voice as he struggled to recite the Jewish memorial
prayer over the coffin for the third time as it was lowered into
the ground. He had recited the Kaddish before they set out
from the Beit Hamidrash and then again by the grave before
the coffin was lowered. But each time he had recited it, the
lump in his thoat had grown thicker and he had strained all
the harder to recite the words of the prayer.

Walter Rubin had put a comforting hand on his shoulder
as he recited the prayer, but that hadn't made it any easier.
He had always thought of Rubin as a harsh but encouraging
teacher, who admired intelligence and effort but who was
too cold and strict to be a father figure, lacking the loving
nature of a real father. When his father had died, he had
borne the psychological burden alone. Rubin had eased the
financial burden.

So now as he got to the end of the Kaddish for the third

40

time, he broke down, unable to continue. Rubin held his hand and recited the last few words for him.

Like all Jewish funerals it was arranged quickly and held as soon as the post-mortem was completed. The decision to conduct the post-mortem quickly had been taken without regard to religious issues. Post-mortems are almost always carried out quickly when the scene-of-crime officer's report suggests the probability of foul play. And one couldn't get more probable than a knife wound in the abdomen.

Jewish law requires funerals to be held as soon as possible after death. The solidarity among the Jewish community was such that even though the Neumans had drifted away from synagogue attendance, they were still treated as part of the community when they needed help, and the rabbi, along with several neighbours, had sprung into action when the news of their bereavement became known.

After the funeral, Rubin drove them home where they began sitting shivah, the seven days of mourning that Jewish households traditionally sit after the death of a member of the immediate family. During that period they would be visited by more distant relatives and friends, who would sit and talk with them about old times. The conversation was seldom morbid, tending to dwell on the life rather than the death, the good times and plans for the future.

'So what have we got?' asked the Detective Chief Superintendent. 'Is it a mugging or is it domestic?'

'It's too early to say,' said Detective Inspector Logan. 'Forensics didn't find anything to tie him to the SOCO swabs.'

They were in the area headquarters: DI Logan from the local police station and the DCS from area level.

'So we can't get the boffins to place him at the crime scene. What about eye-witnesses?'

'Well, no one's come forward yet,' said Logan. 'We've checked the street security camera that covers the side street where Philip Neuman says they split up, but there are too many Japanese tourists in the way. Personally I think we're going to have to assume that it's non-domestic.'

'That means I'm going to have to assemble an AMIP team,' said the DCS reluctantly. Logan knew what was bugging his superior. Putting together an Area Major Information Pool team meant taking experienced officers off other duties. Also it might necessitate overtime and sending out batches of samples to the Met Lab or even one of the regional labs. Nowadays, under the new policy of making every penny count, the Home Office labs, including the Met Lab, functioned as separate entities, billing the police for their services. As such, the ever cost-conscious DCS had to weigh the pros and cons of any course of action that might significantly draw on the services of the labs, or which might involve shelling out for overtime.

'I know, sir. But there's nothing to suggest it's domestic. It took place in the street and there's no proof they were together at the time.'

'And what cause did the PM show?'

'A single stab wound to the stomach, just below the liver.'

'Angle of penetration?'

'Upward and slightly towards the median line.'

The DCS shifted uncomfortably. He had wanted to wrap the case up in forty-eight hours, but it was becoming increasingly apparent that this wasn't going to happen.

'OK, I'll tell you what you do. Go along to the kid's house with a policewoman. Don't bring him into the nick. Question him *in situ*, so he can see the home he shared with his brother and the things they touched and shared. Don't pile on the pressure, just ask him a few questions. Get a feel for if he wants to come clean, and if so, keep him talking.'

'HOLMES equipment?' asked Logan, leaning forward hopefully.

'You can have a terminal in the pre-wired room,' the DCS replied grudgingly.

'Operator?'

'Only one. Day shift. You're unlikely to get any information that can't wait until morning.'

HOLMES was a Computer Network. It stood for Home Office Large Major Enquiry system. It was now in the process of being upgraded in a big way. But for any given investigation, resources were still scarce.

Many of those who attended the funeral had also come back home with them. But they would not participate in the 'meal of condolence' that Rubin's sister was cooking. This was the first meal that they had eaten since being notified of the death, it being a Jewish tradition that the mourners fast from the time of notification of the death until the completion of the burial. It was also a matter of Jewish law that a visitor does not take food from a house in mourning and a tradition that visitors bring food to the house to spare the mourners the need to go out and deal with such mundane matters as shopping for food.

They sat in the living room, amid the grey upholstered furniture and oak sideboard and table. The mirrors were covered. A Jewish family in mourning were not supposed to look at their exteriors, but to contemplate their inner selves and look with hope towards the future.

Miriam identified with this tradition, but her son, seated on his low stool, was feeling alienated from it. She knew that since the death of his father he had not merely drifted away from Judaism, but had developed more than a passing interest in another religion, equally old but native to northern Europe. She had asked him not to wear his silver pentacle neck-chain at the funeral. But now, almost as an act of defiance, he had put it on again.

He looked over at his mother. She appeared to be engaged in earnest conversation with a man on the other side of the room. Walter Rubin was standing there too, and a pretty young WPC was standing just a few feet away. The stranger and Miriam Neuman appeared to be arguing, or at least disagreeing. The boy caught Rubin's eye and the teacher signalled him with a gesture of the hand to come over.

He broke off the perfunctory conversation with the ageing great-aunt who had plonked herself next to him and walked over to where his mother, Rubin and the unknown man were standing. It was Rubin who was the first to speak.

'Phil, this is Detective Inspector Logan of the Golders Green police station. He'd like to ask you a few questions about Tony. You don't have to do it now. But he just has a couple of quick questions which might help the police. If you'd like to answer now I'm sure the inspector would be most grateful.'

'OK,' he said, confused rather than afraid. He'd already answered a few questions from a CID sergeant yesterday evening, about when they had split up, not to mention having to surrender the clothes he was wearing last night and give a blood sample. It was only 'routine', they had assured him. 'Just to eliminate you from the inquiry,' they had said more than once. But he had caught fragments of muted conversations in which words like 'DNA' and 'alcohol level' were mentioned. He assumed that the questions they had already asked were the most important ones and that everything else could wait. He didn't really see what more he could add. But if the inspector wanted more information, he saw no reason not to give it. Anything to break the monotony of this ordeal of being surrounded by wizened old aunts and uncles whom he hadn't seen in donkey's years and wouldn't care if he never saw again.

'We can go into another room if you'd like,' said the inspector.

He noticed that the inspector seemed nervous. He was surprised at this. He always thought that policemen were supposed to be in control of the situation. Or maybe it was just embarrassment. It probably wasn't every day that he had to intrude on a funeral or a period of mourning.

'Let's go upstairs, Inspector,' he said.

'OK,' said the inspector. Then he turned to Miriam Neuman. 'Perhaps you'd like to come too?' he asked.

'What do you need her for?' the boy snapped.

The inspector looked embarrassed, but said nothing.

44

'It's all right,' said Miriam Neuman in a conciliatory tone. 'I'll wait down here.'

'I'd rather you came with us, Mrs Neuman,' said the inspector.

'*I* could come up with you,' Rubin volunteered.

'I'd rather speak alone,' said the boy.

The Inspector again looked uncomfortable at this, but Phil's mother showed no support for the Inspector in the look she flashed him although Rubin's look was rather more ambivalent.

'OK,' said Inspector Logan. 'You lead the way.'

He led the inspector upstairs and into the bedroom, followed by the policewoman. He knew that the police conducted interviews and searches in pairs so as to protect themselves from false accusations by criminals. He sat on one of the beds, leaving the inspector and the policewoman to choose between the other bed and the swivel chair by the small desk. The inspector turned the chair round to face the bed and sat down. The policewoman hesitated for a moment before sitting down on the other bed. She seemed to recognize the sensitivity of the matter, but decided in the end that if Phil objected to her sitting on Tony's bed he would have said so.

'First of all, I should introduce PC Woodward.'

'Isn't that *WPC*?' asked Phil.

'We don't use the W any more,' PC Woodward replied.

'You know, of course,' Inspector Logan began, 'we think your brother was killed by a mugger.'

'I know.'

'You sound sceptical,' said the inspector.

He could tell by his tone that the inspector was prompting him to talk freely. But he had little to say and he didn't like these games.

'I didn't say so. They told us he was stabbed and that he didn't have a wallet or watch on him and so it looked like a mugging.'

The inspector leaned forward.

'I'm glad you mentioned that. You see, it's the watch

that I really wanted to talk about. You told Sergeant Angus yesterday that your brother was wearing a gold Rolex watch. Is that correct?'

'That's right.'

'I was thinking that was rather an expensive watch for a young man to have, especially as I understand your family have been having some financial difficulties since your father's death.'

'Tony was always saying things were tight. But I think that was just his panicking temperament. That's because he didn't understand mathematics. He did his arithmetic in his head and always erred on the side of caution. That's probably how he managed to buy the watch.'

'I don't understand,' said Logan, leaning forward even further.

'Well, he was always saving up money for a rainy day and then buying things like there was no tomorrow. He saved up money like a squirrel, built up a nest egg and then treated himself to some shmonce or another.'

'Shmonce?' the inspector repeated, raising his eyebrows.

'A Yiddish expression. It means a cheap little trifle, a frivolous purchase.'

'A Rolex watch is hardly a cheap little trifle, Philip,' said Logan.

'Well, it was certainly a frivolous purchase.'

The boy felt Logan's eyes upon him and became uncomfortable.

'So you think the watch was just something he bought on impulse after saving up his money,' said the inspector. 'Is that it, Philip? An impulse purchase?'

'I think so,' he echoed. He noticed that while PC Woodward was saying nothing, she was watching him the whole time, and her attention seemed to be focused on his pentacle neck-chain.

'OK,' said the inspector, standing up. 'That's really all I wanted to know. Well, thank you very much, Phil, you've been a great help.'

They noticed a look of relief on the young man's face,

as if these few simple questions had been more of an ordeal than he wanted them to know.

The inspector led the way downstairs, exchanging a brief eye contact with the WPC before walking on ahead of her. He followed them downstairs and saw them out, nodding politely as they thanked him again for his co-operation and told him how they realised how painful this must be for him. When he turned round he found himself confronted by his mother. She had an implacable, knowing look on her face, as if to say: *I know what they were asking about.*

'You shouldn't be standing, Mum,' he said.

She shook her head coolly.

'I'm fine.'

'The doctor said that with those tranquilizers you should be careful —'

'I haven't taken another tranquilizer.'

The look remained implacable.

'It was nothing, Mum. They just wanted to ask some routine questions. You know the sort of thing: where we went, what time we split up. Things like that.'

The look on her face told him that she didn't believe him.

'We have to talk,' she said.

'OK,' he replied, swallowing fearfully as he nodded.

Bournemouth had special memories for the Neuman family. It was where Jeremy and Miriam had gone for several of their holidays. This was in the austere early years of their marriage before the kids were born. Then they had returned there several times with the kids. Once they had started to prosper they took their annual holidays in Israel. But they still remembered those early years when they used to eat their home-made sandwiches on the beach or ran and played in the gardens by the River Bourne.

Miriam had decided to stay at the hotel. She was content to sit by the swimming pool, reading a light romance and trying to remember the good times. She would have been happy to have talked with her son but he seemed in no mood to talk to her. He was eating himself up with guilt over the fact that he had split up with his brother on that fateful day, and nothing she could say would offer him any comfort. Time might ease his pain, but words would only scratch at the scar and make the pain cut deeper.

So he went off on his own. At first he strolled aimlessly on the beach and even lost a couple of pounds in coins at the amusement arcade on the pier. Then, when the novelty had worn off, he wandered through the well-tended lower central gardens with their neatly trimmed grass and meticulously laid-out flower beds, watching the brook trip along the stones. But there were too many people around, too many holidaymakers and children running here and there, reminding him of his own childhood and the good times that he had shared with his brother. And now it was all gone. So he walked up into the central gardens where people were thinner on the ground and the grass was mowed less often, though still well tended. He ambled along by the brook, heading for the upper gardens, rough and overgrown, where he could find genuine solitude.

It had been a hard week and he sensed that his problems were far from over. The hardest part hadn't been the search of the house or having to hand over his clothes, or even giving body samples. The hardest part had been having to go into the mortuary and formally identify the body. He hadn't wanted to do it, but it was either him or his mother. And he couldn't let her do it. So he went in and looked down at the body. The pain of seeing his brother lying dead on a slab had almost broken him. He felt responsible. Yet he couldn't talk about his feelings to anyone.

It was hard to imagine the rest of his life without his brother. They had done so much together, exchanged so much knowledge and lived so much on each other's inspiration. It was Tony who had taught Phil about genetic engineering, about how easy it was to use enzymes to cut the DNA that coded for a protein or group of proteins and then splice it into another species so as to induce that species to produce the protein. He had said, half jokingly, that one day it could be used to produce people with chlorophyl in their skin, enabling them to photosynthesize. 'That's why you hear about aliens from other planets being little green men,' he added, completing the joke. 'They need to be able to photosynthesize in order to survive the long journey.'

Tony had always been able to find humour in science. To him it was never a dry subject, but a source of infinite fun.

And the exchange of knowledge had worked both ways. It was Phil who had taught Tony about computers, about hiding files on line and encrypting them to protect them. Tony had been particularly interested in a refresher course on Pretty Good Privacy encryption after he had started to meet the people that he had told Phil about.

The question was, did any of this have anything to do with his brother's death? The murder had all the hallmarks of a mugging. Why should it be anything else? And yet, as soon as he had heard the news his first thought had been that it was an attempt to guarantee the silence of someone who could incriminate dangerous and powerful people.

The West End of London was not like America. Muggings were not par for the course. Muggers were more likely to prey on women, who were weaker and more vulnerable. And muggers seldom killed their vicitms because usually they didn't need to. Why would his brother put up a show of resistance if he was mugged? He was not a physical person by any means, hardly what you would call a man of action. Certainly, he was physically fit. They both were. But he wasn't the type to indulge in heroics with an armed adversary. And he was wise enough to realize that a knife was as deadly as a gun at close quarters.

Why, then, would he put up a fight? The answer was obvious. But he couldn't bring himself to admit it. He tried to find some other explanation. Perhaps the mugger killed him to stop him describing him to the police. But that made no sense. If that had been his motive why didn't the mugger simply conceal his face? Did this mean that he killed everyone he mugged? If so, then one would expect far more victims with a similar modus operandi. Were there any? Or did he just forget to cover his face on this occasion? Or did his brother pull the mask off the mugger's face? Perhaps the mugger heard other people coming and couldn't take the chance of the alarm being raised before he got clear. Yes, that was the most likely explanation. But at the back of his mind there was an element of doubt, as if this explanation also didn't quite ring true. And there was a still more logical explanation.

He decided that he couldn't let it rest.

It was a week later when Mrs Neuman and her son returned to their house. The boy couldn't remember afterwards whether the taxi journey from the station had been accompanied by a genuine sense of foreboding or just the depression that accompanies the end of any holiday. Miriam had tried to perk him up with idle chit-chat, but that had only made him all the more irritated. The only thing he knew was that his mood had been sombre on the way home and turned to horror when he and his mother arrived.

The house had been ransacked, turned over from top to bottom. His mother was too distraught to speak, but he rushed through the house from room to room to see what had been taken. The two televisions were still there, as was the main stereo and the one in his room. He checked his mother's bedroom to find her jewellery still there in the locked lower drawer of the dressing table. The only thing missing was Tony's desktop computer. Phil's laptop had gone with them to Bournemouth and was still intact. But that was irrelevant. What they were after had been on Tony's machine. The question was, did they want to find out what was on the computer, or did they merely want to make sure that no one *else* found out?

4

'Those who deal with the law did not know me . . .'

Jeremiah 2:4

Police Area Command HQs, in reality, never seemed quite like they did on TV. There was none of that sense of urgency, as if something big was going down. It was more like an endless stream of work as enquiries were moved from one pile or tray to another, rather like a rumbling old factory production line. Of course, this wasn't a weekend or Christmas Eve. Still, he expected to encounter a sense of urgency when he walked in, but instead all he saw was people quietly going about their business with none of the hustle and bustle of the popularised TV image. He suspected that being a cop was even more boring that being a lawyer. But he wouldn't have confided that thought to anyone.

He had spent a few days in the British Museum library looking through back issues of *Fortune* and *Business Week* for articles about the La Contessa takeover. Now he felt that it was time to speak to the police officer in charge of the missing person inquiry. He was now confident that he understood Fabian Digby the businessman from the articles almost as well as he understood Fabian Digby the person from Veronica Digby's description of his behaviour.

They had told him at the reception desk that he would have to be escorted to see Detective Chief Inspector Karen Rousson. He first had to fill out his details in an entry book. When he finished, the top copy was torn off and inserted into a plastic wallet with a metal clip that became his entry badge. He was led to a bank of lifts by a young uniformed constable, tall and very thin, with an intense, serious look about him. He was a sort of young Abraham Lincoln, but without the beard.

As he breezed through the open-plan office, with its shoulder-high partitions, he looked around. The staff seemed busy, but not in an intense way as in the trading room of a stock brokerage or an investment bank. The pervading atmosphere appeared to be one of cool efficiency and purposefulness of action combined with an economy of movement.

He was led to an enclosed office and asked to wait while the constable went in. A few seconds later he emerged, holding the door half open.

'You can go in now,' he said.

'Thank you,' Freeman replied as he entered.

Inside the room, Freeman saw a blond woman sitting with her back to him, talking on the telephone, one hand resting on the desk as she looked out of the window. As she turned, offering him the first glimpse of her profile, her saw her for what she was, a full-figured beauty. She was almost tall enough to strut the catwalk, but her feminine figure would have disqualified her. She was fit and strong, like an athlete, with all the power of a coiled spring locked up inside her and ready to snap if her trigger was activated. She would not have made an easy victim for a lawbreaker. An opportunist criminal, trained in the art of taking the line of least resistance, would do well to steer clear of her.

After a few seconds of silence, as she listened to the voice on the other end of the telephone, she sprang to life again.

'OK, well, tell him that if the CPS turns him back on to

the street, *they* can explain it to the tabloids when he does it again.'

She slammed the phone down as she turned to look at Freeman. Freeman felt self-conscious. He knew that he was smiling, and also that he couldn't stop himself.

'DCI Karen Rousson,' she said firmly and in a tone clearly lacking patience. 'What can I do for you?'

He felt aroused by the sight of her, impressed by her appearance. He never liked the waif look that homosexual fashion designers had foisted upon the public as stand-ins for the adolescent boys they have in mind when they design their clothes. There was something exciting about her angry face and athletic appearance. It was a pleasing contrast to the overpaid, anorexic beanpoles that strutted the cat-walk. She looked as if she would be as much at home with a group of football players or stockbrokers as in a beauty salon. He could almost see her as a contender on *Gladiators* or even as a gladiator herself. She was a woman at home in a man's world, yet still most manifestly a woman.

'I understand that you're the person to speak to regarding a missing person.'

'Well, we don't have a missing person's department or bureau as such,' she said, with gentle stress in her voice. 'But I *am* in charge of the inquiry into the disappearance of Fabian Digby, which I understand is what you're here about.'

'I stand corrected. I was wondering if you might be able to help me. I've been asked by the Digby family to make some discreet enquiries into his disappearance. Enquiries with people who might not talk to the police.'

He handed her his card, wondering why his words had produced a flicker in her eyes.

'If you're in a position to make discreet enquiries that we aren't, it should more properly be if *you* can help *us*,' said Karen, perusing the card.

'I suppose that too,' Freeman conceded.

'So you're an attorney,' she said looking up from his card with a mocking smile.

'Exactly,' he said, wincing at her choice of words. Even

though solicitors had now gained partial access to the crown and high courts, they preferred to be called lawyers rather than attorneys. In Britain, the word attorney had somewhat condescending connotations, unless capitalized and used in conjunction with the word 'general'.

'In this case,' he continued, 'I seem to be acting more as a private detective.'

She looked at him for a few seconds, as if trying to size him up.

He let her take her time about it.

'It doesn't cost extra to sit,' she said finally, breaking the silence.

Freeman sat and spoke cautiously.

'Could I ask you something?'

'Shoot,' said Karen.

'Is it usual for a missing person's inquiry to be headed by a Chief Inspector?'

She thought about this for a moment.

'It can be anyone from a uniformed constable all the way up to a DCS. It depends on the facts of the case. A missing child gets high priority. A missing adult who's known to be *compos mentis* gets little more than a constable on the beat taking notes for the record unless there's some evidence of foul play.'

'Is there evidence of foul play in Digby's case?'

'No direct evidence. But the fact that he disappeared leaving a fortune behind while on his way to a meeting is inherently suspicious.'

'So how did the case reach you?'

'Well, Digby's big in the international arms trade and has several key political contacts. There was no sign of foul play on the one hand, but no sign of a pre-planned departure on the other. That suggests involuntary disappearance and those further down the ladder decided it was too hot to handle, so they passed it up the chain of command until the file ended up on my desk.'

'And that's where the buck stopped,' Freeman summarized.

'Exactly.'

'So you didn't see any need to pass it higher?'

'Not at this stage.'

'But would it be fair to say,' asked Freeman, 'that Digby's disappearance is now presumed to be involuntary?'

'I wouldn't go so far as to say presumed,' the DCI replied. 'We're still keeping open minds at this stage. But considering that he was on his way to an important meeting and never made it to his car, we accept that there's a strong chance that foul play was involved. At any rate, something certainly happened to change his plans.'

'You mentioned that Digby had interests in the arms industry,' said Freeman. 'And that he had a few major political contacts. Could this case have national security implications?'

'If it had I probably wouldn't be on it. They'd be handling it from the Yard.'

'So you're saying that Special Branch aren't involved in this case at all,' said Freeman cautiously.

'That's right.'

'And the Security Service?'

'MI5 don't tell us what they're doing,' said DCI Rousson. 'They just tell us to hand over everything we've got.'

'And they haven't done that yet?' asked Freeman.

'That's right.'

'Or told you to stop investigating.'

'That's right.'

'And they would have done if you'd been stepping on their toes.'

'Probably.'

'So we can reasonably infer that they aren't investigating?'

'You can infer what you like, Mr Freeman. But it could simply be that we haven't found out anything that we aren't supposed to know, so they aren't unduly troubled by our investigation. But on the other hand, if you have the capacity to make enquiries that we can't, then *you* might end up stepping on their toes. And they can turn rather nasty if that happens.'

'Is that what you think is going down?'

'I'm not saying that's what's happening. I'm just saying that's what *could* be happening. If MI5 are on the case I'm just as much in the dark as you are.'

'But the one thing that I – and the Digby family – can rest assured of is that the disappearance of Fabian Digby is being taken seriously?'

He studied her carefully.

'Very seriously.'

'Then would it be fair to say that although you're heading the investigation, you're reporting periodically to someone higher up the chain of command?'

'My DCS,' replied Karen with a trace of irritation. Freeman sensed a modicum of resentment at having to report to a superior. Or perhaps it was just resentment of the particular superior in question.

'OK. I hope you don't mind that I've approached the matter in this way, Ms Rousson. But the fact that the Digby family asked me to make these enquiries suggests that they aren't sure how vigorously Fabian Digby is being looked for.'

'As I've already assured you, Mr Freeman,' said Karen, not without some further irritation, 'we *are* looking for him and we are taking his disappearence as probably involuntary.'

'Can you tell me what lines of enquiry you're following?' said Freeman, trying to keep a straight face. 'So that I can avoid duplicating your work.'

'Mr Freeman, look very carefully at my forehead.'

Freeman was bewildered by this remark, but he looked anyway. There was no denying, it was a very pretty forehead.

'Yes?' he said, tentatively.

'Do you see the word "sucker" written there?'

He blinked, quickly adjusting himself to the fact that he had just heard a humorous quip delivered deadpan by a member of the Metropolitan Police. The blinking gave way to a smile and the smile to what was almost a roar of laughter as he realized that DCI Karen Rousson had seen straight through him. Of course there was no way that the police were going to tell a representative of the Digby family what lines of enquiry they were pursuing. Apart from anything else, the Digby family were technically all suspects until the case was resolved, or at least until they were satisfactorily eliminated from the inquiry.

'OK,' said Freeman, cupping his hand over his mouth. 'You got me there. But I was wondering about the facts of the disappearance itself. Like when he was last seen. Things like that.'

'We already told the Digby family about that – or at least Alan Nielsen, Digby's personal secretary.'

'I understand that Digby was on his way to a director's meeting of La Contessa.'

'So we were told, Mr Freeman.'

'Who told you?'

'Half a dozen members of Digby's personal staff.'

'And how do we know he never got there?'

'We talked to the directors. They sat there for over an hour twiddling their thumbs waiting for him. It was actually one of the directors who called the police in the first place.'

'Which one?'

'Edward Fielding.'

'The MP?'

'That's right.'

'I don't suppose I could speak to them?' asked Freeman tentatively.

'That's between you and them.'

'You see, Alan Nielsen told me that they were meeting to discuss sales strategy, and I was wondering why non-executive directors would discuss sales.'

'You think they were lying?' asked Karen.

'It's a possibility,' said Freeman.

'Now perhaps *you* can help *me*,' she said.

'I'll try,' replied Freeman, leaning forward eagerly.

'I'm a policewoman, not an expert on business matters. So perhaps you could help me unravel the background behind

Digby's business activities, which might help me put his disappearance into some sort of perspective.'

'I'll help in any way I can.'

'I understand that there was a bit of a takeover battle over La Contessa.'

'Yes, that's right,' said Freeman. 'The former CEO of the company fought Digby tooth and nail over control.'

'Why was that?' asked Karen. 'He didn't own the company, did he?'

'No, but he knew that if the deal went ahead he'd be out on his ass. The company was underperforming and the shareholders were already getting restless.'

'What was his name?' asked the DCI.

'Who?'

'The chief executive.'

'Mike Artagnon.'

'Artagnon?' Karen echoed.

'Half French, half American,' Freeman explained.

'Do you know anything about him?'

She picked up her pen.

'Graduate of the Sorbonne and Harvard Business School. Cut his teeth at Global Communications and Computing under the tutelage of Hank Exmoor, rose to be president of GCC Europe . . .'

He paused to let Karen's pen catch up.

'When Exmoor retired from GCC, he left to head up La Contessa. It had a few good years when the company experienced heavy growth, way above inflation. But then things turned sour. The company started to experience growth pains and Artagnon couldn't hack it. First he tried to diversify, like he learned from Exmoor at GCC. But the acquisitions fared no better than the parent company. Then a recession set in, women stopped buying perfume, and the company had to dip into their cash reserves to keep the creditors at bay.'

'And they became insolvent?'

'No, they had cash in hand to weather the storm, but all that cash that Artagnon had been planning to use on more mergers and acquisitions ended up going down the drain or plugging the debt hole. That's when Digby stepped in.'

'That's what I wanted to ask you about,' said Karen. 'I heard somewhere that Digby didn't have that much cash in hand either. That he had to look for outside financing. I was wondering if you know anything about who financed the takeover. I understand that there's been some gossip about secret Arab investment and suchlike.'

'Yes, the rumour mill's been working overtime on this one,' said Freeman. 'There's no reason why it should be secret if it is the Arabs. They're allowed to invest here. A foreign investor can own a British perfume company.'

'Hasn't it all been rather sensitive since the BCCI scandal?'

'Well, the Arabs have never been very popular here,' Freeman acknowledged. 'In the seventies they were blamed by drivers for high petrol prices. Now, because of one scandal, they're seen as crooks who bribe Members of Parliament to ask questions in the House or to instigate official investigations into their competitors. They're thought of as hijackers and terrorists by the working-class oiks, and as greasy crooks by the old-money Park Lane establishment bankers.'

'And the yuppies?' asked Karen.

'The yuppies do business with anyone if it looks like a good deal. But Digby wasn't a yuppie.'

'So you don't think the takeover was backed by the Arabs?'

'No,' said Freeman with quiet finality.

'What if there was more to it?' she asked cautiously.

'How do you mean?'

'Like a quid pro quo.'

'Could you clarify?' he said.

She clenched and unclenched her fingers, wondering how far to go.

'Well, we often hear about the Arabs being involved in secret arms deals. You know, trying to buy weapons that are on the restricted list. Or even some cases where the government has breached its own guidelines and regulations in order to give help to one side or the other in some inter-Arab dispute.'

She was struggling to express herself. He could see that.

'So I was wondering if this could be a cover for something like that.'

'It's rather hard to disguise a laser-guided missile as a bottle of perfume,' said Freeman, sceptically.

'Maybe it's chemical weapons,' said the DCI. 'They could be disguised easily enough.'

'Yes, well, I'll tell you what,' said the lawyer. 'If you hear about La Contessa Perfumes shipping supplies of perfume Iraq you'll know that there's something very fishy going on.'

'So there's no need for me to call in Special Branch just yet?' asked Karen with a smile.

'Not in my opinion. It's all just Square Mile gossip.'

'All right, then, but that still leaves my original question unanswered. Who *is* backing the takeover? Digby Holdings didn't have that kind of liquid assets. And they offered cash not paper.'

'How do you know all this?' asked Freeman.

'I checked it up with the SFO.'

He realized that she wasn't quite as ignorant as she portrayed herself. She had already researched some of the basic financial information at the Serious Fraud Office. But was she pumping him for information that the SFO didn't have? Or was she pumping him to find out his role in the affair?

'Digby's family don't seem too sure themselves about how the deal was financed. Initially he offered a partial share swap – a mixture of cash and paper. But the shareholders didn't go for that. You see the directors were already fighting off a hostile takeover bid from a corporate raider. The raider – Claude Udal – was probably looking for a greenmail settlement, but he was holding out for a high price and the company would have had to have held a fire sale to make it. The directors knew they'd be out on their arses if the takeover went through. But it was a bull market and there was a short-term debt crunch. They couldn't borrow except at high rates. So they couldn't do a Pac-Man defence.'

'Pac-Man defence?' asked Karen.

'Turning on the enemy, like in the video game. In the context of the market it means trying to get control of the raider's company either with a stock swap or a leveraged buy-out. In this case, it was the company that was *backing* his bid. The terminology goes back to the days of Bendix and Martin Marietta. But Digby didn't have the liquid assets either, you see. La Contessa wanted to take on "poison pill" or fat man provisions —'

'Fat man?' Karen enquired, eyebrows raised.

'Bad debt to make the company less attractive. But they were warned that this might make their legal position somewhat precarious. So their only hope was a white knight defence.'

'A friendly takeover,' said Karen, uncertainly.

Freeman smiled. She had evidently done her homework with the SFO quite thoroughly.

'That's right, and the only white knight in town was Fabian Digby.'

'But his initial offer didn't appeal to the shareholders,' said Karen tentatively.

'Right again, and with Claude Udal yapping at their heels time was of the essence. Most observers thought that in the end the directors would settle for a greenmail payment. But it seems that Digby was really anxious to get the company because he came up with a higher bid and all in cash.'

'But who backed him on it?' she asked, homing in yet again on the unanswered question that formed the central point of her inquiry.

Freeman hesitated.

'The immediate backers were three Caribbean banks. Hell, they had to tell the Monopolies and Mergers Commission *something*. But we think that the bankers may have been getting a guarantee from some of their secret depositors. And there wouldn't be any record of that here.

61

It would be like a time deposit made there for the specific purpose of enabling the banks to put up the money. And there needn't even be any record of the agreement at the bank either. They could simply have a gentleman's agreement: "We'll deposit the money and you put up a loan for Digby to buy out La Contessa."'

'So it could be anyone.'

'Absolutely anyone.'

'Well, I can see why they'd be ready to up the money,' said Karen. 'La Contessa has a bloody good marketing gimmick for their main product.'

'You mean the offer to buy back the one-ounce bottles of Gold for an ounce of gold as long as the seal is unbroken?'

'You know about it?' asked Karen.

'I did my homework,' replied Freeman. 'How do *you* know about it?'

'Oh, it's been advertised *ad nauseam*,' said Karen deprecatingly.

'I hadn't noticed. Then again I don't read women's magazines.'

The DCI ignored the condescension.

'It must be costing them a fortune.'

'So far it hasn't cost them a penny,' Freeman replied.

'How come?'

'No one's taken them up on the offer.'

'I wonder why not?' responded Karen, confused.

'They're selling Gold, the perfume, for more than the price of the precious metal – four hundred dollars a bottle or the sterling equivalent.'

'What *is* the price of gold?' asked the DCI. 'The metal, I mean.'

'Lately it's been fluctuating between three-sixty and three-eighty.'

'I wonder if the perfume is being bought by speculators as a long-term hedge against inflation and an increase in the price of gold,' she suggested facetiously.

Freeman smiled. DCI Rousson had been playing ignorant on financial matters. But she had slipped with her last

62

remark. It was obvious that she knew more about business than she had let on. He suspected that her conversation with the SFO had been long and thorough and that she had taken detailed and copious notes and studied them in depth thereafter. She was evidently trying to find out how much *he* knew. He decided to tell her.

'There's no sign of any impending inflation to hedge against – hence no reason for gold to go through the roof now. Inflation is under control. The price of oil is low and stock markets are booming. Even if gold-mine production is lagging behind jewellery demand, the Dutch and Swiss banks are selling off large chunks of their gold reserves and the Japanese are no longer buying it. Having said that I have to add that the price of silver *did* go up briefly and it dragged gold with it. Gold stood at three hundred and ninety dollars an ounce for one day and it hit four hundred before coming down again. But there's no reason for it to stay that way, even with steady economic growth. In a managed recovery, the inflationary pressures won't be that great. And if they are, people will go for the soft commodities or the high-tech stocks in the bull market.'

He studied her, as if trying to see how much of what he had said she understood. If she really was a financial tyro, it would have gone over her head. But she seemed to be nodding appreciatively. If she hadn't understood, she certainly wasn't advertising her ignorance.

'Then I suppose,' she said, 'it must be ordinary women, trying to liven up their drab lives.'

'You'd think ordinary women wouldn't have the money to buy something like that,' said Freeman.

'You obviously don't know women, Mr Freeman.'

This time it was Freeman's turn to ignore the sarcasm.

'What do they do with the stuff?'

'Try and make it last a year,' said Karen matter-of-factly. It was as if she were holding something back. Freeman decided to press her gently.

'Do they manage?'

'Apparently not. I've heard of at least one case of a

marriage breaking up because of the wife's use of the credit card to buy a second bottle in three months. But the perfume seems to be pretty powerful stuff. I've heard that it draws men and women to it like drones are drawn to the queen bee.'

'Men *and* women?' asked Freeman, leaning forward slightly.

'That was the strangest thing about it. I mean, there are all sorts of crazy stories flying about and it's hard to separate the rumour from the fact. And a lot of it is straight from the tabloids. But according to some reports it does attract men.'

'But as you said, Ms Rousson, these *are* just tabloid reports.'

'Of course,' Karen acknowledged. 'But they come from more than one source. And there's more. Women seem to like the scent in its own right. Some women have reported using it even when they aren't going out with men, just because it makes them feel good.'

'Has it been subjected to any sort of chemical analysis?' the lawyer enquired.

Karen hesitated, as if struck by the remark.

'I don't know. But there's a lot more to it. Several women have reported unsolicited lesbian approaches by other women since they started using it.'

Freeman detected a certain amount of haste in the way Karen had spoken after the initial hesitation.

'Were those police reports or tabloid articles?'

'The latter. But one of my friends told me a similar story. She didn't know why she did it. She isn't a lesbian. She said she just wanted to be near this other woman but couldn't really explain why.'

'That sounds very strange,' said Freeman. 'I also read in one of the men's magazines that they were planning to do an aftershave.'

'I wouldn't know,' said Karen mockingly. 'I don't read men's magazines.'

Freeman momentarily wore a smile of happy surrender.

Karen was a good sparring partner and he enjoyed this kind of verbal jousting, whether in court or elsewhere.

'One of them did a scratch-and-sniff market research poll of several thousand men', he added. 'It showed that eleven per cent would buy the aftershave even if it was exactly the same as the perfume, including the price. And *ninety-seven per cent* of the men who responded said they'd buy the aftershave if it cost less than twenty dollars.'

'And if La Contessa doesn't produce one,' said Karen, 'then half a dozen imitators will come out of the woodwork.'

'With Gold, they already have. There are six copies on the market, including one that's suspected of being La Contessa's own. They usually just change one ingredient by a small quantity to avoid infringing proprietary rights and then carve a chunk out of the market.'

'I know,' said Karen. 'I've seen them.'

'So far they don't seem to have got it right,' said Freeman

Karen seemed doubtful of this.

'A Gold clone called Gilt's been doing pretty well. I've seen women who can't afford the real thing cleaning it off the shelves.'

'Well, *most* of them just aren't selling well,' said Freeman. 'I mean, I don't see then in the shops like you do, but I've read the business magazines and, apparently, people buy one and then don't repurchase. They're just not getting any reorders. You're right about Gilt being the exception. It's made by some obscure Cayman-registered company. Some people are speculating that it's a cut-price version of the real thing from a La Contessa subsidiary. The press have labelled it Fool's Gold.'

Karen shook her head in amazement. She seemed impressed by the way Freeman had all the information at his fingertips.

'OK, so they're making a good profit. So that would explain why someone would want to buy the company —'

'Well, actually, it doesn't explain it,' Freeman cut in. 'They only launched Gold after the takeover.'

'Inside information?' asked Karen. 'About the perfume, I mean. Let's suppose someone knew how good it was so they decided to buy up the company before the product hit the market.'

Freeman nodded.

'Possibly. That might explain why the deal went through a secrecy filter.'

'But there's nothing behind it.'

'No, but if you're looking for a suspect start with people who would have known about how good the perfume was: people inside the company.'

Karen looked confused.

'But surely they wouldn't have had the money for a buy-out.'

'No, but they might have had friends. You know the way it goes: a little bit of inside information for a piece of the action.'

'Understood,' said Karen, nodding. Freeman rose. 'Oh, and Mr Freeman,' she said, following him to his feet.

'Yes?'

'If you come up with any information relevant to this inquiry, I'll expect you to pass it on to me.'

'Of course,' said Freeman.

He started to turn. But her voice caught him in mid-sweep.

'And if I even suspect that you're holding something back, I won't hesitate to use my police powers to bring you into line.'

He turned back.

'You don't mince your words, do you?'

'No, Mr Freeman. And my bite is worse than my bark.'

5

'All who make idols are nothing, and the things they treasure are worthless.'

Isaiah 44:9

'So you were the first one to enter the house, Phil?' asked Inspector Logan.

'That's right.'

He was in the kitchen, together with his mother Miriam, Inspector Logan and PC Woodward. He noticed now for the first time that PC Woodward was only a few years older than he. At the shivah he had been too distraught. Miriam was being comforted by PC Woodward, while other policemen dusted for fingerprints in the main rooms. They seemed to be doing a thorough job, and he wondered if every burglary was investigated with this degree of thoroughness.

'Did you notice anything missing immediately?' asked Logan.

Strictly speaking Logan was investigating the murder, not the burglary. But when the Neuman name came up at the station it was passed on to the incident room where the murder of Tony Neuman was being investigated. Inspector Logan and Superintendent Morley had immediately been alerted.

The chaos seemed to have affected the boy too. He was

evidently confused and disoriented, almost to the point of suffering. It was like the aftershock following an earthquake, and probably one aftershock too many for Phil's precarious mental stability.

'Not at first. Everything was in complete and utter disarray, but all the obvious things were still there: television, video, stereo.'

'And then what did you do?' asked the inspector.

'I called out to Mum and sprinted to our bedroom.'

'Why did you do that?'

'Well, I wanted to see if the desktop computer was missing.'

'Did you have any reason to believe that it would be?' asked Logan.

'When a place is burgled, the burglars usually go for the valuables. That can usually mean either jewellery or electronic equipment.'

'But you said they hadn't taken the TV or the stereo,' said Logan, in a mildly accusing tone.

'Yes, but they might have only been able to take one thing. Pound for pound and cubic inch for cubic inch, a computer is worth more than a stereo or video. Also, they sometimes go for the chip.'

Logan looked puzzled, or at least tried to.

'The chip?'

'The microprocessor. The main chip in a computer. It's the single most valuable part and it can be carried away in someone's pocket.'

'But weren't you afraid that the intruder might still be in the house?'

'We were away for a week. It would be strange if an intruder decided to burgle the place just at the time when we were about to come back.'

'But you said nothing was missing. Maybe the intruder was lying in wait for you, for all you knew.'

'That sounds fine in retrospect, but it isn't what I thought at the time. All I could think of was looking to see what had been stolen.'

Logan noted that the boy had a good vocabulary. He was clearly well educated and knew how to express himself eloquently.

'And the only thing missing was your brother's desktop computer?'

'That's right.'

'Presumably that was easy for the burglar or burglars to take,' said Logan, 'and they didn't even have to open it up as they would if they wanted the microprocessor.'

'That's if theft for gain was their motive.'

He regretted saying it afterwards.

'What else would it have been for?' asked Logan.

The inspector noticed Phil looking over at his mother, who was now being led out of the room by PC Woodward. She had just expressed a wish to lie down and Logan sensed that Phil would now feel able to talk more freely.

'I was just wondering if this burglary has anything to do with . . . Tony's death.'

'I doubt that very much,' said the inspector. 'We actually get quite a lot of cases like this.' There was an I-know-more-than-you-do tone in his reply.

'How do you mean?'

'I mean Jewish homes being burgled after a bereavement in the family. It's customary for Jews to take a short holiday away from home after the week of sitting shivah is finished and professional burglars read the *Jewish Chronicle* to find out who's going to be away and when. Then they hit the place at just the right time.'

Logan saw Phil almost wince when it dawned on him how careless he and his mother had been. Whether it was a regular burglary or something more sinister, it was evidently done by someone who knew what he was doing.

There was a lull in the conversation just as PC Woodward returned and took her seat at the kitchen table.

'She's lying down now, Phil,' said the policewoman. 'She took a sleeping tablet so she should sleep for a few hours.'

He nodded a gentle 'thank you' and started playing

nervously with his neck-chain, while Inspector Logan and PC Woodward eyed him appraisingly.

'What exactly is that symbol you're wearing?' asked PC Woodward in a disarmingly gentle voice.

'Oh, this?' The tone was slightly nervous. 'It's a silver pentacle.'

Logan's ears appeared to prick up at that moment.

'Any particular reason for wearing it?' he asked.

'Like what?' This time the tone was defensive.

'Oh, I don't know,' said the inspector, groping for the right word. 'A gift from a relative perhaps? A fashion state-ment of youth? You thought it might attract the babes?'

He was greeted by a contemptuous smile, as if dismissing his pathetic attempt to talk in a way that he misguidedly thought of as 'cool'. Logan realized that it wasn't going to be easy. He was on a fishing expedition, and it stood out like a sore thumb.

'It was a symbol of the Pythagorean Society in Ancient Greece.'

'The Pythagorean Society?'

Inspector Logan had a carefully cultivated way of probing by repeating the last thing the other person said. It was what they call an open question, as distinct from the closed questions such as those asked by professional salespeople when they make their pitch or lawyers when they conduct a cross-examination.

'A society of mathematicians in Ancient Greece who used to meet in secret to discuss mathematics and philosophy.'

'In secret?' said the inspector, smiling. 'No doubt they were afraid that people might think of them as nerds.'

The remark made a noticeable impact, but not on the subject at whom it was aimed. To him, it was like water off a duck's back, and the return of the contemptuous smile confirmed this. But Logan could see that PC Woodward was embarrassed by his display of insensitivity and the inspector felt momentarily embarrassed.

The policewoman decided to kill the silence by venturing a comment.

'And because you're into mathematics you've adopted it as *your* symbol,' was all she could offer. She leaned forward earnestly, awaiting Phil's reply.

'Exactly.' But by now he was playing games of his own. 'Of course, it's also a symbol of Wicca.'

Inspector Logan, who had been about to speak, was cut short before he could utter a sound, and for a few seconds his mouth hung open, like that of a slobbering dog. But, a seasoned veteran of the soft-interrogation game, he recovered his composure quickly.

'Wicca?' he repeated, raising his eyebrows.

'An ancient English religion. It was driven out by proselytizing Christians who burnt its followers at the stake.'

'I thought they only did that to Jews,' said Logan.

'And to pagans,' the boy snapped back. The inspector's mixture of feigned ignorance and pseudo-scholarship was beginning to bore him.

'Oh, so you're a pagan too, then?'

The inspector's game of prompting was designed to provoke anger. For with anger came carelessness.

'Wicca is a pagan religion.'

Logan detected more than a modicum of irritation in the tone.

'You mean paganism isn't just one religion,' he said.

'No, Inspector. Paganism is a whole group of religions. Pagan is the name that Christians applied to any people who worshipped the local gods. You see, in the ancient times, before monotheism, there were different gods for different regions. When people moved to a new region they adopted the local gods. It was a bit like obeying the laws of the local government, like we do today when we emigrate or go on holiday abroad. Later they developed this concept of the family god, which was usually a stone effigy. Remember, Abraham's father was an idol-maker according to Jewish tradition.'

'I didn't know that,' the inspector replied. 'But what's all that got to do with being a pagan?'

'Well, the idea of the family god in the Middle East gave way, in turn, to the idea of a single universal God for everyone. Hence the monotheism of the Zoroastrians, which gradually spread, first to the Jews and then to others. But in Europe, and in other places, when the Christians arrived, they found people worshipping the local gods. The Latin for "locality" is *pagus*. And so the people who worshipped these Gods were called pagan.'

'That's fascinating,' said the inspector, clearly anxious to move on. But by now the boy was having fun at his expense. Logan had let the genie out of the bottle with his petty quibbling over paganism, and now it looked like the subject of his enquiries had turned the tables and was enjoying himself by letting loose with a barrage of blarney from both barrels.

'Of course, the word pagan was often used to mean a country-dweller. And of course pagans are also called heathens. Heath is a Germanic word for an open patch of grassland and so people who worshipped the gods of the land were called heathens.'

'I always thought of pagans as people who have orgies and sacrifice animals,' the inspector chimed in, looking as if he hoped to rattle Phil a little.

'Those are just myths. We may not have the same sexual hang-ups as the followers of monotheistic religions, but we're no more sexually promiscuous than they are. We're just less hypocritical about it. We don't feel guilty about our physical instincts. And contrary to popular urban myths, Wiccans don't practise animal sacrifice – not that the critics who accuse us of the practice are vegetarian. Most of them are perfectly willing to eat the produce of factory farming. But that's the way things go with religion. The gods of the old religion become the devils of the new. And the followers of the old religion are also demonized.'

'I don't think Christianity or Islam demonized the *Jewish* God.'

'No, just the Jews. We were always getting it from one side or another.'

'We? I thought you said you consider yourself a pagan.'

'I was brought up as a Jew. But I'm a pagan by conviction.'

'But don't Jews oppose the polytheism of paganism?'

The inspector noticed a flicker of excitement in Phil's
eyes, as if he were surprised by this first trace of genuine
philosophical insight on the part of the inspector.

'They do. But I'm not a theological Jew. Not even
an ethnic one. I don't think of religion as an ethnic
characteristic.'

'Then what are you?'

'I'm a cultural Jew and a theological pagan.'

'But isn't there some antagonism between Judeo-Christian
culture and your pagan convictions? I mean, how did your
brother feel about all this?'

Logan was trying to lead the discussion back to Tony.
But his subject – he felt it premature to think of him as
a suspect – seemed more anxious to dispel the inspector's
myths about his belief system. It was as if he were tired
of being misunderstood and more than a little angry that he
never got the time to clarify his position.

'I never really asked him. But there's no antagonism
from my end towards anyone. I just live according to what
I believe and respect others' right to do likewise.'

'But how does your mother feel about all this?'

'She accepts it as my right to decide for myself. She
said that if I wanted to worship a horned god that's my
business.'

The inspector seemed to pick up on this.

'A horned god? You mean the Devil?'

'You're putting the cart before the horse, Inspector.
The North European image of the Devil was *constructed*
with horns so as to match the pre-existing horned god of
witchcraft. There's nothing in the Hebrew Bible that says
anything about the Devil having horns.'

'Did you say *witchcraft*?' asked the inspector, latching
on to the word, almost as if it were one of the proverbial
horns of the God/Devil about which they were arguing.

'Witchcraft, Wicca, wisecraft,' said the boy perfunctorily. 'It's all the same thing.'

'And that's what you believe in.' For a change, it was a statement with barely an interrogative tone behind it.

'That's right.'

'And what you *practise*.'

'That's right.'

'I see,' said Logan.

'I wonder if you really do, Inspector.'

'Well, you've summarized it pretty well, young man. You worship a horned god that got turned into a devil somewhere along the line.'

The patronizing reference to his youth fell on deaf ears.

'Not just the horned god. Also the Earth Mother.'

'The Earth Mother,' Logan repeated, throwing his head back. 'That would be what? The pagan goddess of fertility?'

The boy smiled jubilantly as the penny dropped.

'That's right. She had many forms before the Christians reconstructed her as a virgin. Like the German goddess Ostara.'

'Ah yes, Ostara,' said Logan, not troubling to hide the sarcasm now that his antagonist had well and truly joined him on the jousting court. 'Perhaps you could refresh my memory, Phil.'

'Ostara, whose traditional name derives from the same root as the female hormone oestrogen. A tradition that was, incidentally, adopted by the Christians when they named their own spring festival as Easter and adopted the Easter egg as its symbol, showing a similar commitment to renewal and rebirth in the season of spring.'

The inspector nodded, as if to congratulate Phil on his scholarship. But then he leaned forward, as if he were preparing to continue with their verbal tilting.

'I thought the Easter egg came from the boiled egg that the Jews eat at Passover.'

He sensed from Phil's face that the boy was impressed that he was still sparring with him after the intellectual savaging

74

he had just been taking from the boy. But then again, that was his job: to ask questions from a position of ignorance in the hope of obtaining enlightenment.

'The tradition came from both sides. Both Judaism and wisecraft are venerable religions and as such they have common traditions rooted in man's ancient needs. That's why they both use the lunar calendar of the hunter as well as the solar calendar of the farmer. That's why they both plant trees when children are born, to give back to the earth in return for its bounty. That's why they both celebrate spring with fertility symbols as a sign of rebirth and renewal. And Christianity inherited its wealth of tradition from both of these ancestors. If Judaism was the father of Christianity, then paganism was the mother.'

'I'm not sure if too many people would be comfortable accepting that,' said Logan.

'Most people are uncomfortable with the truth Inspector.'

'Tell me something, Phil. Did these religious differences ever crop up in your rivalry with your brother?'

'Inspector, my rivalry with my brother was a friendly rivalry.' He felt a tear forming at the corner of one of his eyes. He wiped it away quickly, hoping the inspector wouldn't see it. 'I don't know why you seem to find it sinister. My brother and I had different interests and we both sought to excel at what we did. But we didn't hate each other. And I seem to remember you saying that you didn't think this burglary had anything to do with my brother's death. So why do you bring it up now?'

'I just thought you might like to tell us something.'

'I've told you all I have to tell you, Inspector. I mean everything I *can* tell you. If I remember anything more, I'll let you know.'

'I'd be much obliged,' said Logan.

It wasn't until he got outside that Inspector Logan spoke again.

'What do you make of all that?' he asked PC Woodward.

They were walking to the car, which the inspector had parked down the road, away from prying and nosy neighbours. There were other policemen still in the house. But Logan and Woodward had done their job, and it had little to do with the burglary as such.

'How do you mean?' she asked, reluctant to venture an opinion without clarification of the question.

'The young man's rather eccentric religious views. Are they just a bit of harmless fun or are are we talking about a psychopath?'

'I don't think his religious views make him a murderer,' said PC Woodward.

'But you were the one who picked up on his pentacle neck-chain.'

'I was curious. But I don't think we should put too much significance on it.'

'I was just thinking about the report that Superintendent Morley's going to be screaming for by the end of the day.'

'Does that mean I'm going to have to type it?'

'If you wouldn't mind, Lara. I was wondering about his response when we asked him about the neck-chain? It seemed a bit defensive.'

PC Woodward inclined her head, in contemplation.

'I think he's an angry and bitter young man. Frustrated with his lot in life and in a state of suppressed rage with the outside world.'

'Thank you, Anna Freud,' said Logan. 'The question I'm really after is whether or not he's capable of murder.'

'I think *Sigmund* Freud would say we're all capable of murder,' the policewoman replied. 'It just depends on how far we're pushed.'

'It's not a psychologist's opinion I'm after, Lara. It's a woman's intuition.'

'I think a lot of what he said was designed more for its shock value than its conviction.'

'How do you mean?' asked Logan.

'I mean he didn't sound like he believed what he was

saying. It was more like reciting a litany of things he's read. As if he was trying to shock us or antagonize us.'

'So he was playing games with us,' said the inspector.

'Evidently,' said Woodward. 'But I can't quite put my finger on what sort of game.'

6

'A man of many companions may come to ruin, but there is a friend who stands closer than a brother.'

Proverbs 18:24

Frustration was welling up in Freeman as his car crawled back to his flat, through the clogged-up streets of the West End. Delays were a normal part of life in London, but he could never get used to them. He decided to make use of the time. In his mind he drew up a list of what he had established so far.

First of all there was no sign of a struggle in Fabian Digby's car. That didn't of course necessarily mean that there hadn't been one or that it wasn't an abduction. But it did mean that it was a less likely possibility. Everything he'd heard about Fabian Digby said he was a fighter. If he disappeared with no sign of a struggle that suggested a voluntary departure. There had been no ransom demand. At least neither Nielsen nor Veronica had told him of one. If there had been they wouldn't hold back. There would be no reason. After all, how could he solve the mystery if they didn't level with him? How could they expect him to help if they kept him in the dark?

Everything spoke of a voluntary disappearance. But Digby didn't tell his wife or Nielsen. That seemed out of character. He would surely have told someone.

And what of the disappearance itself? Was it involuntary, as Nielsen assumed? And if so was he kidnapped or dead?

He realized that he would make no headway with these idle speculations. But there was one thing to do first. Nielsen had given him a lead and he ought to chase it up as quickly as possible. He changed lanes and started driving to Kensington. The Israeli embassy was to be his next destination.

It took him ten minutes to get there and twenty minutes to get through security. Inevitably and understandably, security was very tight here as in all places connected with Israel. First, it took a quarter of an hour for the receptionist to locate the man he was looking for. But at least the man agreed to see him. However, he then had to wait another five minutes for the man to come to the reception/security desk to escort him to his office. Even with closed-circuit TV cameras in all the offices, they didn't want visitors wandering around the corridors on their own.

'So how exactly can I help you?' asked the short, squat, bull-shouldered man who sat opposite him across the desk in the small windowless office, after listening to Freeman's five-minute pressure-cooker explanation of Fabian Digby's disappearance and the events surrounding it.

'You always did like to get right to the point, Yaniv,' said Freeman, grinning. Yaniv Orgad had been in Central Reconnaissance, the same land commando unit as Freeman, in the Israeli Army, more than fifteen years ago. Central Reconnaissance was one of Israel's most élite combat units, alongside Golani Reconnaissance, the paratroopers and the naval commandos. Now he worked in the Israeli embassy as a 'cultural attaché'. Freeman remembered Yaniv as an expert marksman and a skilled practitioner of *krav maga*, an Israeli form of unarmed combat developed by Imi Lichtenfeld a Polish-Jewish veteran of the First World War. Most interesting of all, Yaniv was a skilled linguist, fluent in five languages and competent in five others. It was this last skill, as much as the combat ability, which gave Freeman grounds to suspect what Yaniv did for a living now, and it had little to do with 'culture'.

'Like I said,' Freeman replied, 'I know that you can't tell me if Israel had anything to do with Digby's disappearance, but at least you can give me some hot or cold clues as to whether it's worth me or the Digby family looking any further. You don't have to say why or what or when or where. Just two words like "drop it" or "keep looking". Just something I can take back to Veronica Digby so she knows whether to keep her hopes up or start rebuilding her life.'

Seated opposite Freeman, Yaniv looked uncomfortable. Freeman had been a friend and a comrade-in-arms. But there were strict limits on what he could say. And Freeman knew that Mossad operatives were constantly being tested to see if they were in danger of being compromised. Already, he knew, Yaniv would have to report this encounter to his controller and in theory it could even lead to an attempt to silence Freeman himself, although the Israeli concept of purity of arms made this unlikely. Under that concept only a conscious and willful enemy of Israel could be individually targeted for death or injury, not an inadvertent enemy or the mere relative or friend of of a willful enemy.

'I don't even know if I can help you that much,' said Yaniv. 'But I'll try. I'll talk to Jerusalem and find out what they know and what I'm allowed to tell you. If they know anything, if they tell *me* anything, and if they authorize me to tell *you* anything, it really will be just two words one way or the other. You and Mrs Digby will have to infer the rest.'

They stood up and shook hands across the desk.

'When should I call you?' asked Freeman. 'Or will you call me?'

'Neither,' said Yaniv. 'You'll come back here in three days and I'll have an answer for you. I'll tell them in security to expect you. Try not to wear anything with metal in it this time.'

'Oh, yes, sure.'

'Oh, and one more thing, Emmett. Please don't tell anyone that you've been here just yet, not even your clients. When I have the answer you can tell them and interpret it according to your own best judgment.'

Freeman nodded slowly, understanding the words and grateful that Yaniv hadn't thrown him out empty-handed.

The drive back to his home was no quicker than the drive to the Israeli embassy. It was now more than a week since Nielsen had hired Freeman and he was beginning to get a feel for the case. He certainly knew a lot more about the man he was looking for, but he had the feeling, also, that he was missing something obvious.

He arrived back at his apartment, a couple of pinewood-panelled rooms: a bedroom that doubled as a gymnasium, and a living room that doubled as a dining room, library and office. He didn't have a permanent real office, just a prestige mailing address and answering service at an uptown executive centre. When he needed an office to meet a client he rented one at the same executive centre for an hour or two – usually a suite with a waiting room and a secretary's office. For a secretary, he hired one of the centre's temps, and for decoration, he plastered the walls of his 'office' and 'waiting room' with pictures and paraphernalia of his trade.

He yawned and went into his bedroom. Somnolence was creeping over him, but he felt as if he had fallen out of touch with the world, and so he switched on the small TV in the corner. He had it permanently tuned to CNN and he liked to have it on in the background when he was working. When he had nothing to do he had it on loud. He left the bedroom door open and went back into the living room.

He inserted his notebook computer into its docking station and booted up the system. For the next twenty minutes he tried to write up a preliminary report. If Nielsen asked him about his progress, at least he would be able to give him something. As he worked on the report it amazed him how little progress he had actually made. Oh yes, with that old stand-by, psychology, he could draw up a list of a few suspects. But at this stage he couldn't even say suspects in what, murder or abduction.

There was one avenue that he could explore which not even the smug, know-it-all Alan Nielsen knew about. Emmett Freeman had friends whom he never met; the same friends who had helped him when he was fighting his desperate battle to clear his name and reinstate his physics degree. He had friends in cyberspace.

It was an on-line contact who had told him to read a book called *Gödel, Escher, Bach*, and in particular the chapter on foreground and background and the difficulty of knowing which was which in some of Escher's paintings. This friendly hint had ultimately pointed him in the right direction in solving the mystery. What was significant was that the member could simply have spoon-fed Freeman with the answer. But instead he gave it in the form of a clue. When Freeman unravelled the mystery he was deemed to have shown enough initiative to be honoured with an invitation to join a group called the Logic Forum.

Relationships within this on-line community were based on reason and trust. It was to these friends that Freeman turned now. He drafted a question simply asking if anyone knew anything about Fabian Digby or the perfume Gold.

7

'Pleasing is the fragrance of your perfumes.'

Song of Songs 1:3

There was a faint chill of autumn in the air as Karen climbed into her car at lunch-time. She knew that the Met Lab was open twenty-four hours a day and she could have sent a uniformed PC, but for this sort of work she wanted to speak to someone in authority to make sure the job was done right, not someone whose skill was limited to measuring the blood alcohol levels of the late-night drunk motorists who wanted to dispute the police version of events. Also it was a bit embarrassing: having perfume analysed wasn't exactly normal police work, even if it was connected with a missing person investigation.

She put the bottle of Gold, still sealed in its box, in the glove compartment. Then she looked around with her usual caution, started the engine and headed slowly into the lunch-time traffic of London's West End, wondering if she could make it to Lambeth Bridge Road and back in less than an hour. She had been thinking about this for some time, even before her conversation with Emmett Freeman. Now it had become all the more important. There was one thing that she had omitted to tell Freeman: she too had used Gold and

83

succumbed to its enigmatic allure. But she was determined
to get to the bottom of the mystery and understand why.

The obvious answers were pheromones or drugs. But
that was perhaps *too* obvious. Surely someone would have
noticed by now, some officious bureaucrat. They would have
sent the perfume to some government lab for analysis and
raided the premises where it was being produced. Or the
environmental lobby would have got on to them. But none
of that had happened.

Were people being paid off, she wondered. Or had the
government looked into it and found nothing. If there was
anything to find they would certainly have found it. And
if not in Britain then in the United States. The American
Food and Drug Administration was known to be extremely
aggressive in its pursuit of unauthorized use of drugs or
claims of medical benefit. Of course, perfume *per se* did
not fall within their remit. But if there were suspicions that
the perfume contained mind-altering substances then they
wouldn't hesitate to have it analysed and would swing into
action if they found any illicit substances in it.

She wondered how much it would cost for the analysis
and if she could get away with it. Under the cost-cutting
policy, the police were given an operating budget and had
to stick to it. DCI Karen Rousson knew that as long as
she stayed within her quarterly limit she wouldn't have
to clear it with her Chief Superintendent. But even if the
tests stayed within the limit, subsequent use of the lab on
this or other cases might push her over the limit, bringing
her entire workload under review. Furthermore, if the tests
were extensive they'd be expensive and might even push
her over the limit now. She realized that she'd have to use
the old 'mountain of paperwork' ruse that was so common
in the Civil Service to get clearance for the deficit without
drawing attention to what had caused it. The basic ploy
was to stick the offending document under a pile of others
about three-quarters of the way down. By that stage the
superior officer would be getting close enough to the end
to rush through it and would probably miss it. But because

it would require his signature, she realized that she'd have to stick in other documents that needed his signature. She was already subsidizing the investigation by using her own bottle of Gold. But she didn't see any reason why she should spend any more trying to solve this case.

She had got caught in a queue at the traffic lights and the learner driver in front of her had been stricken by a stalled engine when the lights changed. So she had a barrage of car horns honking away behind her in protest, as if she alone in all the whole world were to blame for the delay. Or as if a cacophony sounding like a modern classic would make it any easier for the learner to restart the engine.

Eventually she gave in to her own anger and got out of her car and walked, not forward to the car in front, but back to the car behind. The driver, who had been angrily honking along with the rest of them, lowered his window and half leaned out aggressively.

'What the fuck's the matter with you?' he asked.

'I can't move until the driver in front of me moves,' said Karen.

'Well, tell 'im to move, then!'

'He's a learner,' replied Karen patiently. 'His engine stalled.'

'Well, tell him to move his fuckin' arse!'

'No, I won't tell him that. In the first place it's rude and in the second place it's stupid. He didn't ask the engine to stall and he's trying his best to restart it. By sounding your horn, you're just distracting him and making it harder for him to concentrate on what he's doing.'

'I don't give a shit what his problem is. I'm late enough as it is.'

'But if you distract him and make it harder for him to restart his car, you'll end up being even later.'

'I don't give a shit about that!'

'Well, if you don't mind being late, then what are you getting so angry about?'

'Look, he's moving!' the raging motorist shouted hoarsely, pointing ahead as he did so. 'You can go now.'

'So I can,' said Karen, smiling sweetly. She turned and walked slowly back to her car, listening with amusement as he cursed and swore at her. Then she closed the door, but made sure not to lock it. She opened the glove compartment, looked in the rear-view mirror and waited. It took only a few seconds for the irate driver to open his door and come storming out. She moved her hand from the glove compartment to her lap, her index finger tensing slightly. When he reached the door he didn't hesitate. He ripped it open and yelled at her.

'Why the fuck aren't you moving, you stupid fuckin' bitch!'

Again she smiled sweetly, showing not the slightest trace of fear, although she felt some. She knew that he was probably reluctant to use violence here. He would settle for intimidation. But she knew that her apparent lack of fear angered him all the more. It meant that his wishes were frustrated. And frustrated intentions were what road rage was all about; that and lack of control.

'Well, I can't move now because my door's open,' she said, showing white teeth and an amused contempt for his frustration.

With the ferocity of an animal that had just been attacked, he reached in and grabbed her by the right lapel of her jacket, trying to yank her out of the car so that he could take a more powerful swing at her with greater freedom of movement. But without resisting his pulling motion she brought her left hand up and sprayed him in the face with CS gas. Then she pulled out her warrant card and flashed it at him.

'Detective Chief Inspector Rousson,' she said calmly as he gasped for breath and rubbed his eyes. 'You've just committed the crime of assaulting a police officer. I can arrest you for that. You might get off with a formal caution, but it'll still go on your record if you're in trouble with the law again. Or I can give you an *informal* caution. Which would you prefer, arrest or caution?'

'Cau . . . Cau . . . caution,' he stuttered.

'All right,' she replied. 'Don't let it happen again.' Then

she pulled the door shut, released the handbrake and drove off slowly, leaving the drivers behind raging and bemused as they saw the car ahead of them stay in place and its driver roll around on the road clutching his left shin in pain, cursing furiously at the 'fuckin' 'ore!'

She looked back in the rear-view mirror and noted with amusement that the other drivers were offering their soul mate no help and that he was effectively taking the brunt of their anger now that they had no one else to pick on. She wondered idly if there would be any repercussions for her action. He could, after all, complain, alleging excessive force. He could cite the fact that she hadn't arrested him as evidence that she didn't think she had a case against him. But then again she could say that she didn't think that the CPS would prosecute because of the cost of prosecution in relation to the likely sentence, and therefore didn't think it worth the bother of arresting him after the initial danger was over. That would certainly conform to the reality of the situation, in which the police force had completely lost confidence in the CPS, while the CPS struggled to make the process of criminal prosecution cost-efficient in the face of judicial leniency.

In any case, if he made a complaint, she could still charge him with assault and battery. Apart from that, the Police Complaints Authority was governed by the same standards as a criminal court: the complainant had to prove guilt beyond reasonable doubt. According to the PCA, any clash of testimony between a single police officer and a single member of the public meant that there was necessarily an element of reasonable doubt, although magistrates' courts took a different view when a single police officer testified against a private citizen.

Karen arrived at the lab and filled out the paperwork, describing what she wanted tested in the 'other' section of the main form. This was not, after all, a standard test. But she was confident that the chemical analysis department of this well-appointed lab could handle it, a view not shared by the receptionist.

'Oh, I don't know if we can do that here,' said the girl at the front desk, a caricature of the dumb bimbo. Karen had been to the Met Lab a few times before, but this girl was new.

'Well, could I speak to your supervisor in that case,' she said.

The girl suddenly looked nervous, as if any suggestion of speaking to her superior meant that she had done something wrong. But she picked up the internal phone anyway and keyed in a couple of digits.

'Dr Sadler, there's a woman here who wants us to do some tests on her perfume . . . Well, she said something about drugs and ferri . . . ferri . . . that's right . . . Oh, I don't know, I'll ask her.' She looked up at Karen. 'What sort of drugs?'

'Nasally and dermally ingested drugs.'

'Ooh, I don't know if I can pronounce that. Here, maybe you'd like to speak to him.'

She handed over the internal phone.

'Hello, Dr Sadler. DCI Rousson here. I'd like to check for various addictive nasally and dermally ingested drugs.'

'And pheromones?' he added, remembering the receptionist's struggle to pronounce the word.

'Yes, that's right.'

'What's the problem?'

'Well, it's not powder or crystals. It's actually a bottle of perfume.'

'Perfume!'

'That's right. You may have heard of it. It's called Gold.'

'I *have* heard of it, including the rumours about it being addictive. I didn't think there was any foundation to them.'

'Well, we don't know if there is,' Karen reassured him hastily. 'But the matter has come up in an on-going investigation and we have to check it out.'

'OK, perhaps you'd like to come through. Room seventeen, at the end of the corridor.'

'Room seventeen. OK. I'll be along in a moment.'

The receptionist was already buzzing the security door before Karen could even put down the internal phone. She walked down the corridor to find herself greeted by a short man in a white coat at the door to room 17. He had thinning hair and gave the impression of one who worked by rote rather than a profound thinker. He introduced himself as Dr Sadler.

It was a cramped office, but Sadler managed to clear her a space on his cluttered desk.

'OK, do you have the bottle with you?' he asked.

'Yes,' she said, placing the bottle of Gold on the desk. 'I'm glad you know about Gold,' she said with relief. 'I was rather embarrassed about bringing it here. That's why I didn't just send it over.'

'My wife's gone crazy over it,' said Sadler, as if dismissing her behaviour as female irrationality.

'So have a lot of women,' replied Karen.

'Don't I know it.'

With the addiction theory put back into the realm of lightweight speculation and his confidence in his world-view restored, Sadler seemed to be rubbing it in, as if he were revelling in this display of male superiority.

'I want you to test for pheromones, for cocaine, for nicotine and for cannabis. Also for opium-based drugs,' said Karen.

'I don't think the nasally ingested drugs are likely to be there.'

'Why not?'

'Well, it's a question of vapour pressure. The vapour pressure of cocaine, for instance, wouldn't be enough to create a "high" unless you held your nose right up against it and snorted.'

'I'm not talking about a "high",' said Karen. 'I'm talking about an addictive effect, a subconscious, insidious addictive effect without any conscious good feelings.'

'Well, I'll look for it, if you want. But I don't think you'll find anything.'

'Just look hard. How much will it cost?'

'That depends on how hard and how thoroughly you want me to look.'

'Give me a ballpark figure,' said Karen.

'Well, there's gas chromatography, mass spectometry and spectroscopy, and that's just for the drugs. For the pheromones I'll have to do radio assays and genetic reaction tests. It could run from a few hundred to a couple of thousand, depending on how comprehensive you want the tests to be.'

Karen almost winced at the sum, but outwardly she kept her cool.

'Do the drug tests first. I'll have to get clearance from God for the pheromone tests.'

'God?' repeated Sadler, confused.

'My DCS,' she replied coolly, realizing she had been a trifle indiscreet.

'OK. I'll have to ask you to fill out a couple of forms.'

Forty minutes later, when the paperwork was done, Karen was back in her car, driving along Chalk Farm Road, having reached a snap decision. She remembered Freeman telling her about Mike Artagnon, the former CEO of La Contessa. She made a couple of quick mobile calls and was now on her way to see him.

Mike Artagnon's London home was a mansion in Hampstead, set back from the road in three acres of ground and rising up on a hill like a fortress overlooking the peasants below. Not that the residents of London's affluent Hampstead were peasants. The house had a cable-car-like lift to take people from the garden entrance to the front door, and as she rode the car Karen had to admit to herself that she was impressed. She knew that Mike Artagnon was not a super-rich man like Fabian Digby. But his net worth was estimated at a comfortable £50 million and he was certainly doing all right for a man who had always managed other people's businesses instead of starting one of his own, belying the old adage that you can't grow rich by working for some one else.

'It was a proxy battle,' said Artagnon. They were seated in his living room, drinking tea and looking out on to the back garden and Hampstead Heath beyond.

'The company was underperforming,' he continued, 'but not by as much as Digby told the shareholders. But it had assets outside the core business that could be sold quickly. In effect, Digby got the company for nothing. He sold some of the assets for more than he paid for the whole company.'

'Why couldn't you do the same thing?'

'What, a fire sale?'

'Yes.'

'And then what? Use the cash to buy back the shares?'

'Either that or give the shareholders a mid-year dividend and create a feel-good factor. Then Digby wouldn't have been able to make the raid pay for itself.'

Mike Artagnon smiled. He didn't know how thoroughly Karen had done her homework after her conversation with Emmett Freeman, and he was decidedly impressed by this display of her keen business insight. What was particularly impressive was that Karen was a policewoman with no apparent background in financial matters.

'I wish I'd had you advising me at the time,' he said, giving her an approving nod.

'I'm an observer by nature.'

'Like shit you are!' he shot back. It was a spontaneous explosion, blurted out by a man who didn't like to see waste. 'You've got a steel-trap mind, young lady, and you're wasting your time as Inspector Plodder. You ought to get out on to the corporate battlefield where the real action is.'

'You think I'm tough enough?' she asked, warming to his praise.

'The question is are *they* tough enough?'

She felt herself blushing at this barrage of unexpected praise.

'Besides,' Artagnon continued, 'it's not about being tough, is it?'

He looked at Karen as if demanding an answer.

'No,' said the DCI. 'It's about being smart.'

'Exactly.'

This time it was Karen who smiled, the embarrassment having completely worn off now that she could see where Artagnon was coming from. He was like a chess player who fought battles against others using his mind rather than his hands. What he yearned for most was a worthy opponent. Of course, he had already been bested by one. But he seemed quite willing to accept his fate lying down.

'So why didn't you fight them?'

Her tone was gentle but taunting, as if she sensed that he needed a fair share of encouragement to open up, just as he had used verbal force to draw the full measure of intelligence from her. She knew that this subject was painful to him. He was a fighter through and through, and it wasn't just because of his name that he liked to call himself the 'Fourth Musketeer'. A fighter never finds it easy to talk about being beaten. He opened his mouth a few times but no words came out. Eventually he overcame his inhibitions and started to speak.

'Any way you look at it, it would have been retrenchment.'

'There's nothing undignified about a strategic pull-back to rally one's forces,' said Karen. 'You'd still have beaten them.'

'We thought of that. But it wasn't so easy. Digby had a tax loss in place from another acquisition to offset against the capital gains from the sell-off. We didn't. Therefore we would have had to have paid capital gains tax and wouldn't have had so much to give the shareholders. In retrospect we should probably have done it anyway. But some of the directors lost their balls.'

He spoke with an accent that was a mixture of French and American, and she remembered Freeman telling her about his background.

'Did you have any idea why he was doing it?' asked Karen.

'I talked about that with Hank.'

'Hank' was Henry Sheldon Exmore, the legendary former head of Global Communications and Computing and

Mike Artagnon's mentor. It was Exmore who had presided over GCC's meteoric rise from minor maker of telecommunications equipment barely in the top one hundred of the Fortune 500 to multinational conglomerate in the top ten. While Exmore was the experienced takeover veteran, still dynamic but no longer youthful, Mike Artagnon had been his eager disciple, presiding over GCC Europe, working with a leading private Franco-Jewish bank and helping Exmore to find targets for mergers and acquisitions, more often than not financed through stock trades. The company's insiders used to call Exmore 'the Wizard of Oz' and Mike Artagnon 'the Sorcerer's Apprentice'.

'I thought it was just a straightforward, old-fashioned asset strip. But Hank said there was more to it than that. Digby had sounded him out about it beforehand and Hank got the impression that it wasn't just a question of going after the assets. But he couldn't figure out what more there was.'

'Had the launch of Gold been planned at the time?'

'Gold? You mean the perfume?'

'Yes.'

'No, that was Digby's baby. It was something he launched after coming on board. We were planning to launch a new perfume, which Digby's people killed – presumably to make sure they got the kudos for the turnaround.'

'What was the new perfume you were planning?'

'It didn't even have a name. We hadn't got round to that stage. We were still looking for a big-name sponsor, an actress or fashion model or something like that. We had one all lined up who then backed out when she discovered that we'd tested it on animals. Something about it not being 'politically correct' – God help us!'

He was smiling again, as if there were some things in life that still amused him, despite his loss of zest for the corporate combat that had once been his *raison d'être*.

'And what about the chemical formula?' asked Karen.

'For the perfume? As far as I know it still belongs to the

company. For all I know, they might have used it for this Gold they've come up with.'

Karen leaned forward. This was an avenue worth pursuing.

'Do you know anything about the effect Gold has been having on women?'

'Like what?'

'Well, like women buying it when they can't afford it? Like women fighting over it? Like men being strongly attracted to women who are wearing it? Like women who were wearing it being subjected to lesbian advances?'

'I heard some of the stories, but I didn't put too much credence in then. I assumed that it was just Digby's propaganda mill putting out tales to show what a wonderful corporate turnaround he'd accomplished.'

'They're true. At least some of them are. I've verified several accounts and heard so many others from so many different sources that I find them credible for the most part. The only thing I don't understand is the reason.'

She decided not to mention her own personal experience.

'That doesn't sound like our perfume. I mean, it was good but not that good.'

'How do you know?'

'We tested it on people too,' he said, smiling again.

'Did it contain pheromones?'

'No. That would have been unethical. And anyway, the state of pheromone chemistry isn't as advanced as many people seem to think.'

'Then you have researched the matter?'

'I think most of the companies in our industry have done *some* research on the subject. Plus we keep our eyes peeled and try to stay abreast of the academic research.'

'What about drugs?'

'What about them?'

'Did you use them in the perfume?'

'No. That's something we wouldn't have even thought of.'

'You thought of pheromones.'

'Pheromones are a matter of ethics. Drugs are a matter of law. We might push against the limits of ethics but we wouldn't gamble the company on a breach of the law.'

'Even if you were desperately fighting a hostile takeover?'

'Especially if we were fighting a hostile takeover – which at the time of developing the perfume we weren't. The last thing you do when you're fighting a war on several fronts is to play with an unstable stick of dynamite in your own headquarters.'

'So you don't have any idea if they're using your formula or have adapted it in some way?'

'Adapting it would have been the quickest way to get something to the market, but I don't see how they could have adapted it to have this effect.'

'They couldn't have just added something?'

'Have it checked,' he suggested.

'I already have.'

She thought she caught the flicker of a smile on his face. But she couldn't be sure.

'And?' he asked, as if dangling a hook before her on which to hang her answer.

'I haven't had the results yet.'

'Let me know as soon as you get them. I'll be most interested.'

He said this with a tone of finality, as if he no longer wished the discussion to continue. Was it that he smelt the sweet scent of revenge in the air? Revenge over those who had bested him in a business duel? Or was there more to his curiosity? Like self-interest? Or fear?

She rose from the armchair and looked out at the garden as he stood to show her to the door.

'It must be nice watching the change of seasons though the French windows,' she said.

'Yes,' he replied with slow emphasis. 'If one has the time for it.'

She smiled inwardly at what he had given away. This was not a man who had given up on life. He might not have a formal post with a large corporation any more, but he was certainly doing something with his time other than wallow in self-pity.

8

*'See if you can lure him into showing you the
secret of his great strength . . .'*

Judges 16:5

It had been a few days now, but he couldn't hide the
restlessness from his mother. Nor could he get over the
frustration of the computer being stolen. It had offered him
the one chance to expose his brother's murderers, not just
with fragments of the facts but with details: names, dates
and places. But now his chance was lost. Not only had the
burglars taken Tony's computer, but they had also stolen
all the diskettes in the house, regardless of which brother
they belonged to. Whoever they were they weren't taking
any chances.

The inspector was a fool. It was clear and plain now. Of
course his brother was killed because of what he had been
working on. It was obvious that he knew too much and they
wanted to silence him. But knowing that for sure was no
comfort in the face of the added realization that the same
event that had confirmed his suspicions had also wiped out
any chance he might have of proving it.

And then he realized that it hadn't. It came to him in a
flash. There was still one other copy. Phil was the more

computer-literate of the two, but they both knew about hiding files in cyberspace. It was Phil who had taught Tony about encrypting files and sending them to oneself via e-mail or uploading them to a bulletin board or to one's personal file area of an on-line information service. They both had accounts with CompuServe and both used them to store back-up copies of files like their personal address books.

He already had the log-on Parameters for both himself and his brother set up on his computer. All he had to do was use the mouse pointer to select the one he wanted from a drop-down list.

Within seconds, he was plugging the internal modem of the laptop into the wall socket and logging on to the CompuServe account. When the software confirmed that he was connected, he clicked on the green traffic light icon and typed the word 'per' in the small box that appeared. This was a shortcut to the personal file area where files would be uploaded. Unlike the forum libraries, this was one place in which he, the individual user, had complete autonomy over what he uploaded.

There were two files there, one with the extension 'pgp', meaning that it was encrypted with the Pretty Good Privacy program. Its full name was 'address.pgp', which meant that it was an encrypted version of his electronic address book. He kept an updated version on line so that if he logged on from anywhere and updated it, it would be instantly available to him elsewhere. The other was called 'pamela.gif'.

He downloaded the second file to his laptop and logged off. The file itself appeared to contain nothing more than a colour picture of an extremely beautiful young actress from a well-known TV series. But there was more to it than that. Tony had used something which he had learned from Phil called steganography.

Steganography is a mathematical technique for concealing digital computer files within other forms of data, such as digital picture and music files – like Edgar Allan Poe's purloined letter. The secret of this approach was the fact that not all data on a computer needs to be accurate. Computer programs need to be stored with 100 per cent accuracy to work properly, while word processing files need to be substantially accurate if they are to be printed out properly with the correct content and layout. But digital sound and pictures need not be stored with absolute accuracy. A slight variation in the colour of a few small points in a larger image or a minute variation in the pitch or tone of a few musical notes will not offend the eye or ear of any but the most demanding connoisseur – and he would have more good taste than to expect perfection from a computerized reproduction in the first place!

By taking the 'bits' of an important file and spreading them out into a computerized picture or sound file in an apparently random mathematical sequence it is possible to conceal information. More importantly, while the picture or sound file is mildly contaminated in a manner that is effectively invisible to the eye or inaudible to the ear, the concealed data can be recovered as long as one remembers, or finds out, the original secret passphrase that was used as the 'seed' for concealing the data in the first place. Of course, one could only use this method effectively if the data being concealed occupied considerably less space than the data *within* which it was being hidden. But music and picture files are large by their very nature. Text files are not. So it was possible for Tony to conceal a digital text file about what he had been doing amid the coloured dots of a picture of a charming young actress in a swimsuit on a California beach. And it rather appealed to Tony's sense of humour to do so.

Under Phil's tutelage, Tony had learned to use a steganography program so powerful that even a mathematics genius with another copy of the same program could not find the hidden files in a picture or music file, or even be sure that any files were hidden there, unless he knew the secret passphrase.

But there were some things that Tony and Phil didn't share . . . and passwords was one of them. Right now that hardly mattered. He grabbed his jacket, scribbled a note and quietly slipped out.

Dr Sadler was slumped in his chair by the window of his office, reviewing the results of the tests. The print-outs were clear enough. It was the interpretation that was giving him a problem. It was the old case of how do you interpret an experiment in which the result comes out as more than one hundred but less than ten? It was that kind of paradox that he faced now.

He had run the initial tests that DCI Rousson had asked him to perform, but what they were telling him made no sense. The gas chromatography yielded a positive result but the liquid chromatography/mass spectrometry/mass spectroscopy gave a negative. Normally the LC/MS/MS test was more accurate than the gas chromatography and could be used to detect even trace amounts. But here the results were paradoxical. The weaker test gave a positive response and the stronger a negative. False positives were unusual with gas chromatography and the more sensitive three-part test was unlikely to miss an amount large enough to be detected by gas chromatography.

He had been racking his brains for the better part of two hours trying to figure it out and had even skipped lunch in an effort to get to the bottom of it.

Suddenly it hit him. There was an explanation for the ambiguity – and what an explanation!

He dived for the phone and called the number of DCI Rousson's regional HQ.

'Hallo, could I speak to DCI Rousson . . . It's Dr Sadler . . . from Lambeth, yes.'

There was a long wait during which efforts were made to connect him to Karen. After a few minutes a voice came back on the line.

'I'm afraid DCI Rousson isn't here,' said the voice. 'Would you like to talk to someone else?'

'Perhaps you could connect me to her DCS,' said Sadler.

'That's DCS DuPaul. OK, I'm putting you through now.'

He felt guilty as he sipped his vodka and orange juice. They were still in the month of mourning and he knew that his mother would be none too pleased about his going out if she woke up and found the note. But he had always believed that life is for the living.

There were plenty of girls on the dance-floor, but he was feeling lethargic, and embarrassed to be there on his own. The dim light, punctuated by occasional colourful and strobic flashes, helped to camouflage his misery. And the powerful rhythmic thumping of the music, with its exaggerated bass, helped to drown his loneliness. But not even the drink, taking its steady hold on him, could numb his consciousness. He was used to going to nightclubs with his brother, where they worked as a twosome, pulling the birds who always came in pairs or threes.

A bitter stab of pain twisted inside his gut as he remembered how he had parted company with his brother just hours before the fatal stabbing. He felt a lump in his throat, but coughed it back and drowned it with a swig of his drink. It was too much. The music was loud and the birds nothing to die for. He might as well cut his losses and call it a night.

And then something happened.

He had been on the verge of leaving when he noticed the girl in the corner eyeballing him. How long had she been watching him? Had she been trying to catch his eye, or was she trying to size him up without being noticed? The fact that she maintained eye contact when he looked at her suggested the former. But it seemed strange. He was good-looking enough, but nothing to write home about.

Why was she watching him?

He realized it was all part of the game. Pick a bloke and try to pull him. If you like him, take it from there, if not, blow him out and move on. A guy could play the same game. You could drift from one bird to another, especially in a place like this with several sections.

But this blonde bombshell seemed to have targeted him even though he was by the bar and not on the dance-floor. Perhaps bombshell wasn't the right word. She was almost his height and her form was 'well filled out'. But there was also a wholesome innocence about her face, as with a fresh-faced American cheerleader. Also, he suspected that the blonde look came out of a bottle. Of course, that was only natural. Like most girls of her age, she wanted to have more fun.

Her age.

That was another thing. How old was she? In this light he couldn't be sure. But she looked more like early twenties than late teens. He'd never pulled an older woman before. The thought was quite exciting.

She rose slowly and started walking to the dance-floor, maintaining eye contact with Phil the whole time. Seizing the moment, he responded by matching her movements, step for step, until they stood inches from each other. Then, with a smile, she began to move and gyrate in time to the music. A second later he was moving and gyrating with her. The music changed, and she turned her back on him. For a minute he was crestfallen. But when she began to edge backwards and rub her back against his groin he felt himself responding, and felt grateful for the low light. He put his hands on her waist and tried sliding them up to her breasts, only to feel her own hands gripping his wrists and gently but firmly sliding them down again. He tried again. Same response. He tried the other direction and discovered that hips were fine, buttocks were a no-no. He tried her arms and found that when he gently stroked her upper arms with his fingers she squirmed with delight and moved back towards his groin.

She was blowing hot and cold, there was no doubt about it. But which way would the wind be blowing at the end of the evening?

The music changed again and she turned around and faced him.

'What's you name?' she asked, shouting to be heard above the noise.

'Phil,' he answered. 'What's yours?'

'Jilly,' she replied.

He realized that they were both lip-reading and neither had actually heard the other.

'Can I buy you a drink?' he asked.

'What?' she replied, not quite keeping up with his lip movements.

He held his hand as if holding a glass and tilted it towards his mouth.

'Yeah, sure!' she said, nodding to make sure that he caught her reply.

They moved to an inner section which housed another bar. The music was quieter there, as there were no loudspeakers, although it still drifted in from round about.

'What would you like?' he asked.

'A screaming orgasm,' she replied.

Hot and cold, he thought. But it was still too early to get his hopes up.

He went to the bar and ordered two screaming orgasms, bringing them back to the corner table that she had managed to grab in the meantime.

'What do you do?' she asked.

'I'm a student,' he replied. He decided not to say that he had just finished his A-levels at an independent school. Now that he could see her clearly, she looked about twenty, and he saw no need to draw attention to the fact that he was only eighteen.

'What subject?' she asked.

'Maths and computing.'

'Where?'

He thought about whether or not to tell the truth, and then decided against the idea. He had already been offered acceptance at all three of his choices, subject to getting two As and a B. And he was sure of getting 4 As.

'Imperial College,' he said, naming the one that he would probably choose. He was still considering the possibility of the Oxford and Cambridge colleges that had made him similar offers. But he didn't really want to leave London, with all of its distractions. It was the distractions that had probably stopped him getting his A-levels a year ago.

'What about you?' he asked.

'I'm also a student – University College, in Gower Street.'

'What subject?'

'Psychology.'

'I don't know much about that, I have to admit.'

She smiled.

'I don't know much about science either.'

They laughed and drank.

It was two hours later when they left the club together, watched by two men in a car. The man in the driver's seat was in his twenties. The other, in the front passenger seat, was in his forties. The girl appeared to be supporting Phil's weight.

'So how about we go back to my place and we get know each other better?'

He was trying to grope her. But she was having none of it, and she deftly brushed his hands away with patience and firmness, but not a trace of anger.

'If you don't come home with me I might not make it home at all.'

'I'll call you a taxi.'

She signalled with her free hand. There were several taxis parked just a few yards away from the club and the one in front responded by starting its engine and moving closer.

'Where to, miss?' asked the driver, lowering his window.

'Golders Green,' she replied.

She opened the door and put Phil in the back, fastening the seat belt for him. Then she closed the door and went back to the driver's window.

'Take him to . . .' She told the driver the address and handed him a twenty-pound note. 'That should more than cover it. Keep the change.'

'Thank you, miss,' replied the driver, smiling.

She watched from the pavement as the taxi moved off and then crossed the road to the car opposite. The two men barely watched her as she got in the back.

'Well?' asked the older man curtly. He seemed to be chiding her for something, perhaps enjoying herself too much.

'He's hooked,' she replied.

9

'Honour your father and your mother . . .'

Exodus 20:12

'So what exactly did my precious stepmother hire you to do?'

Nicola Digby was lazing in a lounger by the heated swimming pool. The air was cool outside, the result of an overnight thunderstorm. But the sun was streaming in through the transparent roof sans cold air. That was what was so amazing about indoor pools. You could have summer inside even when it was autumn outside.

'She wants me to look for your father.'

'My father will turn up when he's ready,' said Nicola in a deep sultry voice. 'Why don't you sit down.'

He sat on the other lounger.

'You can go,' she said, but not to Freeman. The over-ample Serbian maid had been hovering in the background, as if it was were unsafe to leave Nicola alone with this stranger. But she left stiffly in response to her mistress's contemptuously voiced order. Freeman waited a dignified few seconds to make sure that the maid was out of earshot before continuing.

'So you think there's no reason to worry about your father.'

'He can take care of himself.'

Freeman found himself looking at her supine form. She was a big girl, taller than Karen but slightly slimmer.

He realized that he was ogling her. And he couldn't really understand his adolescent reaction to her. He had seen beautiful women before. Seen them, and admired them. When the mood was right and his wallet full, he had scored with them too. But now he found himself lusting after both Karen and Nicola like a horny teenager. He couldn't understand what the matter was with him. At thirty-five his libido should have been on the decline. That's what all the textbooks said.

Maybe it's a mid-life crisis, he told himself. But he knew that it wasn't that. A mid-life crisis is when you look back on your life and wonder where all the good years went. Freeman didn't feel like that. In his case it had been an early-life crisis. He had spent the best years of his life fighting to clear his name and restore his honour. And now his mind was no longer sharp enough to produce cutting-edge papers on theoretical physics. It was true that Einstein had produced his paper on General Relativity at the age of thirty-six. But that was after ten years trying to advance the work that he had done a decade earlier when he had outlined the basics of special relativity and quantum mechanics. Also it was his *last* great paper. From then on he had spent his life in a kind of limbo trying to formulate a 'Unified Field Theory' which he never quite accomplished.

Ironically, Freeman's own wilderness years had been in his youth, and it was now at the beginning of his middle years that he was starting to give meaning to his life. And to do so he had embarked upon a different vocation: the practice of law. It was in this capacity that he was gaining fulfilment, *and*, in some cases, settling old scores. In the process he had gone head to head with the authorities and ruffled quite a few establishment feathers.

Now he was trying to help a woman find her missing husband. A life full of incident, with a string of worthy successes behind him. What more could a man want?

Well, maybe a wife, children . . .

Still, at least he had all the material comforts that he could want, having just added an extra seventy-five K to the kitty. That was more than most men had.

'Has he done this sort of thing before?' he asked.

'What?'

'Disappeared?'

'No.'

'Then why do you think there's nothing to worry about?'

'Because he's that sort of man.'

'How do you mean?'

'He didn't hire bodyguards.'

'No, that's exactly —'

'He didn't need them. He was fit and could easily match any man half his age in any physical context. Once a couple of teenage louts were bothering me. They were both close to six feet tall and young and athletic, but that didn't stop him wading in like Flint. He just walked up to them and beat the shit out of the pair of them. He didn't take any crap from anyone.'

'So he must have made a lot of enemies.'

'No one that he couldn't handle.'

'You're very sure of that.'

She sat up and propped herself on her arm.

'Look, you realize that this is a complete waste of time. In a few days he's going to turn up looking as fit as a fiddle and you and Veronica are just going to have a lot of egg on your faces, especially when you have to explain all that money.'

'What money?'

'Your fee, and don't bother asking me how I know.'

He said nothing, trying to figure her out.

'You're not her lover, are you?'

Freeman was shaken by that one.

'Who?' he asked.

'Veronica's.'

'No, Nicola, I'm *not* her lover.'

He realized, too late, that there was something strangely

intimate in the way in which he had spoken her name. He wondered if she had noticed it too. But this time it was Nicola's turn to remain silent. She lay there on her back, watching Freeman with a sultry look on her face. He realized that he couldn't hide his mood from her. She could tell that he was turned on by her. He sensed that it gave her a perverse delight to look at his crotch and watch the evidence of his feelings which he was desperately trying to suppress.

'Tell me about your relationship with your brother,' he said.

'You make it sound like incest,' she giggled.

'I was wondering how you get on with him.'

'Fine. When we see each other.'

'You mean he has his interests and you have yours.'

'Right.'

'I expect he's the serious, scholarly type. Into his scientific studies and suchlike.'

'Oh, don't you believe it. That's just an act he puts on. He's into partying and dating as much as anyone of his age. The thing about your average nerd is that his libido is as big as that of any macho lout. He's just a bit shy about expressing it, and usually a lot less successful about indulging it, at least until he gets older.'

'Are you talking about your brother,' asked Freeman, 'or nerds in general?'

'The latter. I'm talking about my brother as he used to be a few years ago. Although I understand that now he's a whole lot better at indulging his lust.'

'But he still has time for studies.'

'Oh yes,' she replied, the hint of jealousy creeping into her voice. 'He's one of those overachievers who has the time for everything.'

'I expect he's also done a bit of dabbling in the stock market,' suggested Freeman, probing gently. That's probably why he gets so much mileage out of his allowance.'

She pouted sulkily.

'If you ask me he doesn't have to dabble in anything.

Daddy gives him at least three times as much as he gives me.'

Freeman was edging forward, slowly.

'How do you know?'

'Well, for a start, he always has a lot more to spend, far more than Daddy gives me. Daddy *says* that we get the same. But I know it isn't true. I have to supplement my allowance by modelling and even that barely gives me enough. It's the old story of the son getting the first bite of the apple, and the biggest.'

'I noticed that you automatically assumed that I was talking about Michael, not your half-brother.'

'Oh, John? I've never really thought of him as a brother. My mother had custody of me and Michael and I hardly ever saw John. Even when I was at home I didn't get to see him much. He was brought up by a good old-fashioned British nanny, until he rebelled and got sent to Holland Park Comprehensive.'

'Isn't that rather far from home? I wouldn't have thought their catchment area extended to the Digby estate.'

'Oh, he doesn't live on the estate. He lives in the West End of London. Daddy has a permanent suite at the Hilton. They come home together at weekends.'

Freeman nodded, grasping the complexity of the arrangement.

'Was it an acrimonious divorce, between your parents?'

'Oh no, no custody battle either. He just found a younger woman and moved in with her. That was before he pulled off his big property deals in Manhattan.'

'Didn't your mother resent it?'

'No, not really. She knew all about his affairs. And he was very generous. She found another man, and then another, and then another.'

'You must have resented that.'

'Now you're being Freudian,' she said, pouting again, this time disapprovingly. 'We learned to fend for ourselves, at least when it came to using our time. Of course, Daddy's money came in handy.'

'Interesting,' said Freeman pensively.

She turned over on to her front, adjusting her position sensuously, as if aware of Freeman's eyes feasting upon her and determined to give him a tantalizing treat.

'If you're going to hang around why don't you make yourself useful,' she said.

'What?' asked Freeman, uncertainly.

'Come over and put some oil on my back.'

He could tell that she was toying with him. Opportunities like this he usually had to work for. It was obvious that she was well aware of the fact that she was God's gift to men. Still, he thought, squirting the oil from the bottle on to her back and rubbing it in firmly, there is always the possibility that God is Greek.

'Why do you think your father gives Michael more money than he gives you?'

'Well, for a start because Mike always seems to have so *much* of it. He's never short of a grand or two if he wants to buy some new car or yacht or whatever. I mean, I suppose it all evens out 'cause I can get men to buy me jewellery. But still, Mike always seems to be rolling in it. You know he has his own private five-seater airplane. You're forgetting my legs.'

He'd stopped rubbing in the oil and had been about to step back, when Nicola's voice had shocked him out of his complacency. He sensed that she enjoyed the power of giving him orders rather more than the tactile sensation of his firm hands sliding their way across her soft body. But he didn't protest. His embarrassment was the product of the strange circumstances rather than the action itself. He squirted more oil on to his hands and began rubbing it into her calves.

'How much does your father give you?' he asked.

'Twenty thousand a month. He says that giving us too much would ruin our characters.'

'Twenty thousand a month sounds pretty good,' said Freeman, feeling somewhat guilty as he thought about the seventy-five thousand that he'd just deposited.

'Not when you're paying off a ten-thousand-a-month

mortgage and driving a Ferrari and travelling and trying to keep up to date with the latest fashions.'

'And buying perfume at four hundred dollars an ounce?'

'Exactly,' said Nicola. 'I mean, you'd think that as it's Daddy's company he'd be able to get me free samples. But he insists that because it's a public company and his group is only the major stockholder, he can't bring home the goodies for nothing.'

'So I guess you have to buy it at Harrods.'

'Unfortunately. And contrary to any gossip you may have heard about me, I hate shopping. I just love *owning*. What about my thighs?'

He had stopped again, and she was reminding him imperiously of his duties. His hands moved up in response to her challenge, and she seemed to squirm when they reached the inner thighs, as if her haughty command had been a dare that she hadn't expected him to take up and now had to live with. As his hands approached her buttocks he contemplated the shapely derrière and wondered if a proverbial spanking would have a salutary effect on her attitude. But he kept his own counsel, deciding that now was not the time to overstep his brief – or hers.

'Reverse mouse buttons,' said the message on the computer display screen. The short young man with dark curly hair checked the box on the screen with a click of a mouse button and then moved on to the next set-up function as he installed the program.

He manipulated the mouse to call up another dialogue box on to the screen with one hand while using the other to stick a fork, held American style, into a piece of pre-cut steak and bringing it to his lips. He liked to call himself a 'twentieth-century Renaissance man,' because he could do two different things at the same time with his hands. But a plurality of talents was not the only thing he had in common with Leonardo da Vinci.

He looked at the upper window on the computer screen. There it was, just as he had thought.

Freeman stood there, patiently. The girl in the clinging T-shirt and little else had just shown him in without even bothering to look at his ID and left him there without a word. She seemed a bit bleary-eyed. Downers probably, he thought.

'Of course, I want all error messages,' the young man said to himself. Again he manipulated the mouse. Out of the corner of his eye he noticed Freeman standing there at the doorway. 'I'll be with you in a moment,' he said.

'That's all right,' said the lawyer. 'I've got all the time in the world.'

Freeman pulled up a chair and sat down, this time without waiting to be asked. He looked around the room. It looked like a study, but it was also packed with computers, short-wave radios and electronic equipment. For such a large house it was strange that anyone should use the room for all these things, especially as there was a bedroom. Freeman had passed the bedroom on the way in. It was, in fact, a very *large* bedroom, with a king-sized round bed on which, he suspected, Mike performed many of his extracurricular activities.

Freeman found himself wondering idly how much these houses in St John's Wood cost.

'I'm just trying to install this program for simulating stress fractures on drums during low-intensity seismic upheaval. I've bought up this chemical waste site and I need a program to calculate the risk factors.'

Freeman said nothing.

'Everyone complains about polluting the environment, but they all take their material comforts for granted and no one bothers to think about what makes it possible.'

Freeman wondered if this was for real or if Mike was just trying to sound macho. At any rate he had no intention of being diverted into a sideshow.

He looked around the room. In addition to the furniture, there were books, tons of them. It probably had almost as many books as the library in Fabian Digby's mansion. Well, perhaps not quite as many, but certainly a lot. But these were no leather-bound classics, with gold-tooled spines and specially milled paper. These were torn and battered paperbacks. They were mostly scientific: computers, physics, biochemistry. There were also quite a few science fiction books: Heinlein, Asimov, Clarke. There were no prizes for guessing where the young man's interests lay.

'OK,' said the young man. 'I'm with you.'

'Michael Digby?' said Freeman, noticing how the man sat in front of the computer as if he were merely an extension of it.

'Mike, please. No one calls me Michael.'

'I'm investigating your father's disappearance.'

'Oh,' said Mike, appearing now to feel slightly embarrassed that he hadn't given Freeman all his attention from the beginning.

'I was wondering if you had any ideas. Or for that matter if you even take it seriously.'

'Why shouldn't I take it seriously?' asked Mike.

'Well, some members of your family seem to think that it's all a storm in a teacup.'

'Meaning Nicola,' said Mike.

'Exactly,' said Freeman.

'Well I do take it seriously. It's not like him. But if there hasn't been any ransom demand then I can't start off from a position of pessimism.'

'You mean you're concerned but not worried?'

'I mean that I can't permit myself to assume the worst. I look at it this way. Even if we all knew where he was, he could still get killed in an auto accident tomorrow. So I'm as worried about his whereabouts as I would be about the dangers that tomorrow may bring to any of us, but no more so.'

'Very philosophical,' said Freeman. He could imagine Mike having some absolutely fascinating conversations with his step-mother.

'Your sister thinks your father gives you more money than her.'

'My sister is a spoilt brat who doesn't know how to live within her means.'

114

'And you do.'

'As you can see.'

'Did you have a friend sleep over?' asked Freeman.

'No, why?'

'I just wondered,' Freeman mumbled, pointing to the bed.

'Oh that. No, I was working on a spreadsheet doing projections for the chemical waste site. It's tricky doing contract work for the denationalized monopolies.'

Freeman got the impression that Mike was showing off. It was as if he was trying to emphasize that he was a businessman in his own right and not just his father's son.

'I was too bushed to go to bed so I just curled up over there. I was going to get back to the computer but I guess I must've just passed out.'

Freeman looked at the three day growth of stubble on Mike's face and realized that he was talking about yesterday, or maybe the day before.

'Didn't it bother . . .' he signalled towards the doorway.

'Oh Julie? No. She doesn't live in. She sometimes stays the night. When I'm in the mood. She also doubles as a housekeeper. It saves on the bills.'

Freeman sensed that this sort of sarcasm was well-practiced. He let it pass without comment.

'Do you have any idea where your father could be?'

'Probably in the Middle East working on a new deal.'

'Do you mean it's true? That story about Arabs financing the La Contessa takeover?'

'It could be. I mean maybe Muslims don't want to admit that they're financing the takeover of a perfume company. Maybe they're afraid of antagonizing the fundamentalists.'

'That does seem like a rather unlikely scenario,' Freeman suggested.

'Well, maybe. But he could still be in an Arab country. They still have money to invest, not as much as in the seventies, but still a fair sum.'

'But why the secrecy?'

'Half the business in the world today is conducted in secret. You only get to hear about the more boring deals.'

'Is it likely that you father would have just gone off without telling anyone, not even his own secretary?'

'No it isn't likely. That's why I'm a little worried. But it's not impossible. That's why I'm not hitting the panic button just yet, even if Veronica is.'

'You think she's over-reacting?'

'No not really. If I were a woman I'd react that way too, especially if I was his wife. But I'm a man and we men have to think rationally.'

'Do you talk like that to the girls you bring back here?'

'Not if they've got college degrees. One has to be politically correct you know.'

Freeman suspected that Mike had his pick of college girls and waitresses alike.

'So do you think I'm wasting my time?' asked Freeman.

'No, I think it's important to have some one looking. But my guess is that he'll turn up in a few days time, with a new deal signed for another corporate takeover.'

'Your father doesn't know that the eighties are over,' said Freeman. It was not a question.

'As far as my father's concerned the eighties won't be over till we've buried the sixties.'

Freeman shifted his position.

'When did you see him last?'

'About a week and a half ago. Sunday dinner at the mansion.'

'After church?' asked Freeman.

'Now you're being facetious,' said Mike.

'Did he have any personal problems?'

'Personal?'

'Yes.'

'As in cigareetes and whasky and wild, wild women?'

'Yes,' said Freeman, irritated at Mike's flippance.

'Not that I know of. I mean he had his mistresses and his pre-dinner cocktails and after-dinner port but he was always in control.'

'No sign that he was losing it?'

'Not a bit.'

'So his disappearance could well be said to be out of character.'

'Yes, but not beyond the bounds of possibility, as it were.'

'OK, if you think of anything that might be of use to me, you can reach me at this number.'

He handed Mike his card with the number of his beeper service. Mike looked at it and the expression on his face changed abruptly.

'*Emmett* Freeman?' he asked, astonished.

'Yes,' Freeman replied, wondering why the name was emphasised with such significance.

'So the Klingon has joined the enterprise,' said Mike, laughing.

'I don't follow.'

'It was an allusion to *Star Trek*,' Mike explained. 'A popular science fiction TV series,' he added, seeing the blank look on Freeman's face.

'I don't see the connection,' Freemen replied, bewildered.

'The Klingons were the sworn enemies of the Federation. Then they made peace with them, and in *The Next Generation* there was a Klingon serving as security officer on the Starship *Enterprise*.'

Freeman knew perfectly well who the Klingons were, being a confirmed Trekkie himself. But the analogy was rather obscure and not altogether appropriate.

'I still don't see what that's got to do with me,' said Freeman, although in truth it was all now vaguely beginning to crystalize.

'You blackmailed my father into hiring you as a nominal consultant. Now you're really working for him. Or perhaps you're just trying to preserve the goose that lays the golden eggs.'

'You *know* about me?' asked Freeman, realizing that Mike must have been about sixteen or seventeen when he was hired by Fabian Digby.

117

'*Know* about you? It was because of you that I decided to study physics.'

'Because of *me*?' Freeman echoed.

'Well because of your letter – *and* my father's reaction to it. That was when I realized the value of a physics degree. Until then I'd been planning to study a more ivory tower theoretical subject like maths.'

'He showed you my letter?'

'Sure. We shared a lot, my old man and me. I can even recite the letter word perfect right now. Want to hear it?'

Freeman was about to say 'no', but Mike launched into it without waiting for a reply.

'"Dear Mr Digby, we are a firm of business consultants who also do *pro bono publico* work to prevent encroachments on civil liberties and individual rights. It has come to our attention that you are seeking certain patents in the field of genetics pertaining to the human genome and discoveries pertaining thereto.

'"Pursuant to the pro bono clause in our Memorandum of Association whereby we are permitted to act on a public interest basis on matters in which our clients have no interests and wherein we have no contradictory contractual or fiduciary obligations, it is our intention to challenge your patent applications in an action before the patent office. The substance of our objections is set forth on the accompanying pages.

'"It is possible that we have misinterpreted your applications or ovelooked the rationale behind it. If so, please feel free to contact us as we have no wish to delay or impede a justifiable application."'

'You missed out the words at the top: "Without Prejudice."'

'I hadn't forgotten. I was more concerned with the subtext. "Hire my one-man firm as a consultancy for a big fat retainer or we'll screw you over good and proper." You know patents are the only area in which someone can file an action to block someone else without assuming any financial risk themselves.'

'That's because they can only challenge after the patent application has been published.'

'What's that got to do with it?' snapped Mike.

'Well if the challenge fails then the patent holder can sue any infringers back to the date of publication.'

'But the person who challenges doesn't have to infringe the patent himself in order to file a challenge. He doesn't even have to show that he has standing.'

'No, but if the challenge fails, then the patent holder hasn't suffered a genuine loss. Because he can backdate his lawsuits against anyone who *did* infringe to the date of publication.'

'But there's always an element of uncertainty,' said Mike. 'The patent applicant has to spend money fighting the challenge.'

'So does the challenger.'

'Oh come off it Freeman. You conducted your own case! All you had to pay was the filing fee for the challenge. My father had to spend a fortune on lawyers. Or would have done if he hadn't caved in.'

'I gather you don't approve,' said Freeman.

'Don't approve?' asked Mike, surprised. 'I *loved* it.' A beaming smile had broken out over Mike's face. 'It was the first time in my life I'd actually seen the old man speechless. I mean, I didn't like seeing him beaten by outsider. But at least for once he was *beaten*.'

'You mean you had mixed feelings.'

'You could put it that way,' said Mike, the smile fading. 'How come you never went back to physics?'

'I found other things to do with my time,' replied Freeman.

'Oh yes, the champion for the weak and the frail.'

'It kills time,' said Freeman.

Mike Digby was unmoved by the mock cynicism, apart from a sense of mild amusement that Freeman was now playing *his* game.

'You mean like the would-be martyr grocer who refuses to convert his scales to the metric system because he doesn't want to bow to EU bureaucracy,' he said with a sneer.

'Or the black kid with dreadlocks who gets arrested by the Met when he refuses to comply with the stop-and-search laws that they rushed through Parliament before Easter,' replied Freeman.

'And while you were playing the crusading hero, men like my father were paying the bills.'

'Your father had a weakness worth exploiting. Winning is the name of the game, after all.'

'I thought you didn't believe in preying on the weak,' Mike jabbed.

'Oh, I don't,' replied Freeman. 'But I see nothing wrong with preying on the weaknesses of the strong.'

10

'A good name is better than fine perfume.'

Ecclesiastes 7:1

'Is that Gold you're wearing?'

It was Jenny, the new PC who had just joined the area HQ full of enthusiasm. Her youthful ambition was obvious, and she hung around Karen always asking for advice or simply hovering like a moth around a fire as if hoping that some spark of Karen's wisdom might set her career alight. She was holding a mug of coffee that she had just made for Karen unsolicited as another excuse to be close to her.

'Yes, it is,' replied Karen.

'Mm, I wish I could afford it.'

She put the coffee down next to Karen's phone. She seemed to be prolonging her presence again, filling the silence with any comment that would justify lingering a moment longer. Karen wondered if she was attracted to her, or perhaps to the perfume.

'Have you got any work to do, Jenny?'

'Oh, yes. Sure.'

Karen watched as she walked away slowly, clearly frustrated by her abrupt dismissal. But it hadn't been intended as rudeness. Jenny's remark about Gold reminded her that she hadn't heard from Dr Sadler at the lab. She picked up the receiver and punched his number.

'Hallo, may I speak to Dr Sadler . . . it's Karen Rousson.'

The girl at the other end asked her to wait, and it was a full two minutes before he came on the line.

'Hallo?'

There was an edge in his voice that she couldn't quite place.

'It's Karen Rousson here. I wanted to know if you had the results of the tests yet.'

Their was silence on the other end of the line.

'Dr Sadler?'

'Yes, I heard you.'

There was note of irritation in his voice.

'Well, are the results in or not?'

'Didn't . . . didn't you speak to DCS DuPaul?'

'No,' replied Karen, confused. 'Should I have?'

There was a palpable hesitation for a few seconds.

'Well, perhaps it would be better if you spoke to him,' he said finally.

'Look, I'll speak to him, but in the meantime can you give me a straight answer?'

'I phoned through and you weren't there, and I wanted to talk to someone senior so I asked for your Chief Superintendent.'

'And?' asked Karen, not quite sure where all this was leading.

'He told me not to do any more tests.'

'Did he say why?'

'Yes, he said it was because of budgetary considerations.'

He rang off, not waiting for her reply. She put the phone down slowly and somewhat suspiciously. Of course, the DCS had the right to countermand her instructions. But he could at least have apprised her of the fact.

She decided to pay him a visit.

'You know the kind of constraints we're under Karen,'

said the bald-headed man, barely looking up from his desk. He was short and round, and every time she saw him Karen was tempted to recite the old nursery rhyme about Humpty-Dumpty.

Detective Chief Superintendent Rex DuPaul had seemed almost conciliatory in his tone, as if he recognized Karen's sensitivity to anything that appeared to slight her authority in these days of political correctness.

'I know, sir. But Fabian Digby is a very important man and I understand that his disappearance is being taken seriously at the highest levels.'

'And so it is,' said DuPaul. 'But that doesn't mean going off on wild-goose chases looking into the chemical composition of the perfume that one of his companies is selling. The man had interests in the arms industry. If his business activities are relevant to his disappearance, that's where you should be looking.'

'*Had* interests, sir?'

'Pardon?'

'You said *had* interests. Not *has* interests.'

'Oh, now don't start playing games like that on me, young lady. Digby sold out his interests in Array-Chamberlain after the Middle East missiles scandal.'

'Well, if he no longer has those interests then why should we be looking in that direction?'

'Because he made a lot of enemies in those dealings. And if he has come to some harm that's where we're likely to find the culprits.'

'You don't think that all this talk about his perfume having addictive properties might be relevant to the investigation?'

'That's just what it is, Karen, a lot of talk.'

'Nevertheless,' said Karen. 'I think his takeover of La Contessa and the enmity it aroused should be properly investigated.'

'Investigated, yes,' said the DCS. 'But that doesn't mean recklessly spending on unnecessary tests. If the La Contessa takeover is in any way relevant to my inquiry about Digby, then the answer is to be found in the people, not the molecules of the perfume.'

'Your inquiry, sir?' said Karen truculently. 'I thought it was my inquiry.'

'Is that what this is all about, Karen? The young ambitious female police officer trying to carve a place for herself and thinking that she's not getting the respect that she deserves?'

She was seething within. Once again he had succeeded in putting her on the defensive even though all she was trying to do was conduct the investigation in the way she thought best.

'It's not about ego, sir,' she said, realizing that just by saying so she was implying the opposite. 'It's about casting our net wide enough to get results. If this investigation fails, I'm going to be the one taking the flak from the press.'

'But I'll be the one taking the flak from Regional Command,' said DuPaul.

'I think I'll be the one to come off worst,' Karen replied bitterly, knowing how department politics played out. He would settle his problem with a secret handshake and a quiet word in the right ears. She would be pilloried in the tabloids for failing to solve the case and probably scapegoated by her superiors to get themselves off the hook. Being a woman, she was not admitted to the clubs that they belonged to.

'Just remember that we all have to operate within a budget. That goes for me as much as for you. I may have a bigger budget, but I also have a bigger patch.'

'Then if I stay within the budget may I conduct further tests?'

His voice took on a deep, grandfatherly tone.

'It would be very embarrassing for the department if it were to come to the attention of the public that we've been spending taxpayers' money analysing the contents of a perfume bottle.'

'There's no reason why it should come to the attention of the public. We don't have to give a running commentary on what we're doing.'

'All it would take is one loose tongue at the lab.'

'They're professionals at the Met Lab.'

'Not the lab assistants,' said DuPaul firmly. 'They're low-paid lackeys.'

'They have so much going through their hands, they wouldn't even notice it. And they certainly wouldn't be able to link it to any one investigation.'

'No, but let's take a worst-case scenario. Suppose this investigation drags on for weeks or months and draws a blank at the end of all that. There's going to be a public clamour for an inquiry into what went wrong. The Digby family will demand it and the press will jump on the bandwagon. The next thing you know, some independent high-ranking officer from another area will be going through our files checking up on how we conducted the investigation. One of the things he'll turn up will be a bill for expensive tests on perfume. Then he'll publish his report and the next thing you know the tabloids will be running headlines saying 'bungling police waste money on perfume tests!'

'I mean, you can see what I'm getting at. Running this sort of test is just *asking* for trouble. It'll be like a time bomb ticking away against us. That's why I got the lab to destroy the results of the preliminary tests and write off the bill. That's the only way we can keep it off the record.'

'You did what?'

'Now don't go all sanctimonious on me. I did it for your good as well as mine. If this sort of thing comes out it could destroy both our careers.'

Karen was left almost breathless by this kind of logic.

'It could also destroy our careers if it comes out that we ignored the tests and got the bill cancelled.'

'But it isn't going to come out. There are only three people who know about it: you, me and Sadler.'

'Why would Sadler keep it under his hat?'

'It didn't come cheap, I can tell you that. Suffice it to say that I owe him a favour.'

'Well, I just hope you've got something that he wants

badly enough. By the way, sir, what were the results of the preliminary tests?'

'Negative. And somehow I don't think that really surprises you.'

She was about to reply when the phone rang. DuPaul picked up the receiver.

'Yes . . . yes . . . I see . . . when was he? . . .'

Karen noticed that his voice had taken on an intensely serious tone and that he was looking straight at her.

'I have her with me now.'

11

'How the mighty have fallen!'

II Samuel 1:19

Neither of Fabian Digby's offspring from his first marriage seemed particularly worried about his disappearance. Indeed Nicola didn't seem worried at all. Why not, Freeman wondered? Had he done this sort of thing before? Nicola said he hadn't. How then could she be so calm about it? Or was it just indifference? If he was dead, how would she be affected? How much would she inherit and how much would go to Veronica? And whatever Nicola stood to inherit, did she know the contents of her father's will? Did Veronica, for that matter?

Mike was a different matter entirely. In spite of what he said, he was worried about his father, at least slightly. That, at least, was more reasonable. But he didn't admit to being on the verge of panic. Did he know something that he wasn't telling? Or was he simply denying his fear, to himself as well as to Freeman?

Fabian Digby's family was a house divided against itself. Was it possible that he couldn't bear to stay in that house any longer? That he just wanted to quit and let the house collapse in the absence of the mighty pillar that supported it? It was hard to credit. The rift that cut across the family was not so great, just the normal feuding between jealous siblings and resentment by a daughter of her stepmother. But it was interesting that Nicola's sibling rivalry was with her natural brother and not with her stepbrother.

In any case, it was hard to see family feuding overloading the stress circuits of a workaholic like Fabian Digby. He certainly wasn't a man to be easily defeated by stress. He fought major battles in boardrooms and at stockholders' meetings. He had conducted hostile takeovers and greenmail raids and it was invariably his opponents who were left scarred and bleeding. It was hard to see him running away from the trivial problem of bickering family members. He would have been more likely to have put his foot down or cracked the whip, or the wallet, and brought them to heel.

More likely one of his enemies had come back from the past to haunt him. He certainly had no shortage of enemies: chief executives ousted when he took over the companies they ran; shareholders deprived of equal benefit when he withdrew a tender offer for shares in return for a greenmail settlement with the management; American taxpayers forced to pay higher taxes to underwrite the banks that over-extended themselves with junk bonds that were issued to finance takeovers and leveraged buy outs and ended up in with huge bad debts on their books. An awful lot of people suffered at the hands of men like Fabian Digby, and many of them, the taxpayers for instance, hadn't even *chosen* to be 'players' in the first place. It was hard to say how far the web of enmity extended. There were far too many suspects for Freeman to check them all out. He knew that he'd probably have to wait until there were further developments in order to make a move. If Digby had been kidnapped, a ransom note would soon be forthcoming.

The doorbell rang. He answered it to find a uniformed police constable standing outside.

'Emmett Freeman?' asked the constable.

'Yes,' said Freeman.

'I must ask you to come with me to the station, sir.'

The constable seemed rather embarrassed, and gave no indication of being poised for action or expecting resistance.

'Am I under arrest?' asked Freeman.

'No, sir. Although if you refuse to accompany me my superiors may seek a warrant for your arrest.'

Freeman knew that as he had not committed an arrestable offence or given reason to believe that he had committed one or was about to commit one, he could not be lawfully arrested without a warrant. Even the excuse of a common-law arrest for causing a breach of the peace was unavailable because he was on private property. However, he also sensed that there was nothing hostile in this constable's intent.

'May I ask who sent you?' asked Freeman.

'Detective Chief Inspector Rousson, sir,' said the constable.

He wondered why Karen should be summoning him in this way.

'All right,' said Freeman. 'May I get my jacket?'

'Of course, sir,' said the constable.

Twenty minutes later he was pulling out a chair in Karen's office as the constable left the room.

'All right, Chief Inspector Rousson,' he said icily, 'perhaps you'll tell me what this is all about.'

'I'm conducting an investigation concerning Fabian Digby —'

'I know that,' said Freeman irritably. He had come here of his own free will, largely out of curiosity. But now he was beginning to feel resentful of Karen's heavy-handed methods, especially as she hadn't volunteered an explanation as soon as he had walked through the door.

'I'm sure you also know that private detectives have no special status under English law. As such you are nothing more than a witness in this case.'

'I don't see that I'm a witness to anything,' snapped Freeman bluntly. 'I was called in on the case *after* Digby disappeared.'

'That may be,' said Karen coolly. 'But the Freeman family presumably told you things that may be of relevance to our enquiries. That makes you a witness.'

'They may have told me things,' said Freeman. 'But in case it slipped your memory I am not a private detective but a lawyer. I may have been requested to make certain discreet enquiries, but I am a solicitor and I've been hired to represent the interests of the Digby family. As such I am protected by privilege.'

'Only insofar as it pertains to statements made by your client. And your client can only be a person such as a family member, or a legal entity such as Digby Holdings. Not the whole family.'

'I could be retained by all the members of the family,' said Freeman. 'But in any case I am not obliged to divulge statements that harm my client's interests – except to the extent that I have obligations as an officer of the court.'

'As no member of the Digby family has been charged with any criminal offence, there are limitations on your privilege.'

'But only a judge can say precisely what they are.'

'Look, let's stop playing games, Mr Freeman. If I find any evidence that you've gone beyond your rights or duties to your client you'll feel the full force of the law coming down on your head. Now, I'm ready to meet you halfway in this matter, but I'll expect your co-operation.'

'Well, why don't you start off by telling me why you had me brought here in the first place – especially as you haven't really asked me any *specific* questions.'

'All right. I'll go first. A little over an hour ago Fabian Digby's body was found floating on the Paddington Basin of the Grand Union Canal.'

Part II

SILVER

'Who chooseth me shall gain all that he deserveth.'

William Shakespeare,
The Merchant of Venice

12

'. . . they have together become corrupt . . .'

Psalms 14:3

'There was always a danger of it surfacing, Michael.'

'Or the tide receding, Hassan.'

A roar of collective laughter rose up from around the oval mahogany table. Mike was always good for a witty rejoinder. They had just finished a dinner of smoked salmon and Beluga caviar followed by Tornedos Rossini, the delicate fillet of beef topped with foie gras and truffles. The plates of fresh strawberries had been removed and they had polished off a jeroboam of Dom Perignon. They were now sipping Chivas Rigal from Czech crystal snifters and the finest Kenyan coffee from bone china cups.

'What does it matter?' asked Hassan, harking back to the last words spoken before the mirth that had echoed across the table. 'All they know is that he was killed. That makes it a murder inquiry.'

'Then it's over to you Rex,' said Mike.

At one end of the table sat the imposing form of DCS Rex DuPaul with a nervous grin on his face.

His smile turned to a frown when Mike's words registered in his mind.

'What have I got to do with it?'

'Well, there's presumably going to be an investigation,' said Hassan.

'There's one already,' said DuPaul. 'We had a little problem. But I nipped it in the bud.'

'What sort of problem?' asked Mike.

'Some chemist at the Met Lab found something that he shouldn't have. But I persuaded him to look the other way.'

'I was speaking about an investigation into the murder of Fabian Digby,' said Hassan.

'Yes,' said DuPaul. 'What I meant was there was already an investigation into his disappearance. The only difference is that now it's a murder inquiry.'

'Does that mean it's no longer in your hands?' asked Mike.

'It's still in my hands,' said DuPaul, injecting an assertive tone into his voice to leave everyone in the dining room in no doubt that he was still in control. 'And I don't see why you're all getting worried. We don't have separate missing persons and homicide sections in the Met. It's all CID and inquiries are set up on an *ad hoc* basis. As area DCS I have the power to decide who heads the investigation unless I feel it necessary to pass it still higher up the chain of command. In practice I think that in view of Fabian Digby's wealth and status in the community, an investigation headed by a DCS would be most appropriate.'

'Is it normal for someone so highly ranked to run an investigation?' asked a stout man who sat close to the end of the table, his fingers interlocked across his cummerbund.

'When the victim is someone as important as Fabian Digby,' replied DuPaul, 'it's quite normal. However, in practice, Edward, the day-to-day matters will be run by a subordinate senior officer, like an inspector or chief inspector.'

'And do you have anyone in mind?' asked Hassan with a wily smile on his face.

'I do indeed,' said DuPaul. 'I believe in maintaining

continuity of investigations. So I'll have my loyal sidekick Detective Chief Inspector Karen Rousson as my deputy.'

'Is that wise?' asked Mike.

'I don't see why not,' said DuPaul, mirroring Hassan's sly grin with one of his own. 'That way I can keep an eye on her.'

'But what good does it do you to keep an eye on her,' asked Mike, 'if you can only find out what she knows after she knows it? By then it may be too late.'

'I can also direct her efforts,' said DuPaul, confidently.

'I don't like it,' said Michael. 'Not unless we can bring the investigation to a definite conclusion.'

'How do you mean?' asked DuPaul.

'I mean you need a scapegoat,' Mike replied coldly.

'You're not asking me to fit someone up, are you?' asked DuPaul.

'What if I were?' asked Mike, smiling.

'You can't be serious. I'm a man of principle. I'm prepared to give the benefit of the doubt to a brother and to suggest the most kindly and most palliating circumstances to the outside world. But I am not prepared to bring false charges against the innocent.'

'It may be necessary,' said Mike.

DuPaul scowled. 'Bearing false witness against one's neighbour goes against the basic commandments of the Almighty.'

'So does murder,' said Hassan.

'The slaying of a traitor isn't murder,' said Mike irritably. Now was not the time to reawaken the policeman's doubts. Turning to DuPaul, he added: 'Surely you can innocently lay the blame at the door of those who are beyond suffering.'

'Such as whom?' asked DuPaul.

'Such as the dead?' suggested Mike.

'Accusing the dead can sometimes hurt the living,' the police detective replied.

'What if the person you accused was less than blameless in some other capacity?' asked Hassan, leaning towards DuPaul.

'What do you mean?' asked the DCS.

Hassan threw back his head in contemplation. 'You could point the finger at someone who's already a suspect in another case. I mean someone who is clearly guilty but who might be able to . . . how do you people put it . . . 'beat the rap' on the other charge.'

Mike and DuPaul exchanged a knowing look.

'Yes,' said DuPaul, nodding uncomfortably. 'There is always that option.'

He did not look happy as he said this.

'And even if he won't beat the rap on the other charge,' Mike added, 'it won't do such a person any more harm to be convicted of a second crime of similar magnitude.'

'I think, that we might all be speaking of the same person,' said DuPaul.

'Would that be the brother?' asked Hassan.

'What?' asked Edward, horrified.

'He means the brother of the victim,' said Michael. 'The victim of another crime, that is.'

'I see,' said Edward, not really seeing at all.

'By the way, Edward,' said Hassan, 'I want you to know that my government is most grateful for the spirit of friendship and co-operation with which you have approached this matter and in particular your self-restraint in regulatory dealings with the La Contessa takeover. I must tell you that this co-operation has not gone unnoticed.'

There was a general perking up and lifting of spirits in the room, as the men at the table sat forward in anticipation of the grand gesture that they all knew was coming.

'Accordingly, on a related subject,' said Hassan, 'I can now confirm that my government will go ahead with the purchase of the eight-billion-dollar arms package from your country. So you may look forward to an extra seventeen thousand jobs for the next five years and plenty of good publicity from the increased revenue. We shall of course apportion the contracts so as to ensure that the lion's share of these jobs are created in your marginal constituencies. We shall also be contributing an extra fifty million pounds to your party funds, which of course you will not declare.'

'We're not *obliged* to declare it,' said Edward stiffly. 'Only the companies that *pay* the money are obliged to declare it, and then only if they're *British* companies.' This was a bit of a sore point with him and he didn't like the mockery in Hassan's tone.

'And I also have something for you personally,' said Hassan. He took out a thick white envelope, put it on the silver tray in front of him and slid it across the table towards Edward. 'Your consultancy fee,' he said.

Edward took the envelope from the tray and put it in his breast pocket, not bothering to open it or count it. He knew that the twenty-five thousand pounds was all there.

'I believe that you *are* obliged to declare that on your register of interests,' said Hassan. 'Although I'd be much obliged if you didn't.'

'It's only a parliamentary rule that says I have to declare it,' said Edward. 'Not a law. And I have no intention of infringing your right to privacy by declaring it. I will of course declare it to the Inland Revenue. They don't require disclosure of the source.'

'I am grateful,' said Hassan.

'We have have some trouble in another capacity,' said Mike, leaning over to Hassan.

'What's that?' asked the Middle Eastern gentleman.

'While browsing the Internet, I came across a message from someone called Emmett Freeman asking about Fabian Digby and Gold. He's the man who was hired to look for him.'

'What did the question say?' asked Hassan.

'Basically he just asked for any information that anyone has on the subject.'

'That means he has very little information of his own,' said Hassan, smiling. 'So he isn't really a threat to us.'

Mike smiled, grateful for the reassurance, and rang the bell to summon the butler.

13

'After this, his brother came out, with his hand grasping Esau's heel . . .'

Genesis 25:26

'It's nice here, Phil.'

A fresh smell rose up from the grass as the sprinklers did their work, but it still looked parched from the weeks of drought

'I know. I used to come here as a child.'

They were walking hand in hand by the boating lake at Regent's Park. He was wearing a short-sleeved Hawaiian shirt, a mass of blue and green colours, but the heat of the sun beating down on him on this cloudless day was still oppressive. He had wanted to wear his straw cowboy hat, but it looked silly. The last thing he wanted was to make a fool of himself in front of Jilly. She was wearing a white halter top and matching shorts. He couldn't understand why she had brought the Walkman along. It wasn't as if his conversation was boring. In any case she had told him that it didn't work when he asked to listen, so he wasn't really offended.

'With Tony?'

'What?' he asked, realizing that his mind had wandered.

'I was asking if you used to come here with your brother.'

138

'And my parents.'

'Before your father died.'

'Well, obviously,' he snapped. 'I'm sorry,' he added. 'I guess I'm still touchy about some things.'

'I thought he died quite a while ago.'

He didn't know how she managed to remember all these details. She seemed to remember things that he didn't remember telling her.

'My brother died less than two weeks ago. That's what I'm touchy about.'

'I'm sorry,' she said quietly.

To their right was the bridge over a narrow stretch of the lake.

'My father used to tell us the story of the three billy-goats and the troll that hid under the bridge, and then when we got to the bridge he would stand in the middle and sing the song that the troll sang to the billy-goats when he confronted them.'

They were at the bridge now.

'How did that go?' she asked, laughing.

'Oh, don't ask me to sing it.'

'Go on,' she said teasingly. Suddenly he ran out onto the bridge and stopped halfway. As Jilly looked on in consternation he crossed his outstretched arms and contorted his face.

'I'm a troll, rolly-roll!' he sang. 'I'm a troll, *rolly*-roll! I'm a troll rolly-roll! And I'll *eat you* for my, *Sup*per!' By this stage Jilly had burst out laughing – more from embarrassment than amusement. Sensing that she was ready for greater physical contact, he ran back to her and put his arm round her shoulder, laughing too. She put her arm round his waist as they walked on past the Baker Street entrance.

'I used to love watching the young couples walking along hand in hand.'

'Your libido must have stirred early.'

'Oh, it wasn't a sexual thing.' He inclined his head back, as if remembering. 'It was more romantic. I used

139

to daydream about walking hand in hand with Corinne Bernstein.'

'Corinne Bernstein?' repeated Jilly.

'From my primary school.'

'One of your teachers?' asked Jilly, smiling.

'God, no! She was the prettiest girl in the class.'

'Did she reciprocate your affections?'

A wry smile came over his face.

'No. She was in love with Robert Perchik.'

'In *love* with him? You mean she had a crush on him?'

'No, I mean they were really in love, or at least thought they were. I mean it was mutual. They both loved each other and everyone knew it.'

'You mean they were an item.'

'Exactly.'

Jilly smiled, and looked at something in the distance. But he was too thoroughly wrapped up in his memories to notice.

'Who was he?' asked Jilly.

'Who?'

'This Robert Perchik.'

'The class brainbox.'

'You mean he was smarter than you?'

Jilly saw the anger on his face as he asked the question.

'He was more of an *achiever* than I was. He always came first in the exams. I started coming about tenth when I joined the school and worked my way up to second.'

'You mean you never quite beat him.'

'I was second to someone else. He and a few of the older kids had moved up a class for part of the year. When we were together again in the last year I was only fourth. He was still first.'

'So you never beat your old rival.'

'Not in the exams,' he said bitterly.

'Was it frustrating?'

'Very.'

She glanced at him.

140

'Because he was smarter or because he had this Corinne Bernstein?'

'Both. I mean, I don't think he was smarter. But I thought so at the time.'

'Why?'

'Well, he always came top in the exams and I never got anywhere near him.'

'So what made you change your mind?'

He realised that she had picked up on the words 'I thought so at the time'.

'Somewhere along the line I realized that there was more to brains than passing exams. First of all, I had more general knowledge than Robert. Then I discovered that I had a talent for physics which of course had no way of showing itself in primary school. Physics was my first passion in life.'

'I thought Corinne Bernstein was your first passion?' said Jilly, grinning.

'Apart from Corinne,' he replied. 'Anyway, I also discovered that I had more creative intelligence.'

They had reached another bridge. It led to a quieter area of the park where the grass was rougher and where people played ball games. There were still plenty of people about, but they were more sparsely distributed in this part. He noticed that it was like the gardens in Bournemouth – the longer the grass the fewer the people. Jilly followed his lead in crossing the bridge.

'How long did this rivalry between you and Robert Perchik go on for?'

'Well, I transferred to the school from another when I was seven. And it was primary school so that was until I was eleven. That makes it five years.'

'Did you ever feel like killing him?'

'*Killing* him?'

'I don't mean seriously plan it. But I mean did you ever fantasize about pushing him down the stairs or shooting him in an old-fashioned shoot-out like in one of those westerns?'

'No. I mean it was an intellectual rivalry. The only thing

I really wanted to do was beat him in the exams. And get Corinne Bernstein.'

'Presumably if you'd done one you'd have done the other.'

'Not necessarily. I don't think she loved him for his brains.'

He stopped at the ice cream stand and bought a 99 for each of them.

'How did your brother feel about all that?'

'He went to a different primary school. It wasn't until we went on to a grant-maintained that we were together at school.'

'No, but I mean about your rivalry with this Perchik? Did he give you any advice?'

'Not really. I mean we were close, but I think we got closer later.'

'But didn't you say you also became rivals?'

'Yes, but not for a girl. Just academically. We each wanted to outdo the other in our respective fields.'

'Is it possible that you were continuing your rivalry with Perchik with your brother, perhaps even without realizing it?'

'I don't think so. I more or less forgot about Perchik after I finished primary school.'

'But it might have been lurking there at the back of your memory.'

He half turned and looked at her.

'Why are you so interested in my childhood? Are you planning on using me as a case study for one of your courses?'

'Sorry,' she said. 'I didn't know it bothered you.'

'It doesn't. I just don't understand why you're so interested.'

She had led him to a secluded patch of grass. Now she stood still as if to indicate that she was tired.

'I guess it just kind of fascinated me.'

She sat down on the grass. He joined her.

'What does?'

'The whole thing. This rivalry between you and your brother. I think there's something kind of romantic about two brothers, both talented but the more talented being eclipsed by the less talented one.'

'It wasn't like that.'

'What? He didn't eclipse you or you didn't eclipse him?'

'We neither of us eclipsed the other. It wasn't that sort of relationship.'

'I guess I'm just fantasizing myself now. I'd find it more exciting if it was like that.'

'How do you mean?' he asked, puzzled.

'Well, like I said, two brothers. Rivals. One of them destined to be in the other's shadow, until one day he rises up and kills his brother like Cain killing Abel.'

'You think I killed him?' he asked incredulously. 'Well, if that's what you think of me you can . . . get lost!'

She tried to recover quickly.

'You know Cain wasn't such a villain as everyone thinks. The story of Cain and Abel was symbolic. It said in the Old Testament that Cain owned the land and Abel owned all the animals. It was an allegory of the transition from hunting to farming. Abel was the hunter. Cain was the farmer. The farmer rose up and displaced the hunter. That's what it was really all about. Maybe it was like that with you and your brother. The old order replacing the new.'

'What makes you think my brother was the old order?'

'Oh, I don't know. But wouldn't it be nice to think of you as someone who stood up for himself. I'd really find that quite a turn-on.'

'You'd like me more if you thought I'd killed my brother?' he asked incredulously.

Her fingers did a gentle tap-dance on his chest. 'Let's just say that if I thought you were tough enough to kill your brother I might just be ready to . . . drop my defences.'

She gave him an inviting smile.

'You're sick,' he said.

'I'm sorry,' she replied, retreating quickly both physically and verbally. 'I guess I came on too strong. It's just that if I'm going to get involved with a guy, I'd like to know at least what I'm getting into.'

'I'm sorry if I've disappointed you. I'm just not the guy you seem to think I am.'

'You must have been stunned when you got the news . . . about your brother, I mean.'

'I was devastated.'

'I can imagine.'

'No, you don't understand. I felt guilty.'

'But I thought you said you had nothing to do with it.'

'Just before he was killed, we argued and split up. Then when I got home I heard that he was dead. How do you think that made me feel!'

There were tears in his eyes.

'Did you have to identify the body?'

'Yes.'

'I guess that's the hard part. You had to see him dead. I guess that makes it harder to remember him as being alive.'

'Yes.'

'Did it disturb you? Seeing him dead?'

'Of course it disturbed me. Looking down at a knife wound at the side of my brother's stomach.'

'I'm sorry,' she said. 'Perhaps I shouldn't keep talking about it.'

In the distance Inspector Logan was smiling. As far as he was concerned Phil had already said enough. At body identifications they never pull back the sheet entirely. They only uncover the head. He wouldn't have seen the stab wound. Not in the mortuary, at any rate.

14

*'Cast your bread upon the waters, for after many
days you will find it again.'*

Ecclesiastes 11:1

'He's been in the water a few weeks so the decompo-
sition's pretty bad,' said the pathologist. 'I'd say four
weeks.'

'That would mean more or less since the day he went
missing,' said DuPaul.

They were walking back from the slab on which the body
lay. There were four of them: DuPaul, Karen, Freeman and
Harvey Hoffman, the pathologist.

'He had one of those digital watches,' said Freeman. 'It's
a pity we can't tell the date and time of death from when it
stopped.'

'That only works on TV,' said Karen dryly.

'What was the cause of death?' asked Freeman.

The pathologist scratched the back of his head.

'A single bullet to the base of the skull. Rear penetration
from just left of the median line to just right of the frontal
lobe where it lodged.'

'Calibre?'

'That's ballistics,' said Karen.

'Is the report in yet?' asked Freeman, looking at the CID man.

Karen remained tight-lipped.

'You can tell him,' said DuPaul.

'A thirty-eight-calibre bullet,' said Karen. 'No unusual markings.'

'A thirty-eight,' Freeman repeated. 'Isn't that the type of weapon that armed police units use when they're guarding embassies?'

Karen looked at Freeman coolly, as if to warn him against annoying DuPaul.

'They use point three-eights all right,' said the DCS. 'But the bullets carry a smaller gunpowder charge than a normal three-eight. It's called a light load, Mr Freeman.'

Freeman knew perfectly well about light load charges, having watched more than his share of American cop shows. He turned to the pathologist.

'Doesn't a thirty-eight bullet to the head usually make an exit, Dr Hoffman? If it carries a regular charge?'

'Usually,' said Hoffman, embarrassed. He didn't want to sour his relations with the police, but this was something that Freeman seemed to know already, and could find out easily enough if he didn't.

'It was probably silenced,' said DuPaul. 'A silencer slows the bullet down.'

'And also this Digby bloke was a hard-head,' added Freeman.

DuPaul gave the lawyer a withering look.

'So it looks like a professional job,' said Freeman, trying to sound more serious and professional.

'Yes,' Karen agreed.

'They usually weight the bodies down on professional jobs,' said DuPaul.

'They did on this one too, sir,' said Karen, 'but the chain broke . . . that let the body break free and float.'

'That seems like awful bad luck,' said Freeman. 'Any possibility that they *wanted* the body found?'

'I doubt it,' said Karen. 'It's just that the chain wasn't all that strong, and it only had to break in one place. It must have happened when it hit the bottom.'

By this stage Freeman had taken Karen aside while DuPaul had helpfully led the pathologist off in the other direction.

'Where did they find the body?'

Karen looked past Freeman at DuPaul, wondering how much she should tell him. She knew that as it was now a murder inquiry Freeman was effectively off this case, although he still had a watching brief for the Digby family. Strictly speaking he didn't need to know anything at all about the murder. But she caught DuPaul's eye and saw the Chief Superintendent nodding at her. So she knew she was cleared to speak.

'He was spotted in the Paddington Basin of the Grand Union Canal. But we reckon that he was dumped slightly further upstream, probably in the Little Venice area of Maida Vale. We've got divers searching the canal bed for the murder weapon.'

'How do they know where to look? The gun wouldn't have floated.'

'We got the oceanography department at Imperial College to run a computer model of the slow current flow in the last four days based on weather reports and standard data. We also got the Met Lab to give us some estimates of when it's likely that the chain broke.'

'How could they do that?'

'They looked at the part of the chain that was attached to his waist. They compared the rust on the surface parts of the chain where it broke with the rust on the cross-sectional part. The cross-sectional part only became exposed to water when it broke. So we can use the rust on the sides to calibrate *when* it broke. Once we fixed the time the body floated, we gave it to the oceanography department. Based on their estimates and computer models we've been able to calculate that the body would probably have been thrown into the water within a certain band, and that's the area where we're looking, in certain selected areas.'

Freeman was genuinely surprised.

'You didn't waste any time, did you!' he said with approval.

'Look, Mr Freeman,' said Karen, resenting the condescension. 'Criminal investigations these days aren't solved by men in cloaks and deerstalkers. They're solved with science and technology.'

'You mean you've moved on from rubber hoses?'

He was smiling when he said it, but he regretted it afterwards. The last thing he wanted to do was fall out with Karen.

'Off the record,' said Karen, 'they still have their uses. But only once you've *got* a credible suspect. They can't help you find one in the first instance. It's like the story about the flea powder salesman.'

'I don't think I ever heard that one.'

'A door-to-door salesman knocks and asks the owner of the house if he wants to buy some flea powder. The owner says he's interested in principle but wants to know how you use this flea powder. So the salesman says, "First you catch the flea, then you tickle it under the arm and then when the flea is laughing you throw the flea powder into its mouth."'

'I like the joke, but I don't get the connection.'

Karen smiled indulgently.

'What I'm trying to say, Freeman, is that first we have to catch our suspect. Then we can think about the rubber hoses.'

Freeman winced.

'Aren't the Digby family credible fleas – I mean suspects?'

'We're checking out their alibis now, for the estimated time of death rather than mere disappearance. But they're not the most likely immediate suspects. If they had anything to do with it, they would probably have hired others. That means they'll have perfect alibis. So we still have to catch our flea.'

'How come you're only checking out selected sites in the area that you've narrowed it down to?'

'Some areas have easier road access. Some areas are more suitable for pushing a body into the canal and avoiding detection.'

'Very thorough,' Freeman commented, nodding encouragingly.

'Police investigation is a science, not an art, Mr Freeman,' DuPaul stepped in. 'That's why we don't leave it in the hands of private detectives.'

Freeman was about to ask if this meant that he was being ordered not to do any further investigative work for the Digby family. As he was a lawyer and not a private detective, they would have found it very hard to back this up. He was prepared to argue the point then and there, but a beeping sound cut into their thoughts. They all checked their liquid crystal display beepers. It was DuPaul's.

'Well, how do you like that,' said the Chief Superintendent as he looked at the message. 'They've found the remnant of the chain and the weights on the canal bed.'

'What about the gun?'

'There's nothing about it in the message. Still, now at least they know where to look. Karen, bring the car round.'

'Can I ride along?' asked Freeman.

'You can follow,' said DuPaul. 'But just remember you're a private citizen. I don't want you crossing the police line and saying DuPaul authorized it.'

'Sure thing,' said Freeman.

'How's it going?'

'Nothing much yet. We've found a few bits and pieces. Old bicycle wheels and things like that. But no sign of the weapon.'

Karen had been talking to one of the police frogmen by the side of the canal while Chief Superintendent DuPaul stood by. Freeman strolled up to them. He had been watching the scene from a distance, trying to gauge who was really in control of the investigation. DuPaul outranked Karen. But he was more concerned with putting in an appearance than actually doing anything. He seemed content to let Karen set the pace and do the legwork. So Freeman felt free to carry on addressing his questions to Karen.

'Do you think they'll find anything?'

'Not really, Mr Freeman. I mean, professionals don't usually keep the murder weapon. It was probably bought on the black market for one job and then disposed of. But he wouldn't have made it easy for us by disposing of it in the same place. Once we have a gun's serial number we can sometimes trace it all the way from the manufacturer to the street supplier. Then if *he* squeals, we've closed the case. But in practice it doesn't work like that. It was probably thrown into the Grand Union Canal somewhere, but God knows where. We'll probably never find it.'

'Then why look?' asked the lawyer.

'There's always the possibility. And if this case goes unsolved and the media jump in on it, I want to be able to say I left no stone unturned.'

Freeman realized that defensive policing, like defensive medicine, was a waste of resources that was caused by the very people who suffered financially because of it: a complaining public for whom everything must be right, with as little contribution from them as possible.

There was a mild splash as one of the divers in his oxygen rebreather came back to the surface. Recreational divers breathe a mixture of oxygen and nitrogen, just like regular air but in different proportions, and have to time their dives to include decompression stops to prevent air bubbles from forming in the bloodstream – the dreaded 'bends'. Deep sea divers working for oil companies or in marine salvage breathe a mixture of oxygen and helium and often have to spend several days in decompression chambers. It is the helium component that produces the squeaky-voice phenomenon often associated with such divers. But naval commandos and police frogmen, operating in shallow water up to a depth of twenty-five feet, breathe pure oxygen from compact oxygen rebreathers. For commandos, the advantage is that oxygen rebreathers leave no telltale bubbles floating to the surface during raids. For the police the advantage was more mundane: the oxygen rebreathers were small, light and unobtrusive. In a canal no more than six feet deep, the frogmen could search with their helmet lamps illuminating the canal bed, without having to worry about coming up for air.

'Hey, Chief Inspector! Take a look at this.'

A diver swam over to the side, holding something in his hand.

'What is it?' asked Karen, walking over.

The diver looked at Karen. 'A watch.'

He held it up. It was made of gold.

'A Rolex,' said the head of the frogman unit. 'How do you like that?'

'What would a thing like that be doing in the water?' asked Karen rhetorically.

'Where else would you find an oyster?' asked the frogman, grinning.

'Could it have come off the victim's wrist?' asked the head of the frogman unit.

'No,' replied Freeman and Karen simultaneously.

'The victim was still wearing his watch,' said Karen. 'An electronic digital address watch.'

The frogman looked disappointed, realizing that he had not made a major contribution to a murder investigation but had just found a piece of junk at the bottom of the canal, albeit expensive junk.

'Let's get back to work,' said the head of the frogman unit, walking back to the canal's edge with the diver.

'Any chance that it would have anything to do with the investigation?' asked Freeman.

'Not really,' said Karen. 'We'll check it out by the guarantee and then turn it in to the local police.'

'If it turns out to be connected to Digby will you let me know?'

'Same time as we tell the press,' said Karen.

'You're all heart.'

15

'Your eyes behind your veil are doves.'

Song of Songs 4:1

'So where did you get the money to take women to places like this?' asked Karen.

A rippling glow of candlelight flickered across the white lace tablecloth in an undulating pattern that almost danced in the evening breeze. Freeman had asked the waiter to open the window to the elements, and the warmth of the night air seemed to mingle with the melodious strains of the Suzanne Vega CD in the background.

'Who says I take other women to places like this?' he replied, smiling.

They were sitting in a luxurious restaurant, a tasteful assembly of dark blue leather panelling and walnut furnishings, by a sheet of glass that looked out on to the vast network of roads and buildings that lay to the south of the river. The occasional traces of movement outside gave Freeman a sensation of sailing, even though they were on *terra firma*.

'It must be costing you a fortune even if it's just me,' she said, swallowing a mouthful of beluga caviar.

From their corner table they could see the lights of South

152

London and an occasional ship passing them by coming up the line from from the estuary. The Thames seemed tranquil tonight. But looking at the gentle rippling water beyond the window, Freeman was reminded that even the stillest waters can conceal the violence and trauma of the most horrific death.

'Well, let's just say that the Digby family paid me very well, and up front at that!'

'Isn't that rather strange?'

He had thought about Karen's question himself, more than he cared to remember. But he had no answer. Of *course* it was strange.

'It's certainly unusual,' he said. 'Though not unprecedented.'

She smiled with wry amusement at his use of words. Like the receptionist who answers her home telephone with the name of her company, Freeman's legal training permeated his everyday speech.

'So what did you want to ask me about?' he continued.

She seemed to have changed since he had last seen her. Then she was somehow 'older' in a way that he couldn't describe. She had seemed like a professional woman, on a par with any man she might come into contact with, full of self-confidence and deadly serious. Indeed, it was her seriousness which gave her that aura of self-confidence and power that she radiated. Now she seemed more like a cheer leader with a bright girlish smile. Her cheeks were shiny, her lips glossy, her medium-length hair perfectly styled. She had been transformed by an unknown force into a beautiful, fresh-faced ray of sunshine. But more than that, her manner was different. She was suddenly 'lighter', less intense and more anxious to have fun. It was as if something had taken ten years off her age since their last meeting only a few days before.

'I was wondering about that perfume, Gold.'

'What about it?'

'I was hoping that we might be able to help each other.'

'We might,' said Freeman, cautiously. 'Would you like to go first?'

She told him about the tests at the lab and about DCS DuPaul's action.

'And you think DuPaul might be covering something up?' asked the lawyer.

'I don't know. I just think it's strange that a man who's such a stickler for going by the book should suddenly change his tune over this.'

'But how would he have found out about what you were doing in the first place?'

'Well, Sadler said he phoned DuPaul.'

'That suggests that he must have found something,' said Freeman. 'Why else would he phone and why ask for DuPaul?'

'The question is what can I do about it? DuPaul is my DCS, and even though I can report a superior officer for a suspected breach of the law, I have very little to go on. I can't prove that any of this happened if the records have really been destroyed.'

'It's not so easy to destroy records. There must be a logging record for when you brought the sample in. If that's in a list form, he can't destroy that without destroying other things. And if it was on the computer it won't be so easy to erase as they might think. Even if they erase it from the hard drive of the server or mainframe, it's probably on a back-up tape that they would almost certainly keep for a couple of months at least.'

'But even if I can prove that he broke the procedural rules, that doesn't mean Sadler found anything.'

'He must have found something. Like you said, he *did* phone Chief Superintendent DuPaul. He must have had a reason.'

Karen nodded. 'I realize that now. I didn't think about it at the time. So what do you think he found? Pheromones?'

'I doubt that very much,' said Freeman.

'Why?'

'Well, first of all because the perfume doesn't seem

154

to be functioning in the way you'd expect if that were the case.'

'How do you mean?'

'For a start you told me that women seem attracted to the perfume in itself, even if they're already very attractive to men. Secondly women who were wearing it have reported lesbian advances by their female friends even though they'd showed no previous signs of homosexuality. If it were female pheromones causing it you wouldn't expect that. If it were male pheromones, you wouldn't expect it attract *men* – but it does apparently.'

'So what do you think is behind it?' asked Karen.

'At first I thought that maybe there was some other drug in the perfume – like cocaine.'

'Then why did you drop the theory?'

'Well, I'm pretty sure,' Freeman replied, 'that with all this publicity about it, some Home Office lab would probably have found it already.'

'Sadler must have found something.'

The plates were cleared away and a waiter brought the *carré d'agneau paloise* for Freeman and the *timbale pampolaise* for Karen. They waited in silence until he left.

'We could try and put the squeeze on him,' said Freeman.

'Isn't that a bit dangerous?'

'Of course it is. We might get a visit from the same people who visited him. But then again that's the idea: get them to show their hand.'

'OK, let's do it,' said Karen. 'We can pay him a visit tomorrow.'

'OK.'

'How did you come to be working on this case?'

'I told you. I was hired by the Digby family.'

'But why you? You're a lawyer, not a private detective.'

'I worked for Digby.'

'So did lots of people.'

'I also have some invaluable, not to say unique, contacts.'

'I presume you wouldn't like to elaborate on that.'

'You presume right.'

'How did you come to work for Digby? Originally, I mean.'

'I blackmailed him.'

'Blackmailed him?' she repeated, surprised.

'Well, not only him. Him and a whole load of business-men.'

'And they didn't have you arrested?'

'It wasn't that sort of blackmail. Basically it was just a way of earning a living after I'd been stripped of my physics degree —'

'Stripped of your physics degree?'

'It's a long story.'

'Which?' she asked, smiling. 'How you came to work for Fabian Digby or how you came to be stripped of your physics degree?'

'Both. Which do you want to hear?'

'Both.'

He spread his hands helplessly and smiled.

'Which do you want to hear first?'

'Well,' she said, licking her lips and flicking her hair back with a tantalizing gesture, 'the business about your physics degree is probably the more interesting. But how you came to work for Digby is probably more relevant.'

'I'm not sure that it is, but I'll tell you about it anyway. Basically I was young, embittered and frustrated . . . in a kind of professional limbo. I had a good brain but no academic degree and little hope of getting one. Officially I was branded a cheat and a liar, so no university or college would touch me with a ten-foot bargepole. But I hadn't spent three years studying like a dog just to work in some menial job. So I decided to hit back at the establishment.'

'The establishment?' she echoed, eyebrows raised tanta-lizingly.

'That vague disembodied mass that wields power over us lesser mortals. I was never a long-haired radical or revolutionary, but that was how I saw the situation.'

'And how did you hit back, if not with Molotov cocktails and sit-ins?' she asked mockingly.

'I see you remember the sixties,' he said with a grin.

'Go on,' she prompted.

'Well, I set up as a patent challenger.'

'What's *that*?'

'A new profession I invented.'

'And what did it involve?'

'Well, basically, patent applications are published before the patents are issued, to give others the right to file objections if they feel that the patents infringe on their patents or are obvious extensions of prior art. What I did was, I went to the patent library in the Southampton Buildings off Chancery Lane and looked up hundreds of patent applications for patents not yet granted. I made a note of any that I thought were weak, especially in the fields of genetics and computers where the emphasis was often in unpatentable software, but where there's a lot of money to be made if they can secure such protection. Then I checked up the financial interests and status of the applicants. If they were wealthy enough I sent them a letter telling them that I intended to challenge their patents, but hinting that I'd be ready to drop the challenge if they hired me as a consultant.'

'That sounds pretty dirty.'

'I was a street fighter, especially after getting screwed by the system. Besides, if they couldn't stand the heat they should get out of the kitchen. Many of the patents were genuinely questionable and I wasn't happy with the way patent law was going.'

'But you didn't challenge them on ethical grounds. You did it to make money.'

'I did it to establish my place in the sun. Yes, I wasn't crusading for justice. But it was a fair fight and when I won I did so through the system – the very system that had kicked me so hard.'

'Did they all give in to you?'

'Not all. Some did, some didn't.'

157

'And what happened to the ones who didn't?'

'I filed challenges to their applications.'

'And did you succeed?'

A self-satisfied gleam appeared in Freeman's eyes.

'In some cases. In others the patents were granted. But I succeeded in enough cases to maintain my street cred.'

'You must have made a lot of enemies.'

'That's true. Fabian Digby was one of them.'

'But I thought you said you worked for him.'

'I did. He was one of those who gave in. But he still thought of me as the enemy. He paid me a retainer but he never actually gave me any real work, apart from looking over a couple of his patents and giving a few second opinions when he wasn't happy with what his patent agents told him.'

'How did you get stripped of your physics degree?'

'It was right after I got it. In my finals I sat thirteen papers and got first-class honours in all of them. But in my first year I'd been a bit of a lazy dog, a bit like Einstein in fact, and so they didn't believe that I could have done so well.'

'That's hardly a reason to strip you of your degree.'

'No, but there was more to it than that. You see, some of my answers reflected the model solutions outlined by the examiner right down to the last detail. Even the mistakes in the examiner's solutions were echoed in mine.'

'The examiner made mistakes?'

'Oh yes. Mistakes which they didn't catch until after the exams were marked. And that proved to be the key to it all, although I didn't know it at the time.'

'How do you mean?'

'Well, there was an inquiry chaired by the head of the physics department. The committee heard that the examiner used an unconventional method of evaluation and that this method was reproduced identically in my papers. So the chairman of the inquiry, who effectively had the power to dictate the verdict to the rest of the committee, concluded that in recreating the examiner's model solutions, mistakes and all, I must have used knowledge of the examiner's solutions that could not have been honestly obtained.'

'I have to admit,' said Karen cautiously, 'that in the absence of any additional information, that sounds like a perfectly logical solution.'

'Does it?' asked Freeman. 'Can you think of any way in which I could have *memorized* that much information unless I had a phenomenal memory, aside from the question of when and how I gained access to the solutions in the first place.'

'But still,' said Karen, 'it does seem rather hard to explain by coincidence alone.'

'Oh, indeed it does,' said Freeman. 'And that's what counted against me in the ten years that it took to obtain formal vindication. The problem was that I didn't see any other explanation myself and I knew I was innocent, so I assumed that it must simply be coincidence.'

'And?' said Karen, realizing with absolute certainty that there was an 'and'.

'And then I had a suggestion from someone I met in cyberspace.'

He was talking about the Logic Forum. But he saw no need to go into details.

'And what was that?'

'Basically that the boot was on the other foot.'

'How do you mean?'

'That it wasn't I who had copied from the examiner but the examiner who had copied from me.'

'I don't understand,' replied Karen, hesitantly.

'The examiner wasn't perfect. He also made mistakes. Even the university acknowledged that. But in the first exam, mine was one of the first papers to be marked. The examiner noticed several of my answers conflicting with his model solutions. But he also saw that my answers appeared to be correct. So he reran the calculations and discovered that I was right. The more he rechecked his own results the more he saw that I was right and he was wrong. So he decided to use *my* papers as his model solutions

159

for marking the others and discarded his original model solutions.'

'That's . . . incredible,' Karen stammered.

'Exactly,' replied Freeman, almost reliving the thrill and exhilaration of solving the mystery that had plagued him for a decade. 'That's why no one thought of it. And of course, the thing was, because I'd *also* made mistakes, his *new* model solutions reflected *my* mistakes. That's why my papers matched the alleged mistakes in his model solutions. Because *his* model solutions were *mine*.'

'But how did you prove it?' asked Karen.

'Actually, once I figured it out, it was quite easy. You see, I wasn't the first person to be marked in the first exam. I was the sixth. So the five people before me were initially marked according to the original model solutions. Only after those five had been marked did he realize that he'd made mistakes and decide to change his marking system to conform to the new solutions. So he had to re-mark the original five papers for the sake of consistency. That means those papers had corrections to the markings on them, and *only* those five. Of course, even then the university authorities were stubborn. They refused to re-examine the papers, insisting that there was no need to reopen the original inquiry. It took me another ten months to get them to look at the papers and check out something that was actually very straightforward. But once they did it, the changes to the markings were obvious. The candidate numbers indicated the order in which the papers were marked. Of course, once he was confronted by the evidence the examiner broke down and came clean. I mean, he tried to weasel out of it at first but he was dead in the water and he knew it, so he squirmed a bit, apologized for hurting me and betraying the university's trust and then rolled over with his paws in the air.'

'You sound like you're still bitter,' said Karen gently.

'Why shouldn't I be? He ruined my life.'

'Surely you can go back to physics now?'

'It's not so easy. I wanted to be a *theoretical* physicist – to push back the boundaries of knowledge like Einstein and

Max Planck. But theoretical physicists usually do their most important work in their twenties. I didn't clear my name until I was in my thirties, and by then I'd been out of mainstream physics for ten years. By that stage my mind was no longer as flexible.'

'It seems pretty sharp to *me*. How else could you be a lawyer now?'

'It's not the same. Modern theoretical physics calls for a special mindset that most people never have, and the few who get it find it hard to sustain past the age of thirty. Einstein did some exceptional work at the age of thirty-six, but that was a continuation of work that he'd been doing for the last ten years. If he'd taken a decade out of physics after his wonder year of 1905, he'd never have come up with General Relativity. You have to understand that cosmology and quantum physics involve certain counterintuitive concepts that it's very hard to wrap one's mind around. I could have done it back then, in my twenties, but I can't do it now. All I can do now is watch from the sidelines while other people come up with the unified field theories and collect the Nobel prizes.'

'But why not go into another branch of physics?'

'Like what?'

'Like the practical side. Like technology. There must be a fortune to be made in that. You could be a businessman yourself, in one of these high-tech fields.'

'I could. But I've developed other interests, like the law.'

'I meant to ask you about that. How did you get from physics to law?'

'Well, it's all the same really. It's all about reason and logic. In my limbo years, while I was trying to fight back, I studied law, informally at first. Then I realized that I had a talent for it, so while I was running my patent-challenging consultancy, I got into the external law programme of the University of London. That meant I studied independently, but sat the exams through the university.'

'Didn't they make any problems over your past?'

'They didn't know about it and I didn't tell them. I was only blacklisted in the science departments of the country's universities, and they had no reason in any *law* department to cross-check against the records from the sciences.'

'So you became a lawyer?'

'That's right.'

'And would I be right in thinking that you use your skills and talents to help the underdog?'

'Most of the time.'

'You mean you don't think of Fabian Digby as the underdog.'

'No.'

'But you're helping him, or at least trying to.'

'When I help the rich and successful they pay through the nose. Underdogs travel free.'

'An eminently worthy code of practice, Mr Freeman,' she said with a radiant smile.

They raised their glasses and drank the house wine.

An hour later, they were walking along together on the Embankment, watching the lights on the other side.

'. . . so then I decided to throw everything into my career.'

'And put romance on the back burner,' he added, as a statement not as a question.

She seemed to ponder for a few seconds.

'I wasn't trying to cut it out of my life. It was just a case of getting my priorities right and not falling into the same trap again. I knew that if I was financially secure and independent then any choice I made from then on would be for the right reasons.'

'Isn't there a danger that you might fall into the trap of loneliness?'

'Is that what happened to you?' she asked.

'I made a bigger mistake. I made the wrong choices to avoid the loneliness trap.'

'I think women can handle loneliness better than men.'

'Do you really?' he asked.

'Why do you think men usually make the first move in the courting game?' she asked with a smile.

'I guess you're right,' he replied.

16

'But if he remains silent, who can condemn him?'

Job 34:29

'So let's consider what we've got. We have a man, Fabian Digby, shot in the back of the head, his body weighted down and dropped into the Grand Union Canal.'

There were eight of them in the incident room from where the murder inquiry was being co-ordinated. Karen was actively leading the session, but Chief Superintendent DuPaul had overall command of the investigation.

'We used our friends at Imperial College to calculate where the body was thrown in, using the chemistry of rust and current flow information. We found a probable site quite near to the Digby estate and we sent down divers in search of the murder weapon. Now, as you all know, we didn't find the weapon but what we did find was the other part of the leg-chain attached to the weight that was used to hold the body down and a gold Rolex watch worth about twelve and a half thousand pounds. Digby was wearing an electronic digital watch, so unless he had the Rolex in his pocket and it came out somehow it clearly didn't belong to the victim.'

'In that case can we hold a raffle to see who gets to keep

164

it?' joked Detective Sergeant Croft, who was assigned to the team.

'If we hadn't found the owner it would have gone to the police benevolent fund,' said Karen. 'However, in the event we tracked him down.'

'Why d'you have to do that if it didn't belong to the victim?' asked Croft, persisting.

'Because it *might* have belonged to the murderer,' said Karen. 'It could have come off the murderer's wrist when he – or she – threw the body into the water.'

'Maybe the victim pulled it off the killer in a last-ditch effort to help identify the killer,' said Croft.

The others in the team laughed.

'Or maybe Fabian Digby just couldn't pass up the chance to grab someone else's property, even in death,' said another.

Again the mirth reverberated through the room.

'It could have come off the murderer while the murderer was struggling with the body,' said Karen, irritated by the levity. 'However, in the event, we have established that it came from someone else who is also dead. We checked the guarantee records with the supplier and found that it came from a young man who was recently killed in a mugging.'

'How d'you find that out?' asked a detective constable at the back of the room.

It was the computer operator who answered. 'We entered it on the HOLMES system and cross-checked it.'

'Was this other killing before or after Digby was killed?' asked DC Sandra Blaine, who had just joined the area command from the Hounslow area of west London. Her job at this session was to take notes and provide them to the trained HOLMES operator, who would isolate the salient points and enter them into the computer database. The HOLMES operator was also there at the session, but she was not skilled in shorthand.

'Very good point, Sandra. He was killed after the established time of Digby's death so in theory he could be a suspect. But in practice we don't believe so.'

'But how would a gold watch taken in a mugging end up in the Grand Union Canal?' asked PC Blaine.

'Again, a very good question,' said Karen. 'The answer is we don't honestly know.'

'Is it possible,' asked Blaine, 'that the mugging wasn't really a mugging but was just made to look that way?'

'Hey, Chief Inspector,' said the young detective constable at the back of the room, 'I think she wants to be a detective!'

'Oh, shut up!' said Sandra.

'Yes, shut up!' said Chief Superintendent DuPaul. He knew that this kind of horseplay was par for the course at these evidence review sessions, but it was growing tiresome.

'Sorry, sir,' said the DC, knowing not to push his luck.

'Has the watch been passed on to the team dealing with the other murder?' asked DC Blaine.

'Not yet,' said Karen. 'But we've notified them through the HOLMES network. The owner of the watch was one Anthony Neuman and it —'

'Did you say Tony Neuman?' asked DuPaul incredulously.

'Yes, sir,' said Rousson.

'That's Superintendent Morley's case,' DuPaul said, with a ring of satisfaction in his voice.

'Does that mean we'll be merging the inquiries, Chief?' asked Karen.

'That would be premature. Carry on.'

'DC Maize, you took plaster casts of tyre tracks at the site. What did you come up with?'

'Well, we compared them to vehicles belonging to the Digby family and some of his associates. There were no matches. We did successfully match some of the tracks to a vehicle belonging to someone who lives in the area, but those were recent tracks and it didn't seem likely that they could have dated back to the time of the murder, or rather the time of disposal of the body. The owner and his wife had alibis, and we've entered the details in the system.'

A door opened, and a young police constable entered with a faxed report which he handed to Karen. She read it with a look of surprise breaking out over her face, and then handed it to DuPaul.

'DNA?' he said, his eyes widening.

'Yes, sir,' she replied. DuPaul smiled smugly.

'It's beginning to look as if there could well be a tie-in with the Neuman case,' said Karen.

'Exactly what I was thinking,' said DuPaul. 'I think I'll have a word with Superintendent Morley.'

'So how do you think Tony's watch ended up in the canal, Phil?' asked Logan.

'I've already told you, Inspector, I don't *know*.'

Logan looked over at PC Woodward. He wondered whether perhaps her softening presence was giving comfort to the Neuman boy. She was sitting there looking stony-faced, just as she was supposed to do, but the fact that she was a woman and gentle by nature meant that the interrogation could never have the same impact as an all-male session. Logan was glad that Philip Neuman was over eighteen. That meant there was no need to have a responsible adult present. Of course, at any time he could ask for a 'brief'. But he was not an experienced criminal and clearly didn't know his rights. All of this could work to their advantage. But so far Philip Neuman was sticking to his story.

'OK, now you say you split up with your brother at what time?'

'I already told you.'

'Tell me again.'

They were trying to wear him down. It was an old police tactic. But there was nothing he could do about it. If he clammed up, it would be a sign of guilt. It's the fear of being thought guilty that keeps the amateur criminal talking. The professional criminal couldn't care less.

'About nine o'clock.'

'*About* nine o'clock,' Logan repeated.

'Well, maybe nine-fifteen.'

'Nine-fifteen,' repeated Logan with emphasis, nodding his head to PC Woodward to write it down, even though the entire session was being tape-recorded.

'Well, that's very interesting, Phil, because we have witnesses who said they saw you and your brother together at ten o'clock.'

'That's impossible!' shrieked Phil, the fear in his voice genuine.

'We've got you every way, sonny. From start to finish.'

'Look . . . it was night . . . it was dark. Maybe it was someone else who looked like me.'

Logan half turned to PC Woodward with a smile.

'How many times have we heard that, Lara?'

'More than I've had hot dinners,' replied PC Woodward, still stony-faced.

'Looks like you'll have to try again,' said Logan, turning back to Phil.

'It was late. I'm pretty sure it was about nine. Maybe they're wrong about the time.'

'Who's they?' Logan squeezed.

'The witnesses.' The tone of the reply was weak, as if he were beginning to crack under the strain.

'Or maybe you are.'

'I'm tired. I hardly slept last night. Couldn't I go home and rest for a couple of hours?'

'You must be joking,' said Logan.

'Well, can I sleep in a cell for a couple of hours? I'm not trying to run away. I'm just too tired to concentrate. That's why I'm getting confused about the details.'

'Ah,' said the inspector. 'So you *are* confused about the details.'

'Maybe it was a bit later than I said.'

'Or maybe it was a *lot* later.'

'I don't think it was. But I didn't actually check the time when we split up.'

'Or maybe you checked the time when you took his watch, and claimed the time when you split up was a bit earlier than it actually was to make sure you were in the clear.'

168

'I didn't take his watch,' said the boy tearfully.

'Then who did?'

'I don't know.' He was making no effort to hide the tears.

'You mean you just left him for dead and then someone else came along and stole the watch from his body?' asked the inspector.

'I didn't leave him for dead! I didn't kill him! Why won't you believe me?'

He broke down on the table, crying into his forearm, his whole body shaking from the violence of the sobbing.

'You know what I think,' said Logan. 'I think you didn't set out to kill him. I think you didn't even carry the knife to kill him. I think you just happened to have the knife, possibly for self-protection on the Tube or something like that, and somewhere along the line you lost your temper with your brother. You said you argued over whether or not to go to a nightclub because you had the money and he didn't. But that doesn't make sense. He had the money for a twelve-and-a-half-thousand-pound gold watch and yet he didn't have the money to go to a nightclub. Come off it! It was the other way round. *You* didn't have the money. So when he decided to go off and have a good time, you lost your temper and pulled out the knife and killed him.'

Logan looked at his suspect, expecting an answer, but heard nothing. He did, however see a look of apprehension on the boy's face. He decided to press on.

'And then you took his watch and put it on. But you realized that it might incriminate you, so you decided to get rid of it. You went miles away from the scene of the crime and then you tore if off your wrist and threw it into the Grand Union Canal.'

'I didn't,' the boy sobbed without looking up. 'I swear I didn't.'

'But you made one small mistake with the watch when you decided to get rid of it. And we can link the watch not only to your brother but also to you.'

The boy raised his head slowly, a look of panic breaking out over his face.

'You were wearing that watch, weren't you? You were jealous of your brother because he was more careful with his money that you were with yours. I don't know how he got the money to buy a gold Rolex, but however it was, you were jealous. You wanted to be like him but couldn't be because you didn't have the skill and the self-discipline. So you decided if you couldn't be like him you would take what was his. You had an argument with him and in the heat of the argument you stabbed him and took his wallet and watch. You wore it on your wrist and it made you feel good. It made you feel rich and powerful. It made you feel as if you had all the things you wanted but couldn't have. And then it dawned on you that it could also be your ruin if you had to explain it. So you raced off to Maida Vale and then threw it into the canal, thinking that it would be the end of the matter.

'But it wasn't, was it? Because police frogmen investigating the Digby murder found it when they were looking for the weapon that was used to kill him.'

The panic on the boy's face was degenerating into a mask of terror.

'That can only mean one thing, Philip. You stole it from his body, wore it to satisfy your unrequited desire for wealth and success and then threw it away when a bit of common sense dawned on you. Only now the game is up.'

Again the boy's head dropped into his forearms, but this time from exhaustion.

PC Woodward took advantage of the lowered head to signal to the inspector that she wanted to talk to him outside. He shook his head angrily, not wanting to lose the momentum. He sensed from long years of experience that he was on the verge of breaking the suspect and he smelt a confession in the offing. He knew that in intra-family murders this was how they were normally resolved. Breaking the flow now, when he had his suspect against the ropes, would throw away everything that he had put into the interrogation so far and waste everything that he had extracted. This wasn't an interview designed to gather evidence; it was an interview designed to extract a confirmation of a near-belief that Inspector Logan already held.

But Lara Woodward, displaying an assertiveness that was quite surprising for one of such low rank in relation to a superior, signalled again and left no doubt that it was vital that they talk.

'Interview suspended at two-forty-one p.m.,' said Logan. PC Woodward switched off the cassette recorder and removed the cassette. They stood up and Logan held the door for her.

'OK, Lara, it had better be good.'

'Sir, I think there's something we're overlooking.'

'And what's that?'

'Where *did* he get the money to buy the gold Rolex?'

'I hardly think that's important right now.'

'It could be very important. They're not a rich family.'

'They own a house in Golders Green,' said Logan sceptically. 'They're not exactly knocking on the door of the workhouse.'

'When Miriam Neuman's husband died, the family lost its breadwinner. They didn't have adequate life assurance provision and they went through a bad patch. Yes, they kept the house, but they had to tighten their belts to do it. And they certainly couldn't afford luxuries like gold Rolex watches.'

Logan's tone become angry.

'And you mean to say you called me out and broke the flow when I was inches from getting a confession for this?'

'Sir, how would a young man without a job, who's just finished school and who doesn't come from an affluent family, suddenly come up with enough money to buy a gold watch worth twelve and a half thousand pounds?'

'I see the mystery that intrigues you in the question, but I don't see that it's relevant.'

'Why don't you answer the question first and then judge the relevance by the answer?'

'Well, I suppose the obvious answer is smuggling or selling drugs.'

'Or *making* them.'

'*Making* them?' Logan repeated.

'Tony Neuman was a chemistry whiz kid. Most drugs call for some chemistry skill, apart from spliff.'

Spliff, he recalled, was one of the street names for marijuana.

'And synthetic drugs like Ecstasy require quite a *lot* of chemical knowledge,' he added.

'Exactly. And any involvement with drugs at the commercial level, selling, smuggling or manufacturing, would bring him into contact with some very unpleasant people.'

The inspector thought about this for a moment.

'And you think the killing of Tony Neuman was in some way drug-related?'

'Exactly.'

'Well, even if that were so, it wouldn't necessarily let his brother off the hook.'

'No, sir, but it might require us to look at the case in a different light. Remember, your entire premise so far has been that he killed his brother in a fit of jealousy. Now if he was part of this drug operation then the question is what was his role and why did he kill him? Philip Neuman is an expert on computers. He even calls himself a hacker. How would that tie him in with a drugs ring? If Tony was making drugs that would explain why he had money for a gold watch while there's nothing in Phil's lifestyle or bank account to suggest that he's rolling in money.'

'And if Tony was involved with making drugs, presumably someone else was selling them,' Logan added.

'And more to the point, if he was making them in quantity, he would have been dealing not with a pusher but with someone higher up the ladder.'

'OK, Lara, you may be on to something here. But this could all be a red herring. Even if he was involved in drugs, his killing could still have had nothing to do with it. It could still have been Phil in a fit of jealous rage because his brother had found a way out of the poverty trap.'

'Maybe, sir. But don't you think we should hold off until we've explored this alternative line of enquiry and gathered more information about where Tony Neuman was getting his money from?'

'I've got a better idea, Lara,' said Logan, letting an element of sarcasm spill over into his tone. 'Why don't I go back in there with another officer and squeeze Philip to see if he bleeds, while you write up your report and we'll get the HOLMES operator to pass on the information to the drug squad.' She looked at him, hurt, and bit her lip as she walked away.

'Interview with Philip Neuman resumed at three-fourteen p.m.,' said Logan. 'Present in the interview room along with Philip Neuman are Inspector Logan and Superintendent Morley.

'Do you wish to be represented by a solicitor?' Morley chimed in, sweeping a strand of red hair away from his face. The boy was put at ease by Morley's mellow northern accent. It was not an accent designed to intimidate, but rather to lull the suspect into a false sense of security and winkle out information. 'For the benefit of the tape, the suspect is shaking his head. Inspector Logan?'

The prime suspect in the murder of Tony Neuman was sitting upright now, no longer sobbing but tired and red-eyed. It wasn't just the sobbing. He wanted to sleep, desperately and hopelessly.

'I'd like to ask you, Philip, why you think the watch ended up in the canal?'

'I've already told you. I don't know.'

'We accept that, Philip,' said Morley, stepping in again, and making it clear that he intended to take an active role in this interrogation. 'But think of it from *our* point of view. Obviously we'd like to find out. We found it at the scene of the disposal of a body in another murder. We want to know if there's any connection.'

'But I don't *know*,' he replied pleadingly.

'OK, that's fair enough,' said Morley. 'But I'm sure you can understand why we want to know, Philip.'

'Yes,' he said, exhausted.

'So perhaps you could help us. *Not* with an answer. Perhaps just with a theory. You're an intelligent young man. Perhaps you could come up with a theory about how the watch ended up there, Philip?'

'Maybe the same person did both murders,' he suggested.

'And perhaps the murderer was wearing it when he threw the body of the other victim into the canal?' Morley offered.

'And maybe the victim of this other murder pulled the watch off the killer before being thrown in,' said the boy.

'No, that wouldn't work, Philip,' said Morley, shaking his head.

'Why not?' he asked nervously.

'Because the other victim was dead before he went in,' Morley explained.

'How was he killed?'

'He?' said Logan.

'The Superintendent said "he went in".'

Morley shook his head at Logan, angry with him for playing games. He wasn't trying to use the 'how did you know' approach – certainly not when they had no grounds.

'He was shot,' said Morley to Phil.

'So it wasn't even the same method,' said the boy gleefully.

'True,' said Morley. 'But that doesn't necessarily mean it wasn't the same killer.'

'I'm not saying it wasn't. I'm just saying it *sounds* like the two crimes were different.'

'You're probably right,' said Morley. 'But we have to check out every possibility. I understand that you and your brother had a certain amount of rivalry.'

'We've been through all that before,' said the boy, his impatience showing, for once, as aggression.

174

'All right, all right,' said Morley, holding up his hand in a conciliatory gesture. 'I don't want to go over all the old ground any more than you do. Besides, if you did want to get revenge on your brother you wouldn't do it with violence, would you, Philip?'

'What do you mean?'

'Well, I mean you're into witchcraft, aren't you?'

'What about it?' The defensiveness was creeping back into his tone.

'It's obvious, isn't it. If you *did* want to get revenge on your brother – now I'm not saying you did, mind, I'm just saying *if* – then you wouldn't have done it with violence. You'd have done it with magic . . . wouldn't you?'

'I suppose so,' he conceded.

'You *suppose* so?'

'Well, I don't know. I mean I never wanted revenge on him.'

'OK, now . . . don't take this the wrong way, Phil, but I noticed that you said "I never wanted revenge on him." You didn't say, "I had nothing to *get revenge about*." I was wondering why that was.'

'I *didn't* have anything to get revenge about.'

'Then why didn't you say so when I first asked?'

'I didn't think about it.'

'Now you see, that's what I'm getting at, Phil,' Morley said in his friendly, almost fatherly manner. 'That's why my friend Inspector Logan here is having such a hard time believing you, even though he *wants* to believe you. Because you say things like "I didn't think about it". Surely an honest man doesn't *need* to think carefully to tell the truth. If a man is being truthful, the truth comes out naturally. It's only when a man is lying – or maybe just holding back *part* of the truth – that he has to think carefully about what he's saying.'

'I just didn't think it worth quibbling about whether I had any reason to want revenge or not. It seemed too petty to argue about.'

'Well, I don't know about petty. It could be what this case hinges on.'

175

'All I can say is you asked me a question and I gave you the answer. Anyway, you said yourself if I *did* want revenge, I'd use magic. Tony wasn't killed by magic.'

'No, indeed he wasn't. He was killed by a knife thrust to his stomach, just below the liver.'

The boy appeared to be thinking for a few seconds.

'When I got home, the police took away my clothes and sent them to forensics. "Just routine," they told me. I didn't think anything about it at the time. Now I'm sure that one of the things they were looking for was blood. I know you didn't find any because I know I didn't kill him.'

'Or because you changed your clothes, Phil,' said Logan.

'Without coming home?' he replied, seizing the initiative.

'You could have had a change of clothes ready prepared.'

'I thought you said it wasn't premeditated.'

'I said I didn't think it was,' said Logan. 'Now I'm not so sure.'

'Did I also have a shower?'

'Let's not forget that there wouldn't necessarily have been much blood, would there?' said Morley.

'I don't know.'

'Well, the knife penetrated *below* the liver, in a straight single thrust. If it had penetrated the liver, the murderer would have been splattered in blood. I think it's fair to say you got lucky.'

'As far as I know, they didn't find any blood on my clothes. Because there wasn't any to find. They took my clothes away to analyse, then presumably in the belief that if I was the murderer they'd find some blood. If you'd found any blood, which you couldn't have because I really am innocent, then you'd have confronted me with it. Or you'd have already charged me.'

'It sounds like you're gloating, Phil,' said Morley.

'I'm just saying that if the evidence says I'm innocent, why don't you accept it?'

'There are a couple of problems,' said the superintendent.

He waited for Phil to ask. But Phil, who was now wising up to their game, said nothing. 'In cases like this, we always take swabs from under the victim's fingernails, just in case the victim scratched his assailant or tore at his or her clothes while trying to defend himself. In this case we found nothing under his fingernails. That suggests that when the attack came, it came out of the blue, completely unexpectedly . . . possibly from someone he knew . . . like, maybe someone he trusted.'

The boy swallowed a lump in his throat, but met the superintendent's eyes without blinking.

'I don't mean to imply that you overlooked anything, Superintendent. But maybe he was attacked from behind.'

'That would certainly explain the knife's point of entry. Of course, it would also explain the lack of blood on your clothes if you were the attacker. Still, it's interesting that you thought of that.'

'There would have been blood on the cuff or sleeve, I mean on the side of the hand that held the knife.'

The policemen noticed that Phil was being quite vigorous in arguing the case. More like a lawyer than a detective. Was this self-defence or sport?

'There *might* have been,' said Morley. 'But again, it's interesting that you thought of that.'

'You seem determined to read something into whatever I say. If I make a point in my favour you say it's interesting that I thought of it. If I don't say something you ask why I didn't say it. It's like a game with you. Whatever I say, you take it as evidence that I'm guilty.'

'Maybe that's because we know all too well about fraternal rivalry. Even the Bible is full of it: Cain and Abel, Esau and Jacob.'

Morley saw a flicker of pain in Phil's eyes, he was sure of it. But before he could probe it any further, his prime suspect spoke.

'I'm tired. I didn't get much sleep last night. I need a few hours' sleep. I'll answer all your questions. I just want to sleep for a couple of hours.'

'You can rest soon, Philip,' said Morley. 'We just have a couple more questions.'

'I don't have to answer them,' came the reply, showing the first sign of defiance since he had been brought here.

'You don't have to answer anything,' said Morley. 'But you've been pretty co-operative so far. Why should you stop now?'

'Because I'm tired, and you're not letting me rest.'

'Well, I'm not going to try and force you to answer anything,' said Morley. 'But I'd like to tell you something. It's really something rather sad . . . about a man who was imprisoned for something that today wouldn't even be a crime. He was a writer. His name was Oscar Wilde. He was imprisoned for homosexuality.'

'What's that got to do with me?'

'Oh, sorry,' said Morley. 'I wasn't trying to imply that you were gay. No, it's just that he was a man who didn't really belong in prison. I mean, he wasn't a hardened criminal, you understand. Not a member of the criminal community by nature. He just did something that transgressed society's standards at the time, the old mid-Victorian values as we call them. Anyway, the point is, while he was in prison he met the kind of people who most of us would prefer not to know, like murderers. And under the influence of this new experience he wrote a poem about the wretchedness of their plight. It was called *The Ballad of Reading Gaol*, and it contained a very famous line. "Each man kills the thing he loves." And you know what, Phil. I think that's what you did. I think you killed the thing you loved.'

He saw tears beginning to form in Phil's eyes.

'And now you're punishing yourself for it more than the system would ever punish you given the extenuating circumstances. You're punishing yourself by bottling it up inside you and trying to live with it.'

He could see the tears streaming down Phil's face as the boy gripped the table for support.

'But the great irony is that the system would be far more merciful towards you than you are towards yourself.

Because the system today isn't like it was in the days of Oscar Wilde. The system isn't so harsh to the tormented young man who kills in a fit of anger that grips him momentarily. And I think that's the way it happened, Philip. I think you just lashed out without thinking and then regretted it a moment later. That's why it was just a single thrust of the knife. Because you didn't mean to kill him. You just wanted to show him you were angry. And by the time you realized what you'd done there was no turning back. So you took the wallet and watch to make it look like a mugging. And then you threw them in the canal at the first opportunity after that, desperate to get rid of the evidence, but also to rid yourself of the very things that reminded you most of what you'd done.

'That's the way it goes, Phil. "Each man kills the thing he loves." I can't bring your brother back from the grave any more than you can. But at least you can lift the burden of guilt by confession. I don't know if your pagan religion sees things the same way. But I'm not sure if you really are a pagan. I think even that's just a front to protect yourself from the pain of knowing who you are and what you are. And if you really want to relieve that pain the only way to do it is to share the truth with others and let others be your judge. Whatever penalty the courts impose on you, Phil, it can never be as harsh as the one you're imposing on yourself by denying it. I think it's time for you to lift that burden, before it buries you under its weight.'

'All right,' said the boy, sobbing profusely. 'I killed my brother. I killed him'

'Why did you confess? You didn't kill him. You know you didn't.'

Miriam Neuman sat before her son in the interview room. They had now charged him and asked him again if he wanted a lawyer. He said that he did but didn't know one. They had offered him the duty solicitor. But he asked instead if they could call his mother. She had rushed down there, phoning Walter Rubin and asking him to meet her there. He had got there first. But the boy made it clear that he didn't want to see him. Just his mother. Superintendent Morley thought this was a classic example of the Jewish Oedipus complex. But he didn't say this to anyone.

When Miriam arrived, they gave them an interview room where they could meet.

'I as good as killed him. If we hadn't split up he would still be alive today.'

'You don't know that. He might have killed both of you.'

'Who?'

'The killer,' said Miriam.

'If we'd been together, it would have been harder for anyone to approach in the first place.'

'It might have been more than one person,' said Miriam. 'You know that.'

'I don't know that,' said her son. 'All I know is, I wasn't with him and he was killed.'

'You've got to stop blaming yourself,' she whispered soothingly.

'I'm not blaming myself. It's just the thought of him dying alone like, that after we argued.'

'I thought you made up.'

'We did, but that was because of him.'

'It might have been a gang,' said Miriam.

17

*'. . . a bribe blinds the eyes of the wise and twists
the words of the righteous.'*

Deuteronomy 16:19

It was almost midnight when Freeman returned home. It
had been a pleasant evening with Karen, but she had made
it clear that she didn't want to rush into anything, and he
respected that. He was surprised to see Alan Nielsen sitting
in his car outside when he returned home.

'To what do I owe this pleasure?' asked Freeman, leaning
towards the half-opened window.

'Business,' said Nielsen, indicating by the speed of the
response that he had seen Freeman in the rear-view mirror
and was not taken by surprise when he spoke. Nielsen got
out of the car slowly.

'You're a very hard man to get hold of, Mr Freeman.'

'I do have a life outside work,' said the lawyer.

Nielsen looked around, indicating that he did not wish to
stand and talk outside. Freeman led him into the building,
unlocked the door to the flat and led Nielsen in. Digby's
private secretary seemed content to wait while Freeman
checked his answerphone messages and made himself a

cup of coffee. He offered some to Nielsen, but the latter declined.

'OK, what's this all about?' asked Freeman.

Without a word, Nielsen lifted an attaché case and put it on the desk.

'What's this?'

'Take a look.'

Freeman spun the case round and opened it. Like the one that was given to him in Nielsen's office on the Digby estate, this case was packed with twenty pound notes, all stacked in neat packages.

'You're paying me *another* seventy-five K?' he asked incredulously.

'No,' said Nielsen. 'This is only fifty.'

'And to what do I owe this honour,' said Freeman, realizing that it could hardly be a reward for his results.

'Mrs Digby has asked me to give you this.'

'May I ask what prompted this extraordinary display of generosity on the part of Mrs Digby?'

'It isn't generosity, Mr Freeman. It's your termination fee.'

'My what?' asked Freeman, confused.

'In view of the fact that Fabian Digby's body has now been found,' said Nielsen, 'this is a murder inquiry, and as such is a matter for the police. This is your fee for closing the books and putting the matter behind you. And also of course for being discreet about the entire matter.'

'You mean it's my thirty pieces of silver.'

Nielsen looked genuinely hurt.

'You're not being paid to betray anyone, Mr Freeman. Quite the contrary.'

'In Hebrew the word for silver is the same as the word for money,' said the lawyer, placatingly.

Freeman could understand why he was off the case. It was one thing to hire someone to look for a missing person. It was quite another to hire someone to look for a murderer. But strictly speaking he had been hired to use his Israeli contacts to find out if the Mossad had anything to do with

Digby's disappearance. Now that his body had turned up the question remained: did they have anything to do with his death? Surely Veronica Digby would want to know the answer to this question? But here was Nielsen standing before him with a pay-off to close the case.

Why? he wondered.

One reason, he realized, was that perhaps they already knew, or at least thought they did. The payment was a bribe to ensure his discretion, his silence. But it was a heavy bit of overkill. He had no reason to be anything other than discreet. When they first called him in, they wanted his discretion to conceal Digby's disappearance because they wanted to avoid a dip in the price of the stock. But now it was too late for that. The death could not be concealed, or even the *cause* of death. And how worried could they be? And what could he know?

Of course he didn't like dropping a case that still had a loose end. But once it was a murder investigation, he didn't have any choice. If the police caught him snooping around they'd come down on him like a ton of bricks.

The look in Nielsen's eyes wasn't one of smug satisfaction. It was one of fear.

Fear, Freeman wondered, or fear by proxy. Nielsen had said that Mrs Digby had asked him to pay the money. So it had come from her – not just the money, but the idea, at least if Nielsen was telling the truth. Had this loyal servant taken upon himself the sum total of the fears of the Digby family? There *were* servants like that. And it was hard to see any reason why Nielsen should be afraid for himself, or how he could raise this money himself.

No doubt Veronica Digby was wondering if the entire house of cards was about to fall apart. She was probably as fearful as any rich widow would be for her financial security if her late husband's empire turned out to rest on a bedrock of quicksand. But paying Freeman for his silence wouldn't make the slightest difference. If there was anything unkosher in the way that Digby Holdings was run, it was sure to come out now, and there was nothing Freeman could do either to help the revelations or to suppress them.

So why, he asked himself again, am I being paid off?

In a sense it was an amateurish move, almost calculated to arouse his curiosity. He looked quizzically at Nielsen, convinced that his puzzlement was showing on his face. Perhaps a probing question would not come amiss.

'Tell me something, Mr Nielsen, why is Mrs Digby doing this? If she wanted me off the case she could simply sack me without paying a penny. I mean, she's paid me more than enough already for what little I did, and there really seems no need to round it up to half a million for interviewing a couple of her stepchildren and talking cautiously to a police detective.'

'Let's just say that Mrs Digby appreciates what you've done for her, what you *tried* to do for her, and she doesn't want you to feel that you're being taken off the case because of any personal failings on your part. Also there are interested parties who wouldn't look too kindly on any continued involvement on your part in this case.'

'You mean the police?'

'I mean interested parties.'

Freeman realized that she would hardly be paying him off in order to stop him getting into trouble with the police. Digby's children, perhaps . . .

'I guess it must be very hard for Mrs Digby right now.'

'It is indeed. It would have been their silver wedding anniversary this week. But she is getting support from family and friends and she's a born survivor. I suggest that you take the money in the spirit of gratitude in which it is intended and move on to other things.'

'Mr Nielsen, what if I were to tell you that I couldn't in all good conscience accept this money? I mean, of course I respect Mrs Digby's right to remove me from the case. But I couldn't accept money from a widow, who is obviously distressed, by taking her money for simply complying with her wishes to withdraw from the case.'

'Your sense of professional ethics is admirable,' said

Nielsen, smiling with a hint of sarcasm in his tone and a trace of a sneer on his face. 'But Mrs Digby is not so troubled by grief as to be clouded in her judgment. She really does want you to have this money.'

'All right, then,' said Freeman, closing the attaché case and putting it down on his side of the desk. 'I always was a sucker for the whims and wishes of a wealthy widow. But I can't help feeling guilty about taking an extra fifty grand for closing the books on a case where I failed my client, especially a case with quite a few loose ends.'

He monitored the expression on Nielsen's face carefully, to see if the secretary to the late Fabian Digby picked up on the threat. The expression remained neutral, except for a slight stretching of the lips that suggested the repression of a smile.

'Oh, I wouldn't worry too much about that,' said Nielsen reassuringly. 'And may I suggest that you do yourself a favour and forget about those loose ends. Oh, and if I were you, I'd signal my withdrawal from the case by going away on a long vacation.'

'To whom would I be signalling it?' asked Freeman.

'Like I said before, interested parties. I hear the weather's nice in Israel at this time of year.'

When Nielsen had left, Freeman felt a wave of desolate loneliness sweep over him. It was the now familiar feeling that he had whenever a case he was dealing with was closed or settled. It was the feeling of having nothing to do, of having free time on his hands. He could have gone to bed, but Nielsen's visit had made him restless. It was preying on his mind.

He made himself another cup of coffee and sat down in front of the television, switching off the main light and leaving only the floor lamp in the corner by the couch to illuminate the room. He had bought the evening paper earlier that day, but hadn't had time to read it. He picked it up and started flicking through it, to see if there was actually anything worth reading. Evening papers were usually characterized by an abundance of loud headlines and a dearth of detail, and he expected it to be the same today. There might be an interesting column, or an intriguing tidbit tucked away just opposite the editorial page.

He had an uneasy feeling when he reached that page. He had shot past something, a headline that barely registered in his mind. He flicked back a page, then another. His eyes scanned both halves of the spread, struggling to remember what it was. Then it hit him.

'Canal watch links brother to murder,' read the headline above the picture and the two three-inch columns. He folded the newspaper over twice to get a better grip on it. Then he read the article though word for word.

'A watch found in the Grand Union Canal has been linked to the 'Soho murder' of 18-year-old schoolboy Anthony Neuman. The watch was found by police frogmen searching for the murder weapon in the killing of Fabian Digby. But identification details from the guarantee linked the watch to Neuman from whom it was thought to have been stolen in a mugging which led to murder. The police have not disclosed how the watch is thought to have ended up in the canal, but they say that it has given them enough evidence to prosecute Anthony Neuman's brother Philip. Philip Neuman was charged earlier today, after several hours of questioning. Philip Neuman has refused offers of legal representation, and it is not clear whether he intends to plead guilty.

'The police have not indicated if they think there is any link to the Fabian Digby case and have declined to answer questions about how the watch came to be found at the site where Fabian Digby was believed to have been thrown into the canal. But sources close to the police say that the Digby inquiry is proceeding independently but with close co-ordination and exchange of information.'

Freeman put the paper down. He didn't believe in coincidence. And he also didn't believe that an eighteen-year-old boy should face the harshness and arbitrary standards of the British legal system without the aid of a professional well versed in its intricacies.

18

*'. . . defend the rights of the
poor and the needy . . .'*

Proverbs 31:9

'I read about your case in the papers, Philip, and I'd like to help you.'

'What makes you think I want help?' asked the boy bitterly.

'I'm not sure that you do,' said Freeman gently. 'But you need help.'

They were sitting in an interview room which the police had made available for them. He knew that he was dealing with someone in a precarious emotional state. Here was a young man who had recently lost his brother and who was now accused of murdering him. If he was guilty then he was surely tormented by the pain of guilt. If he was innocent then he was tormented by fear – the fear of being disbelieved piled upon the pain of having lost someone whom he probably loved.

'Maybe I don't deserve help.'

'Everyone deserves help. And no man can judge himself. Even if his judgment is harsh it might not be fair.'

The boy smiled.

187

'So you're a philosopher too.'

Freeman returned the smile. He had broken the ice and now had a chance of getting through.

'So will you let me represent you?'

'How do I know I can trust you?'

The voice was cool, but not cold, as if deep down inside he wanted the reassurance.

'I'm bound by the ethics of the legal profession. I know, I know. On the TV they make us look like a load of crooks. But contrary to what you may see on the screen, we lawyers aren't all a bunch of rogues and shysters. We're decent, honest, hard-working people paid to do a job according to certain clearly defined rules. Those rules say that we have to represent our clients within the bounds of honesty. Sometimes the people we have to represent are lowlifes, but that's the way the system works. Once in a while we get a case in which we find ourselved standing up for someone who really deserves a champion, and that's what makes it all worthwhile.'

'But what if your client is guilty?' asked the boy.

'I'll explain all that to you in a minute. But first of all I want to know as a matter of record if you want me to be your lawyer.'

'I don't know if I can afford your fees.'

'I'm ready to waive my fees,' said Freeman, sensing that it wasn't really the fees that the boy was worried about.

'What about the barrister? Don't you have to instruct a barrister to actually argue the case in court?'

'Not any more. They changed all that a few years ago. Solicitors now have the right of audience in the crown court if they pass certain exams, which I have passed. Of course, if the case merits it I might have to instruct a barrister, at my own expense if necessary. But it might not come to that. We might be able to nip it in the bud.'

'How do you mean?'

'They have to show at least some of their evidence at the committal proceedings in the magistrates' court. If we can challenge their evidence there then we might be able to show that there isn't a case to answer.'

'You're one of them, aren't you?' said the boy sneeringly. The hostility had now returned.

'One of whom?' asked Freeman, puzzled.

'Why should you be ready to pay a barrister out of your own pocket? Why should you be ready to help a stranger with your own money?'

Now Freeman was beginning to understand the nature of Philip's reluctance to accept help. It was neither financial constraints nor guilt which had erected this invisible but all too tangible barrier between them. It was cold grey fear and suspicion. He was afraid of something – or someone – and he didn't know whom to trust. It was the classic paradox of the koan or Zen riddle. He was boxed in on all sides and didn't know which way to turn. So he closed in on himself and rejected all offers of help from the outside. And, just as someone was finally breaking through and winning his trust, Freeman had blown it with an excessive display of generosity. So now the portcullis was dropped, the drawbridge was raised and a frightened boy had once again retreated behind a moat of hostility into his castle of isolation.

'The reason I'm offering to help,' said Freeman, 'is because I think I *can* help. I was hired by the Digby family to find Fabian Digby and when his body was found I was ordered off the case after having been paid most generously. I like to feel I've done something to earn that money. As you were charged partly on the basis of evidence found in the search for evidence of Digby's killing, I feel that by helping you I may be justifying my fat fee for my unsuccessful efforts to find Digby.'

Freeman noticed that a flicker of life had appeared in the boy's eyes when he mentioned the Digby case, as if it meant something to him. He knew that coincidences were possible, but he had been sceptical from the beginning about this linkage being merely coincidental and now he was sure of it.

189

'If you . . . represent me . . .' said the boy hesitantly, 'can I be sure that there isn't any conflict of interests?'

'What sort of conflict of interests?'

'Well, like the Digby family.'

'Like I said,' Freeman explained, 'I'm no longer representing them.'

'But what about privilege? I thought that it applies even after a case is over.'

'It does.'

'But doesn't that mean that you can't reveal, or make use of, anything that they said to you at the time, even if it's of benefit to me?'

'Oh, I see,' said Freeman smiling, realizing what Philip was getting at, realizing also how smart Philip Neuman was in matters that went beyond his scientific field.

'The only person I represented was Mrs Digby and I was hired in an investigative capacity. In fact she didn't say anything that I think could in any way help you, or for that matter anything that isn't on record somewhere in the public domain. But if a conflict of interest does arise then I'll have to resign from the case and that will alert your new lawyer to the fact that there's something to look for. But all this can be avoided if you're open and candid with me right from the start.'

'OK,' said the boy, swallowing nervously and nodding.

'However, before we go any further,' said Freeman, 'I should tell you that if you tell me you're guilty then I can only represent you in a plea in mitigation. I cannot argue that you're innocent if you tell me you're guilty. Basically I can only argue the case in accordance with what you tell me. Whatever you tell me, I have a professional duty to act on the assumption that it is true for the purpose of arguing the case, however preposterous I may find it. However, if you tell me that you're guilty, but that you want me to argue that you're innocent, then that goes beyond the bounds of professional ethics and I cannot do that. The reason I'm telling you this is because many people accused of a first offence think they can say to me something on the lines of: 'I'm guilty but I want you to get me off.' The reality is I might be able to get you off if you're guilty and they have a weak case, but I cannot even *try* to get you off if you *tell* me that you're guilty. Is all that clear?'

'Yes.'

'OK, now with that in mind, I'll tell you what I'm going to do. Firstly, I'm going to go out and tell the officer in charge that I'm now your brief. I'll get the bare facts of the case from him. Then I'll come back in here and we'll go over some basics. Then I'll prepare some arguments for the remand hearing and we'll see if we can get you out on bail. OK?'

He had said this encouragingly, in the tone of an assured, polished professional who knew what he was doing. This was an important part of the process when working with clients who were not used to dealing with the law, and he noticed with relief that his client was warming to him and beginning to trust him.

'OK,' said the boy, nodding again.

He had been waiting for twenty minutes and was beginning to get frustrated. This was blatant impertinence. He held the whip hand, yet *he* was being kept waiting. It had all been done in a very gentlemanly fashion, but he knew that he was dealing with someone dangerous. That was why he had insisted on a public place. Well, what could be more public than Trafalgar Square?

He sat on a bench, watching tourists feed the pigeons. For the umpteenth time he looked at his watch. Finally he saw a man walking towards him. But it was not the man he was expecting. It was someone familiar.

'Hallo, Dr Sadler,' said the man.

'What are you doing here, Chief Superintendent?'

'Oh, I often come here at lunch-time,' said Rex DuPaul. 'Why? Are you surprised to see me?'

'Not at all,' said Sadler nervously. He wondered if DuPaul was on to him. He was doing the dirty on a colleague. Trying to cash in on knowledge gained in the course of his work for personal gain. Could DuPaul have rumbled him?

No, he told himself. It's just a coincidence.

'Let's take a walk,' said DuPaul, quietly, looking at the lions by the fountain rather than Sadler.

'A walk?' repeated the scientist edgily.

'Yes. I have something I want to talk to you about.'

'What is it?' asked Sadler, the fear bringing a flush of crimson to his cheeks.

'I think you know already,' said DuPaul.

Sadler stood up nervously.

'Look . . . I wasn't breaking the law . . . I was . . . Oh God.'

He broke down, trembling. DuPaul put an almost comforting hand on his shoulder.

'It's all right,' said the DCS. 'I'm not going to turn you in. I just want to talk to you.'

'You mean it?' said asked Sadler nervously, his spirits picking up at the prospect of the lifeline that DuPaul was throwing him.

'Of course. I wouldn't lie to you. You have my word I won't turn you in or rat on you. This conversation, and everything to do with it, won't go beyond *us*. But I need to know a few things. Let's walk.'

He pointed towards one of the entrances to the Underground station. Sadler started walking, realizing that even though his chance to make a fortune had slipped through his fingers, at least he wouldn't be going to prison.

It was half an hour and a cup of coffee later before Emmett Freeman was sitting with his client again.

'OK, they weren't all that co-operative but they filled me in on the bare bones of their case against you. I say the bare bones because I'm sure they've got more. They just aren't telling me. What they've got is this. First of all, several witnesses claim to have seen you and your brother together *after* the time when you say you split up.'

The boy started to speak, but Freeman silenced him with a gently raised hand in a 'hold off' gesture.

'Secondly,' he continued, 'they have your confession, which admittedly you gave after considerable pressure and then immediately retracted. Thirdly they have evidence from you and others that there was an intense rivalry between you and your brother. Fourth, they have a psychological profile of you by a leading criminal psychologist who says that you match the profile of this type of killer based on your eccentric religious views and other statements that you made to various police detectives.'

Freeman noted that Phil looked puzzled at this, as if he didn't really understand it. But there was more to come, and he wondered what the impact of his next revelation would be.

'Fifth, and this is potentially the most damaging, you made statements indicating that you knew the state of your brother's injuries even though, according to a member of staff at the mortuary, the sheet was only pulled back far enough for you to see your brother's face.'

'Who did I make a statement like that to?' asked the boy incredulously.

'A young lady called Jilly.'

'She told the *police*?' he asked incredulously.

'She *is* the police,' Freeman replied.

Freeman saw the blood draining from Phil's face.

19

'Extortion turns a wise man into a fool . . .'

Ecclesiates 7:7

'OK, I'll let you come along for the ride,' said Karen. 'But let me make one thing clear, Mr Freeman. *I* do the talking.'

'Sure thing, boss,' said Freeman with a grin. 'I'll just stand around looking tough.'

'Good idea,' said Karen, ignoring his sarcasm. 'I thought from the moment I first saw you that you'd make a good gorilla.'

He chuckled at the thought. Playing a Chandler-style gumshoe wasn't exactly what he'd studied law for, but he'd already accepted the role when he agreed to look for Fabian Digby, so it was only natural that he should continue now. In the course of just a few days, they had effectively become verbal sparring partners, and Freeman wondered idly if this would lead anywhere further. He remembered vaguely that a lady barrister in the sixties had married one of her clients only to divorce him a few years later. Of course a lawyer and a cop was somewhat different. But still, not exactly a union made in heaven.

'Are you sure this won't lead to trouble with your superiors?' he asked.

194

'It's a risk I'm prepared to take,' said Karen.

'Why don't we just phone him?'

'It won't have the same effect. Trust me, I've had several years of practice interrogating people who had no prior warning they were going to be questioned. It's the element of surprise that counts, and the knowledge that he can't put us off or say he's busy. Once we go in there he'll be trapped. He'll know he *has* to answer us.'

Freeman nodded appreciatively and watched the world tick over at a snail's pace through the windscreen. They were crawling along through a traffic jam, and it was only the presence of Karen that stopped Freeman from showing his mild road rage, the old 'what the hell does that guy think he's doing?' routine. He had done it once, even though he was only a passenger, and she had made it clear by her disapproving look and leaning away from him that she wasn't impressed.

Philip Neuman had told him essentially the same story as he had told the police before his confession, that they had split up at nine or nine-fifteen and he didn't know anything about what had happened to his brother until he got home in the small hours of the morning. Freeman, who had learned to read clients, believed that the boy was telling the truth. But like with all clients, there is a tendency, even if they are innocent to hold something back, some embarrassing detail, some minor fact that they think is liable to be misunderstood. They don't realize that their lawyer is there to help them. Or they take it too literally when the lawyer tells them that he can only represent them in accordance with what the client tells them to be true and are restricted by anything the client tells them and constrained not to argue against it.

Whatever the secret was, Philip Neuman was holding something back. But it was hard to say what. He had told him that his brother was working on something with some unsavoury people but he didn't know what. It was pretty damn obvious to Emmett Freeman that Tony knew exactly how to make all manner of illegal drugs, and given his sudden increase in wealth it was more than likely that he was doing so. But he may also have known something about pheromones, and they had to check things out with the see-no-evil, hear-no-evil, speak-no-evil Dr Sadler.

When they arrived at the Met Lab and parked the car, Karen was the first to go in, not waiting for Freeman to play the gentleman and open the door for her. She was in quite an aggressive mood and Freeman sensed that it was not an act. She was genuinely angry with this man for taking her money and then double-crossing her.

She let two swing doors practically hit Freeman in the face as they made their way to the reception desk.

'We'd like to speak to Dr Sadler,' she said forcefully.

'I . . . I'm afraid you can't,' the girl stuttered.

'Tell him we want to see him now. Tell him it's DCI Rousson. He'll agree to see me.'

'No, you don't understand,' said the girl, sobbing slightly. 'Dr Sadler was killed this morning, in a mugging.'

They were seated in a café near the lab, Freeman, Karen and the receptionist, whose name was Alice. It was Alice's lunch break and they found her relatively pliant when they suggested that she come with them for some lunch. It was obvious that she was bottling up her feelings inside and wanted to get something off her chest. Now seemed like the right time to speak to her. They couldn't afford to lose the momentum again. She sat there next to Karen, holding her handkerchief tightly in one hand, occasionally raising it to her nose. Freeman sat opposite. The seating arrangement had been orchestrated by Karen, with the lawyer meekly following her deft, unobtrusive hand signals.

'I heard about it in the morning, from his daughter,' said Alice.

She was still sniffling, but the sobbing that had greeted them when she had first broken the news to them had passed. Now there was just that bitter lingering of memories of someone she had worked with but hadn't really been all that close to. It was more the reminder of how fragile and mortal we all are that which was putting the strain on her.

'Did she tell you any details?' asked Freeman.

'No,' said Alice. 'And I didn't want to ask.'

'Alice,' said Karen gently, resting her hand lightly on the woman's forearm, 'do you remember a few days ago I came in with a small sample of a perfume that I wanted analysed?'

'Yes,' said Alice weakly.

'And you remember that Dr Sadler was going to do some tests on it, like liquid chromatography, mass spectroscopy and mass spectrometry?'

'Yes,' said Alice again, squeezing her handkerchief.

'I was wondering if you knew the results.'

'They were bad people,' said Alice.

'Who were?' asked Freeman. Karen waved a hand at him angrily, to silence him. This was an occasion when a woman's touch was needed. As far as Karen was concerned, it would have been better if Freeman wasn't here at all. But it was too late for that.

'I don't know,' Alice sniffled.

'But you said they were bad people, Alice,' Karen gently encouraged. 'How would you know that?'

'He said so.'

'Who,' Karen prodded. 'Dr Sadler?'

'Yes.'

She started to sob again.

'Did he say who these men were?' asked Karen.

Alice shook her head.

'Did he tell you anything about them?'

Again the head shook. Freeman was looking around, monitoring for signs of anyone watching them. If Sadler was killed because of what he knew, then they could all be in danger.

'Did he tell you anything?'

There was a hesitation on Alice's part, a hint of an inner struggle, and then finally the words came out.

'He said he was finally going to have his day in the sun.'

'Finally have his day in the sun?' Karen repeated.

'Yes.'

Alice clutched her handkerchief tightly, knowing that they were going to probe further, as if clinging on for comfort, like a child clinging on to her favourite doll when she has to go into hospital.

'Was that all he said?'

She shook her head.

'What else, Alice?'

Again, Karen was gentle but firm. Freeman realized that she would have made a great courtroom lawyer. But then again, as a police detective she was probably used to prising the truth out of people.

'He said it was even better than the lottery.'

'Did he say what he found when he analysed the perfume?' asked Karen.

'He . . . he said something . . . but I . . . didn't understand it.'

'Can you remember what he said?'

This, thought Freeman, was Karen's first mistake. Up until that she had been doing great, but here she was giving Alice an 'out', an opportunity to say that she didn't know. What she should have asked was 'What did he say?' But it was too late now.

'He said . . . something about ambiguous results with the drugs tests.'

'Ambiguous results? Did he say in what way?' This was Freeman. Karen waved her hand at him angrily. She knew, and Freeman realized she was right, that with Alice's eyes half closed it needed the one-to-one voice relationship to win her trust and gently ease the truth out of her. He realized that he too had made a mistake and than their investigation might have to pay the price for their impatience.

'He said the gas chromatography was positive for cocaine but the LC/MS/MS was negative. He said it didn't make sense because the second test was more sensitive. He tried it several times to-check it, but got the same results every time.'

'Did he say what he thought was causing it?' asked Freeman.

Having jumped in he saw no reason to hold back.

'He said it might be a cocaine-like molecule that wasn't exactly the same . . . some sort of new organic compound.'

'Did he say anything about this compound?' Freeman persisted.

'He used some long word . . . I can't remember.'

'What sort of word?'

She shook her head.

'I don't remember.'

'Well, what did it sound like?'

She started crying again, leaning her head on Karen's shoulder for reassurance.

'It was something . . . like . . . macro . . . macro . . .'

'Macromolecule?' asked Freeman.

'Yes. That was it.'

By now she was slumped on the table, sobbing into her arms. Karen put a comforting hand on the back of her head and gave Freeman a disapproving look.

'OK, thank you,' said Karen. 'I'm sorry we had to put you through this.'

'You know, you can be very cruel,' said Karen as they got into the car.

Freeman looked at her blankly. 'What's your problem?' he asked casually.

'Couldn't you see that she was in pain? And scared?'

'I've got a client who's in pain and scared. You know, client . . . as in someone I'm paid to represent. As in . . . have a duty to defend to the best of my ability . . . as in . . . legal ethics.'

'All right, I get the point. That doesn't mean you have to trample all over that girl's feelings. Would you do that in court?'

'You mean would I want to risk alienating the jury? No, of course I wouldn't.'

'So you didn't have to be so harsh,' said Karen flatly.

'There was no jury to alienate.'

She lowered her voice. 'The point is, if it had been in court you would have trod more gently. In other words there *was* a gentle way to go and you didn't take it. You could have got the same results without shaking her up like that.'

'I'm sorry. I guess I got a bit impatient. Just remember my client is going through a lot worse than what she's going through. He still hasn't got over the murder of his brother and now he finds himself accused of doing it himself.'

'Perhaps if you didn't think in terms of the adversarial system, you'd see that just because someone isn't your client doesn't necessarily mean that she's a hostile witness.'

He held up his hands like an outlaw surrendering to the sheriff. He knew she was right. By letting him come with her she was effectively helping him prepare his defence of Philip Neuman even though, as far as the police were concerned, Philip was guilty.

'The point is well taken, Detective Chief Inspector.'

She smiled, an almost maternal smile, accepting his apology, then turned the key and brought the car engine to life.

'I don't see why we can't both go in there together,' said Karen, in a tone of protest, as the car pulled up in Kensington.

'Because Yaniv doesn't know you, and he's not going to talk in front of you. He wasn't all that happy about talking to me, but he said he'd try and find out. So when I go in there I have to go alone. But don't worry. I'll fill you in on whatever you need to know afterwards.'

'Thanks a lot,' she snapped, pouting girlishly as he got out of the car.

She watched with silent anger as he walked off into the distance to the gates that protected the grounds of the Israeli embassy.

'Fabian Digby was a friend of Hassan Abed Zaidan.'

Emmett Freeman and Yaniv Orgad were seated in Yaniv's office, a windowless room at the back of the embassy. Yaniv was wearing a short-sleeved blue cotton shirt and light jeans and had one foot on a large pot containing a dark green plant. He could almost have been in an office in Tel Aviv but for the lack of windows. Only air-conditioning kept the temperature bearable.

'*Hassan* Abed Zaidan,' Freeman echoed. 'Brother of Ismail Abed Zaidan? The Minister for Arms Procurement in Bahakabir?'

'That's right.'

'What sort of a friend?' asked Freeman cautiously.

'I think you've already pretty much figured that out. Hassan financed the takeover of La Contessa. Digby was the front man.'

'Any particular reason why?'

'Digby needed the money,' said Yaniv. 'The Arabs probably just wanted to keep a low profile. They're always being accused of buying up the West.'

'So Mossad wouldn't have had any reason to oppose the deal?'

'Not in the least. I can tell you that Mossad had nothing to do with the killing of Digby.'

'Do you know anything about these alleged addictive properties of Gold?'

'We've heard about it. But we haven't checked it out.'

'In that case I have something to tell you.'

Freeman explained about the meeting with Alice at the Met Lab and what she had told them.

'I'm glad you told me that,' said Yaniv slowly. 'It might be worth checking out.'

20

*'Even if I were innocent my mouth would condemn
me.'*

Job 9:20

'OK, now when we go in, you're not to look down or look
nervous. You look at the magistrates when you address them
and you look at the clerk of the court when he asks you your
name. You answer in a firm and confident voice, just like
we practised. But you don't sound arrogant. OK?'

Freeman was giving the boy his last-minute pep talk
before they went in to face the magistrates for the committal hearing. The lawyer was pleased that his client had
developed so much confidence in him, after the initial period
of mistrust. He suspected that this was because he had been
so effective in securing bail from the remand hearing in the
face of strenuous objections from the police.

But he couldn't escape the feeling that his client was
holding something back from him, as clients often do –
even the innocent ones. He just wished he could put his
finger on it. The last thing he needed was to have the
prosecution pull some surprise on him in court. And it
didn't matter if it happened in the crown court or here.
The press would be here and any surprises that occurred

in court would be reported in the newspapers and would be read by the public, including the future jurors.

Aside from that, he didn't want this case going to the crown court. He was determined to have the case thrown out now if he could. The trouble was, the prosecution did appear to have a prima facie case.

The boy stood fidgeting nervously. He felt uncomfortable wearing a suit and tie. He hadn't worn one since his bar mitzva . . . well, not counting his father's and brother's funerals.

A man in a gown strode into the anteroom and looked around briefly.

'Philip David Neuman,' he said, looking at the boy, who sat between his mother and Freeman. Freeman stood up and signalled his client to do likewise. The boy stood. They were instructed to follow the man.

'That's the bailiff,' Freeman explained as they walked behind him.

They were led into the courtroom, the accused into the dock and Freeman to the table just in front of the dock.

The court seemed smaller than the boy had expected, the furniture made mostly of lightly polished pinewood and brown plastic making no real attempt to imitate leather.

The clerk of the court rose and addressed the accused in a stentorian tone.

'Are you Philip David Neuman?'

From the dock, the accused looked briefly at Freeman, but a forbidding look and a sideways flicker of the eyes from the lawyer forced him to look instead at the clerk.

'Yes,' he said.

A bailiff signalled him to sit.

'Proceed, Mr Stewart,' said Roger Trent, the stipendiary magistrate who sat alone on the bench.

The prosecutor, a white-haired man in his late forties, rose slowly.

'Your Worship, I appear on behalf of the Crown, m'learned friend Mr Freeman appears on behalf of the accused. The accused is charged with one count of murder, the particulars of the indictment being that on or around the hour of ten o'clock on July the third of this year, the accused fatally stabbed his brother Anthony Aaron Neuman in the abdomen causing death immediately or soon thereafter, and then removed from his person a gold Rolex watch and his wallet which he subsequently discarded into the Grand Union Canal.

'It is the Crown's case that there had long been an intense jealousy on the part of Philip Neuman towards his brother and that this jealousy spilt over into murder on the night of July the third of this year. The Crown wishes to enter into evidence written depositions from the doctor at University College Hospital who pronounced the deceased dead upon arrival and signed the death certificate and the forensic pathologist who conducted the post-mortem. The Crown also wishes to enter into evidence a written statement made by the accused to the police, a tape recording of the interview culminating in that written statement, statements from Detective Inspector Logan and Detective Superintendent Morley, the two police officers who conducted said interview. We submit that such evidence is sufficient to justify committing the accused for trial in the crown court.'

Freeman rose slowly to his feet, giving the prosecutor time to sit in accordance with the etiquette of the court.

'Your Worship, I am not prepared to waive my client's right to a full 6(1) hearing. While I have no objection to the depositions from the medical personnel, I most strenuously object to the depositions from Inspector Logan and Superintendent Morley. I wish to cross-examine these two gentlemen, especially Inspector Logan. And I would similarly object to the statement and tape recording of the accused unless these pieces of evidence are supported by statements from the police officers responsible for obtaining them, again especially Inspector Logan, who was also present at the immediately previous interview with the accused.'

'For what purpose?' asked the magistrate. 'Surely the only reason these two witnesses' testimony is needed is to establish that the accused's statement was obtained in accordance with the Police and Criminal Evidence Act.'

204

Roger Trent was a burly man of average height wearing a tweed jacket. Although a stipendiary magistrate, he was the picture of the amateur Justice of the Peace, the country squire or retired colonel with a shooting stick and shotgun, trampling in wellington boots across his small country estate in search of poachers, hillwalkers and New Age travellers.

'My understanding, Your Worship,' explained Freeman, 'is that the prosecution contends that this statement by the accused is indicative of guilt inasmuch as it is a voluntary, self-incriminating statement given by a mentally competent adult who was fully apprised of his rights. It is the contention of the *defence*, however, that the conditions affecting the accused at the time were such as to render him incapable of thinking rationally or logically and that accordingly his statement is indicative not of guilt but of a combination of physical exhaustion and mental pressure.'

'Is it your contention,' the magistrate asked slowly, 'that there were specific improprieties by the police or actual breaches of PACE?'

'No, Your Worship,' Freeman replied slowly, knowing that he had to choose his words carefully. He could insist on a full 6 (1) hearing as a matter of right, but he had no wish to offend the magistrate whom he was counting on to set his client free at the end of this hearing. 'But we submit that the accused was under extreme mental pressure arising quite naturally from the circumstances of the recent loss of his brother and his own feelings of moral – as distinct from legal – guilt arising out of the circumstances of that loss. We further submit that the accused had had very little sleep in the period prior to his statement to the police and, as a result, his statement reflected a mind temporarily disturbed by sleep deprivation.'

'Accusing the police of depriving the accused of sleep is a very serious matter and amounts to an accusation of a breach of PACE,' said the magistrate. 'I hope you are prepared to support that accusation with evidence, Mr Freeman.'

The prosecutor, Leonard Stewart, was smiling smugly,

finding it hard not to gloat over the fact that Freeman had apparently painted himself into a corner.

'I am not suggesting that the *police* deprived the accused of sleep,' said Freeman.

'That's what it sounded like to me,' the magistrate cut in.

'I am suggesting that in the period *prior* to his arrest, the sleep pattern of the accused had been disrupted by his personal circumstances and therefore that although the police conducted the interviews in strict compliance with PACE, the end result was that my client made his statement after having had very little sleep in the preceding twenty-four hours. I am not suggesting any impropriety on the part of the police regarding the formal rules of interrogation under PACE.'

'In that case why do you need to call the police as witnesses?'

'In order to establish that the accused *requested* to be allowed to sleep during the interview and to show, by reference to his demeanour during the interview, that he was extremely tired.'

'I see,' said the magistrate, furrowing his brow in mock concentration. 'Then I assume it is your contention that the purpose for your insistence on a full hearing is to show simply that Crown does not have sufficient evidence to justify committal for trial?'

'That is correct, Your Worship.'

Freeman sat and the prosecutor rose, with his typical, and well-rehearsed, majestic flourish.

'Your Worship, I feel I should point out that the evidence I have outlined so far is only part of the Crown's case. We have much additional evidence that can be presented if necessary.'

'You have every right to present it,' said the magistrate.

They all knew the game that was being played out here. Freeman was trying to get the Crown to show its hand by presenting as much of its case as he could force them to present. This would enable him to assess their strengths and their weaknesses, to formulate a strategy to use against them and possibly even to increase the stress level on their witnesses, especially the lay witnesses who could put Philip and Tony together after the time at which Phil had said they had split up.

'Unfortunately, Your Worship, not all the witnesses were asked to attend today,' said Leonard Stewart. 'I only have the two interviewing officers available to testify. If I were to call these two, would that not obviate the need to call any of the other witnesses?'

'That depends on the strength of their testimony,' said the magistrate. 'And on how well they stand up to Mr Freeman's no doubt thorough and vigorous cross-examination.'

Freeman and the magistrate exchanged a smile. It was no secret that there was no love lost between Freeman and Roger Trent. But the magistrate retained a grudging respect for him, and the lawyer had learned with practice how to use this to his advantage.

'I am much obliged, Your Worship,' said the prosecutor, reluctantly. 'The Crown calls Geoffrey Logan.'

The doors to the witness anteroom were opened.

'Call Geoffrey Logan,' the bailiff intoned.

Detective Inspector Logan was led into the courtroom and sworn in. The prosecutor looked down at his notes and then up at Logan.

'You are Geoffrey Logan and you are a detective inspector in the Metropolitan Police.'

'That's correct,' said Logan.

Several more questions were asked to establish where he worked and his involvement with the murder inquiry. They were followed by a series of routine questions about the interview with Philip Neuman after his arrest and specifically the final one where he confessed. At the end of a fairly anticlimactic direct examination, Leonard Stewart said quietly, 'No further questions,' and sat down.

'Mr Freeman,' said the magistrate, frowning in order to suppress a smile. He actually quite enjoyed Freeman's cross-examinations, and this was one of the reasons he

had acceded to his motion about the statements. Freeman rose.

'Prior to the final interview with you and Superintendent
Morley, did you interview the accused in the presence of a
PC Lara Woodward?'

'Yes,' said Logan hesitantly.

'And at that interview did Mr Neuman tell you that he was
tired and ask to be allowed to sleep for a couple of hours?'

'I believe he did, yes.'

'And did you allow him to sleep at that time, Inspector?'

'No, I did not. It was only about two-thirty or a quarter
to three in the afternoon at that time.'

'Inspector, did I ask you your reason for not letting him
sleep or simply whether or not you did?'

'You asked me whether or not I did, but I assumed you
would also be interested to know the reason for my decision,
in the interests of justice.'

The magistrate looked over at Freeman, poised for an
objection to the reply and ready to issue a reprimand to the
witness. But no objection came.

'And did you ask Mr Neuman the reason *why* he wanted
to sleep at that time?'

'No, sir, I did not.'

'Not even in the interests of justice?' asked Freeman.

In the space of a second Logan became decidedly uncomfortable.

'No, sir,' the inspector replied, his facial muscles pulled
taut.

'I see,' said Freeman. 'So you showed not the slightest
interest in why the accused wanted to sleep at such a time,
but you assume that we should be interested in why you
denied him the right to sleep.'

'He *said* why he wanted to sleep,' said Logan, rather more
forcefully than he intended. Freeman knew that he had his
subject in a situation that chess players call *zugszwang*, a
position from which it is one's turn to move, but whatever
move one makes only worsens one's situation.

'And why was that, Inspector?'

'He said that he hadn't had much sleep the night before.'

'And you know that when one gets too little sleep the previous night, it usually catches up with one the following afternoon.'

'I didn't know that,' said the inspector, not troubling to hide his hostility. 'But I'll take your word for it.'

'Oh, you've never been on a dawn raid in the course of your distinguished career, Inspector?'

'I've been on more than my fair share, if anything.'

'And you've never felt tired the following afternoon?'

'We don't have time to get tired,' said Logan, almost bristling with professional pride. 'The nature of police work doesn't allow it.'

Score one for Inspector Logan, thought Freeman.

'But why, if he told you why he wanted to sleep, did you not allow him to do so?'

'Because I didn't believe him, Mr Freeman.'

'Well, why would he lie about such a thing?'

'Because he wanted to avoid answering questions about his brother's death.'

'But didn't he have the right in law to *refuse* to answer questions, Inspector?'

'Yes, of course he did.'

'And didn't you inform him of that right when you arrested him?'

'Of course.'

'Then why would he need to make an excuse to avoid answering questions. Why not simply refuse to answer them?'

The inspector blushed, stymied for an answer. There was nothing he could say really. Philip Neuman had not been forced to answer any questions. But his request to be allowed a couple of hours' sleep had been rejected, in strict accordance with the interrogation procedures laid down by PACE, and yet it still looked bad.

'Well, he might not have wanted to make it explicit that he was refusing to answer,' Logan volunteered, 'because that could have counted against him in court.'

'But that would only have bought him a few extra hours. You could have asked him the same questions later.'

'But he might not have realized that he could refuse to answer. He might have forgotten the words of the caution.'

'In which case his statements were not really voluntary.'

'Well, it's not our fault if he forgets his rights.'

'No, but the credibility of his statements as truthful depends on them being genuinely voluntary.'

'No one forced him to answer.'

'But you didn't let him sleep.'

'I've already explained that,' Logan snapped.

'Have you, Inspector Logan? Have you really? If you genuinely thought that Philip Neuman was *not* tired and that his request to sleep was just a ploy to avoid questioning, then would that not suggest a certain amount of cunning on the part of the accused?'

'Yes,' said Logan smugly. 'It would.'

'And yet you felt that in spite of his cunning you were on the verge of getting a confession.'

'Who says?'

'Well, why were you so anxious to continue the questioning? You'd been at it for some time yourself. You must also have been tired.'

'Like I said, I don't get tired.'

'But to go at it like that, you must have sensed that you were making progress.'

'I felt that I was.'

'And yet you also believed that your prime suspect was being very *cunning* in his efforts to avoid questioning, when he could have simply clammed up and refused to answer. Isn't that something of a contradiction?'

'Not at all,' said the inspector confidently. 'The fact that he resorted to the subterfuge of pretending that he was tired when he could simply have clammed up just goes to show the extent to which he was no longer thinking straight.'

'But if he wasn't thinking straight, then in what sense could his confession be said to have been voluntary?'

Leonard Stewart rose to his feet, prompting Freeman to sit.

'Your Worship, I have refrained from objecting until now because I was wondering what Mr Freeman was getting at and hoping that he would eventually get to the point. But I see now that there *is* no point. Suspects often give themselves away when they're no longer thinking straight. That doesn't make their incriminating statements inadmissible. As long as the interrogation was conducted in accordance with PACE, the statement is admissible. How much weight to attach to it is a matter for the jury to decide, when the case is heard in the crown court.'

The prosecutor sat and Freeman returned to his feet.

'Your Worship, m'learned friend is right in that many incriminating statements are made by suspects while they are disoriented. But he forgets that there are two basic types of incriminating statement. One is the incriminating *denial*, given by the suspect who still wishes to conceal his guilt but who incriminates himself in the course of his denial *because* he is confused and disoriented. The other is the voluntary confession, freely given by someone, either because he is genuinely remorseful and regrets what he did or, more rarely, because he is proud of what he did and wishes to boast about it.

'In the former case, the self-incrimination comes about because of the suspect's confusion. There is no danger to the cause of justice if such a person incriminates himself by the divulgence of detail which suggests that he had knowledge of the crime peculiar to the perpetrator and the investigative authorities.

'However, in the case of a formal confession of guilt, especially one lacking the divulgence of characterizing details of the crime, a *different* standard applies. The statement must be truly voluntary. Now, I think m'learned friend would agree with me that if Mr Neuman was speaking from a position of confusion and disorientation, as this witness's testimony strongly suggests, then any formal confession

211

he made at the time could not be construed as voluntary. Therefore strong doubts attach to its authenticity.'

'I must confess, Your Worship,' said the prosecutor, again on his feet, 'that I find it hard to follow m'learned friend's convoluted argument.'

'I must confess that I *too* am somewhat confused,' said the magistrate. 'Perhaps you'll explain it again, Mr Freeman, this time in plain English.'

'What I'm saying, Your Worship, is that the witness and m'learned friend are confusing the two different types of self-incrimination. It is possible that my client was a devious yet confused person who incriminated himself unintentionally by making careless statements. Or he could have been a person tormented by guilt who incriminated himself intentionally by a freely given confession to unburden himself of the guilt he felt for the terrible crime of fratricide. But he *couldn't* have been *both* at the same time. M'learned friend and this witness would apparently have the court believe that my client was both anxious to *confess* and anxious to *conceal* his guilt. That is clearly a blatant contradiction! If my client's request to be allowed to sleep was the device of a cunning person who wished to *conceal* his guilt, then his confession could not have been the voluntary confession of a guilty man who wanted to *lift the burden of guilt from his soul.* Conversely if he was not a cunning villain trying to conceal his guilt, then his request for sleep was genuine, sincere and truthful. But if it was genuine and sincere, then it means he really *needed* to sleep as he claimed. And if he was in need of sleep, as he claimed, then any confession he made at the time when he was deprived of sleep was not truly voluntary and therefore utterly worthless.'

'I see your point now, Mr Freeman.'

'I am much obliged, Your Worship,' said Freeman, sitting down and leaving it to the prosecutor to salvage this part of his case.

'Your Worship,' Leonard Stewart almost pleaded, 'surely this is a matter of the weight of evidence, for a jury to decide.

'The jury would certainly have to decide on the weight
to attach to the accused's statement if the case goes to trial,'
said the magistrate. But whether or not to commit the case
to trial depends on whether or not *I* am satisfied that there
is a case to answer. And I can tell you now that in view of
this point about the accused not being allowed to sleep, I
have grave doubts about the reliability of this confession.
As the confession is the mainstay of your case as outlined
so far, I would therefore strongly suggest that you consider
presenting additional evidence in support of committal.'

The prosecutor was wiping the sweat from his forehead.

'In that case, Your Worship, could I request that we
adjourn for lunch at this time so that I can arrange for
a couple of other witnesses to come here and testify this
afternoon.'

'Very well,' said the magistrate. 'This court will adjourn
for lunch and resume at two-thirty.'

The judge rose.

'All rise!' the clerk intoned.

Almost two hours later, they were in the courtroom again,
and a witness who was introduced as 'Jilly Smith' was in
the witness box.

'Could you explain first of all,' asked the prosecutor,
'what your assignment was, with regard to the murder of
Anthony Neuman?'

'My assignment was to befriend Philip Neuman and get
him to talk about the case and find out if he killed his
brother. If so, then I was supposed to get him to talk
about it and disclose details that only the murderer would
know, apart from the police, that is. I was wired to record
our conversations and they were all recorded and the tapes
logged, indexed and transcribed.'

From the dock, a young man's eyes were transfixed upon
her. She looked much older now to the young man who
watched her, almost as if she were a different person from
the girl who had befriended him so gently and then betrayed
him so painfully.

213

'And how did you go about befriending him?'

She described how she had picked him up at the nightclub and danced with him all evening and then met him again for coffee and a movie, and then in the park, making sure to keep the meetings in public and, after the first one, during the day, so as to avoid situations in which sex became a reasonable possibility. Police officers were not permitted to engage in sexual activity to gather evidence, although they could hold out the promise of it to achieve that objective.

'Now, when you went for that walk in the park, do you remember substantially how the conversation went?'

'Yes,' said Jilly.

'I'm going to hand you a transcript and I will ask you to identify it.'

He handed several copies of the transcript to the clerk of the court who showed it to the magistrate. The magistrate perused it and nodded to the clerk, who then proceeded to hand copies to the witness and to Freeman.

'Now, do you recognize the contents of this transcript?' asked the prosecutor.

'Yes,' replied Jilly. 'This is a transcript of my last conversation with Philip Neuman.'

'With the court's permission I am going to play a tape recording of this conversation. The transcript will show that it is an identical conversation.'

He played the tape and all parties listened intently until the final words:

'Did it disturb you? Seeing him dead?'

'Of course it disturbed me. Looking down at a knife wound at the side of my brother's stomach.'

There were a few more words on the tape. But the prosecutor switched off at this point.

'Your Worship, I would at this juncture draw your attention to the forensic pathologist's report describing the injuries. I should also like to recall Inspector Logan to give some additional evidence.'

'Why was he not asked to give this evidence already?' asked the magistrate with irritation.

'It required this witness's testimony to establish foundation. It pertains to the fact that the accused showed, in his statements to this witness, knowledge of the crime which he could not have gained from merely seeing the body in the mortuary. I seek to call Detective Inspector Logan to confirm this.'

'Mr Freeman?'

'No objection, Your Worship.'

'Do you have any further questions of this witness, Mr Stewart?'

'No, Your Worship,' said the prosecutor.

'You may cross-examine, Mr Freeman.'

Freeman rose slowly as Leonard Stewart took his seat. He looked at Jilly carefully. He could see that she was nervous. She was a young police officer and presumably quite inexperienced. This was probably her first major case, and consequently the first time she would be facing serious cross-examination. She had probably faced some cross-examination before, but this was a murder case. A lawyer – *any* lawyer – would do more than just go through a few standard questions by rote. Every facet of her testimony, every aspect of her memory would be mercilessly probed. She knew this, had presumably been warned of this, and was nervous. If the case went to trial he would have to test her for cracks, now and at the trial itself.

He could play it a number of ways. He could go at her hammer and tongs and try to shake her, with the added benefit that even if he couldn't break her he could frighten her so that she would be even more nervous at the trial. He could go easy on her now so that she wouldn't be prepared for what he could subject her to at the trial. He could try to probe her to see how well she stood up to cross-examination, and possibly also go on a fishing expedition for exculpatory evidence, safe in the knowledge that if he found nothing, there was no jury to be influenced against his client by the failure of such an attempt.

He decided that he would probe her gently. Judging by the way his client looked at Jilly, and she at him, there was

always the possibility that she might actually be on his side
– might actually *want* to help him, and might be persuaded
to give testimony favourable to him about their discussions.
Certainly there was ammunition to be used in the transcripts,
which he had been given earlier.

'Miss Smith, at one point in your conversation you said
to my client: 'Let's just say that if I thought you were tough
enough to kill your brother I might just be ready to . . . drop
my defences.' Is that correct?'

Jilly blushed. They had heard it on the tape, but it was
different when everyone's attention was drawn to it.

'Yes,' she said nervously.

'What did you mean by this?'

'Well, it was meant to imply that I was ready to give
Mr Neuman sexual favours if he admitted to killing his
brother.'

'"Sexual favours if he admitted to killing his brother,"'
Freeman repeated. 'But didn't you say in your evidence in
chief something about "making sure to keep the meetings in
public and, after the first one, during the day, so as to avoid
situations in which sex became a reasonable possibility"?'

Jilly's face was bright red by now.

'Yes, I did say that.'

'Well, how do you reconcile offering the accused sexual
favours in return for a confession with your claim that you
were taking steps to avoid having sex with him?'

'I wasn't actually going to sleep with him if he confessed!'

'But I thought that was precisely what you were offering
if he confessed.'

'But I had no intention of actually doing so,' she said
desperately.

'Oh, I see,' said Freeman, as if enlightenment had only
just dawned on him. 'You mean it was a *false* promise?'

Jilly remained silent.

'Well, Miss . . . er . . . *Smith*.'

'Yes.'

'So that although you said in effect that you would have

sex with him if he confessed you actually had no intention of doing so.'

'That's right,' Jilly replied, her irritation showing.

'So in other words when a person says something in order to get something they want, it isn't necessarily true?'

Leonard Stewart had been poised to object, but seeing Roger Trent lean forward with a keen look of interest on his face, he thought better of it and silently backed off.

'Yes,' replied Jilly weakly, realizing that she was going to get no help from the prosecutor.

'Just as a young man might admit to committing a murder in order to impress a young . . . *lady* . . . so that he might obtain sexual favours.'

'Yes.'

Inexplicably – or perhaps understandably – she looked over at the dock as if she wanted to apologize. But Freeman continued relentlessly.

'So that even if Mr Neuman *had* confessed under such circumstances, his confession might well have been false?'

'I suppose so,' said Jilly, sniffling a little. She was on the verge of crying by now, but Freeman was not prepared to back off. There was no jury here to feel sorry for her and he preferred her to do her crying here and be emerge tough enough to face this line of questioning without tears in the crown court. The questions touched upon fundamental issues about the scope of legitimate police enquiries and were effective in their own right, no matter how she answered them. If she toughened up between now and then and answered the same questions in the crown court with a hint of defiance or an air of arrogance, so much the better for his defence and the prospects of jury sympathy for his client.

'And you were aware of this even at the time when you set out to elicit such a confession, were you not?'

'Yes,' said Jilly, a few tears now showing in the corners of her eyes.

'So what made you think that such a confession would have any value?'

'The idea wasn't just to get a confession. It was to get the

217

accused, or the suspect as he then was, to make incriminating statements indicating knowledge of the crime.'

'Yes, you've already told us that. But you also set about getting an explicit admission of guilt which you yourself admit would have been worthless. And the thing I'm still trying to find out is *why*? Why did you set out to get an explicit admission of guilt if, by your own admission, such a confession would have been worthless?'

'Those were my instructions,' she responded flatly. It was clear, painfully clear, that she was now on the defensive. Freeman had already made his essential point and he could very easily have let her go. But he knew that her testimony had prepared the ground for another piece of incriminating evidence and he was determined to probe further for weaknesses. It was precisely in order to discover flaws in the prosecution's case that he had pushed so hard to have the witnesses called instead of merely taking depositions.

'I see. So you were just following orders.'

Leonard Stewart was on his feet in an instant.

'Your Worship, I really must object. Counsel is now using veiled Nazi analogies to mock the witness and ridicule her testimony, presumably in the hope that it will gain favourable press coverage before the trial.'

'Not at all,' Freeman replied with a smile of wholesome innocence on his face. 'I was merely trying to establish that the orders came from above to establish foundation to ask those who were responsible for *issuing* the orders – at the appropriate juncture, of course.'

'Yes, I think I'll allow the question to pass, although it was more in the nature of an observation than a question, as it had already been constructively answered. Proceed, Mr Freeman.'

'Would it be fair to say, Miss Smith, that this was an attempt to cover both sides?'

'I . . . I don't understand,' she said hesitantly.

'Well, you couldn't be sure if he'd make any incriminating disclosures when you set out, could you?'

'Obviously not. There was no way we could know in advance exactly what he'd say.'

'So by setting out to get him to make an explicit admission of guilt you were effectively increasing your chances of getting *something*?'

'I suppose so.'

'And indeed it wasn't until after you failed to elicit a clear-cut admission of guilt that Mr Neuman made the statement about seeing his brother's injuries. Is that not so?'

'Yes.'

Again the reply was hesitant and betrayed the underlying nervousness.

'So is it not possible that it was because of this failure to extract a confession that you and your colleagues decided to convert an innocent statement about his brother's wounds into an incriminating statement, through the expedient device of reinventing the events at the mortuary when he identified the body?'

This time Stewart positively *leapt* to his feet.

'Your Worship, Detective Inspector Logan has not even testified about the events at the mortuary and counsel is asking for speculation from a witness who had nothing to do with the events at the mortuary and wasn't even involved in the investigation at that time.'

'Yes, I would agree,' said the magistrate. He turned to the defence counsel. 'Mr Freeman, your question is somewhat premature and clearly aimed at the wrong party. If you wish to put this question to the appropriate witness at the proper juncture that will of course be another matter.'

'As Your Worship pleases,' said Freeman, realizing that his point had hit home and stung.

'And at that stage the mortuary attendant folded back the sheet sufficiently to reveal the face but no more than that.'

Once again Detective Inspector Logan was in the witness box, being questioned by Leonard Stewart.

'And so there is no possibility that he saw the nature of his brother's injuries at that time?'

'That's correct.'

'Thank you, that's all. Stay there, please, I think my learned friend may have some questions for you.'

The prosecutor sat and Freeman rose in the familiar routine.

'Inspector, at what stage did Philip Neuman become a suspect in this case?'

'Well, he was a suspect from the beginning, in the sense that we hadn't ruled him out and he had been with his brother before the murder by his own admission. I assume you mean when did he become the prime suspect.'

'OK, when did he become the *prime* suspect?'

In the trial phase of the proceedings the golden rule is never ask a question to which you do not know the answer in advance. However, committal proceedings like this were made for fishing expeditions and Freeman intended to fish with a fine-mesh net rather than a line and bait.

'It was after the second interview, when he revealed that he was a practitioner of witchcraft and had a fierce rivalry with his brother.'

'And at the time when he identified the body, he was merely a suspect?'

'That's correct.'

'And the reason he was a suspect at that time was simply because he was closely related to the deceased, hadn't been formally eliminated and had been with him before the murder?'

'That's right.'

'And for no other reason.'

'I beg your pardon?' said Logan, hesitantly.

'He was a suspect, *at the time*, for *no other reason* than because he was a close relative of the deceased, had not been formally eliminated and had been with his brother in the period leading up to the murder? Just *those* reasons at the time?'

'Yes,' said Logan, wondering where this line of questioning was leading.

'If there *had* been any other reasons for considering him a suspect at the time, would you still remember them?'

'I think so, sir,' replied Logan, smiling indulgently, as if talking to a not very bright child. 'That is my profession, after all.'

'All right, Inspector. Now, you've told us that when Philip Neuman identified the body, he was not shown enough to see the nature or extent of the injuries. But didn't he ask about how his brother died, either at the time, or even before that – I mean about where and how he was stabbed?'

The inspector hesitated. It was obvious that if Philip Neuman had asked about the injuries and the manner of death then he would have been given *some* sort of answer, even if it was of a general nature, and that would give rise to the possibility that he had been told the extent of the injuries or at least had been told enough to infer their extent and nature.

'Not that I recall,' said Logan, taking what he thought was the safe route.

'But surely it would have been most unnatural *not* to have asked how his brother had met his fate?'

'I can't say what's natural and what isn't, sir. I can only say that he didn't ask.'

'But, Inspector, if he *didn't* ask how his brother died, would that not have been so unnatural as itself to have aroused your suspicion?'

'Well, I suppose it wou . . .'

The inspector trailed off, realizing that he had fallen into a trap. Now it was Freeman who smiled indulgently.

'Well, Inspector?' the lawyer persisted.

'If I had thought about it at the time, I suppose it would have made me more suspicious of him. But there are many things to think about when one is conducting a murder inquiry and I didn't think about it at the time.'

Very adroit, thought Freeman, realizing that the inspector's nimble footwork was pretty nearly getting him off the hook.

'But surely if Mr Neuman was already a suspect, and if

you had him in your company, then you would have been noting what he said, and what he didn't say, with a view to determining how likely a suspect he *was*.

'Not when I had many other aspects of the case to think about,' said Logan, trying to project the image of an overworked professional.

'But did you not say, earlier in your cross-examination, that if there had been any other grounds for considering him a suspect then you would still remember them?'

The inspector was blushing, trying desperately to recall exactly what he had said. Finally he remembered and smiled with relief.

'Remember them, yes, but only if I noticed them at the time.'

He heaved a visible sigh of relief, grateful that there was no jury present. Although he had wriggled and jumped off the hook, any juror witnessing his display would have had grave doubts about his honesty. Now he realized that Freeman had made a mistake, by warning him of what to expect when the case came before the crown court. The magistrate was, by virtue of his profession, favourably disposed towards the police and would therefore overlook the squirming posture and the desperate tone and focus only on the words.

'So you didn't notice the accused's failure to ask any of the usual questions about how his brother died?'

'No, sir,' said Logan, realizing how unreasonable it sounded.

'Even though it's your job?'

The inspector remained silent. He knew that Freeman would have a whole bag of tricks and traps once they clashed swords again in the crown court. He knew also that the lawyer had not made such a mistake after all. For it was he, not Freeman, who had committed himself to a particular version of events. Freeman was free to ask what questions he liked at the trial, and no one on the jury would know about, or be influenced by, his failure to repeat questions that he had asked at the committal proceedings.

But Logan had painted himself into a corner by saying that Philip Neuman had not asked about how his brother died when he identified that body. That fact would seem suspicious to any jury and would imply prior knowledge of the crime. But Inspector Logan's self-confessed failure to pick up on it as grounds for suspicion would not ring true. And it was too late for Logan to say that Philip *had* asked about how his brother died, aside from the fact that such an admission would undermine his efforts to use Philip's statement to Jilly as a means of incriminating him.

'No further questions,' said Freeman, holding the inspector's venomous gaze without blinking.

21

'A corrupt witness mocks at justice . . .'

Proverbs 19:28

'He's putting up quite a spirited defence, Michael,' said Hassan.

'I told you he was good,' said Michael, watching the ducks waddle across the grass by the pond.

'I'm just worried he might be a threat to us,' said Hassan, scooping up a handful of salted peanuts from the silver bowl in front of him.

DuPaul leaned forward on his lounger.

'I don't think there's the slightest danger of that.'

Even in Bermuda shorts and a Hawaiian shirt under a seemingly tropical sun, Rex DuPaul couldn't avoid full consciousness of the fact that he was still in England. He would have liked to have hopped on an aeroplane to the Riviera, to really get away from it all. But it was just a weekened in this quiet, grassy surburban estate in North London. And in Rex DuPaul's line of work there *were* no weekends.

'But he's making mincemeat of the prosecution,' said Michael.

'The prosecution isn't really that important,' said the

detective chief superintendent. 'It doesn't matter if Philip Neuman is convicted of killing his brother or not. The danger was never about there being an open file. There's an open file on the Digby murder even now. The real danger always was that the press or public might start to see the link between Digby and Tony Neuman. So far that hasn't happened.'

'I thought the watch was found when they were looking for the Fabian Digby murder weapon,' said Hassan, unable to follow DuPaul's reasoning.

'That may be, but no one has assumed that there was any actual linkage between the two. As far as the press and public are concerned it's just a coincidence.'

'And what about from the law enforcement point of view?' asked Michael, eyeing DuPaul coolly.

'I've come under no pressure to merge the investigations. The Fabian Digby inquiry is still proceeding along a separate track and no one in the Neuman investigation has asked for our help in any way apart from formal testimony to maintain the continuity of evidence regarding the watch.'

'What about your deputy on the Digby investigation?' asked Michael, again eyeballing the policeman with a piercing stare.

'DCI Rousson?' DuPaul replied defensively. 'What about her?'

'Has she been asking any questions about the Neuman case?'

'No. She also sees the Neuman case as separate. But she's been seeing —'

The DCS broke off, realizing that this was something he did not wish to share with the others.

'Been seeing whom?' asked Michael.

'The Neuman boy's lawyer,' DuPaul replied quietly. He was evidently hoping this revelation would blow over without any further attention. But Michael had a keen sense of danger and didn't drop things like that in a hurry.

'Can't you order her to stop?'

'Not without admitting that the cases are linked,' said

DuPaul, 'precisely the thing that we don't want to do. Besides, they started seeing each other before Freeman became Philip Neuman's brief, when he was investigating Digby's disappearance.'

'Who? Philip Neuman?' asked Hassan confused.

'No, Emmett Freeman!'

Michael was surprised to hear DuPaul addressing Hassan so forcefully. They usually both deferred to him. Michael would sometimes correct him on a point, but it paid them both not to forget that Hassan commanded a fortune that made even Digby's wealth seem insignificant. That was not because Hassan was such a wealthy man personally, but rather because he was the manager for a vast fortune of a very rich ruling family from a country that had a bountiful abundance of oil and an insatiable appetite for Western heavy weaponry.

'The question is,' said Hassan, 'if he continues with his involvement with the case, is there not a danger that in his efforts to discover more, in order to help his client, he will find out about the gene splicing?'

'It's hard to see how he can,' said DuPaul. 'With the death of Tony Neuman and the theft of his computer and diskettes the trail must have gone cold. Tony Neuman isn't around to point the accusing finger and all his computer diskettes and the hard disk have been not merely erased but melted down in a furnace. Isn't that right, Michael?'

'That's right. I used one of the extraction furnaces at the reprocessing plant to destroy the diskettes and the hard drive.'

'So you're saying that there's nothing by way of evidence for him to find. Is that right?'

Hassan looked alternatively at Michael and DuPaul. But it was DuPaul who looked away.

'Yes,' he said.

'What about the perfume itself?' asked Hassan.

'There's nothing we can do about that,' said Michael. 'Unless you want us to withdraw it from the market.'

'That wasn't what I was getting at,' said Hassan. 'I think Rex knows what I'm talking about.'

DuPaul forced himself to meet Hassan's eyes.

'My deputy, DCI Rousson, did send out a sample of the perfume for lab analysis as you already know. But I halted the analysis on budgetary grounds.'

'*After* Dr Sadler found out what's in the perfume,' said Hassan.

'But *before* he could tell anyone. He contacted me first, as the head of the inquiry, and I got him to destroy the paperwork on the grounds that it would not be in the public interest for people to think we were using taxpayers' money in this way.'

'And you bought him off with a bribe,' said Hassan. It was more of a question than a statement.

'I did what I had to do,' said DuPaul.

'Meaning you bought his silence temporarily and then killed him.'

'I did what I *had* to do,' said DuPaul. 'Besides, black-mailers are the scum of the earth. They *deserve* death.'

'I'm glad to see you've got over your inhibitions,' said Michael.

'Can we be sure that all the paperwork was destroyed?' asked Hassan.

'It's almost certain,' said DuPaul.

'It's the almost that worries me,' Hassan continued. 'What if DCI Rousson whispers a word in Freeman's ear? What if Freeman decides that the two cases are linked? What if he tries to get hold of the lab report?'

'Like I said,' said DuPaul, 'I ordered it destroyed.'

'*Ordered* it destroyed. But what if it wasn't?'

'You're worrying over nothing, Hassan,' said the Chief Superintendent. 'I made it clear to Dr Sadler how important it was to destroy it and I'm quite sure that he did.'

'But *my* understanding is that there's a *lot* of paperwork involved in these matters.' Michael stepped in. 'Like the log book when the sample was first brought in. He can't have destroyed all of the documentation. And if someone is really determined they'll find a paper trail. The fact that the lab report is missing will only heighten their suspicion. And of course, even if it was wiped from the computer, it might still be on the hard disk and the back-up tapes – as we all know only too well.'

'Perhaps I can be of some assistance,' said a voice in the corner.

All eyes turned to Edward, who had been sitting there quietly, listening to the discussion as it developed with a mixture of amusement and fear. He liked to be the one who kept his head while others about him were losing theirs. But he was apprehensive about his own capacity to persuade either Michael or Hassan. They all had a lot to lose, and with the exception of DuPaul they had no understanding of how officialdom and public policy actually worked. Michael was a businessman who knew how to play the game of working both ends of Whitehall against the middle, but only how to play it from the outside. Hassan was the sidekick of a foreign potentate who knew about bribery and baksheesh but didn't necessarily know, in the British context, who to bribe or how to make it look like a legitimate transaction, except with Edward's own patient guidance.

'Paperwork involved in a police inquiry is covered by public interest immunity,' he said. 'That immunity, which was created by the courts, not by Parliament, is quite sweeping and all-embracing and there's no way that Freeman would be able to get his hands on any of the loose paperwork from the lab analysis of Gold.'

'I thought you British prided yourselves on being an open society,' said Hassan with a sly grin.

Edward scowled at the sarcasm.

'You're confusing us with the Americans,' he said. 'The immunity is so all-embracing that a few years ago, a black youth whose murder conviction was quashed on the grounds that it was unsafe and unsatisfactory wasn't allowed to bring a civil action for conspiracy to pervert the course of justice and misfeasance in public office against the police officers who falsified his confession. The judge ruled that the police were protected by a rule of *absolute immunity* conferred as a matter of public policy and that falsifying evidence counted as part of the investigative process. Now you can't get more all-embracing than that!'

'I remember the case,' said DuPaul with a wry smile. 'The judge answered the argument that there was no public interest in protecting those who created false evidence by saying that the argument missed the essential point, and that the real point was that the public interest was the protection of those who might otherwise be falsely accused of such conduct.'

'That's not exactly the same type of case,' said Michael, irritated by the way that Edward and DuPaul had teamed up.

'What Edward and I are trying to say,' DuPaul explained, 'is that the courts look most favourably on the police, and I can tell you from my own experience that that goes for juries as well as judges. When a journalist was shot in the head five times by police officers, the police officers were acquitted of attempted murder, even though the victim didn't have anything on him that looked like a gun. The victim was in the company of the suspect's girlfriend and the police got their story out first, saying that he looked like the suspect and the suspect was known to be violent. In classic tradition, the judge directed the jury that they shouldn't assume that because an innocent man was shot someone necessarily had to pay for it. The jury accepted it and that was the end of the matter. When IRA suspects were freed by an appeal court that's always been slow to acknowledge miscarriages of justice unless the evidence is overwhelming, the police officers who obtained their confessions were subsequently acquitted of conspiracy to pervert the course of justice. The public are well disposed to the police in spite of a few scandals here and there. They aren't going to believe the worst of the police just because a lawyer desperately trying to save his client starts throwing accusations about.'

'That doesn't mean there's no danger to us,' said Michael.

'I still think we'd be better off if we dealt with the loose ends like Freeman and DCI Rousson.'

'That's a ridiculous idea!' snapped DuPaul, realizing that reason and patience were failing to get the message across. 'Do you think it would end there? The deaths of the lawyer defending Philip Neuman and the policewoman investigating the murder of Fabian Digby? That would just create more suspicion and more public interest and press scrutiny. No, we're going to have to ride out the storm and let it blow itself out.'

'Let's just hope that we're not facing the wrong way when the wind changes,' said Michael.

'I swear by almighty God that the evidence I shall give shall be the truth, the whole truth and nothing but the truth.'

'State your name and occupation.'

'I am Dr Saul Albion and I am a forensic psychologist.'

Saul Albion was the second of Leonard Stewart's after-lunch witnesses. He was the picture of a polished professional. Tall and silver-haired with square-rimmed spectacles, he looked like an accomplished expert in his field before he even opened his mouth. At one time he had even sported a grey beard, which added to his aura of intellectual accomplishment, but he had shaved it off several cases ago, on the advice of a 'sartorial counsellor' who had advised him that beards reduced one's trust level by being associated with religious leaders and revolutionaries. There was no point being thought professionally accomplished if one was also thought of as dishonest. In most cases it was not his intellect which was at issue, only his integrity.

Leonard Stewart was now looking the picture of self-confidence himself. Freeman wondered if this was simply because he was mirroring the attitude of Saul Albion or because he was now calling his star witness. The police had told Freeman about Saul Albion and he didn't think there could be any surprises from him. He knew Albion well enough, having crossed swords with him a couple of times before. They had come out one-all. But Freeman's victory had been won first, so it was Saul Albion who had improved his performance with time. Perhaps that was what the police were counting on. But Freeman suspected that there was something more: they had some other evidence against Philip, something they had not yet let on about.

'Could you tell the court about your qualifications.'

Freeman rose.

'Your Worship, the defence is ready to waive a recital of the witness's qualifications at this stage of the proceedings. We acknowledge that he holds a doctorate in psychology from University College and many years' experience in the field of forensic psychology.'

The prosecutor smiled. This effectively meant that Freeman was not going to challenge Dr Albion's credentials, at least not at this stage in the proceedings. In a way this was good for the prosecution, because there would be some limited reporting of the proceedings in the press, and this would effectively mean that elements of the prosecution case would come over strongly and be effectively implanted in potential jurors' minds long before the trial. But on the other hand, it meant that Albion wouldn't be prepared for the particular questions that Freeman would ask. And Freeman could always vary his style.

Leonard Stewart rose slowly as Freeman sat, and half turned to his adversary.

'I am much obliged to m'learned friend,' he said graciously. Then he turned to Saul Albion.

'Dr Albion, did you in the second half of July of this year analyse transcripts and tapes of police interviews with Philip David Neuman?'

'I did,' the psychologist replied in his characteristic ringing tone of self-assurance.

'And what was the purpose of this analysis?'

'To determine if the psychological profile of Philip Neuman matched the psychological profile of the murderer of Anthony Neuman.'

'Could you tell the court, please, who determined the psychological profile of the murderer of Anthony Neuman?'

231

'I did.'

'And how did you prepare this profile of the murderer?'

'By looking at crime scene evidence and determining what sort of psychological attributes the known elements of the crime indicated.'

'And what did you determine to be the essential attributes of the perpetrator of this murder?'

'Judging by the single knife thrust that was almost ritualistic in the apparent precision of its placement, and the careful way in which left hand was placed across the chest after the watch was removed, I would say that the perpetrator was someone obsessed with ritual, possibly religious ritual. Also, that there was some feeling on the part of the perpetrator towards the victim. The removal of the watch in itself suggests that robbery was the motive. But based on the fact that it was found to have been discarded I would conclude not merely that this was a deliberate attempt to make it look like robbery but that there was an element of jealousy involved, as if the perpetrator wanted to *be* like the deceased, or even had tried to be, but failed.'

Freeman was smiling because he could see that Roger Trent, the magistrate, looked bored.

'And what conclusions did you reach in preparing your psychological profile of the accused, Philip Neuman?'

'Well, there were some remarkable similarities. First of all there was the paganism. As we all know paganism is a very ritualistic religion – even more so than the Judaism, in which Philip Neuman was brought up. Furthermore Philip Neuman professed to being a practitioner of witchcraft, a *particularly* ritualistic form of paganism. That is fully consistent with the positioning of the hands that I mentioned before. I would also say that the mere fact that Philip Neuman had abandoned the Judaic ethic means that he had lost some of his inhibitions against acts which are reviled by the Judeo-Christian ethic, but not condemned to the same extent in the old religions which were born of societies such as ancient Rome or old England in the pre-Christian days of tribal warfare and barbarism.

'I also detected a clear and intense rivalry between Philip Neuman and his brother, and although he tried to represent it as a sort of mutual rivalry, there were certain statements made by the accused to the police officer known as Jilly Smith that suggested that he was frustrated by his past, unhappy with his lot in life and saw others as having done better than he had. Again, he didn't mention his brother by name, preferring instead to hide the true direction of his feelings behind the façade of Robert Perchik, but it was clear that Robert Perchik was just a fantasy figure whom he had constructed as a representation of his brother.'

'Dr Albion, were you able to determine anything about Philip Neuman's attitude to the death of his brother after the fact?'

'I detected signs of pain and regret that could be construed as remorse. For example, his anger at the suggestion by Jilly that he had killed his brother could be taken as a sign that he felt guilty for having done so.'

'Now, there is one small flaw in this entire scenario, which I'm sure m'learned friend is going to make much of in his cross-examination.' The prosecutor glanced quickly at Freeman. 'Jilly Smith did offer, in effect, to have sexual relations with Philip Neuman if he admitted to killing his brother. Does this not call into question the theory that he killed his brother?'

'No, not at all. First of all, it is not beyond the bounds of possibility that he actually surmised that Miss Smith was a police officer, or at least guessed at the possibility, and was therefore adopting a deliberately cautious line in what he said to her. I gave Miss Smith very precise instructions as to what to say but it is very hard to anticipate every possibility and she could have given herself away by nervousness or mannerisms without even realizing it. Secondly, Philip Neuman's denial could also be a reflection of his feelings of guilt. He realized by that stage that he had done wrong and didn't want to admit to anyone else – or even himself – that he had killed his brother. And he certainly didn't want to derive any *benefit* from the fact that he had killed him. So he denied it when she offered him sexual favours in return for an admission of guilt, indeed he denied it *especially* because she was offering something in return. If she had offered him nothing there is always the possibility that he would have confessed.'

'Now let us turn to the confession that he eventually *did* offer,' said the prosecutor. 'My learned friend will no doubt put to you that the fact that the accused denied his guilt dozens of time while under police interrogation and that he had not had much sleep in the period leading up to his confession shows the confession to be unreliable. How would you respond to this?'

'Well, first of all I would point out that he was questioned in the afternoon and the alleged deprivation of sleep was self-inflicted in the period prior to his arrest. Moreover, the fact that he had the presence of mind to deny his guilt so many times while in police custody in spite of his protests about lacking adequate sleep the night before suggests that he was in full control of himself and not subject to constructive coercion or lack of free will. Thirdly, the fact that he denied his guilt many times before admitting it suggests that he was in conflict with himself. The real battle was being waged not between Philip Neuman and his police interrogators, but between Philip Neuman's base instinct for survival and his moral conscience which recognized that he had committed fratricide and had his brother's blood on his hands. He was facing a cruel inner turmoil and it happened to be played out in a police station. I am convinced that had he not been interrogated by the police that day he would soon thereafter have walked into a police station on his own two feet and confessed without waiting for any interrogators to put specific questions to him.'

'I see. Thank you, Dr Albion. No further questions.'

Leonard Stewart sat down, looking characteristically smug. Freeman rose slowly, giving no sign of any intention to put the witness under pressure. But he noticed Albion's jaw tightening, as if he wondered what was in store for him this time.

'Dr Albion,' Freeman said, smiling. The psychologist inclined his head in greeting. 'You have testified that you compiled your psychological profile of the prepetrator of the murderer based on crime scene evidence, is that correct?'

'Yes,' said Albion.

'And *only* on crime scene evidence.'

'Of course, otherwise it wouldn't be a true profile of the perpetrator.'

'Quite so,' said Freeman. 'So would it be fair to say that you created a written record of this psychological profile before the accused came under investigation?'

'Well, I don't know when, precisely, he came under investigation, but my understanding is that he came under investigation right from the outset, inasmuch as he was the brother of the deceased and had been with the deceased a few hours earlier.'

'So that by the time you were brought in on the case, the accused was already a suspect?'

'Well, again, I don't know what the police suspected. But I didn't know anything about the accused at the time.'

'So you're saying that you created a written psychological profile before you knew anything about my client?'

'That is correct.'

'And when would this be?'

Saul Albion threw his head back, as if contemplating.

'Oh, I would say . . . about July the eighteenth.'

'That would be the day after the burglary was discovered,' said Freeman.

'I'm sorry?' tendered Albion, genuinely confused.

'Oh, nothing,' said Freeman. 'I was thinking out loud.'

'Well, please don't!' the magistrate bellowed. 'It is most disconcerting, especially for those of us who prefer to think for ourselves.'

Both the prosecutor and Saul Albion were smiling at the sight of Freeman being put in his place, the psychologist even going so far as to nod a polite 'thank you' in the magistrate's direction. But Freeman merely ignored their glee and continued smoothly.

'Now by that stage, the police had already interviewed Philip Neuman twice, as well as taking body samples from him.'

'I know nothing of that, Mr Freeman,' said the psychologist, still smiling.

'And do you also know nothing of Philip Neuman telling the police about his practice of Wicca, or witchcraft at it is sometimes known.'

'That is correct. I did not hear anything about this until afterwards.'

'But when you eventually *did* make the comparison between your profile and the accused, one of the transcripts you looked at was WPC Woodward's notes from the interview on the day the burglary was discovered.'

'When it came to the comparative stage of the profiling process, that was *one* of the transcripts that I looked at.'

'But at the time you were called in, that piece of evidence already existed.'

'In retrospect I know that to be the case,' replied Albion, choosing his words very carefully. He knew well enough what Freeman was getting it: that he had prepared his psychological profile of the murderer not solely on the basis of crime scene evidence, but also on the basis of known information about Philip Neuman. There was no way that Freeman could prove this. But equally there was no way that anyone could disprove it. The point was that Freeman could establish that it was *possible* and let the jury's imagination do the rest. He had done this the first time they clashed. Albion had fought him off the second time. But now Freeman was taking advantage of the committal proceedings to probe for weaknesses. The most important one, which he had already uncovered, was that by the time Albion was brought in on the case, the police were already focusing their attention on Philip Neuman. So it would look very unlikely to a jury that the police would tell Albion nothing about Neuman while getting him to compile a psychological profile of the murderer. It would seem more likely that they would tell him about the suspect and ask him how credible a suspect he was.

'Dr Albion, in your evidence in chief you stated, "Judging by the single knife thrust that was almost ritualistic in the apparent precision of its placement and the careful way in which the left hand was placed across the chest after the watch was removed, I would say that the perpetrator was someone obsessed with ritual, possibly religious ritual." Tell me, Dr Albion, why did a single thrust of the knife into the stomach suggest a ritual-type killing?'

'Well, first of all I wouldn't go so far as to say a ritual-type killing. I would prefer to say a killing with ritual elements. Remember that I didn't say the killing was a ritual killing but only that it suggested someone *obsessed* with ritual.'

'Be that as it may, Dr Albion, the question remains the same: *why* does it suggest that?'

Albion tensed up and then relaxed.

No, he thought, he hasn't hurt my credibility. He hasn't made me the laughing-stock of my profession. He's simply asked me for clarification. That's all.

'Most stabbing murders, other than spontaneous intra-family murders, involve more than one thrust of the knife.'

'What about spontaneous murder in the course of a mugging?'

'Well, my understanding is that it wasn't a mugging. The watch was found discarded, as if it had been taken to make it *look* like a mugging.'

'But the watch was only found after my client became the prime suspect.'

'Even without the watch, the direct nature of the stab wound, almost straight rather than at an angle, suggests an element of premeditation that is not consistent with a spontaneous killing occurring during the course of a mugging.'

'But it doesn't necessarily imply a *ritual* killing either.'

'Not in isolation. You have to understand that it's all about probabilities. The single straight thrust of the knife didn't make it a ritual killing, but it made mugging or a rage attack less likely. The positioning of the hand added to the likelihood of ritual killing.'

'Don't many ritual killings involve slashes, such as to the throat or multiple thrusts of the knife?'

'They can, but they don't have to.'

'So the fact of a single straight thrust of the knife is not a distinguishing feature of ritual murder?'

'Not on its own. But there's also the position of the hand, as I keep mentioning and as you keep ignoring.'

'The witness will confine himself to answering the questions,' said the magistrate.

'If the purpose of the attack had been to kill, would there have been any *need* for more than one stab wound, given that the single stab wound was so effective?'

'No, but to be sure of killing with a single thrust, the attacker would have had to have had some detailed knowledge of anatomy. I asked Philip Neuman several questions about human anatomy and was able to establish that he has no such knowledge, ruling out that possibility.'

'*Why* does it rule it out?'

'Because he couldn't have done it as a premeditated murder without such knowledge.'

'But someone else could, couldn't they?'

Saul Albion's face went a bright shade of red. He had shown prejudice and effectively dealt a body blow to his own credibility.

'Yes, if you look at that fact in isolation.'

'And by the same token if Philip Neuman lacked the knowledge of anatomy sufficient for a premeditated killing then jealousy or no he could not have done it with the intention of killing?'

'No indeed. My theory is that he killed his brother in a fit of anger and then decided to steal the watch.'

'About the placing of the hand. Could it not simply have been placed across the body after the watch was taken?'

'Yes, but the question is *why* was it placed there. A ritualistic act is one explanation.'

'But only *one*, Dr Albion. And not the only one. The thief or killer had taken what he wanted. Now all he had to do was put the arm down.'

'But why not just drop the arm, Mr Freeman. That is why I suggest either a ritualistic act or affection for the victim. Possibly both.'

'Couldn't the hand have been put there out of some instinctive sense of tidiness?'

'Now I suppose you're going to say the killer was a Virgo,' mocked Albion, grinning broadly.

'Is that any more absurd than your hypothesizing that he was a pagan?'

'In my opinion.'

'But then again, you didn't say in your profile of the killer that he was a pagan, only that the killing had ritualistic elements.'

'As does paganism,' said Albion flatly.

'As do Judaism, Christianity and Islam,' said Freeman. 'But we'll get on to that later. First let me ask you this. You said of the Rolex watch, and I quote: "Based on the fact that it was found to have been discarded I would conclude not merely that this was a deliberate attempt to make it look like robbery but that there was an element of jealousy involved, as if the perpetrator wanted to *be* like the deceased, or even had tried to be, but failed." Why do you not simply conclude that the watch was taken to make it look like robbery?'

'It was discarded far from the scene of the murder. That suggests that the murderer wore it for a while and then decided to get rid of it, possibly when he panicked or realized that it could incriminate him.'

'But why does that suggest the jealousy of an acquaintance rather than the greed of a stranger?'

'Because a stranger would not have been afraid to be seen wearing it in the way that an acquaintance would. A stranger would not be likely to meet someone who would recognize the watch or be suspicious of it.'

'But the killing was reported in the news, national as well as local. Maybe he feared that he would attract suspicion *as a result* of those reports if he continued wearing the watch. And whether it was a mugging or an assassination made to look like a mugging, maybe he discarded the watch on his *normal* route or in an area *he knew well.*'

'There is nothing specific to support that viewpoint,' said Albion, writhing awkwardly.

'But as an explanation of where and why the watch was discarded, it is at least as possible as your theory about jealousy.'

'Only when viewed in isolation.'

'Now let's turn to this matter of Philip Neuman's paganism, which seems to have you so fascinated. You said earlier that the practice of witchcraft is "fully consistent with the positioning of the hands". What does this phrase "fully consistent" mean?'

'Well, I should think it's self-explanatory,' said Albion.

'Let me see if I've understood, Dr Albion. Are you saying that the positioning of the hands is not consistent with any explanation *other* than paganistic ritual?'

'No, of course not!' the psychologist snapped. 'As you well know, all I'm saying is that it is *fully consistent* with that explanation.'

'Oh, I *see*!' said Freeman mockingly. 'You mean it is consistent with several explanations of which paganistic ritual is *one*.'

'Yes,' said Albion. 'It is consistent with several explanations and one of them is indeed paganistic ritual, which in turn is consistent with the lifestyle of the accused, along with several other facts which I have already pointed out!'

'I shan't warn the witness again,' said the magistrate out of the side of his mouth.

'Is paganism in fact more ritualistic than monotheistic religions?'

'In my opinion,' said Albion weakly.

'More ritualistic than a Roman Catholic Mass or a three-part Jewish Sabbath service or Muslims praying five times a day?'

'Those are just prayers and services, not rituals.'

'What about circumcision and baptism? Aren't they somewhat ritualistic?'

'Well, circumcision is part of the Jewish tradition. He was brought up as a Jew,' said Albion, smiling smugly, until he realized that he had alerted Freeman to another response and would no longer be able to spring it this again at the trial.

'But he turned his back on that tradition, didn't he?'

'So he said.'

'Well, which is he, Dr Albion, a committed witch or a crypto-Jew?'

'I don't know.'

'If you don't know, then on what basis can you draw conclusions about him?'

'As a professed practitioner of witchcraft he is a likely suspect.'

'Because the victim's hand was placed across his chest?'

'Yes,' said Albion, realizing that it was sounding increasingly absurd. 'Together with the fact that the accused had apparently abandoned the Jewish ethic.'

'Ah, yes,' said Freeman. 'The archetypal barbarous pagan with no inhibitions against murder.'

'It isn't an archetype,' said Albion, not waiting for the next question. 'It's a realistic characterization based on pagan literature.'

'Which presumably you have read in some detail.'

'I do my research thoroughly,' said the psychologist, gaining in confidence.

'So thoroughly that you concluded that *north* European pagans were more violent than their Christian or Moorish counterparts in ancient times.'

'Well . . . in *ancient* times they were all barbaric and cruel by today's standards,' replied Albion with a deprecating gesture of his hand.

'Quite so, Dr Albion, and such things as slavery or the death penalty for stealing more than five shillings were par for the course in *many* cultures.'

'Exactly.'

'But do you have any proof that modern practitioners of wisecraft are more likely to kill than modern monotheists?'

'Wisecraft?' repeated the psychologist, confused.

'Another name for Wicca or witchcraft,' said Freeman. 'I thought you did your homework.'

'In my opinion, a readiness to kill is more part of the pagan culture than it is of the culture of monotheism.'

'I'm not sure that Salman Rushdie would agree with you.'

'I'm talking about the West, Mr Freeman.'

'Northern Ireland? Sarajevo?'

'Those are *political* disputes!'

'What's that got to do with it?'

'Political disputes very often blind people to their innate sense of moral duty.'

'But pagans, you would have us believe, have no such innate sense of duty to begin with?'

'Well, perhaps innate is the wrong word. But certainly pagans have a different attitude to killing, if only because they have a different attitude to death.'

'Oh really, Dr Albion. In what way?'

'They believe that death is part of a merging with a great natural whole.'

'Don't orthodox monotheists also believe in life after death?'

'But most monotheists are not orthodox. They just have that underlying seed of the Judeo-Christian cultural inhibition against the commission of murder.'

'Do you have any documented statistics to show that in proportion to their numbers more murders or violent crimes are committed by pagans than those who profess to monotheistic faiths?'

'No, but you can prove anything with statistics.'

'Well, in *this* case it would seem that you *can't*. No further questions.'

Freeman sat down triumphantly.

The prosecutor then called several witness to testify to the finding of the watch and the identification of its ownership via the guarantee records. Then he called his final witness of the day, a scientist in the DNA analysis section of the Met Lab. Freeman realized that this was to be Leonard Stewart's surprise evidence. The defence lawyer looked back at the dock, in time to see his client sit forward with interest when the witness's area of expertise was stated for the record. But it wasn't just interest. It was fear.

'Professor Wade,' the prosecutor began. 'You conducted an examination of the watch together with an assistant, is that correct?'

'Yes.'

'And what did you find?'

'We found a single hair follicle trapped in the winder mechanism, possibly a hair from the arm or wrist that had got caught there when the wearer closed the winder, perhaps after adjusting the time.'

'And what did you do with this hair?'

'Well, the root was intact so we were able to analyse its DNA.'

'And how did you go about doing this?'

'We looked for so-called Variable Numbers of Tandem Repeats using a test called Restriction Fragment Length Polymorphism or RFLP for short.'

He started to explain the test, but the magistrate held up his hand.

'There's no need to explain the details of the test. I am familiar with it. Just tell us what you found.'

'Professor Wade was more disappointed than relieved at this, having brought several colourful charts and a pointer with him to help in his explanation.

'When I compared the DNA with that of the accused at six loci, two bands at each locus, I found inclusions, more commonly known as matches, at every locus.'

There was a rustling sound from the dock. Freeman looked round to see his client frantically scribbling a note.

'Allowing for an allele probability of point zero seven,

or seven per cent,' Wade continued, 'the likelihood of this degree of matching by chance is less than one in a million million.'

There was a gasp from the spectators' section.

'No further questions,' said the prosecutor, unable to conceal his delight at the knowledge that this would make the final edition of the evening papers.

As the prosecutor took his seat, the red-faced accused handed his hastily scribbled note to his lawyer. Freeman looked at the note and rose, quickly, determined to counter the influence of this evidence before the adjournment.

'Professor Wade, when you said the possibility of such a match occurring by chance was less than one in a million million, did you mean between members of the same family or between strangers?'

'Between strangers.'

'And what is the possibility between people who are directly related to one another?'

'Well, it depends on what sort of relationship.'

'Indeed. Don't monozygotic twins in fact inherit *identical* DNA from their parents?'

'Yes, but Philip and Tony Neuman were not monozygotic, despite the physical resemblance.'

'Nevertheless, the likelihood of a match by chance is higher amongst *any* siblings, is it not?'

'It is.'

'And isn't it a fact that the probability of a match by chance at a single locus using two bands is estimated to be about point two five or twenty-five per cent?'

'As a rough order of approximation, yes.'

'So the likelihood of a match by chance between siblings in the case of six loci is one in four to the power of six, which is one in four thousand and ninety-six?'

'Yes, but that is just an approximation.'

'And that's in the case of siblings in general, not specifically twins.'

'Yes.'

'Then is there not a fairly substantial possibility that

this hair follicle came from *Tony* Neuman and not Philip Neuman?'

'No,' said Professor Wade quietly.

'What do you mean, no?' asked Freeman, puzzled by the professor's quiet defiance.

'Because we also had a reference blood sample taken from Tony Neuman at the mortuary and marked by the pathologist for continuity,' said the witness triumphantly. 'We took a DNA sample from this blood and ran it in a parallel channel alongside the samples from Philip Neuman and the hair follicle sample and we found three bands that didn't match the hair follicle sample or the sample from Philip Neuman – in other words three *exclusions*. This proved conclusively that the hair follicle could *not* have come from Tony Neuman.'

Freeman looked over at Leonard Stewart to see him grinning like a Cheshire cat. Then he looked back at the dock. But his client wouldn't meet his eyes.

PART III

LEAD

'Who chooseth me must give and hazard all he hath.'

William Shakespeare,
The Merchant of Venice

22

*'The judge will decide the case, acquitting the
innocent and condemning the guilty.'*

Deuteronomy 24:16

'You're going to have to start telling me the truth!' said
Freeman. '*If* you want me to save you.'

'I'm *telling* you the truth,' said the boy, sobbing into
his arms.

They were in the boys' bedroom at the Neuman household in Golders Green. Miriam Neuman had indicated that
she wanted to stay with them, in case she had something
to contribute.

'He's *my* son!' she had told Freeman forcefully. 'The
only one I've got left!'

But Freeman thought that Phil didn't want to talk in her
presence, and he sensed that whatever Phil was holding
back, he had a better chance of extracting it from him in
a one-to-one face-off than a three-way family conference.
So she made herself a cup of tea and sat in the living
room tensely, while the men went upstairs to discuss
the case.

They both sat on chairs which they half turned to face
each other. Freeman saw the tension on his client's face

249

and knew that the boy was expecting a grilling. He would
not be disappointed.

'OK, now, let me give it to you straight, Phil. I can only
help you if you're honest with me!'

'I *am* being honest with you.'

'OK, then you tell me how come they found a hair
follicle from *your* wrist in the winder of your brother's
watch if you didn't take it from him and wear it.'

'OK, look, I may have tried the watch on once. It must
have been from then. They can't say when the follicle
got there.'

'Do you expect them to believe that?'

'They will if you make them.'

'Do you expect *me* to believe it?'

'Whose side are you on?'

'Look, don't be cheeky, Phil, or you can find another
lawyer.'

'I'm sorry. I just don't understand why you don't believe
me. Objectively speaking, they can't place the hair follicle
getting caught there at any particular time.'

'No, but how did it get stuck in the winder? You must
have not just tried it on but changed the time.'

'I may have played with the time . . . for a joke. I can't
remember.'

'Well, you'd better remember.'

'Look, Mr Freeman, you're not being entirely fair with
me.'

'You're stepping out of line again,' said the lawyer in
a warning tone.

'No, listen. Just listen for a minute.' He sounded hasty
and nervous, as if there was something he wanted to get
off his chest. 'When you first came to me and offered to
represent me, you told me that you were limited in what you
could say or try to prove on my behalf. You said you could
only set out to prove something if I told you it was true. Now
I've never been in trouble with the law before and I don't
know all the ins and outs of the legal system, but I'm pretty
smart for my age and I think I can read between the lines.'

He paused, looking at Freeman for a response.

'Go on,' said Freeman, encouragingly.

'OK, well, I understood that to mean that lawyers often represent guilty clients, but they can't do it if the client says he's guilty. Isn't that right?'

'Not entirely. They can plead in mitigation, but they can't argue that he's innocent.'

'OK. I also understood it to mean that even if the client is innocent, they can't lie for the client or make out a false defence.'

'That's right,' said Freeman, puzzled, but just beginning to comprehend.

'Well, if that's the case, then you were hinting before that if I have something to hide, something that goes against my defence, I mustn't tell you. Speaking hypothetically, of course. So why are you coming on so strong now and demanding that I tell you the truth?'

Freeman sat forward, intrigued. 'Because if you send me out there unprepared, then I won't be able to put up the best defence for you. Now, having said that, I take your point. There are certain circumstances in practice in which a client might have a better chance of getting away with it if he lies to his lawyer and the court. And there may also be circumstances in which the client has something to hide that might emerge if he presents an honest defence. Like the wealthy businessman whose truthful alibi is that he was having it off in the sack with his secretary at the time of the offence. He might stand to lose more by telling the truth than by lying. Even if it leads to him being convicted of an offence like driving without due care and attention.

'Not that I'm endorsing such dishonest behaviour, you understand. But I can envisage circumstances when it might be in the client's best interest. Only I can't see that it applies in *this* type of case. So perhaps you'll enlighten me. Tell me *why* should one need to present a bogus defence? What could you possibly have to hide? *Hypothetically*, of course.'

'Well, let's say the client is afraid. Let's say he knows

something about the people who killed his brother, but
those people are dangerous . . . and powerful. And he's
afraid of them.'

'Afraid that they'll kill him?'

'Possibly.'

'Why?'

'Because he knows too much.'

'About what?'

'Let's just say . . . about what his brother was doing.'

'With these dangerous people?'

'Yes.'

'But if he knows too much then there's a danger that
they might kill him anyway. After all, they want to stop
him talking. If he knows too much he's a threat to them.
Even if he doesn't talk today, he might talk tomorrow. If
these people are as dangerous and powerful as you say,
then they would surely want to kill him *before* he talks.'

'But what if they don't know how much he knows?'

'How do you mean?'

Freeman was leaning forward eagerly now. He was getting somewhere and he wanted to keep up the momentum.

'Suppose that, before he died, his brother left details of
the entire conspiracy on a computer file.'

Freeman recalled the details that Mrs Neuman had given
him when he first took the case.

'This would be the computer file that these people were
after when they burgled his home and stole his computer
and diskettes.'

'That's right.'

'OK, but if they stole the computer and the diskettes,
where does that leave his brother?'

'Let's say there was a copy?'

'On your laptop?' asked Freeman, his eyes widening with
interest.

'No, in Tony's personal file area on CompuServe.'

'You mean he used it as a back-up system?'

'Let's just say . . . hypothetically.'

'OK,' said Freeman. 'What next?'

'Well, let's say further that I had a copy of his access password and was able to access his CompuServe account and download the file.'

'You mean you've got the details of this whole conspiracy?' asked Freeman, his eyes now alive with the fire of excitement.

'It's not so easy. The file was encrypted.'

'When you say encrypted,' Freeman asked, his enthusiasm now tempered with restraint, 'do you mean with one of those simple passwords like in a word processor or file compression program, or something more powerful like PGP.'

'More on the lines of the latter. You see the file itself was a large graphics Interchange Format file. But he used something called steganography.'

'Stenography?' asked Freeman, bewildered.

'*Stega*nography. A system for hiding data files within picture or music files.'

'I don't understand,' said Freeman, although given his own scientific background he was beginning to.

'Picture and music files are fault-tolerant. You can change the least significant bit of many of the bytes in those files without noticeably changing the content. Steganography is a method of hiding data by distributing its bits in place of the low-order bits of a music or picture file.'

'And to recover it afterwards you simply extract those bits from the file and reconstitute them in a new file?'

'Exactly, Mr Freeman. Only the thing is, the bits aren't placed in the picture or sound file in linear fashion. They're distributed in a pseudo-random sequence using a passphrase.'

'So the only way to recover the hidden data file is to know the passphrase.'

'Exactly.'

'And I don't suppose you were close enough to your brother to know his passphrase.'

'I was the one who taught him about steganography,

253

and one of the things I taught him was not to share his passphrase with anyone, not even me.'

'Yet you knew his password for CompuServe.'

'That was different. We sometimes used each other's computers. So we set it up that our CompuServe passwords were stored on each other's machines. We both had premium accounts which gave us twenty hours a month on line. We weren't going to cheat each other by using each other's accounts, if that's what you mean.'

'So what you're saying is you've got a file from Tony's personal file area on CompuServe which you *think* has secret information about this conspiracy. But you can't actually retrieve the information.'

'That's not exactly what I'm saying, Mr Freeman.'

'Well, then, would you please spell it out. Because I'm getting rather tired of this sparring and I'd like to come up with a credible defence before we open tomorrow morning.'

'You said before that the only way to recover the file is to know the passphrase. But that isn't entirely correct. You can either know it, or you can guess it.'

'What do you mean, "guess it"? You mean you can guess the phrase that your brother chose?'

'Not exactly. But there are some very good passphrase guesser programs available on the market or in shareware.'

'But there must be tens of thousands of possible passphrases.'

'And these programs cycle *through* them by the thousands, taking them from standard sources like Shakespeare and Winston Churchill.'

'You mean your brother chose a standard phrase rather than something original?'

'Even a standard phrase is hard to guess if you use a mixture of capital and lower-case letters in it. But a good passphrase guesser tries all the permutations of capital and lower case as well. Only it has to actually test every possible password by trying it out and seeing if it finds any coherent text with recognisable words. I ran it for nine days.'

The boy seemed to be suppressing a grin, almsot as if he were trying to tantalize his lawyer.

'Cut to the bottom line, Phil!' snapped Freeman, losing patience. 'Do you know your brother's passphrase or not?'

'I do. And I've already looked at the file.'

'Well, let's see it, for God's sake.'

The boy switched on the laptop computer and waited while it went through the cycle of 'booting up' its system files. Thirty seconds later he was using the trackball and control keys to open a file. Then he turned the computer screen towards Emmett Freeman and leaned back.

Freeman pulled his chair over to the writing desk so that he could sit close to the screen and proceeded to read through the file while his smug-looking client went over to one of the beds and sat down, ready to unwind now that he had finally got the story off his chest. Freeman's mouth dropped open as the nature of the conspiracy unfolded. The file described the recombinant DNA process and named the company involved. But, interestingly, it did not name the conspirators. Freeman was curious about the file's history. He knew that this word processing program kept a log of when a file was created and when it was last modified. Without letting the boy see what he was doing, he looked at the 'Summary Info . . .' in the file menu. The file had been created several months ago, but what was far more interesting was the 'Last Modified' date. It was given as '20/07/97', seventeen days after Tony Neuman had been killed. File creation dates could change if a file was opened on one disk and resaved (as distinct from copied) to another. But the file creation date was when Tony was still alive. The modification date was over two weeks after his death. This could only mean one thing. Philip Neuman had modified the file! The question was, had he added something to it or taken something out?

'I do solemnly, sincerely and truly declare and affirm that

the evidence I shall give shall be the truth, the whole truth and nothing but the truth.'

'State your name and occupation.'

'My name is Philip David Neuman,' the accused stated in the clear tone that Freeman had coached him in, 'and my occupation is student – if that's still considered an occupation,' he added with a cheeky grin on his face.

'Kindly refrain from levity Mr Neuman,' said the magistrate in a quiet but authoritative tone.

'I'm sorry, Your Worship,' said the accused, remembering Freeman's advice about this being the man who would decide whether he would go free today or go on to face a criminal trial in the crown court.

Emmett Freeman rose and straightened his papers, giving his client time to get relaxed and accustomed to being up there on the witness stand.

'Mr Neuman, the deceased in this case, Anthony Aaron Neuman, was your brother, is that correct?'

'Yes,' said the boy weakly.

'Speak up,' said Freeman encouragingly. He knew that the volume at which a witness speaks plays a major part in their credibility.

'Yes.'

'Now would it be fair to say that you and your brother were very close?'

'Yes.'

'So close that you knew what sort of things he was getting up to?'

'Yes.'

'And could you tell the court, please, what he was doing in the period leading up to his death?'

'He was engaged in some scientific work for a large corporation.'

'Now when you say scientific work, could you explain what you mean?'

'My brother was very good at chemistry and biology and he was skilled in what is called recombinant DNA technology.'

'Recombinant DNA technology,' Freeman repeated. 'Is that what is better known as gene splicing?'

'That's right,' said the boy, gaining in confidence as he noticed that he was getting the respectful attention of those around him.

'And could you tell us, in layman's terms, what this entails.'

'Well, all the characteristics of any living organism, be it a plant, a bacterium or an animal, are contained within the DNA. It is, if you like, the *blueprint* for the organism. It contains the instructions to make it. These instructions are translated by a process of several stages into the making of amino acids that make up the proteins that make up the being.'

'All of this is well understood by the court,' said Roger Trent, reluctant to disturb the boy with his impatience, but anxious to expedite the proceedings.

'All right, but what isn't so widely known, by the layman, is that when a plant can be used to produce a certain substance, like, say, morphine or cocaine, it's one particular sequence of the DNA that produces that particular substance.'

'And what is the significance of that?' asked Freeman.

'The significance is that it has long been possible to isolate certain sequences of DNA by cutting them in selected places with what are known as 'cutting enzymes'. These are the same enzymes that are used to cut DNA for use in DNA profiling. The point is that one can cut out sequences of DNA that produce particular substances, such as antibodies or drugs, and splice them into the DNA of other organisms.'

'And what use is this?'

'Well, some organisms are hardier and less vulnerable to the environment. In some cases a valuable substance is produced in quantities that are too small and it is needed in larger quantities. It can be done to give food crops a protective coat against ice. It can be used to increase a person's immunity to certain specific diseases. It can be

David Kessler

used to mass-produce medicines that can only be extracted from their natural source in small quantities.'

'And how was your brother using it?'

'He used it to extract the DNA for the active ingredient of the coca plant, that is cocaine, and splice it into an aromatic plant that can be used in the production of perfume. The plant looks no different to its usual form on the outside, but it has different properties.'

By this stage everyone in the courtroom was sitting bolt upright, except for those few who were *really* interested, who were sitting forward. But all eyes were on the accused, and they were now hanging on to his every word.

'And what does this mean in practice?' asked Freeman.

'It means that this aromatic plant contains a macromolecule including a cocaine-like component. Drugs work by interacting with molecules in the brain called receptors. A simple way to think about it is to imagine a key designed for a particular lock. If the key fits the lock it works, if it doesn't fit the lock then it doesn't work. This macromolecule is like a skeleton key with a special extension to fit the lock that responds to cocaine. In other words the macromolecule matches the cocaine receptors. If the genetically engineered plant were used in the creation of a perfume, the perfume would contain the macromolecule and produce a mild form of the same effect as cocaine. Because of the low vapour pressure, the effect would be very mild, but it would still be addictive. It's just that the users wouldn't be aware of why they felt that way.'

'But couldn't someone simply use the coca plant in the production of a perfume to achieve the same effect?' asked Freeman.

'Like I said, the effect would in any case be mild and they'd have to use a lot of it. Furthermore, if their production facilities were searched, the cocaine or coca plant would be found there. In contrast, if you were to search the facilities where the perfume was being produced using this genetically engineered aromatic plant, you wouldn't find any cocaine or coca plants. That's the difference.'

258

'And to the best of your knowledge is this process actually being used?'

'Yes, by the company for which Tony did the work.'

'And which company is that?'

'La Contessa.'

A gasp went through the courtroom.

'And in which product is it used?'

'A perfume called Gold.'

A bigger gasp.

'And with which person in La Contessa did your brother actually have contact when he did this work?'

'The man whose body was thrown into the Grand Union Canal at the same spot where someone threw away the watch that my brother was wearing when he died: the late Fabian Digby.'

The collective intake of air almost rustled the clerk's papers.

'How did you feel when you heard the magistrate say they were dismissing the charges?'

They were on the steps of the courtbuilding, running the gauntlet of press and television reporters.

'I'll let my lawyer answer that.'

Before they left the courtroom, Freeman had whispered in the boy's ear and told him to say this and not to answer any questions directly.

'My client is very happy to have been vindicated and spared the pain and suffering of a trial. My client suffered a deep and severe loss when his brother was murdered and these false accusations and the publicity surrounding them have only added to his torment. My client and his mother hope now that the press will leave them alone and allow them time to grieve for their loved one, something that they have never really had time to do until now with all the investigative pressures upon them. My client has expressed the hope that he will not be subject to media pressure.'

Freeman knew that it was only a matter of time before

the Neuman family were bombarded by calls from the press offering them large sums of money for their story, and quite possibly also from agents and publicists. But he also knew that if what his client had told him was true then they were in danger. Of course, he had now given the impression that all the information had been placed in the hands of the police and that they had nothing more. But if Phil started talking to the press then those who had chosen to silence his brother might come after him too. So it was agreed all round that they would say nothing to the press, at least for the time being.

'Do you think your client would have been convicted if he'd gone to trial in the light of such damning evidence as his own confession?' asked a man from a red-banner daily tabloid.

'No honest jury would have convicted a man on the strength of a confession alone.'

'What about the DNA evidence?' asked a reporter from a more middle-brow Sunday tabloid.

'We all know about cross-sample contamination and contaminated equipment in Home Office laboratories. The DNA could have come from his brother and got contaminated through careless handling. Apart from that, all the DNA evidence purported to show was that my client had worn the watch at some stage. That hardly makes him a murderer.'

'So who does your client think murdered his brother?' persisted the reporter from the Sunday tabloid.

'That's for the police to investigate now that they have all the material. And we hope that now they know they won't just take the easy route to closing the file, they'll get up off their backsides and start doing their job.'

'Do *you* have a theory about who killed Anthony Neuman, Mr Freeman?' asked the red-banner tabloid reporter.

'Whoever killed Fabian Digby,' suggested Freeman.

23

'. . . truth has stumbled in the streets, honesty
cannot enter.'

Isaiah 59:14

'So who did?' asked Karen.

Freeman took advantage of the fact that he was positioning
the tray on the wooden rest to think about this question
for a minute. He had been sure, when she accepted his
invitation, that he was on to a good thing. But now it was
beginning to look as if all she wanted to talk about was
the case. She had given him gentle encouragement when
they had dinner together, but treated their relationship as
strictly professional when they went to the Met Lab,
and it wasn't clear by that stage whether she intended
the relationship to go any further. To some extent the
picture was complicated as a result of Freeman becoming
Philip Neuman's solicitor of record. But if she hadn't
wanted to complicate matters, then why did she bring
him along to the lab at all? Was she pumping him for
information?

'Presumably someone to do with La Contessa or the
takeover,' said the lawyer, as he started carving the suc-
culent chicken. He had roasted it to perfection, a golden

brown with mildly spicy aroma that made the mouth water like Pavlov's proverbial dogs.

'But surely the person who had the most to lose was Digby himself,' she argued, as she scooped Brussels sprouts on to both their plates. 'I mean, he was the one who owned the company and he must have known what Tony Neuman was doing. He was the chief beneficiary, after all.'

Freeman started depositing the sliced pieces of chicken breast on to Karen's bone china plate while she used a large tablespoon to put the finely cut golden-brown roast potatoes on to his.

'He was the chief beneficiary as far as the outside world knew,' said Freeman. 'But remember that there's still that unsolved mystery about where he got the money from. He didn't have enough in liquid assets for this sort of deal and, as I told you before, it's widely believed that he was fronting for others.'

'I thought you said that was just "Square Mile gossip"?'

Freeman smiled, pleased that Karen had remembered his words.

'We know that he had backers. It's just that until Philip Neuman's committal hearing it wasn't clear how sinister the whole thing was. Now we know what they were doing, the question of who financed the deal becomes a matter of paramount importance.'

'The fact that your client managed to dig up some dirt on your former client doesn't necessarily mean that the murder of his brother had anything to do with it. He could have been using that as a smokescreen.'

'Counsel for the prosecution evidently didn't think so.'

'What are you getting at?' asked Karen.

'Don't you think it's strange that he was so quick to drop the charges after Phil Neuman blew the whistle on La Contessa?'

'That could just mean that he had the dirt on them and they were pulling strings behind the scenes to cover up the affair. That doesn't mean he didn't kill his brother.'

'The fact is the evidence showed that his brother knew things that were a threat to certain powerful interests – powerful enough to kill a man like Fabian Digby.'

Karen swept a strand of blond hair aside and looked Freeman in the eyes.

'How do we know that the evidence was genuine?'

'What do you mean?'

'Maybe he forged it. We know your client is a computer whiz kid. Maybe he just typed up the entire document, based on a few fragments that he overheard or a few chance remarks that his brother made. I'm not saying it wasn't true but how did he get the file?'

Freeman told her about the encrypted file that Tony had uploaded on to his personal file area on CompuServe and how the data file was concealed with steganography.

'And how did he retrieve the file?' asked Karen sceptically.

'He downloaded a passphrase guessing program from the Internet and ran it for several days at a stretch,' explained Freeman.

'You'd think a whiz kid like that would have written his own.'

Freeman smiled bitterly, remembering his own years as a student, and the accusations that had once been levelled against him.

'Einstein used to say never bother to commit to memory anything you can look up.'

'OK, so let's say that Digby was part of this conspiracy to sell an addictive perfume. Who would have killed him?'

'The people he was fronting for, perhaps.'

Karen pursed her lips, her eyes focused on a spot on the tablecloth as she pondered this theory. What would have seemed outlandish only a few days ago now seemed quite plausible.

'So you're saying that if we find out who financed the deal then we'll find out who killed both Anthony Neuman *and* Fabian Digby.'

'*Exactly*,' said Freeman, 'or at least who was behind the

killings. If they hired a professional we may never know who the actual culprit was.'

He put his plate in his place setting and sat down, waiting for her to start eating. He felt so much more at ease in his own home than he did faking sophistication in a high-class restaurant. At heart he was really a family man without a family, and sitting here in his home, opposite a beautiful woman, he felt almost as if he finally had what had always eluded him in the years of chasing the pot of gold at the end of the rainbow: a woman to share his life with, and not just the one-night stands of the yuppie singles circuit. The decade of hard graft after he acquired and then lost his university degree and the consolidation of his position when it was finally restored had all taken their toll on his personal life.

He had a small but comfortable home and he had money put aside for a secure future. But what he didn't have was all too clear and made all the more painfully obvious now that he was getting a glimpse of it. For Karen was not like the girls he pulled in bars and nightclubs. She hadn't come here on the first date and she had insisted on bringing her own car rather than being picked up. She was a career woman, but he had seen on her desk a picture of two young children whom she said were her nephew and niece. He couldn't escape the feeling that Karen too was looking for something more than just a career.

'So how do we go about penetrating the wall of secrecy behind the La Contessa deal?' She asked, breaking the silence and cutting into Freeman's daydream.

'It won't be easy. The deal went through Caribbean banks – and they have tougher secrecy laws than Switzerland.'

'Your Mossad friends must have some information,' she said with an encouraging smile.

'Like I told you,' said Freeman, alerted by her tone to the fact that from her point of view this was still business more than pleasure, 'they informed me that they couldn't tell me anything. Just like I suspected.'

'The Digby family seemed to think otherwise.'

'What makes you think that?' he asked.

'Because they asked you to investigate. They wouldn't have done that unless they felt you were in a good position to get results.'

'OK, I'm going to take a chance on you. I suppose that now that my client's in the clear it's the least I can do. They told me that the takeover of La Contessa was financed by the government of Bahakabir. Fabian Digby was apparently a friend of Hassan Abed Zaidan, the brother of Ismail Abed Zaidan.'

'And who,' asked Karen with cool anger, 'is *Ismail* Abed Zaidan?'

'The Minister for Arms Procurement in Bahakabir. One of the most powerful men in the Middle East and one of the richest men in the world.'

'And why didn't you tell me this before?' she asked through her teeth.

'I had a client in jail awaiting trial for murder. I had grounds for believing that the cases were linked and a duty to help my client.'

'Oh, I see,' said Karen angrily. 'So while I was sharing information and co-operating with you, you were keeping things from me and not trusting me.'

'Look, at the time . . .' He paused and took a deep breath, realizing that his voice was rising in volume to match her angry tone. He had no reason to be angry, even if he had nothing to apologize for either. 'At the time, I had a client accused of murder. I had a duty to him, a legal and professional duty to present the best case for him and to do nothing to prejudice that case. I was whistling in the dark, wandering up and down blind alleys, putting feelers out and trying to get to grips with the case. For all I knew the Hassan-Digby connection might have led slap-bang up against evidence that incriminated my client.'

'And for all you knew your client might have been guilty! It's still by no means certain that he wasn't!'

'But I still had a duty to defend him.'

'Then you should have been straight with me! And

not led me to believe that we were working together.'

'We *were* working together,' said Freeman, his tone
almost pleading.

'But towards different ends! I was trying to catch
criminals. You were trying to secure an acquittal or a
dismissal of charges for your client!'

'But you knew that,' said Freeman helplessly.

Her face was now bright red with anger.

'Look, I put my career on the line telling you my doubts
about the way Chief Superintendent DuPaul handled the
business with the Met Lab and you couldn't trust me with
a piece of information that you got from your Mossad
friends.'

'I'm sorry,' he said, holding his hands out in a gesture
of appeasement.

'I'm sorry too,' she said, her napkin throwing on to
the table like a prizefighter throwing in the towel. 'I
thought we had a relationship going here. It seems I was
wrong.'

And without another word she got up and grabbed
her jacket.

'Karen?' said Freeman, leaping to his feet and following
her to the door. But she didn't even turn to meet his eyes,
or let him see the tears gathering in hers. She opened the
door and quietly but quickly slipped out. He was about
to go after her, but the phone rang and he grabbed the
receiver on impulse.

'Emmett Freeman!' he snapped in anger at the ill-timed
call.

'*Ata coh-ess*?' an interrogative tone came back at him
in Hebrew.

'Yaniv?' he asked tentatively, surprised that his Mossad
contact should call him at home. 'No, of course I'm
not angry.'

'I think I may have something for you.'

'Can you tell me?'

'Not over the phone.'

'How about the Internet? I can tell you my PGP signature for confirmation and send you the full key by e-mail.'

'No, you'll have to come in.'

'Now?'

'Are you kidding? It's Friday. Come in on Sunday morning.'

'You work Sunday?'

'Just like Israel!' said Yaniv, wishing Freeman could see his smile.

'I don't think we can afford to do it DuPaul's way any longer,' said Hassan, puffing on his thick Havana cigar.

They were sitting in the garden again, but this time there were just two of them: Hassan and Mike.

'I don't see any prospect of doing it any other way,' said Mike.

'What's the matter?' asked Hassan. 'Are you going soft?'

'Soft has nothing to do with it,' snapped Mike angrily. 'The press are still following him around. There's no way I can get at him without being seen.'

'Send someone else. I can help you find someone.'

'You know I'm not like that. I always do my own dirty work.'

'Still trying to prove something?' Hassan mocked, the grin beneath his moustache taunting Mike.

'I've already proved all I need to prove. But I'm my own man and always will be.'

'So what do you intend to do?'

'Just because Phil Neuman's off the hook for killing his brother doesn't mean we can't put him on the defensive.'

'What do you have in mind? Framing him for killing Fabian?'

'That would be a bit tricky. But many people don't believe he didn't kill his brother.'

'Can he be tried again?'

'It never got to the crown court, so it probably could. But that's not the point. Even if he's in the clear as far as the law is concerned, he can still be hounded. He won't be the first man to be hounded by the press and public even when he's been cleared by the courts.'

'Perhaps. But I don't see how you can orchestrate it.'

'You're forgetting, Hassan, one of our brothers owns some significant holdings in the national press.'

The bedroom seemed different when he returned home after the committal hearing. What had once been 'our bedroom' was now just 'my bedroom'. At least that was how it felt. The real change had occurred a month ago. But it was only now, after the scab of his bereavement had been scratched away by others, before it had even had the chance to heal, that it was finally driven home to him. That he was now alone and that his best friend had been taken from him for ever.

It was the same two beds, their headboards against the same pale blue wall, the same walls adorned by pictures of molecules, program flow charts and bikini-clad young women. And yet it was different. It was now his lonely world instead of the warm, friendly world that he once shared with his brother. Strangely, the room seemed smaller now, more cramped, less spacious, even though he no longer had to share it. Time was when he and his brother had to edge past each other to get to opposite ends of the room. Now there would be no more of that amusing, even comical holding in of their breath to glide past each other as one went for the phone and the other went for the wardrobe. It was strange really. His brother had died weeks ago. And he had not been on remand during the committal proceedings. And yet it was only now, when all the legal shenanigans had been played out, that he finally found himself facing this black hole, this depressing emptiness, this nameless void.

At least, he told himself, I've avenged my brother. I've avenged him by hitting out at those who killed him. I've hit them where it really hurts, in their bank accounts. I've hurt their interests. I've hurt them in the way that damages them most. I've launched a frontal assault on their greed.

And yet, he told himself, that isn't really enough. They still haven't been caught, and probably never will be. Besides, he thought, I've only used half my ammunition. I have more to throw at them.

But before he could carry this thought any further, his emboldened heart was struck once again by a stab of fear. They've killed once – indeed more than once. And they could kill again. Already I've angered them by exposing their secrets with La Contessa. Already they're going to have to lose money taking Gold off the market. And there will be an investigation by the police, and heads will probably roll. They'll probably choose their own scapegoats and throw them to the wolves.

But they had more up their sleeves. For he knew what Emmett Freeman didn't. What he had chosen not to tell his lawyer. There was more than one file concealed in that picture. The first gave a technical description of the process as it related to the coca plant and to the aromatic plant that was used in the production of Gold. But it was the second file that he had held back, for he knew all too well what it contained.

He pulled his laptop computer out from the drawer by the bed and put in on the bureau. With a brisk gesture he opened it and switched it on, hopping impatiently from foot to foot while it booted up. Then he opened the second file and stared at its contents, although he already knew them all too well. Amid the welter of molecular diagrams and sequences of the letters A, C, G and T was a description of a chemistry process that consisted of using cutting enzymes at certain points of the DNA of the cannabis sativa plant so as to isolate the codon sequence for one of the active ingredients, followed by the insertion of that DNA into the DNA of the mango plant.

This in itself was not significant. DNA splicing as such was routine and countless specific examples of it could be described, which in many cases would be little more than academic exercises. But this was the work of someone

269

who had already shown a large multinational company how they could use the DNA from a nasally ingested drug to produce an addictive perfume, and, more importantly, they had done it. That same young genetics expert had isolated the DNA for one of the active ingredients of a drug that can be both smoked and orally imbibed and had identified an insertion point in the DNA of a plant that could be used to produce a soft drink – a soft drink with a tranquillizing effect.

More to the point, the work had been done for the same people who had created Gold. The question was, when and where were they going to market the drink?

'They've been having secret meetings with the daughter of the leader of a Pacific island. They don't usually talk business with women so we were alerted to the fact that it was something big.'

Yaniv took a sip of his Turkish coffee as Freeman threw the dice across the olivewood backgammon board. The embassy wasn't open to the public on Sundays, but some of the staff used it to catch up on their workload. In Yaniv's case this meant feeding limited volumes of information to his old army buddy over a game of *sheshbesh* and a cup of *botz*.

'I assume you're not going to tell me which island?' said Freeman, smiling.

'You assume right,' Yaniv replied, returning the smile.

The only light in the room came from the skylight and the only home comfort was the huge green-leaved potted plant in the corner.

'Any idea what these meetings are about?'

'We've used laser microphones and pieced together quite a bit. She's the daughter of an ageing dictator. She and her siblings are worried that the country is going to fall into disarray when the old man dies, so they're looking for some way to maintain order.'

'You mean because of rifts within the family?'

'Partly that and partly because the people are getting

restless. The death of the old man might be just what the people need.'

'And is Israel backing the old man?'

'No, we're not. We would be if the Americans were, but it's no longer politically correct and they don't need him. They'd rather not be associated with another moribund dictator.'

Again Freeman smiled. He was always impressed by Yaniv's command of the English language.

'Well, if this leader was so tough, why didn't he teach his children how to follow in his footsteps? Was he afraid that they'd do a King Lear on him?'

'No, he taught them all right. But we've seen strong leaders toppled before. And they don't know how to handle large-scale unrest.'

'I'd have thought that if they don't know anything else then they'd have the sense to fall back on the tried and tested methods.'

'The trouble is that they depend on exports to America and Europe. We all know that the Western liberal press run things in cycles. Different dictatorships take it in turns to become the pariah of the moment. This leader isn't just powerful, he's also corrupt and very rich. So are his kids. They have a finger in every pie, a hand in every deal. It's well known that if a foreign company wants to do business there, they have to cut a deal with one of the dictator's kids. They have fortunes that would make the Digby heirs turn green with envy. The last thing these spoilt brats want is to become isolated internationally and boxed in by sanctions when their old man dies and when they can't be sure that the army will back them if the treasury dries up.'

'So what's the score?' asked the lawyer, knowing that Yaniv had more to tell him and hoping that it would be interesting.

'Emmett, have you ever read *Brave New World*?'

'Aldous Huxley? Of course. Why?'

'You remember how they kept the lower orders happy? The deltas and epsilons?'

271

'Hypnopoedia? Couldn't be used effectively for intellectual education but worked like a charm for *moral*
education.'

'Exactly . . . and something else.'

Freeman threw his head back for a moment and tried
to remember a book that he had enjoyed so much in his
adolescence.

'Oh yes, Soma.'

'Soma,' Yaniv confirmed. 'The drug that gave people a
sense of euphoria and well-being. They all used it, even
the alphas and betas. But the Deltas and Epsilons had it
strictly rationed, given to them at the right time, and in
one scene it was sprayed into the air to quell a spontaneous
demonstration.'

'And in *Island* they chewed Moksha,' added Freeman,
wondering, belatedly, if this would divert the conversation
into a discussion about whether the books were philosophi-
cally contradictory. But Yaniv ignored the diverging road.

'They've got their own soma to deal with the deltas and
epsilons,' said Yaniv.

'And what is it?' asked Freeman, sitting forward eagerly.
'What *is* the "soma"?'

'They've apparently worked out a plan to produce and
sell a soft drink that has a pacifying effect.'

'*How?*' asked Freeman, knowing full well that if such
a drink existed it would have been produced by the KGB
or CIA a long time ago.

'Using gene splicing. Inserting an active ingredient of
cannabis sativa into the mango plant.'

'Tony Neuman?' asked Freeman incredulously.

'It may well have been the last thing he worked on before
he died.'

'But Phil never told me!'

'Perhaps Tony Neuman never wrote it down,' Yaniv
suggested.

Freeman felt himself becoming short of breath.

'Or perhaps Phil didn't want me to know.'

He was on his feet, picking up his mobile phone.

'Wait a minute, Emmett, you're winning the game.'
'I have to go. I've got to talk to him.'
'What's the problem?'
'If he held something back from me, God know's how he's planning to use it.'

24

'Your brother's blood cries out to me from the ground.'

Genesis 4:10

It was a long walk back to his car. Security was tight in Kensington, especially after the most recent bombing. If he'd parked any closer it would probably have been towed away. They didn't make special concessions for Jaguars.

He wasted no time getting in and bringing the engine to life in a hurry. He swung the steering wheel round and headed off into the weekend traffic. He remembered a time when Sundays used to be quiet days, almost like Saturdays in Jerusalem. But Sunday trading and the new culture of consumerism wrought by multicultural pluralism had changed all that. What had once been dreary days of staying at home or strolling in the park had now become days of commerce and big business. Freeman preferred it that way. When he wanted solitude he would go to the countryside.

But the downside of all this was that the road was now a shared resource, even on Sunday. And car ownership in general was increasing. What had once been open stretches of road were now congested thoroughfares, like the clogged-up arteries of an old man whose diet includes too much cholesterol. It did Freeman no good to have a car that could do nought to sixty in seven seconds if he didn't have a clear road on which to unleash that power. And it wasn't just his male ego that was on the line here, it was the well-being of his client.

But suddenly it hit him. He had another tool of the nineties at arm's reach. He slotted his mobile phone into the recharging holder linked to the car battery, put the speaker on and keyed in the number of the Neuman household.

'Yes?' an anxious woman's voice answered.

'Miriam Neuman?' said Freeman.

'Oh, it's you,' said Mrs Neuman, disappointed.

'I was phoning to speak to Phil,' said Freeman, realizing from her reply, and her tone, that he was too late.

'Oh, Mr Freeman,' she sobbed. 'I don't know what to do. He stormed out half an hour ago.'

'Stormed out? Why?'

'It was after he read what they said about him,' she answered, still crying.

'What *who* said about him?'

'The Sunday papers.'

'*Which* Sunday papers?'

He had read one of the Sunday broadsheets and seen nothing about Philip Neuman or the case.

She told him the name of the middle-brow tabloid that her son had read.

'And what did it say?' asked Freeman, puzzled more than frightened by this new development.

'It presented what they called the case against him. It said it wanted to give readers the chance to consider the evidence that was never put to the jury.'

'And what did he say about it?'

Freeman had been in a mild panic about Phil's safety as soon as Yaniv had told him about the genetic engineering on the mango plant. But now he was growing increasingly concerned.

'He said they presented the evidence against him but

didn't even bother asking him for his side of the story.'

'Did he say where he was going?'

There was a few seconds' hesitation.

'He said something about having it out with them.'

It was like cross-examining a witness for the other side. He was getting nowhere. Only he couldn't lead, because he didn't know the answer.

'With whom?'

'He didn't say.'

'Can you remember his exact words?'

'He said, "I'm going to have it out with those bastards who set me up."'

'That was it?'

'That's all I remember.'

'OK, thank you,' said Freeman.

'Do you have any idea where he could be, Mr Freeman?'

'No, but I'm going to get the paper now. It might give us a few clues.'

'But there's something else . . .' The line started to crackle. 'Mr Freeman?'

'What's that?' asked the lawyer.

'There was something I didn't tell you . . . something I've known for a long time. Perhaps we should have told you earlier, but . . .'

The line started to crackle again.

'Hallo, Mrs Neuman! I can't hear you!'

'. . . I said that Phil . . .'

The crackling continued unabated. He was driving between tall buildings and this sort of thing often happened. By the time he got clear, the connection had been broken. He decided not to call back. He had a pretty good idea of what Miriam Neuman was going to tell him. It was more important that he should find out where the boy was going. And Mrs Neuman had made it abundantly clear that she didn't have a clue about that. So he drove on and decided not to call her back until he had some good news.

276

He stopped off at an Iranian-owned newsagent and bought the Sunday paper that Miriam had told him about, and there it was, emblazoned across the front page. The actual story was on pages seven to nine. At the top it read: 'Who killed Tony Neuman?' The main headline, set against a large picture of Freeman and his client leaving the courtroom, read, 'The case against Philip Neuman a jury never heard.'

Freeman went to a nearby café and ordered a cup of coffee. He sat alone at a corner table letting the coffee cool while he read the story. Some of it was old hat, but not all of it.

Philip Neuman was quite clear that he had separated from Anthony by nine-fifteen at the latest . . .

The first witness to call his alibi into question was pizza waitress **Sandra Giles**. She told the police that she saw the brothers together at 9:35. She said she knew them from previous occasions when they had bought pizza there and that Philip actually waved to her. *But Philip Neuman claimed that they had separated at least 20 minutes earlier than that. A jury would have had to consider who was right, Philip Neuman or Sandra Giles. If they decided that Sandra Giles was right, they would have had to decide if Philip Neuman was mistaken or lying.*

The wording angered Freeman. As a lawyer he knew full well that human memory is frail, but most people would assume otherwise. If Sandra Giles said she saw Phil at 9.35 then she must have done, they would assume, for what reason would she have to lie? If she was right and Phil said they had already split up he must be lying. The possibility that she might be mistaken, or that Phil might be mistaken about the time rather than lying, would not be considered by a jury in practice. Her affirmative recollection of Phil waving would weigh heavily in the jury's judgment. A good lawyer would be able to point out that if Phil waved to her then he knew that he had been seen and could easily have said they split up after that time to avoid being contradicted by a witness who, according to her own statement, had not only seen Phil but had *been seen by him.*

He took a sip of his coffee, but it was not sweet enough. He added an artificial sweetener tablet and carried on reading.

It was at about 9.47 according to **Jenny Eleanor Harrison** that she saw Anthony and Philip Neuman for the first time. She said that they were walking around the Leicester Square area as if trying to decide what to do. She said that they were wearing matching white button-down shirts with long sleeves and dark trousers.

His lawyer's memory stopped him in his tracks when he read this. He looked back at the testimony of Sandra Giles. She had described the boys as wearing white T-shirts.

He wondered if these identifications were based solely on the fact that the boys were twins. Maybe there was another set of twins in the square. Or two. Maybe they were wrong about the time. Maybe one was wrong about the time and the other wrong about the people she saw.

To a layman the case seemed so convincing. To Freeman, with his legal experience, it was potentially a case of mistaken identity. And then there was the hidden side of police procedure.

'I think it was the same boys, but I'm not sure . . . I think it was after nine-fifteen, but I'm not sure . . .'

'Listen, madam, we think this boy has killed once and will probably kill again if he isn't stopped. We've got several other witnesses who saw him at the crime scene or leaving the crime scene just after, but we can't prove that he lied about splitting up with his brother. Without that the jury won't convict him. That's not the only piece of evidence we've got against him, we've got plenty of other evidence. But we can't use it all.'

'But I'm . . . not sure.'

'We understand that, madam, and we wouldn't ask you to testify to anything if you're not sure of it. All we're asking you to do is look at the picture again . . . try to remember if there was anything that might remind you of the time . . . because if we can't nail this bastard there's a strong chance that he'll kill again.'

'Well . . . it might *have been him . . . I might have been mistaken about the time . . .'*

'Thank, you madam. I know it must have been hard, but it's the duty of every good and decent citizen to help us put this young murderer away before he kills anyone else . . .'

And the police could keep that up for hours.

Yes, he understood the finer points of police procedure well enough. Sometimes they actually led to real murderers being convicted. But on countless other occasions they had led to miscarriages of justice. And the police never seemed to realize this. Even if the appeal court set aside the conviction years later on the grounds that it was unsafe and unsatisfactory – something that the appeal court was always slow to do – they would still convince themselves that they were right and the appeal court wrong.

They tended to think in standard patterns. For ninety-nine per cent of crimes this was fine, because most crimes fell neatly into these patterns. But there was that one per cent that defied the trend and conflicted with the norm. It was in these cases that miscarriages of justice occurred. And with so many crimes being committed, one per cent meant a lot – a very rich and fertile breeding ground for miscarriages of justice.

Thanks to my courtroom technique, thought Freeman, and a bit of co-operation from my client, I managed to spare him that. But now he's being hounded by the press. I've seen this sort of thing before. Usually the press don't linger too long on one individual. They pick their potential pariah, manufacture his image, milk the story for all it's worth and then move on. But sometimes they find a theme worth going back to. And in this case it's worse because it's not just a cash cow worth milking, it's probably being orchestrated by powerful interests.

Of that he was quite sure. Whatever Philip Neuman might or might not have done, other people were involved up to their necks in this sleazy saga. Other people had financed the takeoever of La Contessa. Other people had paid Tony Neuman for the genetic engineering of the aromatic plant that had been used in the production of Gold and for the genetic engineering of the mango plant. Other people had suffered substantial losses as a result of the revelation of what went into Gold, and now its production facilities were being closed down and lawsuits were being launched against the Digby-held corporation as pressure mounted up on the Bahamas and Cayman Islands to freeze the company accounts.

There was no doubt that the moving finger was stirring up a hate campaign against Phil as a smokescreen to cover their own transgressions. This story had the hallmarks of conspiracy written all over it.

He had seen it all before, the camouflage that distracted public attention from the real issues. The story falsely accusing football fans of urinating on the dead at Hillsborough. The story about a formerly homeless *Big Issue* salesman making lots of money selling the magazine and not paying tax on it, as if this were the norm rather than the exception – and giving four different figures for the man's alleged earnings. Not to mention the countless stories making fun of the Duchess of York. At the same time, the real scandals, like cash for questions, secret political funding and the withholding of evidence that might help the defence in criminal trials, were buried in brief sentences or ignored altogether in an orgy of titillation and manufactured stories. In some ways the interests of the corrupt were best served not by eloquent apologists but by the daily portion of bread and circuses delivered by tabloids that were owned by, or beholden to, the very interests they were trying to protect behind this wall of camouflage.

And Philip Neuman was their latest victim.

But the question was, where had Phil gone?

If Freeman's assumption was right, Phil knew who had killed Tony. If Tony kept a record of his genetic engineering with the coca plant and Gold, then it followed that he must have kept a record also of what he did with cannabis sativa and the mango plant. But Phil hadn't shown him that. And Phil had edited the file that he had shown him.

It was probably in the same file!

He realized now what had happened. Phil had cut the section about cannabis and the mango plant from the file and presumably resaved it separately. That would explain why he had edited the file. And the file probably also stated the names of the conspirators. But Phil had moved that elsewhere too.

So Phil had probably now gone to confront the shady people behind this conspiracy and put himself in danger. The fact that he had some evidence against them would not protect him, quite the opposite if anything. They didn't kill for revenge at being exposed. They clearly preferred to use character assassination to draw the flak away from their own camp. But they had already shown that they were prepared to kill to protect themselves from exposure in the future.

And if Phil was going to confront them with evidence of their next scheme, he would be putting his life in their hands.

He thought about the two crimes, the one that Phil had been accused of and the one that related so closely to his original investigation: the murder of Fabian Digby.

Were they committed by the same person?

Certainly they were committed by the same interests. But they were carried out with different methods. One was a stabbing and the other a shooting. One was made to look like a mugging and the other was concealed altogether so that, had it not been for chance factors, the body might not have been found. On the other hand the reason the watch was found was because police frogmen were looking for the gun that killed Digby in the place where they believed his body had been thrown into the canal.

What was the likelihood, Freeman wondered, of two people disposing of evidence from their crimes in precisely the same place like that? One person throwing the watch in at that point and the other the weighted body of Fabian Digby? Was it possible that both actions were carried out by someone who knew the area well? Someone who lived in the area?

But why, then, were the crimes so different? Why was one stabbed in the stomach and the other shot in the back of the head? The stomach wound was just below the liver and had it been a little higher would have left the perpetrator covered in blood. Hardly the actions of a sensible man. On the other hand, perhaps it was a man who knew all too well what he was doing and knew exactly where to place the knife. A stabbing would look like a mugging and would at least be quiet enough to let the killer make his getaway. A shooting would draw immediate attention to the scene.

And what of the shooting? What was it the pathologist had said about that?

'Rear penetration from just left of the median line to just right of the frontal lobe where it lodged.'

That sounded more like the work of a professional, or at least someone who knew what he was doing and wanted a clean job with a minimum of fuss or uncertainty.

Then it hit him! All of a sudden the truth dawned on him. He felt that flush of shock, followed by the goose bumps and chill of absolute certainty. He saw, all of a sudden, not only the common features of the two killings, but also where those common features pointed.

He raced to his car and brought the engine to life with a roar. If Phil confronted the killer, he might be lucky, or it might cost him his life.

'You can go through now, Mr Neuman,' said the butler.

'Thank you.'

He walked through the lobby into the library, closing the door behind him.

'Hallo, Philip.' said the man, seated on a leather couch.

'Hallo, Mike.'

The boy sat down on the black-upholstered armchair and looked around at the opulent luxury of the library, the lustrous leather-bound books. It reminded him of the luxury that he aspired to.

'So what did you want to see me about, Philip?' asked Mike evenly.

'I'll come right to the point. I found out about your scheme.'

'What scheme?'

'Your scheme to create an addictive soft drink with sedative properties.'

Mike folded his arms smugly.

'And how would I do that?'

'You wouldn't. If you had the skill to do something like that you wouldn't have had to recruit one Tony Neuman into your corrupt organization.'

'*My* organization?'

'*Your* organization.'

'What makes you think it was mine?'

'Figure it out.'

'Well, as I see it, there are two possibilities. One is that Tony told you before his untimely demise. The other is that he wrote it down somewhere and you found it.'

'I've got a file on my computer spelling out every detail: what he did, who he did it for, how you intend to use the drink.'

'And how *do* we intend to use it?'

'Your trial balloon are the children of a corrupt South-East Asian dictator who want to retain power when their father dies. They probably think the people will start resisting when the old man dies and they think they can use the drink to keep them passive.'

'Quite the little political sophisticate, aren't we,' said

Michael with a sneer. 'But you said it was our trial balloon. What do you think we'll do after that?'

'Who knows. There are probably loads of dictators who'll pay for it.'

'You seem to know quite a lot, Philip.'

'More than you realize.'

The Jaguar screeched to a halt outside the house in St John's Wood and Freeman sprinted out. He raced up to the doorbell and slammed the side of his fist against the porcelain button.

He heard the ringing of the doorbell and then, without waiting for a response, he pounded on the door.

'Open up, Mike, I know you're in there!'

He pounded again, knowing that this was the door to the garden and that Mike might not hear from within the house.

'Come on, Mike, the game is up!'

'Excuse me,' said a squeaky female voice.

Freeman looked round to see an officious old lady staring at him from the doorway of a house a few yards away. She looked more curious than afraid.

'Are you looking for Mike?'

'Yes, I am,' said Freeman.

He looked at her, waiting for a response. She appeared to be studying him through her bifocals.

'He went back to live in his father's mansion after that terrible business.'

'You mean he doesn't live here?'

'Not since his they found his father's body in the Grand Union Canal.'

'OK, thank you,' he muttered.

'You recruited Tony for your father. You found out what he could do and you set up the scheme. It was all part of your effort to prove that you were as good as your father. You must have been elated when you found someone who could create the addictive perfume and

284

you saw your chance to step out from the shadow of your father.'

'You seem to know a lot about me,' said Mike.

'You confided in Tony.'

'And he evidently confided in you.'

'But you couldn't market the perfume effectively without an established manufacturing and market infrastructure. So you needed to take over an existing organization like La Contessa, and quickly. But even your father didn't have the money for that, at least not in ready cash. So he brought in Zaidan while – ah – while Tony worked on the genetic engineering.'

His emotions were beginning to show, the pain and anger spilling out. But he was determined to have it out with Mike.

'So you and your father worked as a team: your father bringing in the money that was out of his league and you bringing in the brains that were out of yours, like a pair of parasites feeding off your betters.'

'Is that a question or a statement?'

'A statement. You met . . . you met Tony on line and befriended him in cyberspace the way paedophiles set up assignations with children.'

'Assignations,' said Mike sarcastically. 'Now there's a long word.'

'Don't patronize me, Mike. You're in no position to mock. Your game is up.'

'What makes you think that?'

'I've got the whole story from start to finish, Mike. And I can prove it.'

He stood up, glowering over Mike, as if to underscore his victory.

'What's that supposed to mean?'

'It means that you daren't kill me, because there's a record.'

'That was what Tony thought. It didn't help him.'

'The other side of the coin is that you thought killing my brother would remove the threat to you.'

'With the aid of the burglary, of course.'

'But you were wrong, weren't you, Mike. Because you didn't manage to destroy all the copies of the file. And so I've got it all on disk.'

'That doesn't prove anything. Anyone can type up some text accusing other people of crimes. That doesn't make it true. There's no way you can prove the authorship of the file.'

'Maybe not, but I can prove the case against you.'

'How?'

'You still haven't figured it out, have you? Police laboratories may sometimes get things wrong, but DNA itself never lies.'

Mike looked up, suddenly aware of the danger that he had overlooked until now.

'You're right,' he said. But before the boy could react, he leapt to his feet and emitted the *kia* or shout of a martial arts exponent as the knife-edge of his hand slashed out in a circular motion and landed behind the ear of his accuser.

There was a thud as the unconscious body hit the ground.

25

'Anyone who attacks his father or mother must be put to death.'

Exodus 21:16

Criminals don't rest on Sunday and for that reason neither do police, especially senior officers. So DCI Karen Rousson was one of quite a few police officers at her desk on a Sunday morning in summer, clearing up the backlog of paperwork that had built up over the preceding week. But it was unusual for the phone to ring on Sunday. So it was with a twinge of apprehension that she picked it up.

'DCI Rousson,' she replied.

'Karen? It's Emmett.'

She took in a deep breath to contain her feelings.

'Yes, Mr Freeman, what can I do for you?'

'Look . . . I've got a problem.'

'Please be specific,' she replied coldly.

'It's about Phil Neuman. I think he's in danger.'

'Why?'

He explained about what Miriam Neuman had told him and what he had figured out about the murders.

'All right,' said Karen. 'But it's premature to start making assumptions. Are you sure he's at the Digby estate?'

'It's the only place I can think of,' said Freeman.

'All right, I'll meet you there. But if you get there first you're to wait for me.'

'Wait a minute, I've got a better idea. I can pick you up in my Jag. It'll get us there quicker.'

'You're not allowed to break the speed limit.'

'I can with a police escort.'

'All right. I'll be waiting for you downstairs.'

She put the phone down, reached for her jacket and handbag and went out. So resolute was she in her stride that she didn't notice that she had swept straight past Rex DuPaul. But he noticed her.

Michael Digby kept his eyes on the road as he drove along a back route, occasionally glancing into the rear-view mirror for signs of activity from the back seat. He knew that he had nothing to worry about. The injection was enough to keep an average-sized adult unconscious for at least two hours. But this was not something he had done before and apprehension was inevitable. He had kept him alive as a kind of insurance. If he was stopped and found with the boy asleep in the back seat he could say he had just fallen asleep or lost consciousness and he was rushing him to hospital.

With the boy dead he would have had some explaining to do. For that reason the killing had to take place at the last moment, just before the disposal of the body. In fact he didn't even need to kill him. He could let nature do the work. It would be a slow, painful death, the kind that the boy deserved. A major money-spinning operation had been closed down because of this young man's interference, and although the real owners had been able to hide behind a wall of front men and banking secrecy laws, the whole affair had brought acute embarrassment on the Digby family name.

Yes, the Neuman boy deserved to suffer. He hadn't merely threatened them, he had damaged their interests. He would wake up to find himself buried alive and would experience all the fear and agony that he deserved in his dying moments.

*　　*　　*

288

'Are you sure the Digby family will even let you in, Mr Freeman?'

'No, that's why I wanted you with me, Karen.'

'What can I do?'

'I thought you might be able to use your police authority.'

'Without a warrant? On private property? When we don't even know that a crime's been committed? As a lawyer you should know better than that, Mr Freeman.'

'Will you cut out this Mr Freeman business! It's Emmett.'

'I think it might be better if we kept things on a professional basis from now on.'

He glanced at her irritably. He hadn't expected her to stay angry this long. He had thought that after a few days to cool off their relationship would be back on track. But now he realized that perhaps he had been wrong about her. Perhaps she didn't want a man in her life at all. Perhaps all she wanted was her career.

'We're here,' she said.

They were at the main gate of the Digby estate. Freeman pressed the button of the intercom.

'Who is it?' asked a voice.

'It's Emmett Freeman. I'm here to see Mike Digby.'

'Just one minute, sir,' said the voice.

It was, Freeman realized, the butler. After about a minute he came back.

'I'm afraid he isn't here, sir.'

The voice sounded deferential, but Freeman couldn't be sure that the man was telling the truth.

'I'm here with Detective Chief Inspector Rousson of the Metropolitan Police. If Mike isn't here I'd like to speak to Veronica Digby.'

Five minutes later they were in the conservatory facing Veronica Digby, who was drinking a cup of tea. She had offered some to Freeman and Karen, but they were too tense even to think about accepting. Freeman was doing the talking. Alan Nielsen was there too, hovering over them like a sort of protector.

289

'We think that your stepson may have been involved in the murder of both your husband and Tony Neuman.'

Veronica did not look surprised, only a trifle sad.

'I should have suspected it before. They were up to something together. I knew that.'

Karen could have pulled rank and taken control of the situation, but she realized that Freeman had already had some contact with the Digby family and might be able to cut to the heart of the matter more quickly.

'You knew it all along?'

'I knew that Mike was involved in the La Contessa deal. I didn't know all the details, but I knew they were working together.'

'Do you know where he is now?' asked Freeman.

'Who? Mike? He moved back in here after Fabian's funeral. I thought he was here.'

'We also think that Philip Neuman came here to see him.'

'I don't know about that,' said Veronica. 'But we can ask the butler. The estate is surrounded by a fence with a barbed wire top. If anyone came here the only way they could have got in would have been through the main gate.' She looked round at Nielsen. 'Alan?'

'A boy calling himself Philip Neuman came here to see Mr Digby not long ago. I saw the butler showing him into the library.'

'Mr Digby?' repeated Karen, baffled.

'Mr *Michael* Digby.'

'Are they still there?' she asked.

'I think they left together,' said Nielsen. 'I heard Michael's car pull out ten minutes ago.'

'Did they say where they were going?'

'No.'

Freeman looked at Karen anxiously.

'Do we have grounds for a police search?' asked the lawyer.

'I can put out an alert for Mike Digby's car, but we can't start searching until we know where to search.'

Freeman remembered the day he had met Mike, when he had first walked into the room. Mike was resetting his mouse buttons as he installed some software. He remembered his words.

'I'm just trying to install this program for simulating stress fractures during low-intensity seismic upheavel. I've bought up this chemical waste site and I need a program to calculate the risk factors.'

Chemical waste site! What a perfect place to dispose of a body!

The lawyer looked at Nielsen.

'Where's the chemical waste site that Digby Holdings acquired?'

'Digby Holdings?' echoed Nielsen. 'Oh, you mean *Mike* Digby. That was *his* baby. He bought it shortly after his father disappeared.'

So that's why he didn't bury his father there. He didn't own it then.

'Where is it?'

'It's fourteen miles north of Stanmore. I can show you on the map.'

Mike stared down at the large clothes trunk. It was certainly large enough for the body, but he wasn't sure it was strong enough. It could probably be traced to him – or at least a trunk of that type could – as he had bought it by credit card. But the whole idea was that it shouldn't be found anyway.

He had driven here via a series of back roads to avoid being seen and had entered by the alternative entrance, concealed behind a small forest, which the previous owners had used to foil environmental campaigners when they wanted to stage promotion-seeking demonstrations at the main gate against the arrival of the allegedly dangerous chemicals.

He had brought the boy in, draped in a blanket on the back seat, with the trunk in the boot of the car. He decided that he would put the open trunk into a hole in the ground, then put the boy in, close the trunk and finally fill in the hole. But first he had to create the hole here in this out-of-the-way corner.

For that he needed one of the bulldozers. Fortunately it was a Sunday and there was only a skeleton staff. The security people were supposed to make periodic checks all around the perimeter. But he was sure they never did. So all he had to do was leave the concrete shed, start the bulldozer and get digging.

'It's lucky this baby has such solid suspension,' muttered Freeman as he drove up the dirt path to the front entrance of the waste site.

Karen smiled. It was such a typical macho approach, bragging about his car at a time like this.

'Karen, this man might be dangerous.'

'That's why we called for back-up,' said Karen.

'It doesn't look like they're here yet.'

A burly, pot-bellied guard wearing nothing but a string vest and filthy jeans stepped out behind the iron gate, which was secured by a heavy metal chain and locked by a huge padlock. He reminded Freeman of the one with the guard dog at the Digby mansion. Except that this one looked fiercer than their guard, or even his dog.

'We're closed,' said the guard as they got out of the Jaguar, in a voice that sounded like it meant business. Karen pulled out her badge and flashed it at him through the bars.

'Detective Chief Inspector Rousson of the Met.'

''Ave you got a warrant?' he asked belligerently.

'I'm not here to conduct a search,' said Karen. 'I'm here to see someone.'

'There's no one 'ere 'cept me and a couple of the other guards. What d'you want to see us for?'

'I don't. I want to see Michael Digby.'

''E's not 'ere,' said the guard, genuinely confused.

'I have reason to believe he's going to be.'

'Well, you can wait for 'im out there, then.'

'Is there another way in?' asked Freeman, looking around for any signs of movement on the site.

'Well, there's the . . .'

He trailed off into an awkward silence. Freeman didn't

think that he was covering for anyone. But he probably wasn't supposed to say anything about the site's security to outsiders. After all, for all he knew the police warrant card could be fake. They could have been gathering information for Greenpeace or Friends of the Earth.

'There's the what?' asked Karen firmly.

'There's a back entrance. We use it to avoid trouble-makers.'

'Where is it?' asked Karen.

The guard half turned and pointed.

'Over there. If you take the road you came on back to the fork and take the left instead of the right turning and then follow the road, it'll lead you to it.'

'OK, thank you,' said Karen.

They got back into the Jaguar and drove off.

The bulldozer was digging away, shifting the earth back into the hole, and he could see that it was almost full. He released the levers and switched off the engine. Now all he had to do was go back to the shed, wash the dirt off his hands and drive back to the mansion.

But as he climbed out of the bulldozer and dropped to the ground he found himself confroned by two people. One he recognized immediately as Emmett Freeman. The other, he recollected after a few seconds, was the policewoman who had been involved in the search for his father.

'Hallo,' he said, wiping his hands on his handkerchief. 'What can I do for you?'

'You can start by telling us where Philip Neuman is.'

'Philip Neuman? I haven't a clue. Why? Is he missing?'

'Look, cut it out, Mike,' said Karen. 'We know he was at the mansion. We just spoke to the butler.'

'Well, I know. That's why I don't understand why you should think that he's missing. He was at the mansion not long ago. I gave him a lift to the station and then drove out here.'

'We think he was on his way to confront you,' said Freeman.

'Confront me? Over what?'

'Over the fact that you murdered his brother.'

'That's crazy,' said Mike with a mocking smile. 'Why should I kill him?'

'For the same reason that you killed your father: because he was a threat to you.'

'Killed my father? Listen, if you're going to insult me I'm afraid I'm going to have to ask you to leave. This is private property and unless you've got a warrant, you've got no right to be here.'

'We know you killed Tony Neuman,' said Freeman. 'We know about the work he was doing for your father, we know you were part of the set-up.'

'Look, I'm not saying that my father's and Tony's deaths didn't have something to do with the genetic engineering of Gold. But why should you think that *I* was responsible?'

'I think your motive was that you were trying to prove something. You liked to do your own dirty work.'

'I don't see why you suspect me in the first place. I mean, isn't there something called *evidence* that's supposed to guide a criminal investigation?'

He had that taunting grin on his face that Freeman had seen before: the one that matched the sarcastic tone in which he was speaking. But Freeman was unimpressed.

'That day when I first saw you, you were reversing the mouse buttons on your computer, making the left button serve as the right and the right button as the left. The usual reason for doing that is because one is left-handed. And of course you had the mouse at the left side of the computer. You were holding a fork American-style in your right hand.'

'So I'm left-handed? So what?'

'Only three per cent of women and five per cent of men are left-handed, and both Tony Neuman and your father were killed by left-handed people.'

By this stage even Karen Rousson was looking at Freeman, surprised.

'How do you know that?' asked Mike.

'Tony Neuman was stabbed just below the liver. The liver

is on the right side of the body and the stab wound was almost straight but heading just slightly to the median line with no lateral movement. That suggested he was stabbed from in front. If he was stabbed from in front to the right side of his body, that suggests that the stab wound was administered by a left-handed person.'

'And my father?' asked Mike, taunting Emmett to prove his case.

'Your father was shot in the back of the head on the *left* side. The bullet travelled towards the right. That again suggests a left-handed killer, or at least that the killer was holding the gun in his left hand.'

'That's hardly conclusive,' said Mike.

'Oh, I know it wouldn't stand up in court,' said Freeman. 'But it was enough to lead us here. And I'm sure that once we've searched this place thoroughly, we'll find Phil. I assume you've already killed him.'

'Actually I've buried him alive. I guess I'm going to have to do the same to you.'

And with these words he produced a gun from his left-hand pocket.

Karen felt a stab of fear. But Freeman had looked down the barrel of guns before and he realized that the risk of Mike shooting them was not as great as she supposed.

'Is that the gun you killed your father with?' he asked.

'That's right,' said Mike proudly.

'I never really understood why you killed him,' said Freeman. 'I mean, I figured out that you did, but I wasn't sure why. Tony Neuman I could understand. He was a threat to you and he probably wasn't happy about the way you were using his skills. But why your father? He was in this deal with you. He had as much to lose as you did. And I thought the whole point of the deal was to impress him. How could you impress him if he was dead?'

'He got cold feet, Mr Freeman. Just like the boy.'

'Fabian Digby got cold feet?' asked Freeman, incredulously. 'I don't think so.'

'Oh yes, of course, the great Fabian Digby! Respected even

295

by his enemies. You all thought he had balls of steel. But you know what, Mr Freeman? He was as human as the next man.'

By now Mike Digby's face was contorted with rage and bitterness. All the pent-up hatred was spilling out. And this made the man dangerous.

'What did he get cold feet about?' asked Freeman.

'We're going to have to call it off.'

A sense of urgency and the stress of fear pervaded Fabian Digby's face as much as his voice, in furrowed brows and lines of contortion that clean living and regular workouts had kept at bay.

'What are you talking about, Dad?'

Michael's voice sounded sceptical and dismissive, as if he sensed that for the first time in his life he held an advantage over his father.

'It's all getting out of hand. The price of gold hit four-eighteen. Some of those bastards started crawling out of the woodwork and buying up bottles of Gold just to trade them in.' He was speaking about the speculators who had pounced when the price of gold metal shot above the selling price of the pefume Gold. 'If it hadn't been over so quickly they would have started cashing in in droves!'

'But it came and went, Dad. And it only cost us two hundred K. Your average Joe Public doesn't respond to the market that quickly. That's why there are so many rich pickings out there for people like you!'

They were standing by Fabian Digby's car. Apart from these two – father and son – the underground car park was deserted, and their tense but muted voices reverberated across the concrete with an eerie and ominous echo.

'But what if it happens again? What if gold overshoots the four-hundred mark for more than a day? We could be wiped out!'

Mike had parked his own car a few spaces away. He could sense that his father was anxious to get to the La Contessa board meeting. But he had to clear up this matter first. He had brokered the project and it was he who had stuck his neck out by promising Hassan that he would hold the project together. They knew only too well about Digby's business credo which held his reputation to be a bankable asset. Fabian Digby had only reluctantly agreed to go along with this whole scheme. If things started to unravel he'd change like the tide to save his skin. And if that happened, Hassan would assume that Mike was playing the turncoat too. Although Mike had taken the initiative on this project, no one really believed that he was completely independent of the father in whose shadow he had lived all his life.

Mike realized that he had to allay his father's fears – or distance himself from him.

'It isn't going to overshoot the mark. It's back to trading in a narrow band between three-seventy-five and three-ninety. If anything it'll go *down*. With inflation under control it could sink to three fifty. Trust me, Dad, there's nothing to worry about.'

'But what if people start investigating? What if they start analysing Gold in a lab to find out what goes into it?'

'Who, Dad?' asked Mike, desperately hurtling towards a tunnel that offered not the slightest glimpse of light at the other end. 'Who's going to investigate? We've got contacts in the police and even in Parliament. They can head off an investigation – or at least warn us if there's one in the offing.'

'A Chief Superintendent and a has-been MP don't have their fingers on all the buttons, or even the pulses.'

'No, but it's a pretty slim chance that the authorities would bother with us. Why would they want to sabotage a successful British export?'

'What about those consumer programmes on TV? They delight in biting the hands that feed them. They get their kicks out of toppling giants and bringing down the very people who put the food in their bellies and the shirts on their backs.'

Fabian Digby was by now fumbling in his pocket, finally producing the electronic key that would open his car.

'You're panicking over nothing, Dad,' said Mike desperately, sensing that his control of the situation was slipping away.

'Perhaps,' said Fabian Digby, opening the car door. 'But it's my neck that's on the line.'

And mine, thought Mike, as he pulled out a .38 revolver and quickly attached a silencer. As his father leaned forward and shifted the road maps on the driver's seat in order to get in, he squeezed the trigger and put nine grams of lead in the back of his head.

'And what did you do after that?' asked Freeman. He noticed that Mike's eyes had glazed over, as if his bragging were tinged with regret. Perhaps his father had been a god to him after all, and not the devil that Mike had made him out to be at their first confrontation.

'I covered his head with a plastic bag, tied it lightly round his neck and put the body in the boot of my car.'

'Why the plastic bag?'

'In case the blood leaked into my car.'

'Weren't you afraid of being caught in the act?' asked Freeman. 'Or at least seen?'

'I acted on impulse. I sensed danger and I responded to it.'

'Just like your father taught you,' said Freeman. He was testing his theory that Mike felt guilty about the murder.

'Oh, no. Everyone said my father was a creature of impulse. But he was a creature of habit. *I* was the impulsive one.'

'And then you drove off to Maida Vale and threw his body into the canal.'

'Not immediately. I could hardly throw his body in during daylight. I took his body back to my place, leaving it in the car, and waited till nightfall before driving out there. Actually I waited till one o'clock just to make sure. And the rest is history.'

'And what about Tony Neuman?' asked Freeman 'What did he get cold feel about? Gold? Or what you were planning to do in that Pacific Tiger with addictive mango juice?'

'Oh, you know about that too?'

'Yes,' said Freeman.

'We asked him to create the genetically engineered mango.

He did it, but then he started asking questions. I told him, because I thought it would shut him up if I reassured him, that we weren't going to sell it in Britain. How was I to know that he was another bleeding-heart humanitarian who gave a shit about the Third World? He started protesting that it was immoral to help a dictatorship, that it was wrong to play with people's minds and deny them their freedom. I told him that we'd only use it to ease over the transition to democracy. He seemed to swallow that. Or maybe he just wanted to believe it. But it was becoming increasingly obvious to us that he was a liability more than an asset.'

'So you killed him,' said Freeman.

'I like to do my own dirty work,' said Mike.

'How come you killed Tony with a knife?'

'I wanted to make it look like a mugging. How was I to know the watch would be found by those frogmen? My father's body wasn't even supposed to float.'

'And what about Dr Sadler?' asked Karen. 'Did you kill him too?'

'He tried to shake us down,' said Mike. 'So I had my accomplice lead him to the slaughter. But as usual, *I* had to do the dirty work.'

'You had an accomplice?' asked Karen.

'Not when I killed my father.'

'But when you killed Sadler?' asked Karen.

'And when I killed the Neuman boy.'

'But *you* did the dirty work,' said Freeman.

'Like I said, he didn't have the bottle to kill the boy himself. He was too squeamish. And when he came to me bellyaching about Dr Sadler knowing too much, I knew that I'd have to do it again. But I didn't know Sadler, and Sadler didn't trust me. So I needed a Judas goat to lead Sadler to the slaughter.'

'And who was this accomplice?' asked Karen.

A shot rang out.

There was a stunned look on Michael Digby's face and seconds later he fell to the ground with a thud.

They looked round to see Rex DuPaul standing there with a smoking gun in his hand.

26

'The voice is the voice of Jacob, but the hands are the hands of Esau.'

Genesis 27:22

'I thought you might need some help,' said DuPaul as he strode up to them.

'How long have you been standing there, sir?' asked Karen.

'Long enough to assess the danger.'

'Is that standard police issue, sir?' she asked, looking down at the gun nervously.

'Oh, yes,' said DuPaul.

'It's a pity you didn't wait a moment longer before shooting him,' she said.

'That's hardly gratitude, DCI Rousson.'

'I'm sorry, sir. I wasn't trying to be ungrateful. It's just that he was about to tell us the name of his accomplice.'

'You know, this is going to sound like a cliché,' Freeman interrupted, 'but we haven't a moment to lose.'

'What do you mean?'

'Mike Digby said Phil Neuman was still alive. He said he'd buried him alive.'

'Did he say where?' asked the Chief Superintendent.

'No,' said Freeman, running up to the bulldozer and climbing in, 'but I have a pretty good idea.'

Within seconds he was operating the machine, learning which control did what and then digging up the ground that they had seen Mike filling in. As he operated the levers, Karen and DuPaul called out directions to him, but when the scoop made impact with the trunk he needed no directions. He heard it and felt it. But he knew he had to be careful. It wouldn't do the boy any good if they killed him with the bulldozer as they tried to dig him up.

'We have to get the box out!' shouted DuPaul.

'Let's just open it and get him out,' replied Freeman, climbing out of the bulldozer cabin.

They used a spade to dig away more earth and then opened the latches by hand. Fortunately Mike hadn't bothered to lock it, presumably because he hadn't expected it to be found.

They looked down into the trunk to see an unconscious form lying there, curled up in the foetal posture. Without waiting for the men to act, Karen half climbed down with one foot in the trunk to check for signs of life.

'He's got a pulse,' she said, reaching down to his neck.

She climbed fully into the trunk, straddling the boy in order to avoid crushing him, and crouched down, putting her ear to his chest.

'He's breathing.'

Freeman sighed with relief. Karen reached up to him as he held out his arm to help her out.

'If you two men could lift him out, we could get him to the shed and call an ambulance.'

She noted that DuPaul had put the gun away.

'So when I said that, his hand just shot out and that's the last thing I remember until you started slapping me and bringing me round.'

He was sitting on a thin mattress that they had found in the shed, sipping a cup of tea. The shed in fact turned out to be more of a concrete bunker, combining a supply depot with an office. They had thrown the mattress on to the floor. The other three were sitting on hard wooden armchairs. Karen had made the tea with an old tin kettle and a portable gas stove that were presumably used when the office was manned during the week.

'Do you know why that set him off?' asked DuPaul evenly.

'Because he understood what I meant,' said the boy smugly.

'And what did you mean?' asked the DCS.

'Tony didn't just meet Fabian and Mike Digby. He met several of the other conspirators as well.'

'He told you that?' asked DuPaul.

'Not exactly.'

'Then how do you know?' asked the DCS. 'And more importantly, who were they?'

'Well, one of them was a man called Hassan. He was the man who financed it all.'

Freeman leaned forward.

'I feel I should step in here. I happen to know from my own independent enquiries that the Hassan in question is Hassan Abed Zaidan, the brother of the Minister for Arms Procurement in Bahakabir.'

'It seems that everyone in this room knows more about this case than I do,' said DuPaul.

'I don't think so,' said Karen.

'What's that supposed to mean?' snapped the DCS.

'It means I think you're in this up to your neck, sir!' she replied, matching his aggression with righteous indignation of her own.

'You have some proof of that, Detective Chief *Inspector* Rousson?'

'Before you shot him, Mike Digby was about to tell us something,' said Freeman.

'As a lawyer you should know that's hardly proof,' the Chief Superintendent mocked.

'There's also Dr Sadler,' said Karen. 'You got him to destroy the report about Gold. And then he was stabbed to death in another fake mugging, like Tony Neuman.'

'Again, do you have proof of that?' he asked, his eyebrows raised in savage mockery.

'There's paperwork to show that I submitted the evidence and applied for the report. There's proof that time elapsed and no report was forthcoming. There'll be discontinuities in the numbering system to suggest that a report was destroyed.'

'That a report was destroyed,' DuPaul repeated in a lawyer's tone. Not that I destroyed it.'

'There is one other thing,' said the boy. 'I told you that Tony met several of the conspirators. You were one of them. Mike Digby wanted to make sure that he was covered if something went wrong.'

'Ah, I get it,' said DuPaul, piling on the sarcasm to the full. 'You're now going to accuse me on the strength of the unsworn testimony of a dead man.'

'Not exactly,' said the boy. 'Like Mike, you seem to be having trouble figuring it out unless it's spelt out to you. My brother and I argued that day because he had money for the nightclub and I didn't. But then, just after we split up, he took pity on me and ran after me. He asked me if I fancied a bowl of lentil soup. It was a reference to the old biblical story of Esau and Jacob – you know, when Esau sold his birthright. And then after that, Jacob posed as Esau before their blind father and stole his blessing as well. You see, it had always been a fantasy of ours to change places, just for a lark, and just then, almost on an impulse, we decided to do it. We exchanged watches and wallets and decided to spend the rest of the evening going our own separate ways, each pretending to be the other.'

Karen's jaw had dropped. And DuPaul was gasping for breath. The only one whose face remained utterly calm and completely fixed on the boy was Emmett Freeman.

'It was a game we always talked about. But until then we'd never got round to playing it. And I'll never forgive myself for the fact that I got my brother killed because he decided to play the game just then. If I hadn't crossed you and Hassan, or if I'd just accepted that I couldn't afford the nightclub without whining and playing on Phil's conscience, he'd still be alive today.

'But I can never forgive you either. I can never forgive you or Mike or Hassan or Edward for this criminal conspiracy that led to you killing my brother. I was greedy. I didn't want to have to worry about money ever again. I didn't want it to be like it was when my father died. But you had no excuse. You and Mike and the rest of you just used your money and power to get more money and more power. And I intend to make you pay for that.'

'It can't be,' gasped DuPaul. 'We were watching you the whole time.'

'We were wearing the same clothes.'

'But the watch. We knew which one was Tony from the watch.'

'Like I told you, we traded.'

'But when? You went into that side street when you argued and then . . .'

He buried his head in his hands, realizing that in those fifteen or twenty seconds when they were hidden by the Japanese tourists the two brothers had simply traded identities to act out their fantasy. And now, as Rex DuPaul looked up, he knew that he was looking into the eyes of the boy he had tried to kill and the boy whose brother he had killed. And he knew that this boy could testify to his involvement in the conspiracy. Along with all the circumstantial evidence, it would probably be enough.

It was all right for Hassan. He had diplomatic immunity. The worst that could happen to him was that he'd be declared *persona non grata*. More likely, the government would whisper in his ear to avoid the embarrassment of a scandal and he would quietly leave without waiting to be kicked out.

But DuPaul knew that he faced the prospect of imprisonment for a long time. For a second or two, he felt his hand itching to move towards his pocket. But reason took over. They had already called for an ambulance and police reinforcements. He couldn't kill all of them. It would be impossible to explain.

What occurred next was more embarrassing than frightening. For at that point, Detective Chief Superintendent Rex DuPaul burst into tears and sobbed bitterly into his hands.

'I never wanted to kill anyone. I didn't want to kill your brother. It was Mike who actually stabbed him. I was hoping all along that he'd change his mind. But I couldn't stop him. You see, Hassan and Mike were calling the shots. Edward and I were only along for the ride.'

It was all over and he knew it. In a way it was a relief. Despite all he had done, Rex DuPaul still knew right from wrong. And he didn't approve of wrongdoing even though he had been lured into it by temptation.

They could hear the sirens in the distance.

'They'll be here shortly, sir,' said Karen. 'Perhaps we should meet them outside.'

'You go,' said DuPaul. 'I'll be out in a minute. I just don't want them to see me like this.'

They got up slowly and walked out of the office and down the corridor to the three steps that led out of the building. They walked through in single file, first Karen, then Tony and finally Freeman. As they walked, Tony remembered the line of poetry that Superintendent Morley had quoted to him.

Each man kills the thing he loves.

It was from Oscar Wilde's *The Ballad of Reading Gaol*. He had looked it up afterwards and wondered if Rex DuPaul also knew it. The full line was:

Each man kills the thing he loves and so he's got to die.

In DuPaul's case, the thing he had once loved was the law. But he had betrayed it. And from the look on DuPaul's face – the look of a broken man – it was clear that he deeply regretted it.

As Freeman stepped out behind Tony and Karen into the light of day, the three of them heard a sharp staccato sound ring out from within the building and then reverberate more softly as an echo. And as the echo faded away into silence, they knew that final judgment had been delivered on Rex DuPaul by the one court of justice from which no miscreant, except the psychopath, ever manages to escape: the court of human conscience.

27

'All streams flow into the sea . . .'

Ecclesiastes 1:7

'I love watching the sun setting over the shoreline,' said Karen.

They were in a small boat, on the Gulf of Eilat. Freeman had decided to take Nielsen's advice and get away from it all. Well, almost all. He had asked Karen to go with him . . . and she had accepted without hesitation. She was entitled to a holiday, and she needed to let things cool off after the stress of the DuPaul affair. Officially she had been cleared, but she had been told that people were out for her blood. Her initial instinct had been to stay and fight, but she was told that if she went away for a couple of weeks DuPaul's clique would be split up and shifted to other areas. She wasn't really sure whether to believe them, but it was made clear to her that she didn't really have a choice.

'What was that?' he asked. She was lying on a deckchair, soaking up the sun in her white bikini at the aft end of the boat, while Freeman stayed at the helm.

'The sunset. It's such a cliché to stand on the shore and watch the sun setting over the sea. But I've always wanted to see it the other way, from a boat looking back on to the land.'

They were staying at a hotel overlooking the lagoon and had rented the boat on impulse while walking round the shops and restaurants of King Solomon's Wharf. They had sailed under the bridge into the Gulf, past windsurfing kids and sun-soaking tourists, and were now out in the open, watching the sun set over the distant red hills that were Egypt. This whole area was famous for its copper deposits which gave the sand and hills their distinctive red colour. Of course, it was even redder on the Jordanian side. But Karen had her eyes glued to the sunset.

Freeman weighed anchor and left the helm. As he did so, he saw the spectacle that had held her in awe. The sea and shore were aflame together in hues of red and orange as the sun descended upon the land from which they had just sailed. It appeared almost as if the sun were spitting out blood upon the water and fire upon the land as it found its resting place for the night beyond the intrusion of human eyes.

'It's a pity they only gave you two weeks' leave,' he said, as he joined her on deck. He lay down next to her on an adjacent lounger, gently brushing her arm on the way.

'I almost didn't take *that*,' she replied. 'God knows what Rex DuPaul's friends are doing to my reputation back home.'

'You think they're engineering a palace coup?' he asked.

'They're probably trying. But I've been assured by people in very high places that my position is secure. They said they need people like me and I guess I still have to trust my colleagues even if there are one or two bad apples. Otherwise I might as well just throw in the towel now.'

'I thought we were going to get away from it all. I thought that's what this vacation was all about. Just you and me together for a week, and let the Devil take the world.'

'That's "let the Devil take tomorrow",' she corrected, laughing lightly.

'Whatever,' he said, Archie Bunker-style.

'You know, I was wondering. How come you didn't seem surprised when Tony came out with the truth like that?'

'Because I wasn't.'

307

'Now wait a minute, hold it there,' said Karen, her detective's suspicions aroused. 'You're not going to tell me you knew all along who he was.'

'I don't know about all along, but I figured it out before you did . . . Detective Chief Inspector.'

He said these last three words with a broad grin on his face. He wasn't seriously trying to compete professionally with the woman that he hoped to marry.

'How did you know?'

'There were several clues that suggested it. It just took a bit of time until I picked them up.'

'Such as what?' asked Karen, as curious as she had been when the entire case had presented itself as a wall of mystery.

'Well, one of them actually came from you. When I told you about him using an off-the-shelf program for guessing passphrases you asked why he needed to download one rather than write one himself. The answer was that he didn't know how to write one because he wasn't the computer programmer, he was the biochemist.'

'Could that just have been because it was easier to use an off-the-shelf program than write one, from scratch?' asked Karen.

'It could have been,' said Freeman. 'But there was something else.'

'What's that?'

Freeman smiled, realizing that he was still way ahead of her.

'He told me that there were lots of passphrase guessers on the market *or* available in shareware. If he actually got one such program *specifically*, then why did he make such a general reference to their availability? Why not just say 'I bought the program' or 'it was a shareware program'? The *real* reason he knew the passphrase was because it was *his* file. And of course he didn't even need the passphrase because he knew the content. He wrote the file in the first place, after all.'

'Hardly conclusive,' she said, her mood cheerful at the prospect of finding flaws in his argument.

Freeman smiled and took her hand.

'Not convinced?' he asked, taunting her gently. 'You know there's more, don't you?'

She smiled, blushing.

'I'm sure there is,' she replied. 'But I think you enjoy teasing me, don't you?'

'When he showed me the file about the coca splicing and Gold I noticed that he'd modified it three days after the burglary. At the time I didn't know what the modification was. All I knew was that he'd modified it in some way. It was only later that I found out that he'd cut the passages about the cannabis and mango splicing. But the *important* thing was that he said he ran the password guessing program for a *nine days* before it found the passphrase that enabled him to open the file. If he tracked down the file in cyberspace after the burglary, like he said, then how could he modify it only *three days* later if it took him *nine days* to decrypt it and open it up?'

'And you really figured it out? Just from that?'

She was smiling at him now, defying him to lie to her. She knew that he couldn't have worked it out from this alone.

'Well, there were a couple of bigger clues staring us in the face,' said Freeman sheepishly.

'Spill it!' Karen shot back, exasperated.

'First of all there was the note he handed me during the committal hearing.'

'What note?'

'The note he handed me after the DNA evidence about the hair follicle. It told me that the odds on a match with six loci and two bands at each locus were much lower in the case of siblings, and there were various other bits of information.'

'So?'

'At the time I thought that was just his knowledge of statistics. But there's a difference between knowing the *subject* of statistics and knowing the specific statistics of a particular subject or situation.'

'I don't get it,' said Karen, her tone showing how completely baffled she was.

'Phil was the mathematician in the family. Tony was the geneticist. A mathematician wouldn't normally know what the odds on genetic matching would be between siblings. But a *geneticist* would. When he handed me that note, what he was disclosing wasn't a *mathematician's* knowledge of the subject, but a *geneticist's*.'

'Now pull the other,' said Karen, the smile returning to her face. It gave her the aura of a sunny personality, something that had been lacking in London. It made her look fun-loving.

'Still not convinced?' he asked.

'Uh-uh.'

'Well, there was also the big one.'

'Which was?' she demanded, like a teacher testing a lazy pupil. 'The hair follicle itself – the hair follicle trapped in the watch winder that matched his DNA. We assumed, respectively, that the result of the DNA test was either the result of laxity and carelessness at the lab, from the defence point of view, or a sign that he really had stolen the watch and then worn it, from the prosecution point of view. That's the polarizing effect of the adversarial legal system – and the blinding effect. None of us considered the obvious answer that he *was* Tony and that the hair follicle got trapped there on an earlier occasion when he was wearing the watch, before he lent it to his brother.'

'And in retrospect it all seems so *obvious*.' said Karen, astounded at the final revelation.

'The truth usually is,' said Freeman.

'The thing that puzzles me is that his mother didn't notice. I read somewhere that mothers can tell even identical twins apart. And Tony and Phil weren't identical, they were fraternal, even if they looked the same to the rest of the world.'

'Yes, but I think you'll find, if you interview her, that she *did* know.'

'She did?' asked Karen, surprised. 'How do you know?'

'Well, at one point, when Tony's life was in danger, she actually tried to tell me.'

'*Tried* to tell you?'

310

'I was talking to her on my mobile,' said Freeman. 'The call broke up.'

'But if she knew, then why didn't she tell anyone? Why did she wait until his life was in danger before telling you?'

'At first she didn't realize because she was drowsy, under the influence of the tranquillisers. But once she cut down on the dosage and regained her awareness she figured it out. Only she didn't tell anyone at that stage, although she confronted Tony. He told her the truth and convinced her that his life was in danger if anyone found out – which in effect it was. So she played along with it. She'd just lost one son, only a year and a half after losing her husband, and the last thing she wanted was to lose her other son.'

Karen was looking at Freeman in a state of half-realization and half-bewilderment.

'How do *you* know all this?'

'I found out at the hospital. While you were interviewing Tony, after the doctor cleared it, I was talking to Miriam Neuman outside. Your colleagues assumed she knew little of what was going on and more or less left her alone. That left the field clear for me to get the story from her side.'

'And you, of course, promised not to tell us.'

'Well, I figured it was for her to tell you.'

'I mean you didn't tell *me*,' said Karen irritably.

'Didn't we agree we weren't going to talk about the case until we got back?' said Freeman.

'Well, we seem to have broken that agreement, don't we?' said Karen with a cheeky grin.

'I won't remind you who broke it first,' the lawyer teased.

'I'm sorry,' said Karen. 'I guess it's the policewoman in me. I can't hold out any longer. I don't like loose ends.'

'I hope you're not regretting coming here,' said Freeman.

'No, I'm not regretting it. I just wish I'd stayed to tie up the loose ends, and then come here.'

'Well, it's no use crying over spilt milk.'

'Perhaps you can make it up to me?'

She was looking at him with appealing eyes.

If I were a judge, I'd grant your motion, he thought.

'How?' he asked cautiously.

'You can help me tie up the loose ends in my own mind . . . here.'

'OK, but you've got to grant me a request in return,' said the lawyer, always alert to the possibility of a deal.

'Within reason,' Karen replied.

'OK.'

'Well, there are two loose ends that I'd like to tie up. First of all, why did Alan Nielsen and Veronica Digby pay you off? What were they afraid of?'

'Basically it was just a case of protecting the Digby family fortune. I mean, I think that Veronica probably didn't know about the genetic engineering and all that but she knew that her husband was getting the money from unsavoury sources. It's possible that after Digby's body turned up, Mike told her the whole story. But more likely he just warned her that there were things going on that shouldn't become known and that I should be paid off. She's a smart woman and she knows which side her bread is buttered. She probably took the hint without Mike having to dot the Is and cross the Ts.'

'OK,' said Karen. 'The other thing was, why did Tony suddenly take it into his head to confront Mike? When he'd tried so hard to make Mike think he was dead?'

'It was when the story accusing him appeared in the paper. When he saw that, he knew that the press would never leave him alone. They'd hound him because he was an easy target and keep throwing the spotlight on the evidence against him while ignoring the evidence in his favour. Then he'd have people encamped on his doorstep, hurling abuse at him in the street and making threatening phone calls. That's what the press do.'

'And of course,' said Karen, 'once he tipped his hand and revealed who he was, Mike Digby realized that *he* was in danger and decided to kill him.'

'Exactly. By the way, what's going to happen to Tony?' asked Freeman.

'Well, he'll probably be a witness against some of the other conspirators, anyone we can round up, basically. Fabian and

Mike Digby are dead. So is DuPaul. Hassan cashed in his diplomatic immunity joker and is now *persona non grata.*'

'Diplomatic impunity more like,' said Freeman.

'That's what it amounts to,' said Karen. 'Of course, the biggest catch of all is Edward Fielding. He's trying to hide behind a wall of parliamentary privilege – not that there is such a thing for extra-parliamentary activities, like conspiracy to pervert the cause of justice.'

'Is that the only thing he's guilty of?' asked Freeman.

'He's probably guilty of quite a lot,' said Karen. 'But the question is how much we can prove. Tony can identify him as having been present at one of the meetings with Hassan and Mike. Also he was a director of La Contessa.'

'That doesn't make him liable in criminal law,' said Freeman. 'You know how politicians wangle their way off the hook when the companies they direct are caught breaking the law.'

'Maybe,' said Karen, 'but he was identified as being at one of the meetings where the genetic engineering was discussed.'

'You think you'll get him?'

'Your guess is as good as mine, Emmett. Your profession is very good at getting people like that off the hook. And judges tend to close ranks behind politicians, especially when it comes to directing the jury. But his political career is over. His constituency party aren't likely to readopt him.'

'Are any more charges likely to be brought against Tony?'

'I doubt it. Technically he would have had possession of prohibited substances at certain times, but he probably won't even get a caution. It's a matter of public policy.'

'I feel rather sorry for him all the same. In a way his punishment is bigger than anything the system could throw at him. He's going to have to live with the fact that it was because he got involved with corrupt and dangerous men in the hope of making easy money that he got his brother killed.'

'That's something he's going to have to handle by himself, Emmett. It's not something you or I can deal with.'

313

'You're right. I just hope he finds help from somewhere.'

'He'll survive,' said Karen.' He's tough.'

'He'll have to be.' Freeman started rubbing sun-tan lotion on Karen's back unlooking her bikini top. 'Mm, that feels good,' she said, turning her head sideways.

'Let's not take the boat tomorrow, Karen. Let's just laze around all day on the beach.'

'OK,' she said with a cheeky grin. 'Just don't ask me to go topless.'